A Pearl for Kizzy

A Pearl for Kizzy

❧

A World War II Novel

Ed Bethune

ALSO BY ED BETHUNE

Jackhammered, A Life of Adventure
Gay Panic in the Ozarks
Anatomy of a Memoir

COVER: Houseboat photographed by Jack Delano, U. S. Farm Security Administration, Office of War Information, January, 1940. Repository: Library of Congress Prints and Photographs Division, Washington, DC.

ISBN-13: 9781533562128
ISBN-10: 1533562121

To children and the sparkle of innocence

Acknowledgments

Writing is a lonely endeavor, but eventually you seek support from others, and this is the place to thank friends and family for their good counsel and encouraging words.

When I wrote *Jackhammered* and *Gay Panic in the Ozarks* I finished the manuscripts before showing them to anyone. I did not want to be discouraged, so I insulated myself from criticism by working in seclusion.

This book called for a different approach. I would need the wise counsel of a woman to help me understand and capture the thoughts and feelings of a young girl. My wife, Lana, filled that role perfectly, and never once did she discourage me. On the contrary, her critiques emboldened me. Without her this story would still be sloshing around in the dark recesses of my mind.

When I finished the manuscript I asked a few carefully chosen people to read it. Their reactions were timely, insightful, and helpful. Judge Robert Edwards of Searcy, Ark., my former law partner, is a longtime circuit judge. Dr. Larry Killough is a retired physician. Julie Killough is my Sunday School teacher. Elliot Berke, a dear friend, is the finest ethics attorney in Washington, D.C. Mike Simpfenderfer of Bellflower, Calif., one of my protégés, has given much to the cause of understanding and preventing child abuse. Jawanda Pulliam Smith, a refreshingly candid woman, loves reading as much as anyone I know. Jim Barden, a playwright, and his wife Mel are longtime residents of New York City; they were in my high school graduating class. Paula Moseley, a longtime friend and political ally, knows and loves the state of Virginia. Adele Fogleman knows what it was like to grow up during World War II. Tess Fletcher, President, and Stacy Thompson, Executive Director of the Children's Advocacy Centers of Arkansas, work around the clock to protect children. My granddaughters Mason Nassetta and Nicole Bethune (a Jane Austen aficionado) have encouraged me to think like a millennial. And my son, Lieutenant Commander Sam Bethune, USN, is my technical adviser for all things military.

The late Pearl Brewer of Randolph County, Ark.—my great-aunt by marriage—deserves special mention. She was born in 1901 and learned scores of old folk songs when she was a little girl. She sang them for me in the summer of 1958, and I got the idea for Kizzy's interest in folk music from this remarkable woman.

Karen Martin, the talented editor of the Perspective section of the *Arkansas Democrat-Gazette*, copyedited my manuscript. She encouraged me and made valuable suggestions as we worked to produce a presentable piece of literature. It is a pleasure to work with her; she makes editing seem like fun, and that is not easy to do.

A Pearl for Kizzy is set in the late 1930s and during World War II. I used the language of that era, including a few crude words, to add realism and show prejudice. I trust readers will understand.

There is no Big Pearl, Jasper County or Cranford County in Arkansas. The little town of Willich in Pennsylvania Dutch country is also fictional. I created these places and my characterizations of culture solely to make a point about how we humans must learn to make the most of our differences.

The *New York Sun Herald*, the *National News*, radio station KPRL, the *Big Pearl Free Current*, and the *Jasper County Bulletin* are fictional news outlets.

"Kizzy's Song" was written by Philip Martin based on a few rudimentary verses that I created. Philip is the chief film and book critic, a columnist, and an editor for the *Arkansas Democrat-Gazette*. He is a gifted songwriter and performer, and has published several poems and books, the most recent being *The President Next Door*, Et Alia Press.

Finally, I constructed the snippets of history that appear throughout the book by synthesizing known facts with my own recollections. It is by no means a full account of our heritage, but I wanted to give readers, particularly those too young to remember, a sense of what was going on at the time. In so doing, I hope that I have done justice to all those who served at home and abroad during World War II.

Table of Contents

"Come away, O human child!
To the waters and the wild
With a faery, hand in hand,
For the world's more full of weeping than you
can understand."

W.B. YEATS

Part One—Dec. 6, 1941

"If all the world hated you and believed you wicked, while your own conscience approved of you and absolved you from guilt, you would not be without friends."

CHARLOTTE BRONTË

I

Fat Daddy's Dancehall

Kizzy snuck out of the dark woods and ran full speed across the old military road to the backside of Fat Daddy's Dancehall. She leaned against the building to catch her breath, but that did not stop the tingly feeling in her heart. The crackle of life inside the dancehall had cast a spell on her. She took a moment to calm herself, savoring the sounds of merriment and country music. Then she squeezed into the narrow space between the building and the snub-nosed bus that had brought Bob Eddy and his Texas Troubadours to Big Pearl, Ark., a quaint town on the Black River.

Farm trucks—the newest being a 1939 Ford half-ton pickup—filled the moonlit grounds around the dancehall. The local preachers called the place a blight, but they could not do anything about it; Fat Daddy's was located just far enough from the nearest church to be legal. Two beat-up motorbikes, a 1932 Indian and a 1930 BSA, were parked near the front door. And a farm wagon, trussed to a pair of mules, stood oddly alongside the bus.

She felt her way along, one hand on the wall, the other sliding along the side of the bus. The old building pulsed with the beat of picking, singing, and foot stomping. But the snub-nosed bus was ghostly still, save for the off-beat clicking sound of a hot motor cooling on a chilly night. When she got to the lone window on her side of the dancehall, she rubbed a spot clean and, giggling to herself, stood on tiptoes.

Kizzy—tallish and full-bodied for a 13-year-old—managed to peep in, but her legs began to ache; tiptoeing was hard. She dropped back on her heels and stamped the ground. *Dang it.* She tried again, stretching as high as she could. But this time, when her legs gave out, she half-jumped, half-pulled herself up onto the wide fender of the bus. She squirmed around to sit cross-legged facing the window, arranged her dress to cover her legs, and leaned back against the hood. The odor of hot-motor stink fouled the fresh night air, but the warmth of the engine felt good. She stuck her chin out in a jerky defiant way. *Ha! This'll work.*

From her new perch she could see almost everything. She recognized a few faces and quickly picked out the bandleader who was wiggling around, singing and strumming a banjo. Bob Eddy was having a grand time and the Troubadours were playing a folk song she loved. It was an early version of "Shortnin' Bread," a peppy tune made famous later on by Gid Tanner & the Skillet Lickers. Kizzy knew the words by heart, so as the dancers clogged she sang along, patting her leg in time to the music:

> *Putt on de oven an' putt on de led,*
> *Mammy's gwineter cook som short'nin' bread.*
>
> *Mammy's little baby loves short'nin', short'nin',*
> *Mammy's little baby loves short'nin' bread ...*

When the song ended, she beamed and started to clap, but whispered a promise instead. *Someday I'll get in to places like this ...*

⚜

Kizzy lived on a houseboat with Cormac Manatt, her make-do stepfather. The run-down scow, more workboat than anything, was the only home she had ever known. And "Down on Black River" is what she said if anybody asked for her mailing address.

River rats like Kizzy and Cormac were not welcome in Big Pearl, much less at a dancehall that cost $3 to get into, money they did not have.

⚜

When the dancers moved in rhythm to a new song, Kizzy saw a head of blond hair that she recognized. It was Stefan, a new friend who had recently moved to Big Pearl. He was standing right down front, as close as he could get to the stage.

Kizzy liked the boy and felt a kinship with him, mainly because the kids at school made fun of his foreign accent. *They oughtn't to make fun of the way he talks. But at least they don't think he's trash, like me.*

When Kizzy was 10, some fifth-grade boys claimed they saw crabs crawling around in her waist-length red hair—a falsehood she quickly squelched by putting her hair in extra-long pigtails. But Horace C. Ayers, a rich town-boy, was persistent. He found another way to make her life miserable and instigated his merciless attack at the beginning of every school year. Horace would sidle up to Kizzy, getting as close as he could. Then he would make a face and announce theatrically, "She smells like a river boat." His running mate, Buster Baggett, would follow up with his favorite line, "No, she stinks like catfish." Other boys—never Stefan—joined in. Many would hold their noses and some would whistle, "Whew," or say "Pew-eee." It was a lie, but Kizzy brushed it off. *I know what they're up to. They mean to keep me in my place.*

The rich town-girls were meaner. They poked fun at her clothes. They called her faded print dresses, especially the ones with blousy sleeves, "catalog clothes." But their sharpest ridicule was for her only pair of shoes, the soiled ankle-high brogans that she wore to school. She despised the shoes but was glad to have them, especially when it got too cold on the boat to go barefooted. The insults about her clothes were the hardest for Kizzy to take because they were true—the shoes *were* ugly and her dresses *were* cheap, old, and tattered. And they did come from Sears, Roebuck.

Kizzy's mother had taught her to forget such insults. "Boys will be boys and the town-girls are just jealous because you're prettier than they are." Then in a lower tone she would say, "MeeMaw was right, we're who we are and there ain't nothing we can do about it." Kizzy hated the last part of that because it too was true; there was nothing she could do about it.

In the eyes of most townspeople, Kizzy was "trash," a "river rat," a "genuine pestilence."

⚜

Four thousand miles to the west of Fat Daddy's, Admiral Isoroku Yamamoto's strike force steamed toward a rendezvous point 200 miles north of Oahu in the Hawaiian Islands. The Japanese Navy—two dozen warships, six aircraft carriers, 20 submarines and five midget submarines—was gathering to launch a surprise attack on the U. S. Pacific Fleet at Pearl Harbor.

In Berlin, Adolf Hitler—smarting from the news that Russia had stopped his German troops on the outskirts of Moscow—prepared to issue two directives: One would order his German U-boats to attack U. S. vessels; the other would open the first Nazi extermination camp in Chelmno, Poland.

The coming tumult would change everything for America, but war would be the least of Kizzy's worries.

⚜

The racket at Fat Daddy's mellowed when the band played "You're the Only Star in My Blue Heaven," a slow dance tune. As the last note of the hit song faded away, the dancers applauded politely and began to mill around. Kizzy thought the band was going to take a break, but the Troubadours surprised her by kicking in with an extra-loud version of the original "John Henry." The dancers let out a whoop. Kizzy whooped too.

"John Henry" was her favorite. It was a sad ballad, but she liked the snappy old version they were playing. She sang along, adding a touch of gloom in just the right places.

Just as she was singing the final lyric, "This belongs to a steel driving man," she began to shiver. She wanted to hear more, but the band was taking a break and the night air of December was getting colder by the minute. She slammed her hand on the fender and muttered. *Dang it.* Then she slid off the fender of the bus and walked slowly across the road to the woods. She paused, entered the thicket, and started down the footpath that twisted its way to the river.

Cormac's waiting for me. Kizzy pushed her hands between her legs and shivered. Strange feelings coursed through her body. *What would MeeMaw say about what he's been teaching me to do?* Then she thought of Stefan, and the rich kids from school. *What would they think?*

Part Two—1936 …

"Every life is a march from innocence, through temptation,
to virtue or vice."

LYMAN ABBOTT

II

Toe-Digging

At first light on what promised to be a sky-blue morning on July 1, 1936, Grandpa hollered at MeeMaw, "Let's go, woman! You and Kizzy—get them tools on board—we got to make some money today." His tinny voice was not threatening and it did not carry very far, but that did not matter. Grandpa was a big man, rawboned and mean-looking. Men feared him, but Kizzy and MeeMaw did not. They had him figured out: Grandpa was a tough man with a soft heart.

"Alright, OK," said MeeMaw as she stepped onto an extra-wide workboat tied snugly to the stern of their houseboat. Grandpa was already aboard, sitting next to an old Johnson outboard that was hiked up out of the water. As soon as MeeMaw got herself settled, 8-year-old Kizzy started handing her the tongs, rakes, lines, buckets and other gear they would need to gather mussels from the muddy bottom of Black River.

"Where's Sarah?" Grandpa asked.

"She ain't going," said MeeMaw. "She's still sleeping."

Grandpa grumbled. "She's more trouble than she's worth."

Kizzy handed the last of the gear to MeeMaw. Then she clambered onboard and sat by her. "She works, Grandpa. She cooks and does other stuff, but musselin' ain't her thing."

Grandpa undid the docking line, and pushed the workboat away from its mooring. "Musselin' ain't her thing? Ha! That ain't it—your ma's just plain lazy."

Kizzy knew better than to argue with Grandpa about her mother's shortcomings. Besides, she did not want to spoil a moment she loved—floating downriver on a still summer morning. The blue herons would be stalking breakfast in the shallows, and the scary alligator gars would roll loudly, stirring the water. And, no matter how quietly they drifted, their slow passing would scare up the native birds—cardinals, bluejays, wood ducks and many others. Kizzy liked to call their names as they flew away; she knew all the birds before she turned 7. The river was in her soul, bone deep. The scenery changed with the seasons, but the smell of the river was constant—fresh, unique, and enchanting.

The workboat quickly caught the main current and Grandpa steered it downriver, using a long single oar as a rudder. MeeMaw looked like she was going to say something, but instead she started singing a folk song. She was a storehouse for Scots-Irish songs that she learned as a girl from a blind uncle. Kizzy thought she had heard them all, but this one was different.

> *One day as I was walking*
> *Through a London dusty street,*
> *A handsome young lawyer*
> *Was the first I chanced to meet.*
>
> *"See here, my little Gypsy girl,*
> *Will you my fortune tell?*

Kizzy interrupted her grandmother. "Ma says my daddy came to Big Pearl with a Gypsy caravan. She says he'll come back to see me some day."

Drifting down the river was the best time to get answers to such questions. Kizzy had figured that out before she turned 6 years old. MeeMaw looked at Grandpa.

He nodded. "Go on with it."

MeeMaw ran her fingers through Kizzy's hair and pushed it back over her shoulders. "It's true, your daddy was a full-blooded Gypsy. They called him Tamás. He latched onto your ma when she was 16 years old. His caravan wintered out west of Big Pearl, but when the Gypsies left here in March of '28 he left with 'em. Sarah ain't seen him since ..."

Grandpa cut her off. "He knocked her up all right, but you turned out pretty. That was the good of it."

MeeMaw pulled Kizzy close and the child laid her head on her grandmother's breast. "Gypsy's ain't all bad, child. They have a way of knowing the mystery of things—that's why they is so good at fortune tellin' and card readin.' I think you got some of that in you, Kizzy."

"Sing the rest of it, MeeMaw."

MeeMaw straightened up a little and then sang, in a soft voice.

> *See here, my little Gypsy girl,*
> *Will you my fortune tell?*
> *Oh yes, sir, oh please, sir,*
> *Hold out to me your hand.*
> *You own many fine farms*
> *Off in some foreign land*
> *It is the little Gypsy girl*
> *That is to be your bride.*
> *I once was a poor girl*
> *But now I'm a rich man's bride*
> *Have servants to wait on me*
> *While in my carriage ride*

"I like it, MeeMaw.

What was Tamás like?"

Kizzy barely got the words out when Grandpa slapped the long oar against the water, making a popping noise. "That's enough of the Gypsy talk; let's get on down the river. We got work to do."

MeeMaw hummed a few other tunes as they drifted south, but she got real quiet after they rounded Cottonwood Bend. And when they were on the straight she said, "We're almost there, but we still gotta go around 'Messican Bend.'"

Grandpa chuckled. "I think we ought to stop and work Mexican Bend."

"No sir! Can't work there. It's haunted."

Kizzy had heard MeeMaw's tale about Mexican Bend, but she played along. "What do you mean, MeeMaw?"

MeeMaw, a tiny shriveled-up woman with piercing grey eyes, considered herself an authority on all things supernatural, particularly haunted places. Just before Kizzy was born, she got interested in fortune telling and Tarot card reading. She asked the Gypsies to teach her how to do it, but they wanted to charge her more than she could afford.

A few weeks later she heard about a book advertised in the Johnston Smith & Co. catalog. It cost 10 cents and promised to reveal the secrets of fortune telling and tell how to make money as a mystic. MeeMaw figured out how to order it and when it came in, she gave a tiny, imperfect pearl to a young river-rat boy who read it to her. He could not pronounce some of the words but that did not matter. MeeMaw learned enough to get her first customer. She made 50 cents and had great plans to make more, but the day law heard about it and threw her in jail.

He let her out the next day when she returned the customer's money. He threatened to lock her up for good if he caught her telling any more fortunes, but MeeMaw did not slow down. She kept telling fortunes to anyone who would let her.

MeeMaw loved the occult. She never tired of talking about spirits, spooks, and haunts, but Grandpa was tired of it—he had heard all her stories.

So when MeeMaw started telling about the "haint" at Mexican Bend, Grandpa started laughing. He knew there was nothing he could say or do that would stop her or change her mind, but he decided to have some fun at her expense. He said other folks were having good luck at Mexican Bend and he wanted to try it. MeeMaw scoffed, raising her voice to a squeaky pitch. Then he said it was silly to skip a good place on the river just because she believed it to be haunted, and that set her off again. Arguing with MeeMaw was like arguing with a stump, but Grandpa got a kick out of testing her stubbornness. Finally, he laughed and gave up because she kept repeating her main argument—it was always a variation of the same theme: "It's bad luck for life if you mess with a haint."

They coasted on toward Mexican Bend and when they started to round it MeeMaw said they had to hold their breath until they got to the next straight.

"Protection," MeeMaw said as she took in a deep breath.

"Bullshit," Grandpa said, but Kizzy took in a deep breath, and she held it as long as she could.

They were almost around the bend when Kizzy saw an odd-looking man standing just beyond the tree line. He was stark naked except for a green derby hat, and he had one finger raised high in the sky, spinning it around as if he were balancing a ball on it. Kizzy gasped to take in a fresh breath and pointed at the man.

"See what I mean," MeeMaw said. "It's hainted."

"Bullshit," Grandpa said. "That's just old Knuckles. He's crazy as a betsy-bug—been living on Mexican Bend ever since they threw him out of the nut house."

"Hainted," MeeMaw said, then she pointed at the man. "He's the only one crazy enough to live here. This is where they lynched that messican way long ago—that's why it's hainted."

Grandpa made another slapping sound with the long oar and pointed toward the next bend. "There now—that's enough of that. We're coming up on Hog Head Bend. You all get ready to do your toe-digging."

⚜

Digging for mussels with long-handled rakes is hard work. Kizzy and MeeMaw could rake, but if they were in shallow places, they liked to toe-dig. They would wade barefooted, scratching the bottom with their toes until they felt a mussel, then they would work it loose and pick it up by hand. They made a game out of it, guessing the size and shape of shells before they pulled them out of the water.

Grandpa raked some, but he got most of his mussels by tonging—backbreaking work that is a lot like using a post-hole digger. He used to search for mussels in deep water using a homemade diving helmet and an air compressor that he made with an old washing-machine motor. The contraption, along with yards of rubber air hoses, once sat prominently in the center of the workboat, but it was no longer there.

Grandpa took it off the boat and quit deep-diving the day he nearly drowned. He accused MeeMaw of trying to kill him by putting a kink in one of the air lines, but she said, "It weren't my fault. It was your stupid contraption—that old washing-machine motor just gave out."

When they finished their day's work Grandpa fired up the Johnson outboard for the trip home. It would be slow going against the current because the workboat was boxy and weighed down by the big pile of mussel shells. But they had had a good day and the grownups were in good spirits. "We done good," Grandpa said. "We got at least $2 worth of shells, and we got mussel meat for the trot lines."

"What about the little pearl I found, Grandpa? What's it worth? You said it's a good one."

"We ain't going to sell it, Kizzy. It's just right to be a 'burying pearl.' I'll put it in the bag with the others and that will give us three."

Kizzy understood the importance of burying pearls. Just a month earlier Grandpa had explained it to her. A poor river rat who had no kinfolks got shot trying to steal a chicken, and Grandpa told Kizzy: "They just rolled him up in an old blanket and buried him in a grave with no marker. That ain't going to happen to us because we got a burying pearl for each one of us—ones we can trade to the undertaker, even Steven, for a bare-bones funeral with a wooden coffin."

Kizzy did not like to think about undertakers and dying, but she was happy that she found the burying pearl. It made her feel grown up.

III

The Rhineland

Stefan's father, Victor Wertz, hunkered over the radio, his dark eyes fixed on the dial. He gently turned the tuning knob back and forth between the low range of 48 and the high of 50, grumbling as he worked. The table-top model, a walnut-encased Lorenz Ordensmeister 3, was top of the line. Victor bought it in Düsseldorf in 1931 and was very happy with it. Even so, he could not keep his hands off the tuning knob.

Eight-year-old Stefan and his mother sat on a nearby sofa speaking in German about his school work. They waited impatiently for Victor to stop fiddling with the radio.

Suddenly Annemarie cupped her hand to her mouth and stage-whispered to Stefan, "He just likes to tinker!" She winked and stuck her hands out, pretending to turn imaginary knobs.

"*Sei doch still, mein schönheit!* I'm not tinkering! I've got the Berlin station, but I have to get rid of the static." Victor gave the tuning knob a final touch and stood at attention, facing Annemarie. "There! It's fixed."

Stefan giggled at their playful bickering. He gave his father a thumbs-up and patted the open space on the sofa. Victor sat down and snuggled up to Annemarie, burying his face in her long blonde hair. She laughed and pushed him away, whispering, "Shhhhh … Listen."

"Welcome to the closing ceremony of the 1936 Olympics." The German announcer took a full minute to praise his fearless leader, "Der Fuhrer,

Adolf Hitler." Then he played the majestic prelude to Wagner's opera "Die Meistersinger of Nürnberg."

"He's a madman, this Hitler." Annemarie said.

Victor nodded once. "Yes. But the American track star has put him in his place. Herr Hitler cannot explain how his mighty 'Aryans' lost to Jesse Owens, a Negro—three footraces and the long jump."

Annemarie joshed, "Go gently, my love. According to Hitler, I am Aryan."

Victor looked down and sighed, "And I am a Jew," Then, after a clumsy moment of silence, he chuckled. "But I'm not advertising it—not these days."

Stefan joined in the laughter, but he sensed anxiety and it befuddled him. He mulled it for a second, and then blurted out, "So I am half-Jew and half-Aryan?"

IV

Independence Day, 1936

A beam of morning sun peeping through a small window on the riverside of the houseboat awakened Kizzy. It was Independence Day. She opened her eyes just in time to see Grandpa grab the water bucket and head out the door. She knew where he was going; it was a morning ritual. Grandpa, wearing worn-out one-Gallus overalls, would walk 50 yards uphill to a hydrant located on the side of the Biggers Cotton Gin. He would fill the bucket with fresh water and lug it back to the houseboat. He did it every day, rain or shine, hot or cold.

Kizzy liked to study the gritty old man. She watched his every move and admired his gumption. Grandpa seldom wore a shirt under his overalls, and he only wore shoes when the ground was frozen or covered with snow.

She got out of bed and put a stick of kindling in the cast-iron cookstove. She tried to be quiet, but that was a challenge. The houseboat had one big room, 30' x 12', cluttered with cooking utensils, oil lamps, and fishing gear—some of it hung on wall hooks, but most of it just piled up. Four rows of shelving on a windowless wall separated the two sleeping bunks, each barely big enough for two people. MeeMaw was still in the bunk she shared with Grandpa, and Kizzy's mother, Sarah, was in the other. They were sleepyheads, unlike Kizzy and Grandpa.

The shelving was stuffed with Depression-era staples: Dry goods, salt, flour, cornmeal, lard, cans of food such as Pet Milk, peanut butter, and beans—lots of beans. A small work table with a built-in metal sink that drained overboard was fastened to the outer wall, close to the cookstove.

When Grandpa got back from the gin he hoisted the water bucket up and sat it by the sink. "Happy birthday, Kizzy. I'm going to get you a rabbit for dinner—a big lean swamp rabbit."

She gave him a hug and whispered. "I'll get some coffee going."

MeeMaw chimed in, "Get a cottontail, Grandpa—them swampers is tough and don't taste near as good."

Sarah rolled over in bed and stretched. "Why're you all getting up so early? The parade won't start before 10:30."

Kizzy loved going to the parade on Independence Day. Her real birthday was July 2, but Sarah and MeeMaw fudged the date when they got her birth certificate. Since Kizzy was born on the houseboat with MeeMaw serving as midwife they figured no one could dispute what they said about the day of her birth. They worked up a strong argument to justify what they were doing. "Why not the Fourth? Nobody celebrates anything on July 2nd."

When Sarah got up, she fixed a pan of spoonbread and stuck the stub of a small candle in it. She put it on the small table in the center of the room and said, "Happy birthday, Kizzy." Kizzy blew out the candle and when they finished eating the spoonbread they all went outside to stand on the tiny aft deck.

It was time for Grandpa's usual Independence Day speech. He puffed up and pointed to the river. "Me and MeeMaw been on this river for 20 years. Some say it's a hard life, and I reckon it is, but nobody tells us what to do and we ain't owing to anybody. We live by the law of the river. We're free, and we aim to stay that way. Happy Fourth of July."

⚜

Kizzy, Sarah, and MeeMaw headed up the hill to town to watch the Independence Day parade, but Grandpa, shotgun in hand, turned toward the woods behind the cotton gin. He had promised Kizzy a rabbit, but he knew he could always get a mess of squirrels in the lowland along the river.

Before he got too far, Grandpa hollered back to them, "Stay away from the day law, Kizzy. They answer to Sully Biggers. He don't like us, and they'll throw you in jail before you can say 'Jack Rabbit.'"

MeeMaw waved for him to go on. He looked like he was going to say more, but he shrugged and disappeared into the woods. MeeMaw looked Kizzy in the eye. "Grandpa's right, young'un. Sully ain't no good. His daddy was a fine man and his granddaddy came to these parts as a preacher, but Sully is taking their money and making a mess of things."

They headed for a place near where the parade would end. It was a good place because there was very little room along the road for people to stand and watch. Most parade-watchers gathered in the heart of the town, around the courthouse, but that was too risky for river rats. If they had gone there, the day law would have run them off for sure.

They settled themselves on top of an embankment and soon the lead horse came into sight, its rider carrying an American flag. Behind the rider a troop of Boy Scouts ambled along, carrying a red, white, and blue banner bearing the message: "Happy Independence Day—Troop No. 3—Big Pearl, Arkansas."

A college band from Memphis, outfitted in purple and gold, came next. They were playing a medley of peppy military songs. Kizzy got so excited that she jumped up and lost her footing. She would have wound up in the middle of the band, but MeeMaw grabbed her just as she was about to slide down the embankment. "Sit down, girl. There's the day law. He's marching right alongside Mr. Sully Biggers' big float."

MeeMaw and Sarah could not read, so they asked Kizzy to read the signs to see what Biggers was up to. As soon as Kizzy started reading, MeeMaw knew the float was not promoting the Biggers Cotton Gin, or the Biggers Bank, or the Biggers Grocery, or the Biggers Construction Company.

Kizzy continued. "Some people are born to be a burden on the rest ... Help correct these conditions ... The American ... I don't know this word—I'll spell it out. E-U-G-E-N-I-C-S." Then she finished reading the sign. "Society."

"I should've known it," MeeMaw said. "He ain't no good—never has been—now he wants to get rid of folks like us."

"That ain't nothing new, MeeMaw," Sarah said.

"No, but this here …," she pointed at the float, "is about how he wants to fix the niggers and Jews and poor people like us so that we can't have babies. I been hearing about it for a good while."

MeeMaw shut up when she saw Sully Biggers nudge the day law and point to where they were sitting. "Uh-oh, he sees us. We better not stay too much longer."

Kizzy heard uncommon fear in her grandmother's voice. "Are you afraid he will try to fix us, MeeMaw?"

"Over my dead body, child." MeeMaw got back to acting like herself after she saw a puzzled look in Kizzy's eyes. "Sully Biggers is a bully … Yes, that's it … It ain't Sully—it's Bully. And it ain't Biggers—it's Bigshot. From now on I'm calling him what he is: Bully Bigshot."

Kizzy clapped her hands and gave MeeMaw a hug.

Some of Kizzy's rich classmates were on the next float, but as it came into sight, she saw the day law coming their way. When he was a few feet below them, he looked up. "You all need to move on—you know Mr. Biggers don't want you here. If you stay I'll have to take you in."

Sarah smiled at the day law, and said in a singsong way, "Now Harry, don't be like that." She batted her eyes and wiggled her ass in a knowing kind of way. "We ain't doing no harm—can't we stay a little longer? My little girl just wants to see the parade—it's her birthday."

The day law stammered and hitched his pants. He looked around to be sure no one was listening, "Well, Sarah, you all can stay a little longer, but then you need to move on."

Sarah winked at MeeMaw and Kizzy. MeeMaw grinned. She understood fully.

Kizzy did not understand the day law's sudden change of heart, but it did not matter. She was happy. She could watch the rest of the parade.

V

The Sturmabteilung

Two uniformed men in their late 20s—Brownshirts, members of Hitler's *Sturmabteilung*—strode briskly along a country road at the east end of the Neander Valley in the Rhineland. They passed several farms, and when they came to an archaic rock bridge the larger man, a *sturmman*, ordered the man of lesser rank to stop. "Wait, the place we are looking for is on this side of the creek." He looked to his right and pointed to an old farmhouse and barn bounded on three sides by an orchard. "That's it. The boy lives there."

The Nazis headed toward the place, and as they walked, they talked. The smaller man said, "These old places are storybook—like a page from *Hansel and Gretel.*

The *sturmman* said, "They should be grateful—the new farm law is going to be good for small farmers. They will prosper—all Germans will prosper—now that the Fuhrer has sent our Army back into the Rhineland. Everything will be better now."

When they reached the front door, the *sturmman* pulled a nightstick from his belt and banged it hard against the door, several times. He waited a minute, and was about to strike again when Annemarie's father opened the door and said, "Yes?"

"We are here about a young boy, Stefan Wertz."

"What about him? He is a good boy. I am his grandfather."

"He is not participating in youth activities, and I must explain the program to the boy's parents. Are they here?"

"The boy's mother is here, but his father has gone to town to sell some eggs and cabbages, and the boy is with him. Can't this be done some other day?"

The *sturmman* gave the old man a look of importance. "I am too busy to make extra trips. I must see the mother."

The old man opened the door and hollered for Annemarie. Then he led the men to the living room and said to the *sturmman*, "This is my land—20 hectares—but they have lived with me for 10 years. We raise vegetables and fruit. I couldn't get along without them."

The Brownshirts were about to sit down when Annemarie entered the room. The *sturmman* looked at her and took a quick breath. Unsettled by her beauty, he struggled to mask the clumsiness he felt.

Annemarie gave him a knowing look, smoothed her dress, and sat down.

She waited for the Nazi to collect himself. "Now, what is this about my son?

The *sturmman* cleared his throat and struck an official pose. "Our records show that Stefan Wertz is 8 years old, but he has not been attending the new village program that is designed to prepare young boys for service to the Fatherland."

She feigned surprise. "That is my fault; I thought it was for older children."

"So you did know about the program?"

"I have heard a little about it, but I make Stefan come home after school to do his chores and practice the violin."

"It is not your decision to make. All children, ages 6 to 10, must participate and record their progress in a performance book. It is for his own good to serve a cause greater than self. When he is 10 he will graduate into the *Jungvolk* and when he is 14 he will enter the Hitler Youth and serve there until he is 18, and then he will pass into the Labor Service or the Army."

She looked to the other Brownshirt. "Are there no exceptions to this?"

The smaller man shook his head. "No, and there are heavy prison sentences for parents who try to keep their children out of the program."

Annemarie's father interrupted. "I have not heard of such a law."

The *sturmman* glared at the old man and launched into a long speech praising Hitler. "Our Fuhrer is standing up for Germany. On March 7, our troops paraded across the Rhine bridges and the French did nothing." He laughed and digressed to explore "French weakness." Then he rambled for another 10 minutes, reciting the Nazi doctrine of "Aryan superiority" and extolling the Fuhrer's plan for a new and better Germany.

When he wound down, he pointed a finger in the old man's face. "It is policy, but it will soon be law! On Dec, 1, the Fuhrer will sign a law requiring all 10-year-old boys to register for the *Jungvolk*. At that time, they will have to pass tests in athletics, camping and German history."

He turned to Annemarie and lowered his voice. "That is why your son must attend the village program for young boys."

She looked down: *These Brownshirts have not asked about Victor, and they have not asked about Stefan's heritage—they have been too busy crowing about the Jungvolk and praising the madman's plan for "Aryan" purity.*

Then she gave a most gracious smile to the Brownshirts. "My Stefan will start attending the youth program. It is a good idea to prepare for service to the Fatherland. *Ya*, it is good!"

With that, the Brownshirts got up to leave, but before they got to the door, the *sturmman* said to Annemarie and her father. "We will be checking on Stefan's progress with the youth program."

❧

Victor and Stefan barged through the front door, laughing and clasping their hands in celebration. Stefan ran to hug his mother. "We sold every last egg and cabbage."

"That's good, son—but it is late and you must practice." Your father and I will come listen to you in a little while, but first we must talk."

When Stefan left the room to fetch his violin Annemarie gave Victor a worried look and motioned for him to follow her outside. Her father was waiting for them on the porch, but said nothing when they sat next to him.

"What is it?" Victor asked.

Annemarie and her father then told Victor about the Brownshirts. He asked a few questions, but listened carefully and when they finished, he slammed his hand against the arm of his chair. "We worried that they would come for me, but they have come for our son. They want to poison his mind, but imagine how they will treat him if they find out that I am a Jew."

Annemarie sobbed. "I cheapened myself." She paused, and then said, "I indulged the idiot in charge, the *sturmman*. I said it was a good idea to prepare children for service to the Fatherland. I am ashamed of myself."

"You did the only thing you could do, and it worked. You got rid of them, but it would be naïve to think that this is the end of it."

The old man spoke. "I cannot imagine life without you and Stefan, but I agree with Victor." He stood up and walked to the side of the porch. He waved his hand from left to right, pointing to the boundaries of the farm. "Our family has lived on this land for generations, but Hitler has made a new law that will not let me pass the farm to a woman or to a male heir that is not 100 percent 'Aryan.'"

"Welcome to the new Germany." Annemarie put her hand on her father's shoulder. "Just last year he passed the Nuremberg law and that turned Victor, a German citizen, into a 'subject' simply because he is a Jew. None of this is right."

Victor joined them at the edge of the porch. "I don't mind being a 'subject,' but that same law also forbids sexual relations between 'Aryans' and Jews. That I will not tolerate." He laughed, but Annemarie did not.

"Not funny, Victor."

The old man put his arms around them and said what they did not want to admit. "You must leave—get out of Germany before it is too late." And when they did not respond, he said, "Gustave will know how to do it. He can get you on a ship out of Hamburg."

"Uncle Gustave?" Annemarie said.

"Yes. We can't talk about it, but my brother hates the Nazis and has helped others get away."

"Your father is right." Victor said, "I have never told anyone that I am a Jew, but it is only a question of time before they find out ..."

⚜

Stefan was practicing the scales when Annemarie and Victor came in from the porch. Annemarie signaled for him to continue, and when he finished Victor praised him, as he always did. "You have a gift, my son."

The boy shrugged. "I like to play, but the scales bore me."

Victor laughed. "You got that from me."

"Are all Jews like that, father?"

Annemarie winced, but Victor took the occasion to tell Stefan that he was proud to be a Jew even though he never talked about it outside the family. He said, "I don't talk about it because there are powerful people in Germany who do not like Jews."

"Why?"

Victor did not try to answer the boy's question. Instead, he said, "Don't worry about it, my son—you are always safe with us."

Annemarie smiled and put her arms around the boy. "Play something for me, Stefan."

Victor wiped a tear from his eye. "Yes. Play for your mother." He looked at Annemarie and then Stefan. "Play the second movement of Mendelssohn's Concerto in E minor ... and, my son, play it with the Jewish half of your heart."

VI

Birdie

"Kizzy." Grandpa whispered to his granddaughter as he sat the water bucket by the sink.

It was just breaking day. Eight-year-old Kizzy was still in the bunk bed, slumbering, but she heard her name and opened her eyes. She stretched a little and looked at the old man.

"Birdie's back."

Kizzy's eyes lit up and she slipped out of the bunk, taking care to let her mother sleep. She and the old man stepped outside to the aft deck and he said, "He was up to the gin, drawing water for 'em—said he came in on the bus last night—says he has a weekend pass."

"I'm going over there, Grandpa."

"Might as well, we ain't gonna get any work out of you until you see him."

Kizzy giggled and skipped across the gangplank to the upriver footpath, running lickety-split to the Barden houseboat.

Grandpa watched her all the way and smiled when he heard her shout, "Birdie! It's me—Kizzy!"

❧

L. W. "Birdie" Barden, like Kizzy, was a lifelong river rat and the best toe-digger on the Black River. He had two baby sisters and two younger brothers, all by different fathers. The itinerant sires could not resist the temptations of Birdie's mother, Shirley Barden, a voluptuous woman who never seemed to age. Her "men friends" would stay on the Barden houseboat long enough to get her pregnant, and then they would disappear, usually in her fourth month.

Birdie could whistle birdsongs better than anyone. He could not read or write, but he loved birds and knew all about them by the time he was 10. That is when his mother gave him his nickname, and it stuck.

Grandpa told Kizzy, "Birdie can whistle them calls better than the mockingbirds." No one in his family cared about the birds, but Kizzy did, and that is why Birdie took a special liking to her. When she was 5 years old and Birdie was 14, Kizzy found a cardinal that was dragging his wing, hopping along the upriver footpath. She gently coaxed the redbird into her cupped hands and took it to Birdie. Together they nursed the bird to health, and it flew away a week later. From that day forward Birdie and Kizzy were a twosome, and he taught her all he knew about Black River bird life, which was a lot. He tried to teach her birdcalls, but Kizzy had to give that up. She had a good ear for the sounds, but she could not pucker her lips and whistle much of anything, much less the high chirpy notes that birds sing.

⚜

Kizzy began to fidget as she waited for Birdie to come out, and when he did she broke into a broad smile. "Hey, Birdie. Grandpa said you came in on the bus last night. How're you liking the CCC?"

"So far, so good. It's hard work, but they gave me some new work clothes and this fine pair of boots—best I ever had, that's for sure."

"You look good, Birdie. I think they are fattening you up."

"I'm eatin' more, that's for sure. Say, Kizzy, whatcha doin' today?"

"Just hanging around here. It's going to be hot as blazes."

Birdie rubbed his chin and gave her a wink. "How's about goin' to the baseball game with me this afternoon? The Pearl Diggers is playin' the Caruthersville Alfalfas and I got some free tickets on account of being a

CCC boy. My buddy from camp says he can use his daddy's A-Model to run us down to Newport."

Kizzy swooned, then said, "Oh, yes. I've not been to a big-time ball game."

❖

The game was a runaway for the Alfalfas, but Kizzy, Birdie and his friend braved the hot August heat and cheered to the very end. Kizzy did not know much about baseball, but Birdie kept telling her, "There ain't no givin' up in baseball. The game ain't over 'til the last man's out."

When they got back to the truck Birdie said, "Let's stop at that drugstore on our way out of Newport. I'm goin' to buy my favorite girl and you a malted milkshake—that'll cool us off. How about it, Kizzy?"

Kizzy swooned again. *This is the best day of my life.*

❖

When Kizzy sucked the last drop of her milkshake through the straw, the two boys teased her about the slurpy noise she was making. She said, "I don't care. I've never tasted anything so good in all my life."

Birdie's friend changed the subject to something that sounded serious to Kizzy. "Say, Birdie, has your mother started getting that 25-dollar allotment from the CCC yet? My folks ain't seen hide nor hair of the one they's supposed to get."

"My maw got it this week," Birdie said. "It's more money than she's seen in a while. It makes the CCC worth doin'."

"Can I go in the CCC when I get old enough?"

The boys laughed. "It ain't for girls, Kizzy."

Birdie turned to his friend. "Kizzy's real smart. She can read and write and does good in school."

His friend looked at Kizzy and smiled. "That's real good." He dropped his head and looked away. "The CCC is learnin' me and Birdie how to read and write."

"That's real good," Kizzy said. "What are you reading?"

Birdie said, "Well, we're still in the first McGuffey but it's goin' good. The man teachin' us says it's OK to try and read other stuff. He says if we come to a word we can't read we oughtn't to give up. He says we should just say 'Moses' and keep on reading."

Kizzy was not sure how to react to that, but she laughed when the boys started laughing at themselves.

As they were leaving the drugstore Birdie pointed to a colorful St. Louis Cardinals baseball poster. It was on the wall next a photograph of Bill Dickey, the all-star catcher for the New York Yankees, and two separate photographs of the Dean boys, Dizzy and Daffy.

The two young men stood as if worshiping at a shrine.

Birdie broke the silence. "Them boys—all of 'em—is Arkansas boys."

There was nothing else to say so they headed home.

VII

Neanderthals

Annemarie and Victor talked secretly for days after the Brownshirts left. At times their fear of Hitler and the Nazis gave way to the excitement of starting fresh in America. But mostly they worried about their son, fretting over the best way to tell the boy about their decision.

Annemarie urged patience. "Let's go slow. I think it will be best to break the news to him gently, in pieces."

Victor agreed, so they decided to wait until the Brownshirts had been gone for a week. Then, with everyone at the dinner table, Victor and Annemarie began to talk in a most general way about the value of living in different places. They carried on about how travel and change can broaden one's perspective, bring new friends, and create new opportunities. Annemarie's father played along, doing his best to fight back tears and stay composed.

The grownups stuck with it for three days, finding new ways each night to broach the subject.

Stefan listened and asked questions, occasionally giving the impression that he might like to move away, but at the end of each discussion he came back to the predictable response of a happy 8-year-old boy: "Yes all that is so, but I like it here, with Grandfather."

On the fourth day Annemarie said to Victor, "We are getting nowhere with this. Stefan is a child, but he is no fool. I think we ought to be more direct. He loves us and will follow our lead."

Victor nodded in agreement. "Let's tell him straightaway that we are going to move to Hamburg and then go to America." He paused, took her hands in his, and said, "But we must be honest when he asks why we are going."

Annemarie winced. "That will be the hardest part, so let's take a picnic to the valley tomorrow. Stefan loves to go there and it is the perfect place to talk about why we need to leave Germany."

⚜

The beautiful Neander Valley lies to the east of Düsseldorf, Germany in the Rhineland. A small river, the Düssel, graces the scene, but the valley is famous for another reason. In 1856 German laborers, digging for limestone, found some bones and showed them to a scientist, Johann Carl Fuhlrott, who recognized them as the remains of a previously unknown type of human. In time, scientists dubbed the remains "The Neanderthal Man."

The Nazis were interested in the famous discovery, but not for scientific reasons. Hitler was not searching for truth. He had bastardized the disciplines of archaeology and anthropology to support his ghastly theory of "Aryan superiority." And he was using the phony information to stoke hatred for Jews and other undesirables.

Many Germans turned a blind eye to Nazi evil, but Victor and Annemarie did not. They could not—their son was half-Jew.

⚜

Victor parked the farm truck in a shady spot and the little family walked over a bridge and into a large park that lay between a grove of trees and the Düssel River. It was a perfect September day, not a cloud in the sky. Annemarie spread the picnic blanket near a quaint old bandshell, close enough to enjoy the baroque melodies being played by a string quartet.

Stefan sat down with his parents, but as soon as they finished eating their lunch he jumped up and ran to watch a nearby soccer game.

"Let him go, Victor, he'll tire of it and then we can tell him that we have decided to move away."

Stefan proved his mother right. He quickly tired of watching *futbol* and started back in their direction, doing his own version of the hop-skip-and-jump.

"Can we watch them fish?" Stefan shouted and pointed to a half-dozen fishermen lining the banks of the Düssel.

"We'll watch them on our way back to the truck, son. But right now I would like to tell you a story about the bones that were found in this place many years ago."

Stefan's eyes widened. "Is it a ghost story, father?

Annemarie smiled and ruffled his hair. "No, but it is an important story." She took a deep breath and said, "Tell us the story, Victor."

Victor pointed to the river and swept his arm to the east, across the reach of the valley. "This is where the workers found the bones of a man that was not like other men. They called him the Neanderthal Man and people began to talk about the ways he was different."

"Did he have horns? Or a tail?

Victor chuckled. "No, son, he looked a lot like us, but he was smaller and some say he was not very smart."

"Was he mean?" Stefan asked the questions of a child, but he was interested, and Victor used the moment to teach.

"We don't know, but people have always fought with one another."

"Why?"

"Sometimes people hate other people."

"Why?"

"Mostly because they are different, but sometimes people hate people who aren't all that different."

Stefan blinked, pondering his father's answer. Then he said, "Why?"

"That's a hard question to answer, Stefan. But there are powerful people right here in Germany who don't like me because I am a Jew."

The boy looked as if he was going to ask why again, but the *futbol* players gave a loud cheer. Stefan turned to see what had happened, and when he saw the players with their arms reaching to the sky he said, "Goal! They made a goal."

Annemarie gave a little cheer and clapped along with Stefan. Then she cut her eyes to Victor. He gave her a quizzical look, but before either of them could speak, the boy said, "Do they hate you, Mother?"

She pointed to herself. "Well, they say I am OK because I am not a Jew. I am a Gentile, but Hitler calls me an 'Aryan.'"

The boy frowned and looked to his father. "Were the bones Aryan or Jew?"

Victor laughed. "Well, nobody knows who they were or what they believed, but if someone says they were Jews the Nazis will not like the Neanderthal Man."

"Why, Father?"

Annemarie answered. "We just don't know why, Stefan. But we have decided we don't want to stay here." She paused and gave the boy a playful push. "We are going to move to America!"

Stefan looked to his mother, and then to his father. "Will Grandfather go with us?"

"No, he wants to stay on his farm. The Nazis are not mad at him—he is not a Jew."

Stefan winced and looked down. Then he jumped to his feet and ran as fast as he could to the soccer field.

"He is hurt," Victor said. "Have we done the right thing?"

"We had to tell him—I think he will be OK, but it is not the kind of thing an 8-year-old boy wants to hear."

They watched as Stefan ran along the sideline, following the action of the players, but then he turned and walked slowly toward his parents.

Annemarie whispered. "He's coming back."

When Stefan got close he said, "Will we go on a big boat?"

Annemarie and Victor laughed, and the three of them wrestled around on the picnic blanket.

"And will I get to see the cowboys and Indians when we get there?"

"Yes, son, we will be happy in America." Victor turned his head as he said the words. Then he stood up, cleared his throat and whispered hoarsely, "But now it is time to get back to the farm."

⚜

Two days after the trip to the valley Stefan was in his room practicing on his violin, playing scales and trying to memorize another Mendelssohn melody. Victor opened the door and entered quietly. He nodded his approval and signaled for Stefan to play on.

When the boy finished the piece, Victor applauded. "Good. You did well, but this tune is more complex than the movement you played for your mother. Let me play it for you—it is one of my favorites."

Stefan handed the violin to his father and lay back on the bed. Victor was the only teacher he had ever had. The boy listened carefully as he played, but he also studied his movements and the expressions on his face. His father had taught him from the beginning: "Show your love for the music."

When Victor finished the tune, he sat by Stefan and put his arm around him. "We told you at the picnic why we are going to America, so I want to show you something." He pushed his collar to the side and carefully pulled out a golden chain and pendant.

"It's pretty. What is it, and what do the markings mean?"

"It's a Jewish symbol. The marks are Hebrew letters. Together they spell 'Chai' which shows respect for 'Life and the Living God.'"

"Where did you get it?"

"My parents gave it to me when I was a child." Victor put the pendant back beneath his shirt and put his hand on Stefan's heart. "I'm proud to be a Jew, son, but these are difficult times in Germany—that is why I have not told anyone outside this family that I am a Jew."

"Mother told me a long time ago that it is our secret—that I am never to tell anyone that I am half-Jew."

"Good boy. It is our secret, but one day we will be free to talk about it, won't we."

⚜

One week later Annemarie was beginning to gather the things they would take to Hamburg. Stefan was at school and Victor was working in the field. It was a good time for her to sort through their clothes and make decisions.

"Annemarie, Annemarie! Come quick!" Her father barged into the house, screaming and crying at the same time.

"What is it?"

"It's Victor. He's hurt. Bad, I'm afraid."

He waved for her to follow him and ran out the door. Annemarie followed but the old man had to slow down to catch his breath. He pointed to a far corner of the farm and shouted. "There! Under the tractor. He was driving up that embankment and it reared up and came back on him."

Annemarie ran as fast as she could. The tractor was upside down and when she got close she could see that Victor was pinned beneath it. She fell to her knees and crawled under the tractor, screaming, "I'm here, Victor, I'm here."

Victor moaned and mumbled something, but she could not understand the words. She pulled a mound of dirt out of the way and got close enough to kiss his cheek and put her hand on his face. But she could also see that the gearshift had pierced Victor's chest. "I love you Victor. I love you."

He was wheezing and struggling for a last moment of life, but managed to turn his head so that he could look into her eyes. "I—love—you—and Stefan." She pushed her way closer and kissed his cheek.

He whispered. "Our son—the—pendant." He gasped and was gone.

⚜

The burial of Victor Wertz was in the family gravesite just a stone's throw from the place where Victor died beneath the tractor. A few of the neighboring farmers attended, but no religious words were spoken. Annemarie's father gave a simple eulogy, and when he finished Annemarie laid her cheek against the coffin and wept.

Stefan had cried all he could. His best friend, his teacher, was gone.

When Annemarie stepped away from the coffin, Stefan drew close and used his finger to trace two imaginary Hebrew letters on the wood:

חי

He stepped back and spoke, too gently for the others to hear: "For Life and the Living God—I will always love you, Father."

VIII

On Needing a Man

On a Sunday afternoon in late September 1936, Sarah and MeeMaw were relaxing on the aft deck of the houseboat, sitting on a small bench. Kizzy had her back to them, sitting at the deck's edge, her legs hanging over the side. Her bare feet dangled in the chilly water, dancing musically as the current swept by. She hummed, and then sang a verse from "Gypsy Girl:"

> *It is the little Gypsy girl*
> *That is to be your bride.*

"Tamás was a good-looking devil, Kizzy," Sarah said. "He'll come back some day if he ain't dead or locked up somewhere."

"Bullshit," MeeMaw said. "If he'd been half a man he would've married you."

"You ain't got no call to run Tamás down about that—you and Grandpa never got married."

MeeMaw bristled. "But Grandpa didn't run off. He takened care of you, and now he's takin' care of your girl."

Kizzy stared at them. "You all stop fussing." She huffed theatrically, picked a tiny sliver of loose wood off the deck, and tossed it into the river.

MeeMaw frowned, then pronounced, as if speaking to the multitudes, "A woman needs a man—particular if she's livin' on the river."

Kizzy shook her head. "MeeMaw … there you go again."

"I ain't fussin' about Tamás no more," MeeMaw said. "I'm just sayin' this old river can be mean and you got to have a man around. You're too young, but Sarah remembers the big flood—it was 10 years ago, in '27. If Grandpa hadn't been here we'd be dead and gone." She playfully poked Kizzy's back. "And you, girl, would never have been born."

"What was it like, MeeMaw? The flood."

"Here comes Grandpa, ask him," Sarah said as she got up and headed off the boat. "MeeMaw's done worn me out—she'd argue with a post."

Grandpa laughed as he came over the gangplank to the aft deck. "MeeMaw—you been preachin' again?"

"No. I was just sayin' the big flood nearly got us."

Grandpa glared at her, and when Kizzy looked away he frowned at MeeMaw and put his finger to his lips. Then he told Kizzy, "We had a bit of a hard time, but it was an extra-big flood. You don't need to be scared about it. The big ones are few and far between. This old boat has been good to us."

MeeMaw huffed. "I ain't been scarin' her, it's the first time I ever said much about it." She stomped across the gangplank and headed up the footpath.

"It's OK, Grandpa. MeeMaw ain't been scaring me with talk about the flood. She saves her scaring for stories about the haints at Mexican Bend and the White River Monster. That's the stuff that gives me nightmares."

"That's just hocus-pocus stuff, Kizzy. She's full of spook stories and superstition. Don't pay no mind to it."

Kizzy got up off the deck and climbed into his lap. "Did you really save them?"

"We made it just fine, Kizzy. Floods is just part of livin' on the river. We have to fare for ourselves. It's a hard life, but we got our own code of right and wrong, and we are free as a bird."

"MeeMaw says Bully Bigshot wouldn't lift a finger to help us. Ever."

Grandpa laughed. "That's a fact. Bully Bigshot won't allow anyone in town to help us 'cause he hates us. He don't care if we drown or get swept away. He just wants us gone. But that's OK. We don't need him, and we don't want nothin' from him or his kind—it's our way."

"It's getting dark, Grandpa." Kizzy jumped off his lap. "The skeeters are coming out."

Grandpa nodded. "Let's get inside." He got to his feet, but quickly sat back down and rubbed his stomach. "Whew-eee! I got the heartburn or something.'"

Kizzy turned to look, but he was on his feet and laughing. "I got to stop eatin' so much grease."

IX

St. Lambertus

On Monday, Sept. 21, 1936, Annemarie got Stefan ready for school, and as soon as he had left the house, she went back to her bedroom. She sat on the edge of her bed, looking at the photograph she took of Victor and Stefan just three months earlier. She had caught them in a playful pose, face to face, a happy moment. She sighed. The picture that had always brought a smile to her face now brought deep heartache. She slumped back on the bed, turned on her side, and pulled the sheet over her head.

Annemarie lay still for an hour, and she struggled in the fog of melancholia, torn between grief and fear. *Victor—my love—you are gone. And now the Nazis want our son. To warp his mind and poison his heart.*

She jerked the cover away and got to her feet. I must put an end to this madness. She called out to her father, and when he did not answer, she went outside to look for him. He was not on the porch, but she found him in the barn, milking the cow.

"Will you take me to Düsseldorf? There is something I must do."

❧

Annemarie's father backed the farm truck up to the barn and loaded it with 10 dozen eggs and one large can full of milk. He tooted the horn and when Annemarie came out of the house he was not surprised to see that she was wearing a black skirt, a black loose-fitting sweater, and a classic black beret that was in stark contrast to her long blonde hair.

He noticed that his daughter was cradling the family Bible against her heart. "You are a beautiful woman, my dear—even in mourning clothes."

"I want to go to St. Lambertus." She gave him a quick look. "And I want to be alone."

"Yes. Of course. I'll drop you off and come back for you when you're ready to leave. I'll go to the market. I've got milk and eggs to sell."

She nodded and they rode in silence until they reached the outskirts of Düsseldorf. They drove a few blocks farther and rounded a corner to head toward the north side of town; suddenly he touched the brakes and groaned. "Look. It's the Army."

A German soldier was in their path, stopping traffic to permit the uninterrupted passage of an enormous convoy of tanks, weapons carriers, and scores of trucks loaded with German troops. The noisy stream of military vehicles and equipment continued for a quarter-hour, but it finally passed and the soldier allowed them to continue.

"What does this mean, Father?"

He squinted. "I don't know, but I'll find out when I go to the market."

In a few minutes he pulled to the curb. "Here you are. I'll come back in an hour."

"That will be perfect." Annemarie got out of the truck and walked toward the church—a 14th-century masterpiece in spite of its twisted, misshapen steeple.

⚜

St. Lambertus Cathedral has a tall spire that is an icon for the city. For centuries, parishioners have told visitors that the wood was wet when the steeple was built, and its drying caused the odd shape. But for Annemarie the twisted steeple was a comforting sight. She was christened at St. Lambertus and took her first communion there. She passed through the great bronze door with its depiction of the Prodigal Son and went into the softly lit interior with its beautiful stained-glass windows. As she moved toward the altar and the carved wooden image of the Virgin and Child she tightened her hold on the Bible and thought of the day when she took the Sacrament of Confirmation.

Father Joseph Stieger recognized her immediately. "Annemarie, how are you, child?"

"I will be all right, Father, but these are hard times. My husband was killed just three days ago and I am worried about my son; he's only 8 years old."

The old priest put his arm around Annemarie and invited her to sit with him.

"We saw German soldiers, hundreds of them, on our way here."

He clasped her hands and hissed. "Hitler took back the Rhineland in March and today the Army is starting its largest maneuver since the last war. These are, indeed, hard times."

"The Nazis have told me that my son must join Hitler's youth program." Annemarie straightened up and raised her voice. "He is a good boy, Father. I do not want that and his father did not want it either." She paused and looked her friend in the eye. "I am going to take Stefan to America."

The priest stammered. "I will miss you, child. But I understand."

"Will you keep that in confidence, Father?"

"Of course I will, Annemarie."

"Now that you know what I am going to do, will you take my confession?"

He nodded and they moved to the confessional booth, where Annemarie told him of her intention to move to Hamburg and do whatever might be necessary to get Stefan out of the country. She confessed that she was prepared to lie, steal, and cheat if necessary. The old priest did not try to change her mind, but he did tell her to say the Rosary every day and pray for God's divine guidance.

When they left the booth he gave Annemarie a hug and left her alone. She went to the altar and prayed for God to forgive her determination to say or do whatever might be necessary to keep her son safe. She paused, and then carried on: *Forgive me Father, for I have lied about my husband being a Jew … and I have taught my son to tell the same lie.* She hesitated and took a deep breath. *And I intend to tell him that he must tell that lie for the rest of his life.*

Annemarie made the sign of the cross and left St. Lambertus, knowing that she would never return.

✤

On the drive home she told her father, "We have been living on the farm for so long that we have been blind to what is happening. Now, with the Brownshirts coming and the Army marching around in Düsseldorf, I see that Hitler is not only evil, he is all-powerful."

He said, "The sight of tanks and troops, heavily armed and marching … it breaks my heart."

"Everything is going from bad to worse. Father Joseph says the hatred for Jews is building. He says people have been saying that things will get better; that it won't affect them. But he doesn't believe that and I can't take the chance. I've got to get going. Victor said we must leave, so I can't mope around feeling sorry for myself. I don't have that luxury. I must go to Hamburg, now! Stefan and I must get out of Germany. Now!"

Annemarie's father was quiet, so she continued. "Just tell everyone, particularly the Nazis, that after Victor's death I couldn't bear to live in a house filled with memories of him."

✤

On Oct. 1, 1936, Annemarie and Stefan arrived in Hamburg. Uncle Gustave Hofmann, a short, sprightly old man with a full head of grey hair, was at the train station to meet them. They collected their luggage and when they had finished the formalities Annemarie said, "I am so grateful for your help, Uncle. I am prepared to do whatever is necessary to get Stefan out of Germany."

"Yes, I know that," said Gustave. He ruffled Stefan's hair and then told Annemarie, "I know how people are getting out, but for now you must get settled. Tomorrow we can talk about what you must do."

X

Cold River

It was breaking day on a cold November morning when Kizzy heard the familiar noises. Grandpa was fastening the clasps on his overalls and tiptoeing to the sink. She pulled the covers from over her head just in time to see him go out the door, water bucket in hand. It was her everyday ritual; watching the old man—shoeless and shirtless—slip quietly out the door to fetch a bucket of fresh water from a hydrant on the side of Bully Bigshot's cotton gin.

Long before Kizzy's birth, Bully caught Grandpa drawing water in mid-day. He threatened to prosecute him for trespass, but Grandpa did not cower. He simply changed his water-drawing schedule from broad daylight to the crack of dawn.

When she was 6 years old Kizzy asked him why he went to all that trouble. He said, "Because we need fresh water, and nobody—especially the likes of Bully Bigshot—is gonna run us off or tell us what we can or can't do."

As soon as Grandpa stepped off the boat Kizzy got out of bed and put a stick of wood into the cookstove. She stoked the coals and soon a fire was warming the room. She fixed a pot of coffee and when it began to perk MeeMaw got up and started making a batch of corn dodgers.

Sarah did not move until MeeMaw started frying bacon and fussing at her. "Get up, lazybones—we got to gather wood this morning. Grandpa is going to chop and we're gonna haul."

When Grandpa got back he sat his bucket of fresh water by the sink and took a seat at the table. "I'm feelin' poorly this morning, but after we eat we've got to get the firewood 'cause it's gonna rain later." He laid a piece of bacon on his corn dodger and took a big bite. He winked at Kizzy and said, "This is some good eatin', MeeMaw."

When he finished breakfast, Grandpa grabbed his ax and started out the door. "Give me about an hour, then you all come and help me tote the wood back to the boat."

Kizzy ran to the door and said, "Can I go with you, Grandpa?"

He looked into her wide eyes and chuckled. "You're my girlfriend and my best helper for sure, but you need to stay here and help MeeMaw. After we get our firewood, I'll take you with me to run our trotlines. I'm bettin' we will have a good mess of fish to sell."

Grandpa got off the boat and headed for the woods. And 20 minutes later Kizzy heard the sound of his ax echoing against the stillness of the river.

Sarah was slow getting dressed, as usual, but when she was ready, the three of them walked across the gangplank and headed for the woods. When they were halfway MeeMaw said, "I ain't heard the ax for a while. I bet he's already worn his self out."

When they got to the clearing where Grandpa was working, he saw them and pointed to a pile of cut wood. "I'm done for the day. You all take as much as you can carry and go on back to the boat." He sat down on a stump and said, "I'll be along in a little bit."

⚜

The women were hovered around the stove warming their hands when Grandpa got back. The boat rocked a bit when he stepped on the gangplank and Kizzy thought she heard him say something, but the noise of firewood clattering on the deck muffled his words. They heard a big splash and MeeMaw shouted, "Uh-oh! Grandpa's in the water."

The women hurried outside, stepping over and around firewood strewn all over the aft deck. MeeMaw shouted, "There he is!"

Grandpa's foot had caught between the boat and its mooring line. His head was under water and he was not moving. MeeMaw grabbed a leg and so did Kizzy, but Sarah pushed her out of the way, so that she and MeeMaw could pull the old man out of the water.

Kizzy cried and screamed, "Grandpa, Grandpa."

The women finally managed to get him on board, and laid him on his back. MeeMaw pushed on his chest and slapped his face. She said, "Grandpa" repeatedly, but after a while she said, "Grandpa is done for—he's gone on down the river … Grandpa's done for—he's gone on down the river." In a few minutes, she quit pushing on his chest. "His ticker's done give out. Let's get him inside out of the cold."

Kizzy made no sound during MeeMaw's attempt to resuscitate Grandpa. She just stood there, catatonic, shivering and crying.

Once they got him inside, Sarah sat on the bed and whimpered and Kizzy got under the covers and sobbed. But MeeMaw—not one to show weakness—stood by the open door looking out. She cussed the river and then launched into a long dissertation about demons and the hand of fate. When she finished her tirade, she broke down and said in a quiet voice, "He was just 56—said he wanted to make it to 60, but it weren't in the cards."

⚜

MeeMaw fished a burying pearl out of a little leather pouch and handed it to the town undertaker that afternoon when he and a helper came to the boat to get the body. The ghoulish little man assured her that Grandpa would get a full-service 25-dollar funeral. When MeeMaw asked him what that included he said, "I'll lay him out in a proper pine box and bury him in the town cemetery and put up a wood marker." When they did not respond, the undertaker said, "If you want me to arrange any preaching that will be extra."

MeeMaw snorted. "We don't need no preaching. The river was the onliest religion Grandpa ever had."

The undertaker said, "Meet me on the backside of the cemetery at 2 o'clock tomorrow—right by the road."

⚜

They buried Grandpa on Saturday, Nov. 28, 1936. The undertaker met MeeMaw, Sarah, and Kizzy at the gravesite. A gravedigger stood nearby, leaning on his shovel, eager to finish his job.

No one from town came to comfort the bereaved or pay respect to Grandpa, but that was common. Townsfolk paid attention to the births, deaths, weddings and sicknesses of their own, but that did not include river rats.

MeeMaw was just about to say words over Grandpa when Birdie and his mother walked up. "Hey MeeMaw. Sarah. Hey, Kizzy. I'm home on a weekend pass and just heard about your grandpa."

Kizzy went to his side, crying. Birdie pulled her close and MeeMaw let loose with the shortest eulogy on record. "Grandpa was my man. He done his durndest, but now he's gone. He's gone on down the river."

⚜

On Sunday morning, the day after they buried Grandpa, Kizzy got up at first light. She quietly took the water bucket from its place by the sink and slipped out the door.

XI

Hamburg

Annemarie had a restless first night in Hamburg. Uncertainty about the future worried her, but Uncle Gustave's splendid home is what kept her awake. Never had she, a farm girl, lived in such luxury. When the first ray of daylight peeped through her bedroom window, she slipped out of bed and headed downstairs, taking care not to wake Stefan.

Uncle Gustave had shown her the principal rooms of Villa Elbe when they first arrived, but Annemarie was eager to nose around the *bel étage*. The high-ceilinged parlor, the library, and the other formal rooms on the main floor were masterworks. It did not take long for her to realize that her uncle—now 67 years old—was a very successful trader and shipper. The objects of art and the plaques and certificates of recognition proved it. *We are in good hands—Uncle Gustave will know what we must do to get Stefan out of Germany.*

⚜

After breakfast, Uncle Gustave asked the kitchen maid to take Stefan to a park across the street to play, and when they were gone, he invited Annemarie to join him in the library. She followed him into the beautiful room, and he showed her to a seat by the fireplace. He then put a finger to his lips and walked back to close the big hand-carved French doors. He fastened the door latch and returned to sit by Annemarie, saying in a soft voice: "It's a shame, but we have to be very careful these days."

She nodded. "I know." She put her hand on his. "Thank you so much for helping us."

"You are my brother's child—I want to help."

Annemarie's lip quivered and she looked away. "I need to tell you about …"

He interrupted. "There's no need to talk about the past. Your father has told me the whole story—about Victor, about the Brownshirts and the boy, and why you must leave. Let's focus on what needs to be done."

"Whatever you say, Uncle Gustave."

"In that case I'll be blunt and get right to the hardest part." He looked her in the eye. "You are a single mother with an 8-year-old boy. It will be difficult if not impossible to get you and your son out of Germany if you don't get married."

Annemarie winced; then she toyed with her wedding ring. "But … why?" She glanced up and said in a shaky voice, "I don't understand."

"It doesn't have to be a marriage for love or intimacy. It could be a marriage of convenience, for practical reasons." He waited a beat, and then explained. "It is easier to get immigration clearances for families."

"I don't … is there no other way?"

"I wish I could say yes, but I can't. The Nazis are getting stronger by the day. There is much to do and we don't have a lot of time."

Annemarie slouched; then she stood up and turned her back to the old man. She stepped toward the cold fireplace, staring into it. *This is not right … Victor … Victor, my heart burns for you. … Stefan … Why? … God help me … I must be strong …*

He let her be, but soon she backed away from the fireplace and stood near him. She put her hand on his shoulder. "How much time do we have?"

"Today is the first of October. If everything goes well, we could get you out of Germany by early spring. After then it may be too late."

"I just lost the man I will love forever, Uncle." She trembled and rubbed her temples. "Victor is on my mind." She broke down when she said his name, but quickly composed herself.

He took her hands and pulled her close. "I understand how hard this must be, Annemarie, but we must deal with the cards that are on the table."

She did not answer for a long while. Then she said, "I have to sleep on this, Uncle. It is a hard thing to think about."

⚜

Annemarie lay awake most of the night thinking about Victor and the decision they had made to get out of Germany before it was too late. When morning came, she and Stefan went downstairs. Uncle Gustave was already at the breakfast table. She caught his eye. "Yes, Uncle. The answer is yes. I will do what is necessary."

"Good." Then he turned to the boy. "Stefan, I have arranged for you to start school at St. Boniface. It is a very good school and you will like it there. Sister Marie is a good friend and she will take good care of you."

Stefan was playing with his food and did not answer.

Annemarie scolded him. "Stefan, you must thank Uncle Gustave."

Stefan did not look up, but he mumbled, "Thank you, sir."

⚜

Uncle Gustave was not a natural-born matchmaker, but as a trader and shipper he knew a number of able-bodied young men who hoped to get married and move to America. Over the next five weeks, he introduced three men to Annemarie, and she did her best to assess each man's potential. Uncle Gustave was patient and understanding, but when Annemarie rejected the third man, he told her, "You are being too particular, but I think you will like the next man. He is a brickmason, and a good one. Just remember, we have got to get this done."

On Sunday, Nov. 15, 1936, 35-year-old Fritz Halder came to Villa Elbe for lunch. Uncle Gustave introduced him to Annemarie and Stefan, who were cordial but not overly enthusiastic. Uncle Gustave cut his eyes to Annemarie and mumbled to himself. *Here we go again.*

⚜

Fritz Halder had come to Villa Elbe because Uncle Gustave assured him that he would like Annemarie, his most beautiful niece. Fritz had heard that line before, but he resolved to keep an open mind. *Who knows? Maybe she will be the one.*

When Uncle Gustave led him into the parlor, Annemarie was standing by the piano. She was wearing an emerald green suit that matched her eyes. And just as he neared her a ray of sunlight shone in, caressing her face as if on cue. Fritz, a strapping man with sandy hair and a pleasant countenance, stumbled through the introductions and prepared himself for the customary small talk. Instead, Uncle Gustave launched into a detailed description of Villa Elbe, telling of its history and describing various pieces of art. Fritz stood mute, fumbling with the buttons on his coat, his heart atwitter. *My God, she is beautiful. How could I be so lucky?*

Uncle Gustave's dissertation finally ended and Annemarie said, "I think the food is ready, shall we sit down?"

The meal was delicious and Fritz did his best to be engaging, but halfway through the meal he lost his nerve. *What if she says no? I am such an oaf. I would not blame her.*

⚜

Three days later, at Annemarie's suggestion, Uncle Gustave invited Fritz to come to Villa Elbe for evening cocktails. That meeting led to others, and some of the meetings included Stefan. The boy was hostile at first, but Fritz took him to the park to watch a *futbol* game and that seemed to help. Then, on a very chilly Saturday in early December, Fritz took Stefan fishing. They did not catch anything, but the outing worked a small miracle.

Five days later, Fritz and Annemarie agreed to marry and on Thursday, Dec. 17, 1936, Father John, Uncle Gustave's priest, came to Villa Elbe to officiate. Stefan and Uncle Gustave were the only witnesses. Annemarie used her maiden name, Annemarie Hofmann, instead of Wertz, Victor's name.

⚜

On Friday, the day after their wedding, Fritz and Annemarie took Stefan on a day trip to a *Kristkindlesmarkt* in the suburbs of Hamburg. Fritz had offered to take them to the famous Christmas market in Nuremberg, but Annemarie did not want to get too far from Uncle Gustave and the safety of Hamburg. Nor did she want to mislead Fritz by agreeing to make an overnight trip.

When Fritz suggested the trip to Nuremberg, Annemarie was gracious but firm. "It's nice of you to offer, Fritz, but our agreement is to live separately until everything is all set. Uncle Gustave says it will take two months to finish all the necessary paperwork—then we will see."

Fritz, smitten with his beautiful wife, could only smile. He had told Uncle Gustave after the wedding, "I am the luckiest man alive."

The *Kristkindlesmarkt* was small but nice. Stefan ran from one concession to another to see all the handmade ornaments and bric-a-brac. Annemarie and Fritz spent most of the afternoon chasing after the youngster, but the wafting aroma of freshly cooked German waffles finally wore them out. They bought three servings and wolfed them down, laughing hysterically when Stefan wound up with syrup all over his face and hands.

Annemarie watched her son and Fritz with a mother's eye. *This may turn out all right. We shall see. Time will tell.*

⚜

It was dark when Stefan and Annemarie said goodbye to Fritz a half-block from Villa Elbe. He climbed on the *Straßenbahn Hamburg* and waived as the tram pulled away.

Annemarie held Stefan's hand, and as they turned toward home she said, "Did you have a good time today?"

He did not answer her question, but posed one of his own. "Will he sleep in your bed like father did?"

They stopped and Annemarie pulled Stefan close. "He can never take your father's place, Stefan. And he is not going to live with us until Uncle Gustave gets all the paperwork ready so that we can go to America."

Stefan scuffled the pavement with his shoe, but said nothing.

Annemarie said, "He is helping us get to America and that is a good thing. Do you like him?"

"I guess so."

⚜

On Sunday, Uncle Gustave came home from mass and found Annemarie in the library. "It was a beautiful service—there is nothing like the last Sunday of Advent."

"I'll be a better Catholic when we get out of Germany," Annemarie said.

"Yes, but right now you must continue to lay low. It is best not to stir interest in all that we are doing. Just today, I learned that the Nazis have sent more Jews to a new concentration camp called *Sachsenhausen*. They arrested them under the guise of being political dissidents or homosexuals, but that is a lie. It was because they are Jews."

"The Nazis scare me, Uncle." She fidgeted with the binder of the book she was reading, and whispered, "I make Stefan promise every day that he will never tell a soul that his father was a Jew."

"Everything is going to be OK, my dear. My lawyers are very good and they are taking care of everything. I don't know how they got all your identification papers changed back to your maiden name but they did, and they did it for Stefan too. That was an important step that cleared the way for you to marry Fritz in your maiden name, and now that he is Stefan's legal stepfather the adoption will be easier to get."

"Adoption? I never talked to Fritz about adoption. We talked about him being a stepfather to Stefan, but there was no mention of adoption."

Uncle Gustave gave her a sheepish look. "Actually, I discussed that with Fritz."

"Uncle!"

"It's OK. He did it of his own free will." He gave a big belly laugh. "You have bowled him over, Annemarie. He will do anything to please you.

Anyway, it is done—he has signed the adoption papers and they are ready for you to sign."

"I have been very standoffish to Fritz—it is what we agreed to, but perhaps I should do more to show my appreciation. What do you think?"

Uncle Gustave pinched her cheek and winked. "I know what you are thinking, but that is not necessary—not right now."

She giggled. "Are you sure, Uncle?"

"Absolutely! Be patient. Do nothing more. Just lay low for two months."

XII

High Water

MeeMaw, Sarah, and 8-year-old Kizzy struggled to get along after Grandpa died; they were determined to survive. MeeMaw made sure of it. Sometimes she used words of encouragement, but mostly she warned them that they needed to work twice as hard now that Grandpa was gone. And she never missed a chance to repeat her mantra: A woman needs a man if she is living on the river.

Sarah changed the most, which is what MeeMaw wanted. On the third day after Grandpa's death Sarah took over the task of poaching fresh water from Bully Bigshot's cotton gin. When Kizzy picked up the bucket and headed for the door Sarah got out of bed and took it from her. "It's too heavy for you, Kizzy. I'll fetch it."

After that, Sarah and MeeMaw became a team. They took turns cooking and cleaning, and they ran the trotlines and sold the fish they caught—catfish, buffalo, crappie, and perch—to the market in Big Pearl.

It was a hard life, but as the days passed they gained confidence. Winter came, but as is often the case in Arkansas, the weather was nice—cool nights and mild days. MeeMaw stopped bitching about how mean the river could be to a woman without a man. Kizzy never missed a day of school, and she hurried back to the boat each afternoon to help the women clean and dress the day's catch of fish. All three of them gathered firewood, and to Kizzy's surprise, MeeMaw and Sarah stopped fussing.

On Thursday, Jan. 7, 1937, MeeMaw got out of bed first and said what she had said every day since Grandpa's death—changing only the number of days: "Let's go girls, it's been 40 days since Grandpa went on down the river—we got work to do."

⚜

On Sunday night, Jan. 10, 1937, MeeMaw said, "Let's go to bed. It's powerful cold, and we gotta run the trotlines tomorrow morning." She took a big warm rock from the top of the cookstove, wrapped it in a small blanket and put it in the bunk bed between Kizzy and Sarah. They snuggled around it and pulled the covers up to their chins. MeeMaw snuffed out the oil lamp and went back to the stove. "Scoot over, girls. Here I come." She wrapped up another warm rock and climbed into bed with them. Kizzy was sandwiched between the warm rocks, with Sarah on one side and MeeMaw on the other.

They shivered, giggled, and scrunched around until each of them found an agreeable position— then MeeMaw spoke for everyone: "Damn, it's cold."

⚜

Then the rains came.

MeeMaw and Sarah ran the trotlines early Wednesday afternoon, Jan. 20, another cold day. Kizzy walked halfway from school to home in bright sunshine, but by the time she got to the boat the skies had darkened and a strong wind was beginning to blow out of the southwest. MeeMaw and Sarah had just returned, and they had a good mess of fish to clean. Kizzy pitched in, scraping the scales off a big buffalo. MeeMaw was skinning the catfish and Sarah was fileting. They worked as fast as they could, but they barely got inside before the storm hit.

Kizzy put a log in the cookstove and they huddled around it, rubbing their hands. The boat began to sway on its mooring, and Kizzy went to the door and looked out. "It's dark as night, MeeMaw!"

MeeMaw chuckled. "Dark as Egypt is what Grandpa always said."

Sarah shook her head. "I never understood what he meant by ..." A bolt of lightning struck near them and lit the sky as if it were day, and the sight of that was quickly followed by a burst of thunder so loud that it rattled the houseboat. Kizzy and Sarah dove into the bunk and hid under the covers.

MeeMaw dealt with her fear in a different way. A mighty wind rocked the boat so violently that she had to hold on to keep from falling. Even so, she made her way to the door and scotched herself into a three-point stance that freed up her right arm. Now in a stable position, MeeMaw made a tight fist and shook it at the sky, uttering mysterious incantations and vile threats. She tailored her messages to fit: One for the wind, another for lightning, and the vilest of all for the deafening thunderclaps. While different, each message to the unknown included some variation of a common theme: "Stop it—I ain't never done nothin' to you."

When the lightning and thunder let up, Sarah said, "Glad that's over." But the words were barely out of her mouth when big chunks of hail pounded the boat. MeeMaw came up with a new message for it, but after a few minutes the hail gave way to a heavy rain and that seemed to tranquilize the old lady.

Scared no more, MeeMaw stopped shaking her fist and plopped down on the bed by Sarah and Kizzy. "Whew-eee! It's gonna be a frog-strangler!"

⚜

At daylight the next day the violent thunderstorm had become a steady, soaking rain—the kind that would last for days.

Kizzy left for school at 7:30 a.m., and when she was gone MeeMaw got a nervous look on her face and said to Sarah, "We better lay in plenty of wood and fill up the water buckets. This reminds me of 1927."

⚜

When Kizzy got back to the houseboat at 4 o'clock that afternoon she could barely get in the door. MeeMaw and Sarah had been gathering firewood all day long and they had stacked the wet wood inside, out of the rain. MeeMaw said it was the smart thing to do, but the stench of dirty clothes, fish, and wet wood led Kizzy to pinch her nose and roll her eyes. MeeMaw fussed at her, "You'll just have to get used to it, Missy."

The rain continued for a week and Kizzy walked to school every day, wearing her slicker and galoshes. They were cheap hand-me-downs—black rubber and heavy—but she was glad to have them. And she was happy to spend the day in school, where it was warm and dry.

✣

On Thursday, Jan. 28, when Kizzy left for school it was cold and windy, and it had been raining off and on—mostly on—for eight days. She pulled her coat collar up around her ears and ran most of the way. And she giggled as she rounded the corner of Biggers Hardware Store, but when she saw the schoolhouse she stopped in her tracks. It was deserted. At first, she thought it might be closed for a holiday that she had forgotten, but when she got closer, she saw a notice posted on the main entrance.

> "Due to rising water on the
> Black River this school is
> closed until further notice."

Kizzy stamped her foot and blew into her cupped hands. *Dang it! It's cold as all git-out. I wish we had a radio to hear about such stuff.*

She peeped in the window, but seeing no sign of life, she turned and started running back to the boat. She retraced her steps, but when she ran around the corner of the hardware store she ran head-on into a fat man. Kizzy fell down, but the man did not. He looked down at her, grumbling because the collision had knocked some papers out of his hand.

Kizzy got a close look at the fat man's face as she got to her feet. He had beady eyes perched beneath a pair of bushy black eyebrows and a bulbous forehead. One small eye was giving her a hard look, but the other one seemed to be looking sideways. Kizzy would have laughed, but the fat man twisted his face into a mean scowl and grabbed her by the arm. That is when she recognized him.

Uh-oh! It's Bully Bigshot.

"You need to watch where you are going, little girl." Sully Biggers reached down, grunting and wheezing, and picked up his papers. "Who are you anyway?"

"I'm Kizzy."

"Where do you live?"

She pointed toward the river. "Down on the river."

He scowled again and flicked his hand toward the river. "Well, get on down there. We got high water coming."

⚜

Kizzy ran all the way home. She told MeeMaw and Sarah about the school closing, and then said, "And I ran smack-dab into Bully Bigshot and knocked some papers out of his hand."

MeeMaw laughed. "Too bad you didn't knock him down."

"He's ugly and mean-looking. And one of his eyes looks sideways."

Sarah smiled, but she did not laugh. "He hates us river people." She sat on the edge of her bunk bed and pulled Kizzy close. "Let me look you over."

"He said there's high water coming. Is that right, MeeMaw?"

"Maybe, but we've had high water before. It ain't trouble unless it gets too high."

⚜

Three days later, on Sunday, Jan. 31, Kizzy asked again. "Is it going to get too high, MeeMaw?"

When she did not answer, Kizzy tried another approach. "Can't you read your cards to see what's coming?"

MeeMaw walked to the door and looked out. "I don't need no cards to tell you what we are in for." She looked at Sarah. "Grandpa never let us talk in front of Kizzy about the big flood in 1927, but he ain't here now and I think we got another one coming. We might as well tell her—she ain't gonna stop asking until we do."

Sarah shrugged and looked at Kizzy. "I was only 16 at the time so I'll let MeeMaw do the telling."

MeeMaw began. "The last big flood was just 10 years ago, in 1927. The water got so high that it nearly flushed Big Pearl down the river. The rich folks, like Bully, built back, but it was hard on the little people."

Kizzy squirmed. "Were you all on this houseboat?" Sarah nodded, so Kizzy asked MeeMaw, "What was it like when the water got so high?"

"We made it. But some folks weren't so lucky. On the worst day of the flood a barge full of logs broke loose and came roaring down the river. There was three boats of river people living about a mile upriver from here and the barge crashed into them and broke 'em loose from their moorings."

"What happened to them, MeeMaw?"

"There weren't anything they could do, child. The current had them."

"Did they die?"

"We heard they drowned because nobody tried to save them." MeeMaw paused, then scowled. "Town people don't care what happens to river people—to them we is just river rats."

Kizzy whimpered and looked away, but MeeMaw saw her tears. "Now I don't know for sure that they died. In fact, all I know for sure is that I saw all three boats floating down this river." She laughed nervously and pointed to the river. "When they came by here they was going lickety-split, and the women and children waved to us like they was on parade. It was plumb sad to see."

⚜

The two women and Kizzy did what they could to keep their mind off of the ever-rising water. They had a fair stock of cornmeal, bacon and beans, but they knew they could not hold out much longer. The gangplank to shore had long since washed away, but Sarah had found a way to get to high ground. She would hold onto the mooring line and pull herself ashore in the workboat that they used for fishing. On Feb. 5, she told MeeMaw that if they were going to get off the boat they would have to do it right away because her technique for getting ashore was getting too dangerous.

"It don't matter," MeeMaw said. "We ain't got no place to go."

"When I was in town the other day I heard that some people are going to a refugee camp over in Jonesboro," Sarah said.

MeeMaw huffed up. "There's diseases and shit like that at those places. We learned that back in 1927. No sir, that ain't for us. We'll stay with the boat—she'll float—she's all we got, and she'll get us through."

⚜

On Feb. 10, a cold gale-force wind came howling out of the north. Sarah and Kizzy hovered by the cookstove to keep warm, but MeeMaw was outside on the fore deck, leaning into the wind and staring at something on shore. Sarah said, "She's been doing that for the last three days, but she won't tell me what she's looking at."

The boat was bouncing around in the wind and MeeMaw lost her balance a time or two, but she stayed at her post—staring, staring. Finally, she came inside and a draft of cold air came with her. She shut the door and revealed her findings: "The water is going down! I been watching it real close for days and I say it's going down! The river is still wild as a March hare, and the wind has piped up, but I believe we are going to make it, girls."

They celebrated with a fine lunch of corn dodgers, bacon, and beans. But the gaiety ended in mid-afternoon when the houseboat lurched and tilted to starboard, throwing MeeMaw and the pot of beans against the wall. Sarah and Kizzy managed to keep their footing, but as soon as the boat settled, they said in unison, "What was that?"

MeeMaw righted herself and looked out. "Our bow line has busted loose, but the line to the aft deck is still holding. Come on Sarah, we got to go out and see what we can do. Kizzy, you stay here."

When they got to the fore deck, MeeMaw pointed to the Sampson post. "Look, the line is still fastened tight around the post, but it has gone slack—must've busted somewhere between here and the mooring post on shore."

Sarah nodded. "Let's go back in and wait for the wind to stop blowing."

"Not yet. We got to get to the bottom of this, Sarah."

MeeMaw leaned over the side to inspect the dangling line, and Sarah held to the bottom of her coat. "Be careful, Mee ..."

A huge half-submerged log crashed into the houseboat, knocking it sideways. Sarah tried to keep her balance and hold on to her mother, but she could not. The thumping noise, as loud as a cannon shot, covered up Sarah's scream and the sound of MeeMaw falling into the river.

Kizzy came on deck and ran to Sarah's side. MeeMaw was caught in the swift current, heading downstream. They screamed and called to her—MeeMaw! MeeMaw!—but there was nothing they could do to save her. She went under and came back up, but she was doomed. She was wearing several layers of clothing as well as a heavy coat. MeeMaw waved to her girls, and the next time she went under—50 yards downstream—she did not come up.

Sarah and Kizzy clung to each other as they made their way back inside. They sat down on the bunk. "We'll be all right, Kizzy." She pulled her child close and they cried for MeeMaw.

⚜

Cormac Manatt, a wandering man, saw the whole thing.

He was living in a hobo camp up on high ground, in the woods behind the railroad depot. Cormac had been on his way south in search of work when the high water on the Black River marooned him in Big Pearl. The camp was in an old shack that the hobos had commandeered as an emergency shelter. A potbelly stove kept the place warm and dry, making it a comfortable place to wait for better times.

Cormac could see the entire riverfront from his vantage point, but he had taken a special interest in the old houseboat that was tied securely to two huge bollards. He reckoned there were three people on board—an old woman, a young woman, and a little girl—and he had come to admire them, particularly the young woman who had figured out how to pull herself ashore in a fishing boat. *Those are tough women. I'm bettin' they'll make it through this flood.*

Cormac was watching them on the day the bow line gave way and the boat swung out into the current. He saw the women go forward to see what they could do, and he saw the big log hit the boat, causing the old woman to fall overboard. He knew she was a goner when she fell in. And he could tell the young woman and the little girl were devastated, even though he could not hear their screams.

It all happened fast, but as soon as the old woman fell in Cormac ran down the path, aiming to help if he could. *They got to get that bow line secured or they're done for.*

When he got to the bollards, the houseboat held only by its stern line was swinging wildly in the current and high wind. The bow line was still attached to the boat, but it was dangling in the water. It had come apart due to chafing, but the separation was at the end closest to the bollard. Cormac started thinking. *If I could get ahold of that dangling line and tie some more line to it ... Hmmm ... that might work ....*

He called to Sarah, who had come out onto the aft deck, "Have you got another mooring line?"

"Yes, can you help us? I've got a little girl on board."

"I'll try."

Cormac grabbed the stern line, eased into the water, and pulled himself to the houseboat. When he got on board Sarah started to say something, but Cormac cut her off. "It's cold as hell—I'm soaked—and we ain't got no time to waste. Get that extra line for me and let's get busy."

He went forward, pulled the dangling line out of the water, and when Sarah brought the spare line to him he tied the two lines together. He pointed to the knot he tied and said, "That's called a Carrick Bend; it'll hold for sure. Now I got to get this end of the line back to shore and get it around a bollard."

Cormac pulled the repaired bow line back to the stern and Sarah followed him, saying "Thank you" over and over. When they reached the aft deck Kizzy was standing in the doorway, shivering and crying. Cormac said, "Hang on, young'un. We're gonna get this fixed."

He tied the line around his waist and slipped back into the water. Then he used the stern line to pull himself back to shore. He undid the line from his waist and hitched it around the bollard that had been used for the bow line. *There! Now I've got to pull the bow in close …*

⚜

Sarah and Kizzy watched as Cormac pulled on the line. Kizzy said, "Who is he, Ma?"

"I don't know, Kizzy. But we're lucky he came along."

Cormac tugged and pulled, struggling for every foot of purchase, and as he worked, Sarah sized him up for Kizzy. "He's taller than Grandpa. I make him six-foot-four at least, and I figure he's around 30 or 35." They watched Cormac work for a while, and then Sarah said, "This is why MeeMaw said a woman needs a man on board."

"He's pretty good-looking," Kizzy said. "But his teeth go every-which-way."

Sarah laughed. "Go inside and dig out some of Grandpa's old clothes, somethin' warm."

⚜

Cormac finally got the houseboat back to where it had been before the catastrophe. He secured the line around the bollard and gave a thumbs-up to Sarah and Kizzy.

Sarah waved, and then she held Grandpa's old clothes up as high as she could. She motioned for Cormac to come back to the houseboat. He gave her another thumbs-up, grabbed the stern line, and pulled himself back through the water to the houseboat. Once again, he came aboard dripping wet, but this time Sarah greeted him with a hug.

"Where's the little girl?" Cormac said.

"She's inside laying down. She's tough, but this has been a hard day. She lost her grandpa in November and now MeeMaw's gone."

"It's a shame all right." Cormac shivered as he spoke.

"Let's get inside. You can get out of those wet clothes and I'll make some hot coffee."

As soon as they got through the door Sarah heard Kizzy crying. She told Cormac to dry off and change clothes and then she lay down beside Kizzy. She put her arms around her and whispered, "Go on and cry, baby. It's all right. I'm crying too, but we got to go on—that's what MeeMaw would tell us to do. It's a hard life on the river. That's what she'd say."

Kizzy fell asleep in her mother's arms. Sarah stroked her red hair and slipped out of bed. Cormac was dry, outfitted in Grandpa's best flannel shirt and a pair of overalls. Sarah said, "Sit down and rest. I'll make that coffee I promised."

A half-hour later, they were sipping hot coffee and talking. As soon as Sarah finished her coffee she took a hot rock off of the stove, wrapped it in a towel, and placed it in Kizzy's bunk, against her belly. Kizzy woke up long enough to give Sarah a kiss, and then she snuggled up against the rock and went back to sleep.

Sarah slipped out of her clothes and got into the other bunk.

Cormac took off Grandpa's overalls and got in beside her.

Sarah's favorite hot rock was still sitting on the cookstove.

XIII

Pennsilfaanisch Deitsch

On March 17, 1937—three months after the wedding of Annemarie to Fritz Halder—Uncle Gustave brought good news to Villa Elbe.

He found Annemarie alone in the library, shelving a book. He tossed his hat on the sofa and made his announcement with great flourish. "The lawyers tell me that everything is in order for your departure to America. They just got word that the U. S. Consulate has issued the necessary immigration visas."

"Oh, Uncle …" Annemarie locked her hands against her breast and smiled, but then her voice quivered. "I have been so worried—you thought the visas would take longer. How …?"

He winked and gave her a mischievous smile. "Well, yes I did … but a little grease makes the machinery of government move faster." He laughed aloud. "I have an ally at the consulate who helps me—he likes grease."

"When can we go?"

"I have booked passage for you, Stefan, and Fritz on the *SS von Hase.* You will leave from Bremerhaven two weeks from today."

Annemarie grinned and stepped close to hug the old man, but she stopped short of him and her smile went away. "Fritz will move in now—I know he must, but I've got to explain it to Stefan. I've been putting it off …"

⚜

When Stefan got home from school, his mother met him at the door and led him into the library. They sat down and exchanged niceties about his day, and then she patted him on the knee. "Good news, son, Uncle Gustave says we can leave for America in two weeks."

Stefan saw her excitement, but sensed that she had more to say. And she did. Annemarie carried on, bubbling about going on a big boat and the thrill of living in America. He liked all of that, particularly the part about the cowboys and Indians. But his mother had not mentioned Fritz, and when he could wait no longer, he asked, "Will Fritz sleep in your bed now?"

Annemarie winced. She took his face in her hands and gently pulled him close and kissed his forehead. "No one can take your father's place, Stefan—but we must be nice to Fritz. He is helping us get to America."

Stefan broke from his mother's arms and ran out of the library. Then he turned and climbed the stairs thinking of the times he had seen Fritz kissing his mother. The image would not go away. *No. Stop it. She loves my father—not you.*

When he reached the third floor, Stefan ran to a small spiral staircase at the end of the hall and started climbing. And when he got to the top he opened a small creaky door and entered his thinking spot—the attic of Villa Elbe. It was filled with Uncle Gustave's memorabilia—curios, paintings, books, and stuffed animals. Things he had collected in a lifetime of travel in Europe and the Near East. It was a perfect place for Stefan to dream. Here he could wander off to strange places or think about things that troubled him.

He went first to the painting of a young couple with a small girl. He had always imagined it to be a family that Uncle Gustave had, or one that he wanted but never got. But today it brought memories of the picnic in the Neander Valley. *My family—Father and Mother and me … not Fritz … they're watching me run, skip, and jump … the futbol game … and Father telling the story about the old bones. He makes me laugh, and Mother is laughing too.* Stefan moved to his right and opened a frayed leather case. He did not take the balalaika out of the case but plucked each of its three strings. *Father—Mother—Grandfather. I love you … family … not Fritz.* Then he closed the case and moved on to his favorite, a stuffed red fox with cunning eyes. He stared into them. *Mother says Fritz must live with us ... he's not my father ... tell me what to do ... Mr. Fox?*

⚜

Later that day Annemarie went for a walk in the park with Uncle Gustave. "Stefan is miserable. He cannot bear the thought of Fritz sharing a bed with me. I should have talked to him sooner, but I kept putting it off."

Uncle Gustave could tell that she wanted to say more, so he listened. Annemarie told him how Stefan ran from her when she said it was time for Fritz to move in. She repeated the story several times, but the old man never interrupted. When she was done, she cried— whimpering first, and then sobbing. He put his arms around her. "It was one thing for Stefan to see you marry Fritz, but it is another thing for a boy to think about another man sleeping in his mother's bed."

They walked a while, thinking—then Uncle Gustave spoke.

"Give him some time. He will never like it, but he will adapt to it. I think he knows it is something he must accept."

"I pray you are right, Uncle. It is hard for me, but it is harder for him. I must be patient because we have got to get out of Germany."

They turned around and headed home, but Annemarie stopped when they reached the portico of Villa Elbe. "There's another thing that is bothering me."

"Go ahead, get it all out."

"We have never told Fritz that Victor was a Jew or that I want to leave Germany because I am scared of the Nazis."

"He doesn't care about that. He thinks you want to go for other reasons. He wants to go to America because he is an adventurer at heart and believes he can make his fortune there."

"Yes, he has said as much to me. But what bothers me is that he doesn't seem to think the Nazis are all that bad. On occasion we have seen some Brownshirts or SS people and he just shrugs it off. He says things are better in Germany than they were during the Great Depression and that people are worried too much about Hitler."

"A lot of Germans are in a deep sleep, dear Annemarie." He rubbed his forehead and looked away. "The truth is you and Fritz are leaving Germany for very different reasons. But in time he will see what we see, and in time he will come to his senses. For now, you must steel yourself to avoid all talk of such things. Get to America—that is the first order of business."

They looked at each other for a moment, then stepped up onto the porch and went inside.

⚜

On the eve of departure at 4 o'clock, Annemarie left Villa Elbe for a walk in the park. She had spent the day packing and writing two goodbye letters, one to Uncle Gustave and another to her father. Now she wanted to be alone, to think and make peace with herself about the love of her life.

She went directly to her favorite spot, a quaint copper-roofed gazebo that overlooked a small pond, and was pleased to see that she would have it to herself. She sat down and smiled as a mother duck marched by, leading her seven babies from one spot to another for some obscure reason.

When the last baby duck marched out of sight Annemarie focused on the difficult issue that had brought her to this place to pray.

Fritz had moved into Villa Elbe the day after Uncle Gustave's announcement that the papers were in order, and Annemarie slept with him that night. She allowed him to consummate the marriage because that is what she had promised to do, and she did not want him to back out of their deal. But in the days since, she had come to believe that she should try to make the marriage work. She realized that their sterile arrangement—the marriage of convenience—might get them to America, but it was a formula for disaster. It would eventually fail and that would bring more heartache for her and Stefan. *After all*, she reasoned, *Fritz is a nice man. He will be a good provider and he seems to be madly in love with me.*

A couple walked by, and when they were gone Annemarie bowed her head. *Lord, Victor is the father of my son and I will love him forever, but I must go on with life and I must learn to love Fritz as much as he loves me. Help me to do that. And give me the wisdom to help Stefan accept Fritz as his stepfather. But let us always hold dear our good memory of life on the farm with Victor. Amen.*

⚜

As the dinner hour approached, Annemarie and Fritz waited in the parlor for Uncle Gustave to come home. Stefan was playing with the chess set, lining the pieces up as he would line up toy soldiers. Annemarie said, "Where's Uncle Gustave? It's unlike him to be a minute late."

The words were barely out of her mouth when the front door opened and Uncle Gustave shouted, "Look who I found wandering around outside! … Surprise!"

Stefan was the first to see the guest. "Grandfather!" He ran to the old man and threw his arms around his waist. He shrieked again, "Grandfather!" Then he broke down crying and sobbing.

Annemarie hugged her father and motioned for Fritz to come close, but her father was busy honoring Gustave. "Thanks to Gustave. He made all of the arrangements—sent me a train ticket and picked me up at the station. That's a good brother for you." Then he shook Fritz' hand and said, "Welcome to our family."

The dinner lasted for two hours, giving everyone a chance to visit and talk about going to America. Annemarie was pleased to see that Fritz and her father were getting along quite well, but she was not surprised. Fritz grew up on a farm, and the two men shared several stories, mostly about the satisfaction of doing hard work "with your hands."

Stefan also noticed their friendliness, announcing abruptly to his grandfather, "Fritz took me fishing when I first got here—we didn't catch anything, but we had a good time."

Everyone laughed, and Annemarie's father gave her a knowing wink. She winked back and mouthed a thank you.

⚜

They got up before dawn on the day of departure. The *SS von Hase* would sail from Bremerhaven, a port city two hours away by train. Uncle Gustave and Grandfather said their goodbyes at the Hamburg station and Annemarie let Stefan cling to them until the conductor said it was time to get aboard. And when the train pulled away Stefan had his nose pressed against the window, waving to the two old men. When they faded from view, he plopped down on the seat and laid his head on Annemarie's lap.

They got to Bremerhaven three hours before the scheduled departure and took their place in the long line of voyagers waiting to clear for passage to America. They shuffled their way along, but Stefan was not satisfied to stay in the slow-moving line. There was too much to see, so from time to time Annemarie had to pull him back to her side. As they neared the control point Annemarie noticed that the officials checking passports and papers were working at a reasonable pace, but two Nazi SS officers standing behind them kept interfering, and that slowed the process.

They pulled two young families out of line and made them report to an office that had a large Nazi flag above the door. Neither family had come back, so Annemarie concluded that the Nazis were looking for someone. She shivered and got a sinking feeling as they inched closer to the officials. When they were next in line to present their credentials, she took out her compact to check her appearance. Then she brushed her hair back, smoothed her dress, and chit-chatted loudly with Fritz about farm work in the Rhineland. Suddenly it was their turn.

"*Deutsche Pass-Kontrolle.*" The Nazi SS officer calling for passports looked over the shoulder of the immigration official and then squarely at Annemarie. She gave him a warm smile to mask the wormy feeling in her stomach. He looked at her, then the papers, back and forth, and finally he stared into her eyes and did not blink. She cringed. But the long stare suddenly became a mysterious smirk, and the SS man waved them through.

⚜

When the *SS von Hase* cleared the Bremerhaven channel and steamed into the North Sea, the captain announced that they would arrive in New York City on Wednesday morning, April 7, 1937.

Annemarie, Fritz and Stefan stood on deck watching, taking their last look at Germany.

⚜

The *SS von Hase* docked at 10 a.m., right on schedule. The passengers disembarked and formed several lines to clear immigration. A dozen protesters, who stood outside the secure area waving homemade signs and chanting anti-Nazi, anti-Hitler slogans greeted them. Annemarie hustled Stefan past the protesters, but he tugged the sleeve of her dress and asked, "Are they mad at us, Mother?"

"No, they are mad at Hitler and the Nazis."

"It's just politics," Fritz said. "They don't really know what is going on in Germany."

He started to say more, but Annemarie gave him a stern look. "This is not the time to get into that."

"Yes, dear."

⚜

The immigration process was arduous, but the American officials did not frighten Annemarie as did the SS officer in Bremerhaven. As soon as they cleared immigration, they made their way to Grand Central Station where Fritz bought tickets to Kutztown, Pa., a small village 115 miles west of New York City.

A redcap helped Fritz carry their luggage and showed them to their seats on the train. Once settled, Annemarie noticed a heavyset man sitting across the aisle from them. He was watching their every move and seemed to be listening to their conversation. Annemarie smiled at him and said, "Hello."

The man answered in fluent German. "I'm sorry, but I heard you talking about the protesters who met the *SS von Hase*. I just want to say welcome to America."

"So you are German?" Annemarie asked.

"Well, I was born in Heidelberg, but I came to America when I was the age of your boy. For the longest time I said I was German, but now, especially when I travel, I call myself *Pennsilfaanisch Deitsch.*"

Annemarie gave him a quizzical look. "I don't understand."

"There is some lingering hostility toward Germany due to the World War and the recent activities of Hitler and the Nazis. You saw an example of it when the protesters met your boat." He hesitated. "You will learn, as I have, that *Pennsilfaanisch Deitsch* has a good connotation and it allows us to sidestep the present difficulty of being German."

"We are going to live in a small village near Kutztown. Don't most of the people there have German roots?"

"Yes, and they do not hide from that. But they also like being called *Pennsilfaanisch Deitsch.* You will see. Be patient—there is much for you to learn."

⚜

When they neared Kutztown on the Allentown and Auburn Railroad, Fritz pulled a folded letter from his pocket and read from it. "Horst Bachmann says, 'I will meet you at the Kutztown Depot if you will telegraph the time of your arrival. I have arranged a place for you in the nearby village of Willich.'"

"Well, you sent him a telegram from Grand Central Station. I'm sure he will be there. Uncle Gustave said he is a good man."

It was just getting dark when the conductor came through the car chanting, "Kutztown. Next stop, Kutztown."

XIV

The Way of the River

On Sunday, April 11, 1937, Kizzy heard the church bells ringing in Big Pearl. She finished her breakfast with Sarah and Cormac, and went outside to where MeeMaw had been standing when the big log hit the boat and knocked her overboard. The townspeople of Big Pearl could also hear the bells, and they would gather to worship and pray. But Kizzy did not know about such things. MeeMaw, her teacher, had never been a church-going woman. She preached a different message that she called "the way of the river."

Kizzy sat down on the deck and let her feet dangle in the water. The current was gentle; the water was warming after a hard winter. She rubbed her heels against the mossy scum on the side of the houseboat, and began to sing one of MeeMaw's favorites:

Lady Margaret was standing in her high parlor door,
Combing back her yellow hair;
And none did she see but Sweet William and his bride,
Who were going to the Roman Fair…

"Kizzy." Sarah interrupted the singing as she walked onto the foredeck. "You need to stop moping around. I miss MeeMaw too, but those old songs always end up with killin' or dyin' and that ain't good for you."

"I like the old songs. MeeMaw taught them to me and I'm singing them for her."

Sarah put her arm around Kizzy and said, as gently as she could, "Well, she can't hear you no more, Honey. She's gone on down the river."

Kizzy shrugged Sarah's arm off her shoulder and stared into the water. Then she got up and acted as if she was ready to go inside. Sarah started toward the aft deck, but Kizzy did not follow. She looked back at Kizzy and started to say something, but decided not to. Sarah just shook her head and went back inside.

Kizzy looked downriver. *MeeMaw? ....Grandpa? ....You all doing any toe-digging? ... Cormac and Ma are sleeping in your bunk ... they wrestle around every night and make lots of racket ...but we're getting along ...*

⚜

On Kizzy's ninth birthday, July 4, 1937, Sarah gave her a surprise party. They invited Birdie's young sisters and his mother to eat birthday cake at a cleared-off spot up by the bollards. Sarah handed Kizzy a present and she tore the wrapping off. *A dress ...I got a dress.*

She giggled and jumped up and down. Then she whispered to Sarah, "This is my best birthday ever. Is Cormac rich or something?"

Sarah laughed. "No, you can thank MeeMaw for this. We cashed in her burying pearl—she didn't need it—and Cormac said we could use the money to get a new trotline and he's got his eye on a used outboard motor that he says we need to work the river."

Later that morning Kizzy dressed up. She put on the 99-cent print that Sarah ordered from the Sears, Roebuck catalog. And they headed up the hill—Kizzy strutting in the lead—to watch the Independence Day parade, but it got rained out.

⚜

For the rest of the summer they worked the river. Kizzy and Sarah liked to toe-dig for mussels, but Cormac got twice as many by tonging and raking. And the new trotline proved to be a good investment. They made some extra money that would come in handy during the cold months.

The long days on the river gave Kizzy and Sarah plenty of chances to talk about Cormac. Sarah said she liked him and praised him for being a hard worker. She said he like to drink whiskey, and had an eye for the girls, but those were natural shortcomings for a working man.

Sarah often stared at Cormac as he tonged and raked, shirtless in the hot sun. And when Kizzy caught her admiring his physique Sarah would explain. "You know what? MeeMaw was right. A woman livin' on the river needs a man."

Kizzy was tempted to ask what they were doing in bed to make all that noise, but she did not.

Summer soon gave way to September, and it was time for Kizzy to go back to school.

XV

Willich, PA.

Fritz pressed his face against the window as their train neared the station, straining to see as far down the track as he could. Soon he got a first glimpse of the Kutztown Depot. "The track is very close to the building. There is an old man waiting." Then, as their rail car rolled to a stop, he turned to Annemarie and grinned. "It's him." Fritz pointed to an elderly man in a dark business suit standing on the small platform, beneath an overhanging roof. "That has to be Horst Bachmann."

Stefan giggled and pushed Fritz aside. "Let us see!" He and Annemarie put their faces close to the window, and when they saw the spindly old man on the platform, they waved and shouted his name. But Horst Bachmann did not see them; he was preoccupied—staring at his pocket watch. Stefan pecked on the window. "Here we are! Here!" Finally, the old man snapped the cover shut on his watch and looked their way. "He sees us, Mother!" They waved again and Stefan danced around as if he had to pee. Horst Bachmann did not wave, but he cracked a small smile, nodded, and politely touched his walking stick against the brim of his black derby hat.

Annemarie whispered to herself, *thank God.*

⚜

Horst Bachmann loaded them and their belongings into his 1936 black Oldsmobile and drove slowly away from the Kutztown station. "I have arranged a place for you in Willich. It is a small village about 15 miles from here."

They talked first about the trip from Germany, and then Horst said to Annemarie, "Gustave told me you lived with his brother on a farm near Düsseldorf. I think you will like this place. It is a 20-acre fruit and vegetable farm, and two acres of the 20 are devoted to the barn and a small two-bedroom house. I own the place, so we can work out a rental arrangement once you are settled."

Fritz smiled. *"Danke schön, Herr Bachmann."*

"Ha! You are welcome, but you must begin now to speak English. Many people here speak German as well as English, and they will help you." Horst pointed to Stefan. "It will be easiest for the boy. The elementary school in Willich is a small one-room school, and the teacher, Katharina Werner, is a good woman who came here from Germany five years ago. She now has perfect English."

Annemarie said, "Forgive me for speaking in German, but Stefan's school near the Neander Valley was also very small. I think he will like it, won't you, Stefan?"

Stefan scrunched down in the back seat and mumbled, "Yes, Mother."

⚜

They turned off the highway and headed up a long, winding one-lane dirt trail. Annemarie caught sight of the farmhouse and barn and turned to Stefan. "It reminds me of Grandfather's farm. I think we will like it here very much, don't you, Stefan?"

He mumbled again. "Yes, Mother."

Horst changed the subject. "Fritz, you will find plenty of work around here. It is just 15 miles to Kutztown, and several other towns are very close. There is a Ford A-Model truck on the farm that you can use for farm work, but you can also use it to drive back and forth to do your work as a brickmason."

Fritz hesitated, and then spoke with a heavy accent, "Thank you, Mister Bachmann."

⚜

On Oct. 12, 1938, 18 months from the day they arrived in Willich, Fritz and Annemarie took Stefan to a traditional Oktoberfest celebration in downtown Kutztown. As they drove near the center of town, they heard an oompah band—the familiar sound of tubas and euphoniums in rhythm with a thumping bass drum.

Fritz parked the truck, and as they walked toward the crowd of merrymakers Annemarie's thoughts turned to Germany—the good times on the farm with Victor and Stefan and the bad times with Hitler and the Brownshirts. Then she thought about their new life in America and the day Horst Bachmann met them at the train station.

They had spent several days unpacking, but quickly realized that they had no time to waste. The 10-acre orchard was in good shape, but eight acres of tillable land needed attention. A neighbor had plowed the field for Horst, but it was time to work the land and get it ready for planting.

They had walked over the entire farm with Horst discussing which crops they should grow, and that conversation produced a long work list and a division of responsibilities. Annemarie would keep the house in order, fix the meals, and shop for seeds and other essentials. Fritz would keep the farm equipment working, and harrow and prepare the eight acres for planting. Stefan would take care of the animals, gather the eggs, and—because the county schools did not meet in April or May—he would help Annemarie and Fritz in every way that he could. Stefan quickly learned that farm work is a way of life for children in Pennsylvania Dutch country.

Annemarie liked Stefan's school the instant she saw it. She was confident he would like it, and she was right. The schoolhouse favored the one he attended in Germany near the Neander Valley—a rectangular white frame building with six windows on each side and two windows on either end.

The yard around the school was grassy and open except for a large oak tree and a one-hole outhouse carefully positioned to account for the prevailing wind. A small bell tower atop the arched roof was directly above a single door that opened to the classroom—a Spartan arrangement of fold-top desks lined up, two deep, on either side of a potbelly stove that dominated the center of the room.

Katharina, the schoolmarm, proved to be a blessing. She was German on the outside—blonde hair in a bun, stocky, and all business—but on the inside she was a work in progress: an immigrant acclimating to American ways. She took a personal interest in Stefan; thus he transitioned from German to passable English somewhat faster than Annemarie. Fritz made steady progress with the new language, but he still resorted to German when he got excited, stubbed his toe, or smashed his finger with a hammer.

⚜

Annemarie's reverie of the farm and their new life in America ended when a smiling young man in traditional Bavarian costume—classic shirt, lederhosen, knee-length stockings, and colorful suspenders—greeted them. He tipped his Alpine hat and handed Annemarie a leaflet:

> "Welcome to our traditional OKTOBERFEST!
> Hitler is trying to rename it.
> He calls it the 'Greater German Folk Festival.'
> But Adolf Hitler cannot change what is in our hearts.
> This festival is ours, not his. It is and always will be:
> OKTOBERFEST"

Annemarie smiled. *Good for them!*

The German immigrants sponsoring the event hailed from Munich, and no Nazi was going to hijack their beloved Oktoberfest. They would celebrate in the finest tradition of old Germany—not Hitler's Germany—with games, native costumes, and lots of German food: *Bratwurst, weisswurst, knockwurst*, black bread, kraut, and beer. And, in a concession to their new home in America, roasted corn on the cob.

They spent most of the day at Oktoberfest, but by sundown they had had their fill. As they drove back to the farm Annemarie said, "I think we have the better of both worlds—Germany and America. Today was nice. It was a good way to remember the best about our homeland, but we are here now and America has so much to offer."

Fritz and Stefan nodded in agreement, but they let her ramble on.

"I must write Uncle Gustave tonight to tell him how well we are getting along—thanks to him and Horst Bachmann."

⚜

St. Andrew's Catholic Church in rural Willich, Pa., paled in comparison to the magnificent St. Lambertus Cathedral in Düsseldorf, the site of Annemarie's baptism and confirmation. But on her first visit to the tiny rustic church—shortly after they arrived in America—Annemarie gasped and murmured to herself when she saw a carved wooden image of the virgin and child near the altar. *My God, can it be?* As she neared the altar she noticed that the sculpture was rough-hewn and smaller; even so, it brought back memories of the Virgin and Child, the famous wood carving at St. Lambertus. She kneeled at the altar, made the sign of the cross, and looked up to savor the image. *Yes. Mother and child. We're in a new place, Stefan. God forgive me for the lies I tell.*

Stefan liked to go to mass with his mother, but Fritz did not. His principal argument for not attending was that he hailed from a long line of Protestants—common people who had become dissatisfied with the doctrines and perceived corruption of the Catholic Church—but Annemarie would not let him get away with that. She would say to him: "There are scores of Protestant churches around here—Lutheran, German Reformed, Dunkards, Moravians, Amish and Mennonites—and you don't go to any of them."

Fritz did not like to fuss with Annemarie, so he adopted a strategy that suited his personality. He would let her skin him with logic, then he would shrug his shoulders, give her a goofy grin, and say nothing. After a while, Annemarie gave up and invited Horst Bachmann to go to church with her and Stefan.

Horst had been a member of St. Andrew's since he came to America in 1908, but he had quit going after his wife died. To go to mass with the beautiful Annemarie and Stefan was a blessing for the old man. He immediately accepted her invitation.

⚜

On Sunday, Nov. 13, 1938, Horst drove to Willich to pick up Annemarie and Stefan for the short ride to St. Andrew's. As soon as they got in the car he said, "Still can't get Fritz to go to church?"

"No, but I can't complain. He is a hard worker. He takes care of the farm and does bricklaying on the side … enough to save a little money." She gently poked Horst and chuckled. "By the way, speaking of money, I am going to start working for Doctor Günther, at his clinic. I wanted to be a nurse when I was a girl, but didn't have the chance to do it."

Horst pondered, and then said, "Doc Günther is a good man, but you take care. He has beds for sick people in his little clinic, doesn't he?"

"Yes, but I'll be fine." Annemarie then turned to Stefan who was in the back seat. "Look, there are your friends."

Horst pulled into the parking lot at St. Andrew's, and as soon as he stopped the car Stefan turned the door handle, but could not get the door to open. Horst reached back and released the lock. He smiled and said, "Try it now." Stefan did and when the door opened, he jumped out of the car and ran full-speed to join the cluster of young boys playing near the sanctuary door.

Horst laughed, and then he looked at Annemarie. "How is he doing?"

"I'm not sure, Horst. We've been here a year and a half. Most of the time, Stefan is my precious little German boy—doing well at school and working hard on the farm. I love to watch him, and I melt when he smiles at me. But I want him to be happy, and there are moments when he seems withdrawn and troubled." She grimaced and looked at Horst. "And it breaks my heart when he is like that."

Horst put his hand on her arm. "He's just 10 years old, Annemarie. It's the beginning of puberty, a puzzling time for boys—and girls too, for that matter."

"I've taken that into account, but Stefan has been through more than most boys. He lost his father in a terrible accident. Then I married Fritz and we moved to America, away from his grandfather and his home in Germany."

"It was the right thing to do ..."

Annemarie interrupted. "Yes. It was, and I am at peace with the decisions I made, but the changes are bothering Stefan." She paused, and then said, "Fritz is good to him, but he is more of a friend than a father. Stefan likes him, but he misses Victor—they were very close."

Horst could see that Annemarie wanted to talk, so he said nothing.

She glanced at Horst, and then she looked down and spoke in a soft voice. "Stefan has not touched his violin since Victor died, more than two years ago."

Horst hummed, but let her go on. And her voice quavered. "It just bothers Stefan ..." She looked away to finish her point, mouthing the words so that Horst could not hear her. ... *It still bothers him for Fritz to sleep in my bed, and I don't know what to do about it.*

"He misses his father, Annemarie. That is normal. In time, he will understand. Just love him. I know you will do that, but you must be patient." He patted her shoulder. "Let's go to mass and pray about this."

⚜

Father Joseph Meissner, a wisp of a man hunchbacked by age, had been the only priest at St. Andrew's for 45 years. He moved carefully around the altar during mass, taking care to keep his balance. But his frailty belied the tone and power of his voice—that of a young virile man. He performed the prescribed rituals in a soothing baritone and delivered his homilies in a booming bass that was easy on the ears. The parishioners at St. Andrew's listened closely to Father Joseph, and they did not care when he drifted from homily to sermon, or sermon to homily. They loved the sound of his voice, and they could tell when he was getting ready to tear into Hitler and the Nazis. On those occasions, the melodious voice would morph into a wild guttural idiolect.

Horst and Annemarie expected Father Joseph to rant about the Nazis when they went to mass on Sunday, Nov. 13, 1938, and it did not take him long to get to the recent news from Germany.

He gently delivered the first words of his homily. "I had intended to speak about the beatification today of Sister Frances Xavier Cabrini—she was, as you know, born in the old Austrian Empire.

"But I must address the latest news from Germany. Jesus taught us to love our brother as we love ourselves, so there can be no excuse for what Hitler and the Nazis did just four days ago. This is on my mind, so hear me out."

Father Joseph held his chin, cleared his throat, and pulled in a deep breath. Then, in the raucous voice he reserved for Nazi evil, he roared:

"On Wednesday—all over Germany, Austria and other Nazi-controlled areas—Hitler's vandals smashed the windows of Jewish shops and department stores, destroying contents and many valuable items. They burned synagogues and desecrated sacred Torah scrolls, and the local fire departments did nothing.

"Hitler's propaganda minister, Joseph Goebbels, fanned the flames, inciting Germans to 'rise up in bloody vengeance against the Jews.' And when mob violence broke out the regular German police just stood by. And crowds of spectators turned a blind eye, and did nothing to stop the violence.

"Nazi stormtroopers along with members of the SS and Hitler Youth beat and murdered Jews, broke into and wrecked Jewish homes, and brutalized Jewish women and children. About 25,000 Jewish men were rounded up and will be sent to concentration camps where they will be brutalized by SS guards."

Father Joseph moved away from the pulpit and wiped his brow. He paused, bowed his head to say a prayer, and then continued in a melodious baritone. "My friends, we who have roots in Germany are now called *Pennsilfaanisch Deitsch* whether we are Catholic, Lutheran, Amish, or whatever. We have learned to live together in peace and make the most of our differences. We Catholics may fuss with the Lutherans about how God saves people from their sins—the doctrine of justification—but we all agree that what is happening in Germany is wrong. We must not be silent. We must speak out against such hatred—such prejudice."

⚜

When they were in the car and headed home, Horst said, "The troubles in Germany continue to mount."

"I am so thankful that we got out of there when we did."

Horst pointed to a stack of newspapers in the back seat. "Father Joseph took his homily from a story that was in Friday's edition of the *New York Times*. It's in the papers that I saved for you."

"Thank you, Horst. I read the papers mainly to practice my English and learn about America, but I am very interested in what Father Joseph said. And I am also interested in the activities of the Hitler Youth and the *Sturmabteilung*. The Brownshirts came to our farm near Düsseldorf to recruit Stefan for the Hitler Youth, and that is the main reason we left when we did."

Stefan chimed in from the back seat of Horst's car. "That's when we went with Father to the place where they found the old bones, wasn't it?"

Annemarie looked at Horst and grimaced. "Yes, Stefan. That was right around the time we picnicked in the Neander Valley."

⚜

Three weeks later, in early December of 1938, Fritz came home late from a bricklaying job in Kutztown. As he sat down for dinner, he pulled a printed black and white flier from his hip pocket and looked at it.

Annemarie asked, "What is that?"

"Oh, when we took our lunch break today a man came by and told us about a new program that sounds interesting, so I went to the meeting before coming home." Fritz handed the flier to her. "The man said it is the way of the future—a way to improve health and make things better."

"Let me see," Annemarie took the flier and read the first few lines aloud:

"Fitter Families
Improve the Human Race
Some people are born to be a burden on the rest
A better society can be created by promoting better bloodlines
6 p.m. Tuesday, Dec. 6, 1938
Willich City Hall
Sponsors: Brandenburg Social Club &
The American Eugenics Society"

"This is garbage, Fritz." She wadded the flier and squeezed it as hard as she could.

Fritz answered, defensively. "The man who spoke at the meeting said the highest court in America and a lot of important people are behind it."

Annemarie stamped her foot and threw the wadded-up paper into the wastebasket. "I don't care what he said. This is wrong. It is not for us to judge our fellow man. It leads to the kind of hatred in Germany that Father Joseph talked about a few days ago—people are now calling it 'The Night of Broken Glass—*Kristallnacht.*' You should go to mass with me instead of going to such meetings."

Fritz saw the look on Annemarie's face and decided to say no more.

XVI

In Loco Parentis

Kizzy woke up early on Independence Day, 1938. It was her 10th birthday, and she intended to make the most of it. She rolled over and then raised up to sit naked on the edge of her bunk. She rubbed her eyes and stretched, and then slipped a clean dress over her head. The cabin was still dark, but it was breaking day on the river. Kizzy tiptoed to the screen door that opened onto the aft deck and carefully lifted it to keep it from squeaking. She pushed it open, inch by inch, taking care not to wake Cormac and her mother. They were in the other bunk bed, naked and snoring lightly; curiously entwined after another night of noisy sex.

Kizzy mused as she stepped onto the aft deck of the houseboat. *He's been living with us a year and a half and they hardly ever miss a night. It must feel awful good.* She stood facing the river and pressed her hands between her legs. A tingly feeling rushed through her loins, and she thought to herself. *It's natural, it's the way of the river—that's what MeeMaw would say.*

Two men in a flat-bottomed fishing boat drifted into sight, interrupting Kizzy's thoughts about sex. The river was still murky with night fog, but it was light enough for her to tell that the men were fishing just for the fun of it. *They're holiday fishermen, casting out and reeling in artificial lures using high-priced rods, and making way too much noise.* When they drifted by the houseboat, Kizzy waved, but the men turned away, purposely ignoring her. She smiled. Grandpa was right. *Just a couple of fancy-pants from town. They wouldn't know how to fish for a living, like we do.*

She stepped close to the stern rail and thought about Grandpa's Independence Day speech. *He used to make it from right where I'm standing. It's a hard life, he'd say. But nobody tells us what to do and we ain't owing to anybody. We live by the law of the river. We're free, and we aim to stay that way. Amen.*

Kizzy sat down on the aft deck and relaxed to enjoy the sounds of the river. She loved to hear the current lapping against the houseboat, the birds tuning up for the day, and the rustle of leaves in the morning wind. But suddenly the music of the river was drowned out by a familiar racket. Kizzy sat upright and looked back through the screen door. *Yep. They're at it again. Mercy.*

⚜

Later that morning Kizzy, Cormac and Sarah were sitting around the table having a late breakfast when they heard Birdie's mother, voluptuous Shirley Barden, call out for permission to come aboard. Kizzy hurried outside to say hello, and saw that Shirley was carrying a dish of food.

"Happy Birthday, Kizzy! I brought you some candied sweet potatoes. It ain't a cake, but I make 'em on the stovetop and my kids love 'em."

Kizzy took the warm dish. "Thank you. This smells real good."

Sarah hollered from inside. "Come on in, Shirley, I've got some coffee made."

"OK, I'm coming." Shirley said as she and Kizzy stepped inside.

Cormac was sitting at the table, shirtless, shoeless, and disheveled. But in a rare nod to modesty he was wearing a beat-up pair of khaki trousers. He took one look at Shirley and said, "Hey, Shirley. Sit yourself down." Cormac, obviously mesmerized by the sight of her breasts, patted the chair next to him.

Sarah did not seem to notice or care, but Kizzy was just beginning to blossom physically, and Cormac's fondness for Shirley's breasts fascinated her. *He looks at mine too. They're little bitty, but he tells me I'm going to be very pretty someday.*

She made a mental note to ask Shirley about such things. *MeeMaw drowned before I started sprouting or I could've asked her. Ma won't talk about her and Cormac doing it, or anything like that. But Birdie's ma knows all about such things. Maybe she'll talk to me.*

Everyone had a scoop of candied sweet potatoes, and then the grownups sang "Happy Birthday" to Kizzy. Shirley went back to her boat, and at 1 o'clock Cormac, Sarah, and Kizzy headed up the hill to Big Pearl to watch the annual Independence Day parade. Kizzy pretended—as she did every year—that the parade and gaiety of July the Fourth was to celebrate her birthday.

⚜

On Tuesday, July 5, Kizzy waited until mid-morning to go see Shirley Barden. When she saw Shirley's little girls playing up by the bollards, Kizzy knew the time was right. Shirley was all alone; this was her chance to get some answers.

Shirley was scrubbing and rinsing clothes and hanging them out to dry on a wire strung across the fore deck when Kizzy walked up and called out to her. "Hey, Shirley, I meant to ask about Birdie yesterday, but we got so busy talking about other stuff that I forgot. How's he doing?"

Shirley invited her to come on board, and when Kizzy was standing on the fore deck with her she said, "He likes the CCC all right, and it's a good thing. But some of 'em are saying there's a war coming and the CCC boys will have to go to the Army." She fed a dress into the rollers of a metal wringer and turned the crank. When the dress got all the way through the wringer Shirley shook it out and pinned it on the line to dry.

Kizzy said, "I wish we had one of those wringers—we have to squeeze the water out of our wash, and it takes longer for them to dry out."

"Yep, it's a handy gadget. I got it from Sears last year for a little over $3."

"Cormac says he doesn't have to worry about the Army because he has one bad eye and flat feet. Maybe Birdie won't have to go."

"Well, Birdie's feet ain't flat and he's got the eyes of a hawk." Shirley turned away from the wringer and started scrubbing a handful of soapy underwear on a small brass washboard. "I don't want my boys going off to no war—they'll just be cannon fodder for the rich folks."

Shirley carried on about the rich folks for another 10 minutes, grieving that they always take advantage of poor boys like Birdie. Kizzy just listened and nodded in agreement. Meanwhile, she was trying to think of a way to change the subject to what she came for: learning what she could from Shirley—a very experienced woman—about sex and growing up, and what to do about it.

Suddenly, a way occurred to Kizzy. "I don't think my ma could put her purifying sheepskins through that wringer—she'll have to keep on wringing them out by hand."

Shirley stopped scrubbing, looked up and laughed. "Purifying? I ain't heard it called that in a while. I call it a curse, myself."

"I ain't started yet," Kizzy said. "But MeeMaw always called it purifying."

"Well, you'll learn about it soon enough. But, when you start, don't use them old sheepskins or rags that your ma uses. Come see me and I'll give you some of my Cellu-ettes. I get 'em from Sears for a penny apiece with the money Birdie sends me from the CCC. They're every bit as good as them high-priced Kotex."

Kizzy thanked her, but she had not come to learn about menstruation or sanitary napkins. She wanted to learn as much as she could about what Sarah and Cormac were doing almost every night, and she could not hold back any longer. The questions rushed out of her, all at once. "You've got five kids. What's it like to do it with a man? What does it feel like? How does all that work? And what does it have to do with what MeeMaw called 'purifying'?"

"Whoa, girl." Shirley laughed and patted her on the head. "It ain't for me to tell you all that. You need to ask Sarah." She then turned her back on Kizzy and started putting more wet clothes through the wringer.

Kizzy slumped, and waited to see if Shirley would answer, but she did not. Kizzy stepped toward the gangplank as if to get off the boat, but stopped and looked back. Shirley was still doing her wash, so Kizzy whined in a soft voice, "She won't talk about it." Then she left the boat, but when she had taken just a few steps, she hollered back to Shirley, "But thanks for what you said about the Cellu-ettes. I was worrying about that."

❦

The land upriver from the bollards and behind Bully Bigshot's cotton gin was a mix of wetlands and higher ground thickly covered with a stand of native hardwoods. Kizzy had gone there often with Birdie to learn about the birds and with Grandpa to hunt squirrels and rabbits. The trails were unmarked, but she knew her way through the thicket by heart. It was Kizzy's thinking spot; a place of solitude where she could connect with the two men she admired and with MeeMaw.

Her short conversation with Shirley Barden about sex, purifying, and the other puzzles of pubescence had produced more questions than answers. She had confronted her mother, but the most she could get out of Sarah was a terse admission that Cellu-ettes, for those who can afford them, are easier to use than the sheepskins and purifying rags she had been using for years. Kizzy had asked about the noises that she and Cormac were making in bed, but she refused to answer. And when Kizzy persisted—saying it sounded like they were having fun—Sarah exploded and brought the conversation to a halt. "It's too soon for you to start thinking about all that."

On Tuesday, one week after her conversation with Shirley Barden, Kizzy headed into the woods just after dawn to watch the critters, listen to the birds, and do some thinking. Sarah and Cormac had been especially noisy the night before and Kizzy could not get it off her mind. Her mother had told her it was too soon to think about sex, but that does not work for a 10-year-old at the doorstep of puberty.

Kizzy followed a narrow path to the last place where she saw Grandpa alive, the small clearing where he chopped wood. She sat down on the stump that he sat on and was about to begin a make-believe conversation with him and MeeMaw when she heard the hoot owls barking and cackling. The monkey-like sounds were coming from the wetlands, not far from where she was sitting, and it turned her thoughts to the many times that Birdie tried to teach her how to do birdcalls.

Birdie knew them all, and his calls were so good that the birds would answer him. She had a good ear for the sounds, but she could not make the high chirpy notes that birds sing.

"I just can't whistle that way, Birdie." And they had laughed about it until their sides hurt. Kizzy would pucker her lips and blow out, but blowing air was all she could do. She tried it time and again, but gave up on imitating birdcalls—until the day they heard a hoot owl.

Birdie made a funny face and punched her on the shoulder. "Try doing that one, Kizzy. Try doing Mr. Owl—you don't have to whistle to imitate him."

Kizzy hesitated, but Birdie showed her how to do it, and insisted that she should try it. Finally, after much goading, Kizzy pursed her lips, drew in a deep breath, and hooted: "Who cooks for you? Who cooks for you all?" Birdie gave her a thumbs-up, but Mr. Owl did not answer.

Kizzy loved to think about that day long ago because Birdie's lessons about the birds went beyond making birdcalls. Birdie could describe all the species in detail. He knew all about every bird, their range, nesting traits, and mating habits. He was a storehouse of information, and Kizzy learned a lot from him. She knew what it meant for the hoot owls to bark and cackle. *There's at least two of them out there and that's how they fuss with each other.*

Kizzy walked to the edge of the clearing and hooted, but the owls did not answer. She hooted again, and when they did not answer, she went back to the stump and sat down. Then she turned her thoughts to the thing that was on her mind so often these days—sex, and the questions that no one seemed willing to answer.

Birdie says the hoot owls mate for life. But his ma and mine ain't done that. Nothing close to it. Kizzy touched her swollen nipples and then rubbed between her legs to get the strange feeling in her loins, the same sensation she felt on the boat the morning the fancy-pants fishermen floated by. *MeeMaw and Grandpa may have mated for life, but they never got married.*

Us river people do it our own way—that's what Grandpa always said. Free as a bird, he always said. Hmmm.

✦

Some two years later, on Wednesday, May 8, 1940, Kizzy was just weeks away from finishing the sixth grade, and she was looking forward to summer. Her teacher asked for a show of hands to see how many girls were keeping a diary, and how many boys were keeping a journal. Some of the rich girls raised their hands, but so did Kizzy. None of the boys raised their hands, so the teacher said, "You all are 12 years old now; it's high time for you to start writing notes about your life."

One of the rich girls volunteered that she had been writing a diary since the sixth grade and proudly held it up for the class to see. Kizzy drooled. It was gorgeous, a genuine pink-leather diary with a gold-plated lock and key. Kizzy had seen them in Shirley Barden's Sears catalog. She whispered to herself. *A beauty like that—even when on sale—would cost at least $2.25.*

Kizzy—not about to be outdone by a snooty rich girl—raised her hand. "I've been writing a diary for two years, but mine is at home." The other girls laughed as if they did not believe her, but Kizzy was telling the truth. She had started a diary a few days after she began to think seriously about sex. But she was not penning her thoughts onto the ritzy pages of an expensive store-bought diary. Kizzy kept her diary on the pulpy pages of a Big Parade school tablet, one of the giant-sized ones. Shirley Barden got them from Sears for her girls, and she always ordered a few extra tablets for Kizzy. They cost 5 cents apiece, and Cormac would give Shirley a nickel every time Kizzy needed a new tablet.

Her first entry was on July 15, 1938, a few days after she had tried to get answers from Shirley Barden and Sarah. *Dear Diary: I've got lots of questions about doing it, but Ma won't tell me anything—she says to wait—and Shirley says it's not her place to tell.*

Her next entries told about her life on the river with Grandpa, MeeMaw, and her mother. She also wrote about the Gypsy father she never knew and how Cormac—who saved them from the flood—was proving to be a hard worker and a "pretty good make-do stepfather." And she wrote a whole page about the day Cormac used Grandpa's old diving helmet to dig mussels and found a small pearl worth $100.

On another day she wrote about the kids at school who were teasing her. *Dear Diary: No matter how good I do at school they keep running me down—calling me a river rat and making fun of me. Ma says they are just jealous. MeeMaw used to say that too.*

But many of Kizzy's diary entries for the two-year period from 1938 to 1940 were about her passage through puberty. These very personal notes were sandwiched in between her comments about school and everyday life on the river.

Jan. 30, 1939. I'm getting some hair under my arms. And my little bitty nipples are sore as all get-out.

March, 5, 1939. I've grown three inches since last summer. I'm bigger than a lot of the girls in my class, even the rich ones.

July 4, 1939. My 11th birthday. Ma says the changes in me are normal, but she still won't talk about the funny feelings I am having.

Thanksgiving, 1939. Those little bitty buds that were so tender are turning into sure-enough boobs. Not very big yet, but not as sore as they were.

Feb. 10, 1940. More hair down there and under my arms and that little pea-like thing at the entry to my fotchet feels good to touch.

March 20, 1940. Boobs are coming right along, but I haven't started yet. Some of the girls at school who are a year younger than me have already started.

April 30, 1940. Grown another inch. I'm now an inch over five feet tall. I keep asking Ma, but she won't answer my questions—still saying it is too early.

⚜

Kizzy was determined to solve the enigmas of puberty. She was looking for someone—anyone—to answer her questions.

Voila! On Saturday, May 4, 1940, just two months before Kizzy's 12th birthday, Sarah saw a strange boat coming downriver. She hollered to Cormac and Kizzy who were inside. "Something's coming down the river."

She got no answer from inside the houseboat, but Cormac and Kizzy came outside when Sarah added, "It looks like they mean to tie up here, closer to us than to Shirley Barden."

Tom Pardee's homemade vessel was more scow than houseboat, although it did have the semblance of a shelter on the forward two-thirds of the boat. The improvised cabin was a conglomeration of lumber, glass, various swaths of canvas and corrugated metal. From stem to stern, the boat was a mishmash of thrown-together leftovers. And trailing alongside was a 19-foot workboat full of tools and musseling gear. The smaller boat had an outboard motor hiked up out of the water, but the larger vessel had no motor at all. A sweating, barrel-chested man in overalls propelled it with an extra-long sculling oar. He grunted with each stroke as he pulled the sculling oar back and forth, walking from gunnel to gunnel over a cleared-off spot on the stern. Cormac admired the man's strength and skill as he expertly sculled and steered the clumsy vessel to shore.

A buxom girl stood on the fore deck with a coiled line in her hand, ready to jump onshore to make the tie-up. When they got close, she screeched. "Hi-dee! I'm Elsie Sue."

Cormac nodded, but said nothing. The big man let go of the sculling oar and the scow coasted to shore. "Hey. I'm Tom Pardee. We're coming down from Missouri, just below Poplar Bluff. Lookin' to rest up and do some musselin' around here for a while."

Cormac stared at him and snarled. "This here is our spot. It's barely big enough for us—we're full-up."

Tom Pardee hollered to his daughter. "Tie it tight, Elsie Sue." Then he lowered his voice and stared at Cormac. "We just want to rest up and work around here for a few days and then we'll move on downriver to Jacksonport—we hear that's the best place for pearling."

⚜

Elsie Sue Pardee was almost six feet tall, full-breasted, wide-hipped, and rough looking. She had the look of a woman in her mid-20s, but an imbecilic manner and childish giggle revealed the truth: Elsie Sue was only 15 years old.

Kizzy disliked her immediately, but she did not let Elsie Sue know it. *She's goofy and dumb as a post, but I bet she knows all about sex.*

And Kizzy was right. As soon as she could, she lured Elsie Sue to her thinking spot in the woods to pump her for information. Elsie Sue was eager to help, but she answered every question with a story, a personal experience. And her storytelling—a babble at best—always ended with the same throaty exclamation: "It feels good!" And every time Elsie Sue said those words Kizzy would get that strange feeling in her loins. *Whoa, there it is again.*

On their third visit to the woods Elsie Sue told Kizzy that she had quit school, and she seemed to be proud of it. Kizzy tried to change her mind about school, but Elsie Sue butted in to tell a story about the time she "screwed two boys, one right after the other." Kizzy thought to herself, *Good grief.*

When Elsie Sue saw Kizzy's reaction she returned to her principle argument for unbridled sex: "It feels good."

There it is again. Dang. Kizzy had had enough. She made up her mind to avoid Elsie Sue, but that became unnecessary when Tom Pardee made a pass at Sarah, and Cormac beat the living daylights out of him in a burst of anger and territorial protection. The Pardee scow left the Big Pearl tie-up on Saturday, May 11, 1940.

⚜

Curly's stinky Fish Market was a fixture on Black River. The tar-papered shack sat on a huge barge docked a half-mile downstream from the bollards. Curly's was a gathering spot for townspeople and commercial fishermen. Cormac liked to bring his catch there because Curly promised honest weights and square dealing—a motto he extolled in big white letters over the store's entry, directly beneath a six-foot-long hand-painted bright-yellow catfish. Homemade signs on either side of the entryway listed the kinds of fish for sale beneath a curious heading: "Special Today—Alive Fish."

On June 5, 1940, Cormac took a big load of fish to the market, and after Curly weighed his catch, he went inside to get payment. A dozen men were in the market, but they were not gabbing and joking—they were huddled around a radio, and that was unusual. Cormac joined the gathering just in time to hear the voice of a British announcer:

"Today, the Germans launched a fresh assault. France is about to fall, and the last of the British Expeditionary Forces—over 300,000 men—have been evacuated from the beaches of Dunkirk. Prime Minister Winston Churchill has issued a call to arms. He said this yesterday in the House of Commons: 'We shall go on to the end, we shall fight in France, we shall fight on the seas and oceans, we shall fight with growing confidence and growing strength in the air, we shall defend our Island, whatever the cost may be, we shall fight on the beaches, we shall fight on the landing grounds, we shall fight in the fields and in the streets, we shall fight in the hills; we shall never surrender.'"

An American announcer in Washington, D. C., followed up with an interview of a congressman who predicted the United States would be drawn into the war, and with that the crowd at Curly's stopped listening and started arguing.

A rickety old man wearing a campaign hat said, "It's going to be just like the World War." Then he started singing snippets of George M. Cohan's big hit. "Over there … over there … and we won't come back 'til it's over, over there."

"Bullshit," said the man standing next to Cormac. "We ain't gonna do that again. It ain't our fight. Let 'em fight it out over there."

⚜

On Oct. 31, 1940, Kizzy got home from school just as Cormac was returning from a day's work on the river. Sarah was not there, so Kizzy tossed her books on the bunk and went outside to the aft deck. Then she waved to Cormac as he steered the workboat to its place alongside the houseboat.

"Do any good?"

"Yep, I just took a load to Curly's. Thirty-eight pounds—not bad."

Cormac grunted as he climbed from the workboat onto the aft deck of the houseboat. He looked around to be sure they were alone, and put his finger to his lips. "Shhh. I got a surprise for you."

"For me?" Kizzy beamed and danced around.

Cormac pulled a Baby Ruth candy bar out of his pocket and handed it to her. "Happy Halloween."

"Thanks, Cormac." She tore the wrapper off and took a bite.

Cormac smiled and started through the door. As he did he bumped against Kizzy and patted her on the butt. "I swear, girl, you're just 12, but you're gonna be prettier than your ma."

XVII

Good Friday

Annemarie left work at Doctor Günther's clinic just before dark on Dec. 23, 1940. She had offered to stay later, but the doctor insisted, "Go on, Annemarie. Enjoy *Kristkindlmarkt* with your family."

"But the clinic is full. I should stay."

"I can handle it. This flu is virulent, but it is nothing compared to 1918. I was doing my residency in Philadelphia back then, and we lost over 700 people in one day."

"Well, I've been working here two years, and this is the first time we have had to cram extra cots into the clinic."

"Go!" Doctor Günther pointed to the door and smiled. "I can handle this. Enjoy yourself. This is the last night for the market—tomorrow is Christmas Eve and everything will close at noon."

⚜

Twelve-year-old Stefan turned and walked away from a cluster of schoolgirls, but not before his persnickety classmate, Manfred, giggled and mouthed a not-so-silent alert: "Your hard-on is showing."

Stefan put his hand in his pocket as he walked away, hoping to escape further embarrassment. *Drats. It's as hard as a brickbat.* He kept walking and talking to himself. *Nach unten. Down.* And it did go down, as quickly as it had arisen, without warning or fanfare.

It was not Stefan's first arousal, but he was still learning and sorting through the mysteries of puberty without Victor, his real father. *Fritz is a friend, and I like him. But I'm not going to ask him about this stuff—he is sleeping with my mother!*

Stefan decided to experiment and learn about such intimacies from his peers.

But for now, he had an appointment to keep. *My thingamajig is finally behaving, and it's time to meet Fritz and Mother at the Kristkindlmarkt.*

⚜

Stefan found Fritz where he knew he would be—drinking homemade brew in the biergarten. He was sitting with a dozen friends at the end of a long communal table, very close to a loud oompah band. The men—singing and swaying from side to side—hoisted their mugs to the tune of "*Schuetzenliesel,*" a favorite drinking song.

When Fritz saw Stefan he guzzled the last of his beer and got up from the table. The other drinkers lifted their mugs to salute his exit, but they carried on with their singing and did not miss a beat.

Fritz said hello to Stefan and wiped his mouth with the back of his hand. "This reminds me of the *Kristkindlmarkt* we went to in that little town near Hamburg." He swept his arm from right to left and described what he saw. "There's clothing, crafts, jewelry, pottery, quilts—a little of everything—and most of it is handmade." He paused. "But let's find your mother. She said she would be helping the women from St. Andrew's. They're baking and selling hot waffles—so we can just follow our noses."

Stefan sniffed, and swooned. He pointed to his right. "It's this way."

Annemarie was very busy when they got to the waffle concession, but she took off her apron and motioned for Fritz and Stefan to follow her. "I want Stefan to see the *fraktur* display, then we can sit down and have dinner."

Fritz and Stefan looked at each other and rolled their eyes, but neither of them said a word. They dutifully followed Annemarie through a maze of concessions until they reached the featured exhibit—scores of handmade decorative documents known as *fraktur*. The colorful drawings with intricate lettering tell of baptisms, births, and deaths. Annemarie said, "They call it *fraktur* because each letter is separated—or fractured—from the next."

She pulled Stefan from one *fraktur* to another, but neither he nor Fritz showed much interest until Horst Bachmann walked up behind them and said, "In the old days it was commonplace to put a person's baptism *fraktur* in their coffin and bury it with them—it was their passport to heaven."

Stefan perked up and gave Horst an incredulous look. "Really? What if they aren't Christian—would they get to heaven?"

Fritz grumped and mumbled, "Superstition."

Annemarie frowned at Fritz. "Let's not get into that." She skipped a beat, and then she barked an order. "No fussing about religion. It's Christmastime." Fritz looked away, chastened. Annemarie waited a second, and then she smiled and pointed to a concession run by the Girl Scouts. "It's time to eat—how about some *bratwurst mit sauerkraut?*

⚜

When they finished dinner Horst invited Fritz to join him for a stein of beer, and Fritz quickly agreed. Annemarie knew from experience that the two friends would drink a few swallows of beer and chat peaceably for a few minutes. After that, they would resume their ongoing argument about religion. Horst, a true believer, would argue for the Catholics, and Fritz, an agnostic, would defend the Protestants.

Annemarie wanted no part of that, so she took Stefan by the hand and pulled him in the direction of the *fraktur* exhibit. "Let's let the men go their way. They are determined to fuss about religion."

They had taken only a few steps when they met three boys from Stefan's school. Annemarie stood back to watch her son interact with his classmates. But they did not say much. Instead, they jabbered nonsensically and made funny faces. They punched each other on the shoulder, giggling uncontrollably, and then they left as suddenly as they had appeared.

"What was that all about?" Annemarie asked.

Stefan gave her a goofy look and shrugged his shoulders.

"I know you are going through a crazy time in your life—12-year-old girls go through it too." He did not respond, so she let her comment soak in. Then she said, "But girls don't show their adolescence by doing dumb stuff like hitting each other and making stupid faces."

Stefan blinked and looked hurt, but he did not speak or cry.

Annemarie started to put her arms around him, but tousled his hair instead. Then she grinned and gave him a friendly cuff on the cheek. "Hey. Let's go get a waffle."

⚜

On Jan. 15, 1941, the situation at Doctor Günther's clinic had improved. When Annemarie arrived for work, the doctor said to her, "Thank God. I think the worst of it is over."

The sick bay was still half-full—three patients were too sick to go home—so the doctor and Annemarie decided to remove the temporary cots they had added. Once the cots were gone, Annemarie and Doctor Günther spent the rest of the day scrubbing and cleaning. And at the end of a hard day's work he thanked her, and said, "You are a blessing, Annemarie."

But one week later Annemarie missed work for the first time in two years. She was feverish and feeling bad when she woke up, so she asked Fritz to call Doctor Günther and tell him that she would not be in that day. Late that afternoon, when the doctor came to the house to see how she was doing, Annemarie was nauseous and her temperature was 101 degrees. Doctor Günther gave her some medicine and said, "I think you may have the flu, but I'll stop in the morning to see how you are doing—we'll know more then."

Annemarie had a rough night, and by the time Doctor Günther got to the house, she was very sick. He examined her, and then motioned for Fritz to meet him in an adjoining room. When they were alone he said, "Something has made her sick, but I am more concerned about something else. She has a hard lump just below her rib cage on the right side, and she has a touch of jaundice. I'm worried that she may have a tumor on her liver, so I think you should take her to St. Mary's Hospital in Philadelphia. I have a friend on staff there. I'll call him to make the arrangements."

"But she is healthy ... and strong ... she will be all right, won't she?"

Doctor Günther frowned. "I pray that she will, but she needs to see a specialist." He put his hand on Fritz's shoulder. "I know she can be hard-headed, so I'll need your help on this."

The two men went back to Annemarie's bedside, and—to their surprise—when Doctor Günther told her she needed to go to the hospital she agreed and did not argue.

⚜

Fritz called Horst Bachmann to tell him what Doctor Günther had said about Annemarie's illness, and when he told him about the lump below her rib cage the old man's voice cracked, and he murmured, "Oh, no." That scared Fritz, but before he could say anything Horst gathered himself and spoke with authority. "Get her ready to travel. I'll be there in an hour, and I will call Father Joseph. He will notify the school and make arrangements with the ladies of St. Andrew's. They will take care of Stefan while we are in Philadelphia."

"But Annemarie will want to see Stefan and tell him not to worry."

"If she insists we can stop at the school on our way out of town, but Father Joseph will know how to handle things if we don't."

⚜

When Horst got to the house Annemarie was sitting in the living room in her nightgown with a knee-length coat draped over her legs. She was peaked and burning up with fever, but said she was ready to go.

They helped her into the back seat of Horst's car, and Fritz arranged several pillows to make her as comfortable as possible. When they pulled away from the house Fritz asked her if she wanted to go by the school to see Stefan.

Once again, Annemarie surprised the men. "Father Joseph will know what to tell Stefan, and the ladies of St. Andrew's will know what to do." Then she lay back and closed her eyes.

❧

Doctor Adolph Becker, a no-nonsense man with a Germanic manner, barked orders to the nurses and motioned for Fritz and Horst to follow him out of Annemarie's room. "My colleague, Doctor Günther, believes the lump beneath her rib cage is a tumor. We'll try to get her temperature down, and if she is better tomorrow morning I will do a thorough examination."

Horst started to say something, but the doctor cut him off. He raised his hand and shook his head. "Find a place to stay. There's no point in speculating. We'll talk tomorrow after I see what we are dealing with." He wheeled and hurried away without saying more.

❧

Horst and Fritz settled into a nearby hotel and called Father Joseph to check on Stefan. The priest told them, "He wants to see his mother, but I told him it might be a few days before she comes home. Tell Annemarie the ladies of St. Andrew's have everything under control—Stefan is OK."

Later, when Horst and Fritz were having dinner, Fritz said, "Doctor Becker seemed cold to me. Do you think he really cares?"

"Günther says he is a genius, and that is what we need. We are not looking for a friendly doctor—we want competence."

❧

Annemarie rallied that night and by morning her temperature was slightly below 100 degrees. Sister Theresa, the head nurse, let Horst and Fritz go in for a short visit, but before they could say a word Annemarie asked about Stefan. And when Horst told her that Father Joseph and the ladies of St. Andrew's were taking good care of him, Annemarie smiled and said, "Thank God." Then she asked Sister Theresa to pray for her, and she did. Annemarie closed her eyes, and Horst bowed his head during the prayer, but Fritz did not. He just stood at her bedside, sobbing and wringing his hands.

⚜

Horst and Fritz spent the entire day in the waiting room. They looked at magazines, talked about life in Willich, the merits of growing fruit instead of vegetables, bricklaying, and the comings and goings of the nurses and doctors. And when they talked about Annemarie and Stefan they praised Father Joseph and the ladies of St. Andrew's, but they did not debate or argue about religion, and that was a first for them.

At 4:30 p.m., Doctor Becker walked into the waiting room and signaled for them to follow him to a small office. Fritz expected to hear the cold, staccato voice of yesterday, but the doctor spoke in hushed tones as he told them the bad news. "This beautiful young woman has breast cancer, and it has metastasized to her liver and to her lymph nodes." He paused. The men were speechless, so the doctor continued. "We'll do what we can to make her comfortable, but that is all we can do."

Horst interrupted. "Surely there is something. What about the Rife machine? A friend told me about it. And he says there are other new cures for cancer. Money is no object, Doctor Becker. I am old and rich and I will do anything, pay anything, to keep this beautiful woman alive—she is like a daughter to me."

The staccato voice returned. "The Rife Machine is pseudo-medicine at its worst. It is a false hope. We are searching for new ways to treat cancer, but it will be years before we succeed." His voice softened again. "I told Annemarie what we can and cannot do, and she says she just wants to go home—to be with her son."

Fritz had been quiet, and his voice cracked as he asked, "How long does she have?"

"Three months. Maybe more, but not much more."

❖

They spent another night in Philadelphia. On the third day of Annemarie's stay at St. Mary's Hospital her temperature was back to normal. Doctor Becker released her, and on the trip back to Willich Annemarie made it clear to Horst and Fritz that she was not going back to the hospital in Philadelphia. "I see no sense in it—I want to spend every day I can with Stefan." And she made them promise to keep secret the diagnosis of cancer. "I'm going to enjoy my life and be as normal as possible. And, when the time is right, I will tell Stefan in my own way." Horst nodded in agreement, and Fritz said, "It is your decision to make—not ours."

❖

Annemarie did her best to be normal. She tried going to work, but Doctor Günther sent her home after the first week. She busied herself with house-work—cleaning and cooking meals for Fritz and Stefan—but she could not hide the nausea and tinge of jaundice that yellowed her face and hands. It was time to tell Stefan, and she knew she could wait no longer.

On Tuesday, Feb. 25, Annemarie called Father Joseph and asked him to come to her house the next day. Horst picked him up and they were in the living room with Annemarie when Stefan got home from school. As soon as her son came into the room Annemarie motioned for him to sit by her on the couch, and when he was next to her she gave him a hug and said, as cheerfully as she could, "This is Ash Wednesday, and since I'm not feeling very well, Father Joseph has come to distribute the ashes. Isn't that nice of him?" Stefan gave Horst a quizzical look, but said nothing.

Annemarie pulled her son close, and when the priest finished the lit-urgy, he placed a spot of ashes on her forehead. "This is a reminder to the faithful of human mortality, and it is a sign of mourning and repentance to God."

Father Joseph and Horst then gathered their belongings and slipped quietly out of the house.

⚜

When they were alone Annemarie gently eased out of Stefan's embrace so that she could look him in the eye. "Father Joseph said the ashes are a reminder that we are all going to ..." She stopped to clear her throat. "Stefan ... I'm very sick, and the doctors say I am not going to ..."

"No, Mother. They are wrong—don't say that—don't say that." He tried to run away, but she would not let go of him.

"You must be brave, Stefan, because I don't have a lot of time." They clung to each other, sobbing and saying nothing until Annemarie took his face in her hands. "And there is much that we need to talk about."

⚜

Early the next day Fritz tried to get Stefan ready for school, but he lolly-gagged around the house, refusing to go. And when Fritz insisted he went into his room, slammed the door, and flopped down on the bed. *This is wrong ... all wrong. ... Father ... now Mother. School? That's wrong too. I just want to be with Mother.*

He drifted away, half-asleep, but soon heard a tapping on his door. He rolled to the side of his bed, and growled, "Yeah!" But instead of Fritz it was Annemarie who answered in a weak, but tender voice. "Stefan?"

Stefan started saying he was sorry before he got to the door. And when he opened it and saw his mother in her nightgown he said it again, and again, and gently put his arms around her.

He helped her to the living room and they sat, clinging to each other. "You cannot miss school, Stefan. Life must go on." But you might as well stay at home today—you have already missed the first bell."

It was the first of their talks. Annemarie took Stefan's hands in hers and reminded him of the day they picnicked in the Neander Valley with his father. "He explained why we had to leave Germany. Do you remember that?"

"Yes, Mother. He told the story about the old bones—about the 'Aryans,' and Jews, and Nazis.

Annemarie took a gold chain and pendant from the pocket of her night-gown and placed it tenderly in his hands. "I was with your father when he died. And his last words were: 'Our son—the—pendant.'"

"That's Hebrew lettering. Father said it shows respect for 'Life and the Living God.'"

"Yes, that is true, but I give it to you as a reminder that your father never told anyone that he was a Jew."

"But he told me he was proud to be a Jew."

"Yes, he was, but terrible things were happening to Jews in Germany and he kept silent to protect you."

"But we are in America now, Mother."

"It is better here, but there are still those who hate Jews. I hear it a lot, and I heard it most recently in Philadelphia. You must promise me that you will do as your father did—never tell anyone that you have Jewish blood."

"I promise, Mother ... I promise."

⚜

Stefan never missed a day of school after Annemarie told him to go, and he hurried home each day to be with her. As time passed, their visits got longer, but they did less talking as the cancer stole her strength and ravaged her body. The handsome woman surrendered the beauty that people see with their eyes in exchange for an inner beauty that only the heart can know.

On the last day that she felt like talking, Annemarie told Stefan a Bible story. "You know; Moses hid the fact that he was a Jew." Stefan had heard it before, but he let her go on. "You can read about it right here." She opened her Bible to a bookmarked page. "See, it is here in Exodus 2. Moses was born in Egypt at a time when the rulers felt threatened by the Jewish people.

The king put the Jews into slavery and ordered his soldiers to kill their male infants. To protect Moses, his family let others raise him as an Egyptian. So you see ... you will not be the first to deny that you have Jewish blood."

Stefan gave her a kiss on the forehead. "I will never tell anyone, Mother. I promise."

⚜

On Good Friday, April 11, 1941, Annemarie died peacefully at home. Doctor Günther, Stefan, Fritz, and Horst were at her side when Father Joseph administered the last rites and said it was altogether fitting for a true believer to die on the day that Christ was crucified.

⚜

On Monday, April 14, St. Andrew's was packed to capacity with Protestants, Catholics, and non-believers. And scores of mourners, who could not get inside for the funeral mass, stood outside to pay their respects.

Later, at the cemetery, Father Joseph blessed the gravesite, and sprinkled it with holy water and incense. He gave a brief version of what he had said at the mass, and then he made his final petition: "May her soul, and the souls of all the faithful departed through the mercy of God, rest in peace."

Stefan compared the elaborate funeral and burial of Annemarie to the simple burial of his father in an unblessed grave—just a few yards from where he had died beneath an overturned tractor. *Only a few neighbors came ... no prayers.* Stefan's thoughts then turned to what he had done just before his father's coffin was lowered into the grave. *The Hebrew letters ... the Jewish symbol ... I marked it on his coffin.*

As the mourners began to leave Annemarie's gravesite Stefan drew close to her coffin and, using his finger, traced an imaginary Christian cross on the wood. And he whispered to his mother. *I love you.*

⚜

Three weeks later, Fritz went to Horst's office in Kutztown. They talked about the farm and Stefan for a few minutes, but soon Horst said. "You seem to have something else on your mind. What is it?"

Fritz hesitated. "Stefan and I are going to move to Arkansas."

Horst blinked, and gave him a puzzled look. "Why on earth would you do that?"

"We want to make a fresh start, far away from here. We've talked about getting away ever since the funeral." He paused to see how Horst would react. The old man said nothing, but suddenly looked older. So Fritz continued, "The memory of Annemarie is driving me mad. I see her everywhere, and Stefan feels the same. We need a change."

"I think it is a mistake, but I am old and change scares me."

"I have a friend there," Fritz said. "He loves it, and tells me there's plenty of work. ... He says they call it 'The Land of Opportunity.'"

XVIII

Nymphet of the River

Kizzy liked to learn, but on May 1, 1941, she moped along as she neared the entrance to the schoolhouse, talking to herself. *It's this way every year. The town girls are wearing their fanciest dresses, with pretty ribbons and bows in their hair, and patent leather shoes. And when school lets out they'll go to Horsey Hairs' house for a May Day party. He has it every year, but he only invites townies.*

Betty Sue Kensett, a poor girl from the country, told Kizzy, "It ain't so bad to be left out. My ma says May Day is for heathens. It ain't for believers. And the maypole is the work of the devil."

Kizzy laughed, but shunning hurts. So when school was over she left the building as quickly as she could. She headed for the river and did not look back. *Silly maypoles. It's kid stuff anyway.*

When she got home, Cormac was just coming back from a day of fishing. He steered the workboat alongside the houseboat and looped a line around a deck cleat. "I've got a load of fish for Curly. You wanna go with me? There's a Baby Ruth waiting for you at the market."

Kizzy perked up. She laughed and jumped into the workboat, and Cormac let it drift downriver toward Curly's. He told about his day of fishing, and Kizzy let him rattle on, nodding from time to time. But she was thinking. *Cormac ain't all that bad. He's paying more attention to me lately, and he treats me like a grownup.*

⚜

On her 13th birthday Kizzy slept late. She planned to laze around until noon, and then walk up the hill to Big Pearl for the annual Fourth of July parade. Sarah was still asleep when Kizzy woke up, but Cormac was up and walking around in his undershorts. When Kizzy began to stir he sat down, and he watched as she pulled her nightgown over her head and tossed it on the bed.

Kizzy had lived with Cormac since she was 8 years old. He had seen her naked many times because it was the way of life on their one-room houseboat, a vessel with no electricity and no connection to city water or sewer. They had lived together in close quarters for almost five years, and it was normal for her to see Cormac in his shorts. And there had been times— mostly on hot summer days—when he paraded around the cabin without shorts, totally naked.

When Kizzy reached for the dress that she was going to wear that day Cormac said, "You're turning into a woman, girl." He had said things like that before, but not when she was naked.

Kizzy felt a strange tingle when he said it, but she did not answer. She just pulled her dress over her head and went outside.

Every day is a new experience for a girl in the springtime of life. As she stood on the aft deck, Kizzy—a nymphet of the river—watched the current lap against the boat, and she thought about Cormac. *He's screwing ma, but he's watching me. There's a difference in just seeing me naked and watching me when I'm naked. And, now he's watching me and saying something to boot. It makes me feel funny, but it's like MeeMaw said: It's natural, it's the way of the river.*

⚜

Two weeks later Cormac again took Kizzy to Curly's Fish Market. He offered to buy her another Baby Ruth, but she said she wanted to try a Milky Way instead. They went outside to sit at a picnic table and Cormac rolled himself a cigarette using Bull Durham tobacco.

Kizzy took a bite of her candy bar and Cormac started talking about getting off the river.

"When you get older I know how we can make big money in the city. But until then we'll have to stay here and work the river, but we need to spend more time looking for pearls—that's where the big money is. A body can't make no serious money fishin' and sellin' shells."

"We find a good one ever so often," Kizzy said. "But most of them ain't much bigger than burying pearls."

"We got enough burying pearls to bury all of us twice. That's not what I'm talking about. I'm talking about going to the city and cashing in, or finding a big pearl that will make us rich—rich enough to buy a piece of land and get off the river."

"What does Ma think about it?"

Cormac put his arm around Kizzy. "I can't talk to her about such things. She ain't interested in my dreams, and she ain't as smart as you." He jostled her a little and then said, "It's just a dream. Let's just keep it between you and me. It'll be our secret."

⚜

Late in the afternoon on a very hot day in mid-August three roughnecks—ne'er-do-wells from Coconut's Pool Hall—came down the trail from Big Pearl, talking and guffawing. They walked past the bollards and stood just a few yards from the houseboat. Kizzy was sitting on the aft deck fanning herself, waiting for her mother to get back from Shirley Barden's boat. The smallest man, who was wearing a big cowboy hat, said, "Say, pretty girl—you want to make a few bucks?"

Kizzy ignored them, and the ugly man in the cowboy hat pushed it back and said, "Hey, pussycat. I'm talking to you." And the other two chortled, "Cat's got the pussy's tongue, cat's got the pussy's tongue."

She looked away, and as she did the ugly one stepped on the gangplank. But he stopped abruptly and froze in place when he saw the shotgun pointed at his head. Cormac was standing in the doorway near Kizzy. He pumped a shell into the chamber and said, "Cat got your tongue, Cowboy?"

The roughnecks took a step back and put their hands up. Cormac said, "Git! And if you mess with her again I'll blow you away."

They ran up the hill, stumbling and tripping over each other. Cormac turned to Kizzy and smiled. "They won't be back, but I can't blame them because you're somethin' to see." He rubbed his chin and mumbled as he looked out over the water. "But them boys is small potatoes."

Kizzy stood up and started through the door, and when she scooted past Cormac he patted her on the butt and whispered, "But don't you worry. Ole Cormac's here, and I'll always take care of you, Kizzy."

XIX

Big Pearl

Germany completed its conquest of Western Europe in the summer of 1940. Hitler gloated, and humiliated the French by forcing them to surrender at Compiegne, a forest north of Paris—the very spot where 22 years earlier Germany surrendered to the French to end World War I.

But Hitler wanted more; he hungered to cross the English Channel and defeat the British. He ordered a *blitzkrieg*, and the *Luftwaffe* bombed the island unmercifully for months on end. But the British did not weaken. Hitler abandoned his plan to invade Britain and turned his attention to the East.

On June 22, 1941, Hitler launched Operation Barbarossa, a massive invasion of the Soviet Union. Three great army groups with over 3 million German soldiers, 150 divisions, and 3,000 tanks smashed across the frontier into Soviet territory.

And on July 2, 1941, *Schutzstaffel (SS) Obergruppenführer* Reinhard Heydrich—a Nazi monster—issued a wide-ranging order directing his *Einsatzgruppen* to execute all "radical elements." His mobile killing units murdered thousands of Russian Jews during Operation Barbarossa, but they also murdered Jews in Western Europe. On July 6, 1941, the *Einsatzgruppen* began to systematically shoot and kill thousands of Jewish men, women, and children in Kovno, Lithuania.

⚜

On Friday, Aug. 15, 1941, Fritz and Stefan loaded their belongings onto their 1938 Ford pickup and drove to St. Andrew's Church. It was just breaking day, and the streets of Willich were empty. Fritz parked behind the church near the entrance to the parish cemetery, a cozy half-acre shaded by a dozen ancient oaks. And as they passed beneath the arched entry the early birds began to sing, giving life to the eerie stillness of morning.

They passed scores of tombstones with remembrances yearning to be read, and when they got to Annemarie's grave, Fritz laid a bouquet of fresh flowers and stepped back to admire her tombstone, a large granite base topped with a hand-carved statue of the angel of intercession. It cost more than Fritz could afford, but Horst paid for it, saying Annemarie deserved the best. Her name and vital information were on the base, carved deep, along with her favorite Bible verse: "Blessed are the pure in heart, for they shall see God. Matthew 5:8."

Stefan wept, as he did every time he visited her grave. But Fritz began to talk to Annemarie as if she could hear him. "Well, we are on our way. We're going to go through Kutztown to see Horst, but then we'll head out to Arkansas."

Fritz shut up when Stefan dropped to one knee and made the sign of the cross. He did not speak aloud, but Fritz knew he was praying.

When Stefan stood up, Fritz continued. "We're leaving Willich now because it breaks our heart that you are gone. Everywhere we go—everything we do—reminds us of you. That's good in a way, but we are taking our memories of you to a new place, and we're going to put this sad time behind us." He looked at Stefan. "Did I say it right?"

Stefan nodded. "She wants us to be happy."

They walked away, and when they passed beneath the archway Stefan blew a kiss to his mother and whispered, "I love you."

⚜

Horst was sitting on his front porch, sipping a glass of iced tea when they pulled into the driveway of his Victorian home, one of the finest in Kutztown. He waved, and when they stepped onto the porch he said, "So, you are on your way?" His voice cracked when he said it.

Fritz said yes, and then he began to talk business with Horst. They discussed the farm, going over everything the new tenant would need to do to make a crop. Then suddenly Horst changed the subject. He began to talk about his age, and his aches and pains, and his love for Annemarie. As he talked, Stefan thought. *He misses Mother as much as I do, and it shows. We're going to move and start fresh, but he's too old for that.*

⚜

After a while, Fritz and Stefan began to squirm and Horst noticed. "I know you want to get going, but I must say one more thing before you go—I'll hate myself if I don't."

Fritz got a curious look on his face, and so did Stefan, but they listened carefully.

"Hitler is ravaging Europe, and now he is invading the Soviet Union. Some Americans are beginning to hate Germans, even those of us who have been here for a long time. The same thing happened during the World War, and I fear it is happening again."

Horst looked directly at Fritz. "When you first came to America you were somewhat sympathetic to the new German nationalism—and you were reluctant to find fault with Hitler and the Nazis. Please take this in the right way: Be careful what you say these days. You are German, but don't talk about it. Do what people around here are doing. It's what they did during the World War. Just say you are Pennsylvania Dutch."

Fritz nodded. "That's good advice, Horst."

Stefan did not respond. *Great! Now I have another secret to keep. I can't talk about being half-Jew, and now I can't say I am German.*

Horst interrupted his thoughts. "So, Stefan, you will go to school in Jonesboro?

Fritz interjected. "No. We're not going to Jonesboro. My friend lives there, but we are going to settle in a little river town that is an hour or so from there."

"Does it have a name?"

"Big Pearl," Stefan said.

XX

Moccasin Bend

Sarah and Kizzy were resting half-naked on a sandy beach, sunning themselves after a hard day's work, when Cormac told them it was time to head back upriver to the houseboat. It was midafternoon on Monday, Aug. 18, and they had spent the day digging for mussels above and below legendary Moccasin Bend. The bend makes a snakelike 180-degree turn in the Black River, and that is how it got its name. But it became a legend in the summer of 1925 when an old river rat found a prize pearl that he sold for $5,000 cash.

Every river rat within 100 miles envied the odd-shaped black man they called Tum Tum; he had what they wanted—the means to buy land and get off the river. But alas, the legend of Moccasin Bend came to a sad ending. Tum Tum—so named because he was rail-thin but had an enormous gut—took his money to Memphis, and after a year of whoring and gambling, he came back to the river, once again a penniless river rat.

Cormac said, "We've had a good day, and who knows? This may be the batch that'll give us a pearl as big as Tum Tum's belly." He started the outboard motor, and held the workboat steady while Sarah and Kizzy found a place to sit amongst the mussels and digging gear.

Sarah winced when she sat down. "Dang! There it is again." She rubbed her belly, down low on the right side, and stretched. Then she put her head in Kizzy's lap. Cormac pushed the workboat away from the sandbar and headed upriver. And as soon as they were underway, Sarah pointed to her belly. "Somethin's wrong in there, and I been feelin' sick and feverish for days."

Kizzy felt Sarah's face. "I think you've got a fever, but it is so hot today that it is hard to tell." She dipped a rag in the river and put it on Sarah's forehead. "When we get home you need to get in bed and sleep it off."

"I need to lay more on my back," Sarah said. But as soon as she moved she screamed and said, "How long's it going to take to get back?"

⚜

It took an hour for them to get back to Big Pearl. Cormac tied the work-boat alongside the houseboat, and he and Kizzy helped Sarah to her bed. "She's really hurting and she's hot as a firecracker, Cormac. We've got to do something."

Cormac grabbed the bag of burying pearls and shouted, "I'll fetch the doctor." He hurried across the gangplank and headed up the hill to Big Pearl.

Kizzy kept putting wet rags on her mother's forehead, but by the time Cormac returned with the doctor Sarah was barely conscious.

The doctor examined her, and when he pressed on her belly she screamed and pleaded with him to stop. He said, "It's appendicitis for sure, but it may be worse. I could operate on her in Big Pearl, but if you've got enough money to get her to the hospital in Jonesboro she'll have a better chance."

Cormac fished two burying pearls out of the bag and showed them to the doctor. "These is worth at least $25 apiece."

The doctor took the pearls from Cormac and said, "I've got a helper who'll take her over there."

⚜

The doctor in Big Pearl was right. Sarah did have appendicitis, but by the time she got to the hospital in Jonesboro the appendix had burst, spilling infectious materials into her abdominal cavity.

The surgeon opened her up and cleaned the abdominal cavity as best he could, but that was all he could do.

He came to the waiting room, and Kizzy knew as soon as he walked through the door that he had bad news. *I can tell by the look on his face. It ain't good. First it was Grandpa—then we lost MeeMaw, and now Ma's bad sick.*

Kizzy tried to be brave. *MeeMaw said we have to be tough, but dang it all—this ain't gonna be easy.*

The young doctor was nice-looking and he had a soothing voice, but Kizzy broke down when he said, "Your mother has peritonitis. We've done all we can do, but it's now out of our hands. If the infection spreads, we won't be able to stop it."

⚜

On Thursday, Aug. 21, the undertaker in Big Pearl met Kizzy and Cormac on the backside of the cemetery. Kizzy saw him right away. *He's standing pretty close to where he put Grandpa five years ago. That scrawny guy with him, the man with the shovel—he's the gravedigger, same one who buried Grandpa.*

No one from town came to Sarah's burial, and when Kizzy asked the undertaker if he could put Sarah right next to Grandpa the undertaker said he could not. "We have to put charity cases in the next open spot—that's how it works if you don't have family plots."

Shirley Barden came to the burial and brought some wildflowers that she had picked on her way to the cemetery.

Cormac made a short speech about rich people getting all the breaks, and when he was done they turned and started to leave. Kizzy said to Shirley, "When we buried Grandpa I was only 8 years old, but I remember what MeeMaw said: 'Grandpa was my man. He done his durndest, but now he's gone. He's gone on down the river.'"

Shirley put her arm around Kizzy, and pulled her close. "Well, that's better than the words Cormac said over Sarah."

Kizzy looked back to where the scrawny man was already shoveling dirt onto Sarah's remains. She made a mental note of the scene, and then she gave a pitch-perfect impersonation of MeeMaw, "My ma tried hard, but now she's gone. She's gone on down the river."

⚜

When they got back from the cemetery, Shirley invited Kizzy to come to her boat. "Come sit with me. My girls are off playing in the woods, and I've got something that'll cheer you up."

"What?"

Shirley pulled a letter from her pocket and handed it to Kizzy. "Here. You read it for yourself. It's from Birdie."

Kizzy unfolded the letter and began to read it aloud, paraphrasing Birdie. It was two pages long and hand-printed. "He's in the Marines! In Hawaii. Says it's pretty there, but not as pretty as it is here on the Black River." Kizzy paused and grinned. "He asks about me. And he says he wrote it himself."

"I'm proud of him, Kizzy. My other boys have joined the Army, but I ain't heard from them in a long time."

"I'm going to write a letter to him, Shirley. Is there anything you want me to tell him?"

"Just tell him I love him. And be sure to tell him that you lost Sarah. She was always nice to Birdie."

Kizzy copied Birdie's address onto a piece of scrap paper. Then she gave Shirley a hug and headed home.

⚜

Kizzy intended to write a letter to Birdie as soon as she got home, but when she crossed the gangplank her thoughts turned to Sarah. *It all happened so fast. One day she was here and the next she was gone. Grandpa was old ... we knew his heart was bothering him. And MeeMaw drowned in the flood—that sort of thing happens on the river. But Ma—she was young, and then all of a sudden she was dead on account of something that doctor called peritonitis. I'm all alone now. There's Cormac, but he's not exactly what you would call family. I've got to get on with life—that's what MeeMaw would tell me to do.*

⚜

Kizzy tried to be as strong as MeeMaw, but it took her several days to adjust to life without her mother. Finally, one week after the burial, she opened her Big Parade writing tablet and started a letter to Birdie. At first she wrote in longhand, but it occurred to her that Birdie might not be able to read cursive. So she started over and told him, in the first paragraph, how proud she was that he had learned to read and write. She also told him, "I just turned 13 and school starts next week—I'll be in the eighth grade and I'm looking forward it."

And then she told Birdie about Sarah dying and how she was now living alone with Cormac on the boat. "Without him I would probably have to go to the poorhouse down in Jacksonport. He's just a make-do stepfather, but I'm lucky he's here. Besides, he's been pretty good to me. And, he says I'm going to be a knockout."

Kizzy mailed the letter, and then told Shirley what she had written to Birdie, but she did not tell her what she had said about Cormac.

⚜

Monday, Sept. 1, 1941, was Labor Day. Kizzy had planned to loaf on the holiday, but at 9 o'clock in the morning she hurried over to Shirley Barden's. When Shirley heard Kizzy calling her name she came onto the aft deck of her houseboat and waved.

"Hi, Shirley. Say, can I get some of those Cellu-ettes from you?"

Shirley motioned for her to come onboard. They went inside and Shirley got a full box of Cellu-ettes off the shelf and handed it to Kizzy. "Here. Take 'em all. I won't be needin' 'em for a while. I'm knocked up again." Kizzy gave her a quizzical look, and Shirley grimaced. "That last guy that was here …"

"Well, are you happy about it, or what?"

"Not really, but I ain't gonna get no abortion. Bully Bigshot's outfit—the one that preaches that eugenics stuff—keeps telling me I need to get one, and they been tryin' to get me to get my tubes tied. But, I ain't gonna do that either."

Kizzy pretended to understand, but she had no idea what Shirley was talking about.

XXI

Eighth Grade

Fritz and Stefan spent the last night of their trip from Pennsylvania to Arkansas at Whitey's Tourist Court in downtown Memphis, Tenn., but they did not tarry. At sunup on Tuesday, Aug. 19, Fritz steered the Ford pickup onto the highway and within minutes drove onto the Mississippi River Bridge. Stefan sat up tall in the seat to get the best possible view of the great river, looking north then south. And when they reached the high point of the bridge Fritz honked the horn three times—long screechy honks—and pointed to the vast lowlands west of the river. "We're here, Stefan. This is Arkansas."

"It looks awfully flat."

"Yes, but this is the Delta. Big Pearl is 140 miles to the west—it's in the foothills of the Ozark Mountains."

They made good speed once they were in Arkansas, even though Fritz had to slow down from time to time for slow-moving farm equipment. Much of it was motorized, but they encountered scores of old wagons—inching along the highway—pulled by plodding mules.

And they saw hundreds of black people working in the fields. Some were chopping late weeds, but in the white-tinged fields the blacks were hunkered down, dragging pick sacks and pulling cotton from bolls that had cracked open early.

Stefan pointed to the workers. "I've seen more Negroes since we've been in the South than I've seen in my whole life." He paused and then pointed to a row of weather-beaten shacks, most of which had several half-naked children playing on the front steps. "Look, Fritz. You can see all the way through those houses when the front and back doors are open."

As they traveled west, the flatlands of the Delta gave way to hill country. And at 11 o'clock they came to the Black River Bridge.

Across the river lay quaint and colorful Big Pearl, a picturesque river town, tucked amongst the hills.

⚜

Bertha Mae Tyler, a weak and moody spinster, was not cut out to be a schoolteacher. Even so, Sept. 2, 1941, would mark the beginning of her 29th year as homeroom teacher for eighth-graders at Big Pearl Junior High School.

Many teachers follow the old adage "Never smile until Christmas," hoping their dour look will intimidate new students, particularly adolescents. Bertha Mae practiced the adage to extreme—she never smiled—but it did not help her keep order; the students knew she was bluffing. Strong teachers discipline unruly students; Bertha Mae did not. Her technique was to whine and carry on as best she could—a mannerism that guaranteed scuffling, arguments, spitball fights, and hair pulling, particularly on the first day of a new school term.

Horace C. Ayers, Kizzy's longtime nemesis, was inciting riot when Stefan walked into Bertha Mae's classroom. The girls were behaving, but the boys were making odd noises and pushing and shoving one another.

Bertha Mae pointed to an empty seat and Stefan sat down just as the bell rang. The boys quieted a little and took their seats, but chaos resumed when Bertha Mae began calling the roll. The students ignored the background noise, and each answered with the customary "Here" as the teacher called their names.

Suddenly, just as she was about to call Stefan's name, the chaos ended. The eerie stillness surprised Bertha Mae. But she collected herself and called the next name. "Stefan Halder?"

"Present." Stefan responded formally, respectfully.

"Present?" Horace C. Ayers guffawed, and his sycophants followed suit. One after another guffawed, mocking Stefan by saying "Present."

Bertha Mae did nothing to stop them, but when she looked at Stefan and opened her mouth to speak the noisemakers shut up. "Where are you from, Stefan?"

"I am from Willich, Pa., ma'am." Again he spoke formally and respectfully, but his accent gave Horace C. Ayers a new angle of attack.

"You sound funny, Yankee-Boy." Horace laughed and goaded his minions to do the same. Then he made a clumsy attempt to sound like Stefan, and be sarcastic at the same time: "I am from Willich, Pa., ma'am."

More laughter followed, and Stefan was not sure how to handle the situation. Just then, an intercessor came to his rescue.

"Leave him alone, Horsey Hairs. Don't make fun of people just 'cause they're different."

Horace gave her the small-eye. He hated the way Kizzy said his name, and he tried to ignore it by guffawing. Then he pointed at her. "You ought to know, River-girl."

Stefan turned to see who had taken up for him, and was surprised to see that it was the girl he had noticed when he first entered the classroom. He nodded his thanks to her. *The redheaded girl ... she's not dressed as nice as the others ... but she's prettier.*

Bertha Mae called the next name on the roll, and the hubbub resumed.

Kizzy waited for her turn to answer. *He seems nice ... like Birdie ... he's not like Horsey Hairs and the idiot boys I've grown up with.*

⚜

When school recessed for lunch Stefan looked for Kizzy, and he found her on the playground, sitting alone in the shade of a large cottonwood tree. He sat down beside her.

"I'm Stefan. Thanks for what you said in homeroom. That guy is obnoxious."

"He's always been that way. Horsey has been pickin' on me since the first grade." She smiled, and then said, "But you *do* have an accent."

"I'm Pennsylvania Dutch. That's just how people talk where I come from."

Kizzy shrugged. "Well, I like the way you talk. Don't let 'em bother you."

"Why did he call you 'River-girl?'"

Kizzy laughed. "He usually calls me a river rat, but he won't call me that to my face 'cause he's afraid I'll whip him." Stefan gave her a puzzled look, so she pointed toward the river and said, "I live down on the river, on a houseboat … been livin' there all my life."

"Miss Bertha Mae should keep better order in the classroom," Stefan said.

Kizzy chuckled. "That's just the way she is. Lots of people complain, but they can't get rid of her."

Stefan looked as if he was going to ask why, but he shrugged instead.

"So you came here from Pennsylvania? Why'd you move?"

"My stepfather got a new job here—he's a really good brickmason." Stefan hesitated, and then lowered his voice. "And my mother died of cancer in April. We just wanted a change."

Kizzy laid her hand on his arm. "I know how you feel. My ma died two weeks ago. Her appendix busted and that was that. We buried her and now I'm living with a stepfather too—well, mine's what I call a make-do stepfather since he was never married to my ma."

"Is your real father living?"

Kizzy shook her head, "I don't know. I doubt it. They say he was a Gypsy—his name was Tamás—but he ran off." She looked at Stefan and asked, "How about yours?"

"He died in a farm accident."

They sat quietly for a while, then Stefan said, "You said they can't get rid of Miss Bertha Mae. Why is that?

"Because she's Bully Bigshot's second cousin."

"Who's Bully Bigshot?"

"His real name is Sully Biggers, but my MeeMaw gave him that nickname 'cause he owns nearly everything in town."

XXII

Boopie

On the first day of the fourth week of school, Kizzy hurried to be on time for her first-period Latin class. She liked her teacher and enjoyed the classic stories, but the *New Latin Primer* forced students to translate from Latin to English by referring to a vocabulary that was inconveniently located in the back of the book. The students griped about that, so it was no surprise when a smart aleck slipped into the classroom and wrote a poem on the blackboard:

> *Latin is a dead language*
> *Dead as dead can be*
> *First it killed the Romans*
> *And now it's killing me*

Kizzy figured that Horace C. Ayers had done it, so she did not laugh along with the other kids. But Horace denied it, and Kizzy began to wonder who did it. *Who's the mystery poet? Surely not.* She turned around to sneak a look at Stefan, and he grinned mischievously. *I'll be danged. He did it.* She chuckled and gave him the "shame on you" sign when nobody was watching. *There's that grin again. Hmmm. There's a little bit of devil in that boy.* But when she asked him about it after class Stefan denied it, and the mystery continued.

⚜

When Kizzy returned to the houseboat that afternoon Cormac was sitting on the aft deck with a blonde-haired woman who looked to be in her late 30s. She wore a colorful print dress that was one size too small for her hips and two sizes too small for her bosom.

"Hey, Kizzy," Cormac said. "This here's Boopie."

"Hi, kid. How're you doing?"

Boopie had a pretty face, but the bleached hair made her lipstick look too red, and the heavy dose of mascara looked odd and did nothing to cover up the blue-black ring around her left eye.

"That's some shiner you got there." Kizzy pointed to Boopie's black eye.

"My man caught me messin' 'round, so he run me off."

"Boopie ain't got nowhere to go, and she wants to stay with us for a while." Cormac cleared his throat and grinned sheepishly. "Me and her used to live together, but it was a long time ago—back before I met your ma."

Boopie looked to Kizzy for approval. "I can help with the cooking. And I've worked the river before. I'll help Cormac fish and mussel while you are in school."

Kizzy thought for a minute, then spoke in a serious tone. "My MeeMaw always said we ought to help those who are hurting. It's the way of the river."

⚜

Cormac and Boopie wasted no time once they were in bed. As soon as the light was out they restarted their old romance, and the noise of sex reminded Kizzy of the many times she had listened to Cormac and Sarah.

The sound of their lovemaking stirred the same sensation she had felt before—an awkward quiver slithering from hip to hip—but Boopie added a new dimension to Kizzy's sex education. Boopie—a preacher's daughter turned hoochie-coochie dancer—liked to describe what they were doing. The salacious tête-à-tête invaded Kizzy's mind, reminding her of what she had learned from the lips of the vile river rat Elsie Sue Pardee: "It feels good."

⚜

Two days after Boopie moved in, Kizzy told Stefan about her. "I feel sorry for Boopie. Her husband got mad at her, beat her up, and ran her off. She doesn't have any place to go so she came to Cormac asking for help."

"It was good to take her in."

"It's the way of the river."

"You say that a lot."

"I say it 'cause it's how I was raised. My MeeMaw was full of sayings about the way of life on the river, and she used to sing songs about it too."

⚜

Stefan and Kizzy began meeting for lunch on school days. In good weather they would sit beneath the big cottonwood tree to eat their homemade sandwiches and visit. Most of the time they talked about school, but they also talked about themselves. Stefan wanted to know about her life on the river, and Kizzy wanted to know what it was like to live in a house instead of on a boat. Stefan asked about gathering mussels, looking for pearls, and running trotlines; she wanted to know about farming. On occasion, they would commiserate about losing loved ones and living with stepfathers. But they did not dwell on the hardships of life, and that was what they liked best about each other.

⚜

Six weeks after they first met, Stefan coaxed Kizzy into singing one of the songs she had learned from MeeMaw.

Kizzy looked around to be sure they were alone, and then she said, "This one's called 'Farewell to Green Fields,' and it's sad."

She sang gently—in shadowy alto—about a man whose wife caused his downfall. And when she sang the last verse—the poor man was going to prison for life—her voice and manner told more than the lyrics. Kizzy sighed; then she pretended to strum a chord on an imaginary guitar.

Stefan wanted to praise her, but he struggled to find the right words. After a clumsy pause, he said, "I love the way you sing, but your voice is too pretty for such a sad song."

Kizzy laughed. "Well, listen to this one." She then sang "Lord Thomas," an ancient song about a man who chooses between two women and in a fit of jealousy one of the women kills the other. The man despairs, and the song ends with him falling on his sword.

She made it seem so real that Stefan winced. "Good grief."

Kizzy giggled. "Most of MeeMaw's songs are about hard living and dying. They pretty much tell the way of the river."

"If I was still playing the violin I'd put some music to those lyrics. They'd still be sad songs, but the music would perk them up a little."

"Ain't no violins around here, Stefan—just fiddles."

⚜

Emma "Boopie" Cartwright stayed a total of six weeks and four days, and then she announced to Cormac and Kizzy that she was going home to her man. They wished her well, and Boopie thanked them profusely: "My man can be mean, but he had a right to run me off." She hemmed, hawed, and then said, "He's got a house and 40 acres." Boopie studied Cormac and Kizzy to see what they thought about that, and then she belly-laughed. "And I ain't no spring chicken anymore."

She gave Kizzy a hug and poked Cormac on the shoulder. "I'll see you all."

As Boopie stepped onto the gangplank to leave the boat Cormac rubbed her bottom and said, "I'm gonna miss you, Baby."

⚜

On Nov. 9, a misty Sunday morning, Kizzy headed to her thinking spot in the woods. She listened, hoping to identify her favorite birds, but there was an eerie stillness. She sat down on Grandpa's stump and thought of Birdie, who would know why the birds were not singing. Then she heard a rustle behind her, and when she turned to see what had caused the noise she saw a doe and her fawn—a little family—quietly making their way through the underbrush. *Did the deer spook the birds? Birdie would know—I wonder how he's doing in Hawaii.* And she thought of her family—her life on the river with Ma, Grandpa, and MeeMaw. *Everything's different now—Cormac's my only family.*

We did right to give Boopie a place to stay, but it ain't fair to Ma that Cormac took up with her. I'm glad she's gone. I wasn't jealous of Boopie or nothing like that, but who was she to have all the fun? Helping folks who are hurtin' is one thing, but lettin' her take Ma's place—that's another ...

Cormac likes me. I know that for sure 'cause he says I'm pretty, and he's always looking at me. If it weren't for him they'd be sending me off to the poorhouse.

⚜

Stefan was running late the following Monday, so he hurried to their noontime meeting place. When he sat down she nodded, but the usually sunny and talkative Kizzy said nothing. Stefan tried to perk her up by telling one of her favorite stories: The time their math teacher paddled Horace C. Ayers, her nemesis. Stefan laughed louder and longer than usual, but Kizzy did not laugh or smile. He unwrapped his sandwich and took a bite. *She's in an odd mood. Something's bothering her.*

"You seem down in the dumps today."

"Just thinking." Kizzy finished her sandwich and leaned back against the cottonwood tree.

"About what?"

"Nothing in particular." Kizzy looked away.

Stefan decided to try another approach. "Got any more songs for me?"

She nodded. "But I don't feel like singing today, Stefan."

They sat silently for a while, and then Kizzy blurted out, "Boopie left— she's gone back to the man who threw her out—can you believe it?"

Stefan did not know what to say, so he just shrugged.

"I guess I understand—she's getting older and needs a place to live—but having a woman on board was good. It reminded me of the way things were when Ma was alive."

"So you are sorry she's gone?"

She looked down and spoke softly. "I guess I'm glad Boopie's gone, but in a way I'm not."

"You're just missing your mother—that's natural."

Kizzy suddenly straightened up, and spoke in a strong voice. "Yeah I am, but death is a close-up thing for us river rats—it ain't no mystery. It's like my MeeMaw always said, "She's just gone on down the river.""

"I think there's more to it than that. My mother's in heaven—she was a good Catholic."

Kizzy squinted and cut her eyes toward Stefan. "Well, what are you? People say us river rats are heathens. Are you a Catholic?"

He looked away. "I don't know for sure what I am."

⚜

On Wednesday, Nov. 12, Cormac was not on the boat when Kizzy came home from school, but she could tell that he had just returned from a day of fishing. The workboat was secure alongside, and two catfish filets lay on the counter by the sink.

Kizzy tossed her books on her bunk and made a fire in the stove. There was a chill in the air and the sun was going down. *It's time to fix dinner. Cormac will be back pretty soon.*

When Cormac returned Kizzy was leaning over the stove, frying the catfish. He tossed his jacket on a chair and said, "Smells good!" And then he drew near and stood close behind her. "The minute I took those fish off of the trotline I put them aside for our dinner—best lookin' catfish I've seen all week." He patted her on the bottom and then sat down at the table.

Kizzy finished cooking and dished up two plates of fried catfish and potatoes. She put them on the table, and sat across from Cormac.

They talked about her day at school and his day on the river, and then Cormac said, "I sort of miss old Boopie."

"She was all right, but she talked dirty."

"She didn't know any better. Your ma learned how to be a woman from MeeMaw, but Boopie didn't have nobody to learn from."

Kizzy stared at her food. *Ma didn't teach me how to be a woman, but I ain't going to say that to Cormac.*

⚜

Cormac found a way each day for the next five days to praise Kizzy's mother as one who knew how to do things the right way. He praised her cooking, her personality, her appearance, but he always wound up contrasting Sarah with Boopie. And he would repeat his explanation of Boopie's shortcomings: "Boopie didn't have nobody to learn from." He made it seem that without proper instruction Kizzy would turn into another Boopie.

Kizzy listened as Cormac wove his web, but she was thinking about Boopie's dirty talk and Elsie Sue Pardee. *Those two are one and the same—I don't want to wind up like them."*

On the sixth day, Tuesday, Nov. 18, as they were getting ready for bed, Kizzy told Cormac, "It don't seem right for us to be talking about sex and stuff like that."

Cormac sat on the side of Kizzy's bunk and stroked her hair. "Well, your ma's gone, so I'm all you've got. It ain't doin' no harm for us to talk about such things, or for me to teach you how to be a woman."

He slipped his hand beneath the covers and traced the roundness of her breast. Kizzy gasped, but gave way. *Feels good—different—been wondering about that.* And when Cormac slid his hand between her legs. She squirmed, and moaned slightly. *He's breathing hard. I am too, but Cormac ain't gonna hurt me—he's just touching it—it's what Ma would have taught me.*

XXIII

Eugenics

Stefan and Fritz moved into a small rent house the day they arrived in Big Pearl. The two-bedroom house had a tiny garden spot in the back yard, but it was quite different from the farmhouse in Willich, and change is what they wanted.

They had moved to Big Pearl to escape the painful memories of the last few months, the images of the terrible sickness that killed their beautiful, vivacious Annemarie. But the move was good for them in other ways. Fritz was earning good money, and Stefan had weathered the complicated business of going to a new school in a strange town. But most importantly, Stefan had found Kizzy, his first girlfriend.

⚜

On Monday, Nov. 24, 1941, Fritz went to pick up his paycheck for bricklaying work he had done for Big Pearl Contractors—Homer "Hoot" Headlee's construction company. Hoot had hired Fritz the day he arrived in Big Pearl, and the arrangement was working out well for both men. Hoot—thanks to his friendship with Sully Biggers—got most of the new construction jobs in Big Pearl, and Fritz proved himself a master brickmason, the best ever in Big Pearl.

The two men got along well outside of work. Fritz called his boss "Hoot," and Hoot called Fritz "Dutch," because he believed him to be a real

Dutchman, a native to the Netherlands; after all, Fritz and Stefan had told everyone since arriving in Big Pearl that they were "Pennsylvania Dutch."

Just as Fritz was about to leave for home Hoot came out of his private office. "Hey, Dutch. Can you go to a meeting with me tonight? It's a group that Sully Biggers started, and he asked me to help him round up a good crowd."

"Sure. What's it about?"

"It's the quarterly meeting of Sully's Eugenics Society. He's been pushing the program for several years."

"I went to one of those meetings a few years ago in Pennsylvania," Fritz said. "It was a big thing back then, but I haven't heard much about it lately."

"Well, Sully keeps it going around here and we need to keep him happy, for business reasons. The meeting is at City Hall, and it starts at 7 o'clock. It'll only last about an hour."

⚜

Later, when Fritz and Stefan had finished eating dinner and had cleaned up the kitchen, Fritz said, "I've got to go to a meeting tonight, but I should be back around 8:30."

"What kind of meeting?"

"It's something Sully Biggers is pushing—the local Eugenics Society."

"Kizzy and the river people call Sully Biggers 'Bully Bigshot.'"

Fritz scowled. "Well, we shouldn't call him that."

⚜

Fritz and Hoot were among the first to arrive for the Eugenics Society meeting, and soon the mid-sized meeting room was almost full. Two local preachers were present, along with the prosecuting attorney and the sheriff of Jasper County. Fritz counted 30 men and eight women, and people were still coming in when Sully Biggers entered through a side door, nodding and waving to the well-dressed crowd.

Most of the men, including Fritz, were wearing their Sunday-go-to-meeting clothes; the women were in their finest dresses, and the hats they wore gave the meeting a formal, churchy feel in spite of a thick cloud of cigarette smoke wafting in the breeze of a ceiling fan.

Sully Biggers wore an expensive three-piece black suit that tried, but failed, to hide his bulk. He waddled to the lectern and welcomed the crowd, but Fritz was not listening. He was getting his first close-up look at Sully Biggers, and the fat man's odd face intrigued him. The bulbous forehead resembled a washboard, and it hovered over an unbroken line of bushy black eyebrows and two beady eyes, one of which was looking sideways.

Fritz was still studying the strange face when Sully's words recaptured his attention. "Tonight we are fortunate to have a special guest. Herman Spence is a well-known eugenicist. He has worked with Wickliffe Draper who—along with the Carnegie Institution, the Rockefeller Foundation, and the Harriman railroad conglomerate—has used his great wealth to support our cause. I met Herman through the great Gerald L. K. Smith, and tonight he is going to talk to us about the goals of one of the great leaders of the modern eugenics movement. Please join me in welcoming Herman Spence."

The middle-aged Spence, a beanpole of a man in a tight-fitting suit, stepped to the lectern to praise Sully as the preeminent eugenicist in Arkansas. "I know of no one who is working harder than Sully Biggers to improve our race through eugenics. His work stems from the research done by Madison Grant as set out in his book *The Passing of the Great Race*. Some who have supported eugenics are getting weak-kneed, but not Sully. He has been a strong supporter of the Better Babies and the Fitter Families programs, and he is still trying to get your legislature to approve compulsory sterilization of the mentally ill and intellectually disabled."

Spence looked and sounded like an elitist because he fancied himself a scholar. After praising Sully, he recited a complete history of the eugenics movement, including the obligatory reading of an opinion written by United States Supreme Court Justice Oliver Wendell Holmes upholding compulsory sterilization laws, which said, *inter alia*, "It is better for all the world ... three generations of imbeciles are enough."

The audience applauded when Spence finished, and Sully Biggers returned to the lectern. "Let me support what Herman has said, and I will put it in plain language. Those rascals in the Arkansas legislature need to get off their duffs and follow the lead of North Carolina and the other enlightened states that have passed compulsory sterilization laws.

"And I want them to go a step further. We need a law that will allow us to sterilize *all* the undesirables. The problem goes beyond the Supreme Court case that dealt with imbeciles. Through scientific planning and intervention, we can weed out the ne'er-do-wells, the lazy, the infirm, and the homosexuals. And, my friends, if we don't act soon, these undesirables— and that includes the Jews and the niggers—are going to corrupt our race."

Some in the audience wiggled around in their seats, uneasy with Sully's rant, but several said, "Amen."

Sully took a deep breath and continued, "You don't have to look very far to see what I am talking about. We have plenty of examples here in Big Pearl. The river rats breed like a bunch of rabbits and we wind up taking care of them at the poorhouse. This has to stop if we want this country to be all it can be. I don't like the war that Hitler and the Germans are waging in Europe any more than the rest of you, but when it comes to eugenics they are doing what we should be doing."

Fritz perked up when Sully mentioned the Germans. *Annemarie was right. This eugenics stuff is wrong. It starts out sounding like a good thing—a way to improve health and make things better—but then it goes too far.*

Sully carried on. "The Germans have an interesting program called Lebensborn, which means 'Fount of Life.' The government selects women to mate with high-caliber German officers and then it provides for the children through adoption. It is based on the same idea as our Fitter Family program, but I mention it because it shows how a determined government can be directly involved in the breeding process, thus improving the race."

Sully answered a few questions, and as he adjourned the meeting he invited the women in attendance to work as volunteers in the Big Pearl Fitter Families Clinic, an organization he started in 1932. "We are about to celebrate our 10th anniversary, but the success of our clinic depends on volunteers like you."

Fritz said goodnight to Hoot and left the building. He made a decision as he was walking home, and whispered a message into the night air: *Well, Annemarie, you were right. I'm done with his eugenics business. I won't say anything against it because Hoot gives me a lot of good work, but I'm not going to any more of these meetings. Stefan is happy here in Big Pearl and if all goes well I'm going to buy a house that I've got my eye on, and we will make this our home forever.*

XXIV

The Library

Sully's grandfather, Carlton Biggers, served with distinction in the army of the Confederate States of America, first as a chaplain, then as a line officer. He led a company of men at the Battle of Kennesaw Mountain in Georgia in June of 1864, but mortar fire mangled both of his legs. He came home to Big Pearl seriously disabled, but as a decorated hero with a flair for business he amassed a fortune. And in 1875, he built a beautiful Federal-style house in Big Pearl that everyone called "The Biggers House."

Sully's father, Carlton Biggers Jr., was born in 1855. "Junior" was a chip off the old block. He joyfully carried on the Biggers tradition of hard work, philanthropy, and Christian service.

The Biggers men had great hopes for Sully, their only heir. But on Sully's 15th birthday, Grandfather Biggers branded him a "cheeky renegade." He told Junior Biggers, "The boy is a selfish, insolent little fart. He shows no respect for family tradition, and he has turned his back on everything we have worked to build."

Junior agreed that Sully was a black sheep, but he stood by his son and turned the family businesses over to him when he graduated from college in 1906. Soon thereafter, Junior's wife died and he became a recluse, living alone in the Biggers House until he drank himself to death in 1920.

Sully was furious when the family lawyers told him that Junior's Last Will and Testament bequeathed $300,000 to the City of Big Pearl for the establishment of a veterans' center and library. The pertinent provision, a tribute written in his own hand, was a codicil to the original will:

> "I regret that I was too old to serve my country in the Spanish-American War or the World War. My father, Colonel Carlton Biggers, fought for the South in the Civil War and came home a hero. He never complained about losing both legs at Kennesaw Mountain, and now that I see men coming home from the war in Europe I am reminded of the great sacrifices of all those who have gone to war for the rest of us. I therefore bequeath the sum of $300,000 to the City of Big Pearl for the construction and operation in perpetuity of a combination veterans' center and library. The center will be a place for our veterans to come and rest, but the library must be open to everyone."

Sully said the bequest was a waste of money. He tried to break the will by claiming that his father was insane, but the probate judge upheld the codicil, noting that it would be political suicide to do otherwise. Sully promised the judge that he would see to his defeat in the next election, and he did. Sully's hand-picked candidate beat the judge handily, but Big Pearl built a beautiful facility, the envy of every town in Arkansas.

The Veterans' Center and Library was completed and dedicated on Memorial Day, 1923, and Sully Biggers was there to take credit, claiming to have encouraged the bequest.

⚜

Olivia Joyce, an only child, was born and raised in Big Pearl, and she loved the library. She was almost 6 years old when it opened in 1923. Her mother, a widow, took her to the dedication ceremony, and that was the beginning of Olivia's lifelong love of books and reading. By the time she was 15 years old she had read most of the children's books as well as the complete works of Jane Austen, Charlotte Brontë, and Jules Verne. But her favorite story was not a novel; it was George Bernard Shaw's play *Pygmalion*.

When she was 14 Olivia got a part-time job shelving books, arranging displays, and coaching young readers. The library—a constant in her life—became her touchstone.

She graduated from high school in 1935 and matriculated to Arkansas State College in Jonesboro where she majored in English literature. In 1939 she graduated with honors and married John Decker, her childhood sweetheart, on the day that he graduated from the United States Naval Academy.

They took their marriage vows in the historic Naval Academy Chapel in Annapolis, and John's classmates, in dress whites, honored them with a ceremonial sword arch as they departed the chapel. The newlyweds honeymooned their way to San Diego, Calif., and when they arrived two weeks later, Ensign John Decker reported for duty with the Pacific Fleet.

Olivia and John had a good life in San Diego. The Navy assigned him to the *USS Yorktown*, and when he was not on duty the young couple explored the many delights of southern California.

In 1940 German U-boats began attacking merchant ships in the Atlantic Ocean. The United States was not at war with Germany, but on April 20, 1941, the Navy deployed the *USS Yorktown* to the Atlantic to participate in "Neutrality Patrols," a wide-ranging operation designed to protect American shipping.

The Deckers faced a dilemma. With war likely, Olivia could stay in San Diego and live alone, or she could move to the East Coast and live alone.

Olivia went home to live with her mother, and on her first day back in Big Pearl she volunteered to work full-time at the library. With her husband in peril on the sea, the library was more important to her than ever.

⚜

On Tuesday morning, Nov. 25, 1941, Olivia went to the library early to have coffee with her longtime mentor, head librarian Mabel Swafford. Mabel also loved the library—it was her life—and she guarded the collections as if they were bound in gold. As they sipped their coffee, she said to

Olivia, "I'm hoping you will give your special touch to designing this year's Christmas display."

Olivia grinned and nodded enthusiastically.

The architect who designed the Big Pearl Library had given it a unique set of six display windows—three on either side of the front entry—to stimulate interest in reading. In 1932 Mabel gave Olivia permission to decorate one of the windows as a Valentine's Day exhibit. The teenager created a huge paper-mâché heart, and then—to the surprise of everyone—painted a jagged black line across the bright red heart and titled the exhibit: "How do you mend a broken heart?" To enrich her theme Olivia arranged rolls of tape, fasteners, and similar hardware on one side of the heart, but on the other side she displayed an array of books—classic love stories.

Mabel got so many compliments from the people of Big Pearl that she asked young Olivia to design all future displays and she did, until she married John Decker and moved to California.

⚜

On Wednesday morning, Nov. 26, 1941, Olivia rolled a library cart laden with books to a stop near the display windows and began to think about the theme she would use for Christmas. She wanted this display to be a masterpiece—a tribute to all the soldiers, sailors, and Marines who were in harm's way.

As she visualized her creation, Olivia saw a young girl standing on the sidewalk outside, looking in. She had seen the poorly dressed girl twice before; the girl always appeared to be interested, but she had never come into the library.

Olivia waved to her and motioned for her to come inside; the girl smiled, but turned and walked away.

Olivia kept her eyes on her, hoping that she might look back, but she did not. As soon she was out of sight, Olivia shoved the library cart aside and hurried outside. *Maybe I can catch her.*

The girl, lingering, had stopped to look into another display window, and as soon as Olivia took a step toward her, their eyes met.

"Hi! I'm Olivia Decker. What's your name?"

"I'm Kizzy."

What a pretty girl—redheaded—probably in the seventh or eighth grade, but she's as tall as I am. She reminds me of my friend Norma Sue—she was poor too—used to wear the same faded clothes and brogan shoes, those awful brogans.

She held out her hand to Kizzy. "Well, Kizzy, why don't you come inside and I'll show you around the library."

⚜

Olivia startled Kizzy when she came outside, particularly when she held out her hand. At first, Kizzy thought she must have done something wrong, but the woman's smile was a nice one.

She ain't after me, and she seems nice even though she's dressed fancy. I figure she's in her early 20s, but it's hard to tell 'cause she acts so grown-up, even more than the teachers at school.

Kizzy took her hand and as they entered the library Olivia said, "I've been coming to this library since I was 6 years old. You'll like it, Kizzy. It's a wonderful place."

Kizzy listened as Olivia gushed about the library, but there was so much for her to see. The two-story building took up an entire city block, and the high ceilings and marble columns made it seem even bigger on the inside. The architects, in keeping with Junior's bequest, had divided the building equally. A wide marble staircase leading to the second floor separated the Veterans' Center—designed for solitude—from the wide-open design of the library.

"I hope I'm not boring you," said Olivia.

Kizzy chuckled and shook her head. "No, ma'am. I've wanted to come in here for a long time."

Olivia led her through the stacks and the reading room, and as she talked, Kizzy studied her new friend. *She's an inside girl—that's for sure. That black hair makes her extra pale, but she's awful pretty.*

Olivia showed her how to use the card catalog, and encouraged her to come back as often as she liked. Then she said, "Do you like to read, Kizzy?"

"I read my school books, but that's about it."

"I love to read," said Olivia. "I learned when I was little that it is the easiest way to see the world and learn new ways to live." She smiled and led Kizzy to the fiction section, and pulled a book off the shelf. "Here's one of my favorites." She handed Jules Verne's *Around the World in Eighty Days* to Kizzy. "It's a lot of fun to read and I guarantee it will open your eyes as it takes you around the world."

"Can I read it here?"

"Yes, but let's make you a library card so you can take it home to read." She motioned for Kizzy to follow her to the checkout counter where Mabel was tending to a patron.

When Olivia asked Kizzy for her address, she said, "Down on the Black River." And when she asked for her birthdate Kizzy said, "July the Fourth."

Olivia laughed. "That's my birthday too—how about that?" She put the checkout card in the book and handed it to Kizzy.

Then she introduced her to Mabel, and said, "Come see me next week and let me know what you think about the adventures of Phileas Fogg and Passepartout."

⚜

On the Friday after Thanksgiving, Nov. 28, 1941, Olivia was working on the Christmas display when Mabel hollered to her. "You have a telephone call—it's long distance."

Olivia took the call, and she was so excited during the call that Mabel could not restrain herself. She asked Olivia if the call was about her husband, John Decker.

Olivia started to play dumb, to have a little fun with Mabel, but she could not hold back. "Yes. That was a friend, a Navy wife." She danced around and babbled. "The scuttlebutt is that the *Yorktown* will be in Norfolk on Dec. 2."

Mabel clapped her hands and cheered, but then she turned serious. "Will it stay there? Can you make a home there, in Norfolk?"

"Nobody seems to know, but if they are coming in—and I'll know more tomorrow—then I want to go to Norfolk to see him." Olivia stopped talking and turned her back to Mabel. She whimpered for a moment, but then she turned around to face her, and the two of them giggled nervously. Olivia took a deep breath, and her voice quivered. "It's been six months."

"I hate war," Mabel said. "People call me a 'spinster,' but I lost my true love in the war. If he had lived, I'd probably be a grandmother by now." She pointed a bony finger at Olivia. "Here's my advice: Pack your bag and get on the next train to Norfolk."

⚜

Stefan waited for Kizzy in the hallway near the school lunchroom; she was late and he was about to give up on her. Then he saw her weaving her way through a throng of students, waving and grinning as soon as she caught his eye.

"What's up?" He said.

"I met the nicest lady at the library, and she wants to be my friend. She gave me a book to read and I've already read half of it. And she gave me a library card. And she wants me to come back and tell her what I think about the book …"

"Whoa." Stefan stopped her in midstream, and then he said, "I've never seen you this happy about anything."

"Her husband's away in the Navy so she's living here, with her mother. This is where she grew up and she's the one that does all those decorations in the library window." Kizzy paused her breathless report, then she continued. "She's working on Christmas decorations, but she told me to come in next week, and I can hardly wait. Maybe I can help her."

"That's good. Back where I came from in Pennsylvania they'll be setting up *Kristkindlmarkt* and the *fraktur* exhibits." Kizzy gave him a blank stare, so Stefan told her about the Christmas market, the music in the churches and the *biergarten*, and the family histories displayed in *fraktur* drawings. Then he said, "I especially loved the Christmas music."

Kizzy listened, but she was thinking about her next meeting with Olivia, then the school bell rang. Kizzy, as an afterthought, said, "You like music as much as I do—so why don't you get out your fiddle and start playing again?"

Stefan mulled it over. Then he said, "I'm thinking about it."

⚜

On Friday, Dec. 5, 1941, Kizzy went to the library to see Olivia. She searched among the stacks and looked in the reading room; then she ran upstairs to see if she might be there. Finally, she gave up and started slowly down the stairs.

Mabel was waiting for her at the foot of the staircase. "Hi," Mabel said as she took Kizzy's hand and spoke to her in a soft voice. "I know you have come to see Olivia, but she is not here. She's gone to Norfolk, Va., to meet her husband."

Kizzy said nothing. She was crestfallen, and Mabel could see it in her eyes. "She told me to tell you she may be back, but it depends on what the Navy has in mind for her husband. I expect to hear from her next week. But if he's going to be stationed in Norfolk, then I'm afraid we will lose Olivia once again."

Mabel paused to see if Kizzy wanted to respond, but Kizzy looked away and said nothing. "She needs to be with him, Kizzy."

"Yes, ma'am." Kizzy took a deep breath, as if she was going to speak loudly, but her voice cracked as she whispered. "I was just going to tell her that I like the story about old Phileas Fogg and Passepartout."

XXV

The Fiddler

Stefan was 4 years old when his father gave him a violin and taught him how to play it. He practiced for hours, doing scales and classic movements, and he was good—so good that his father called him "my little prodigy." Stefan's mother did not play, but she loved to listen.

In Stefan's fondest memory, Annemarie is running her fingers through her hair as if the long blonde strands were strings on a violin. His father, Victor, is in the same vision, and they are watching Stefan—listening and admiring—as he plays Mendelssohn. He is 8 years old, and when he plays the last chord of his favorite concerto his father says, *"Glückwünsche und bravo, liebe Stefan."*

But the idyllic memory was bittersweet; Stefan could not separate it from the horror he felt the day he came home from school and learned that his father—his teacher—had died in a freakish farm accident.

Eight-year-old Stefan did what children often do to protect themselves from pain. He plucked the offending memory from his mind's eye. He quit playing the violin. He did not want to see it, touch it, or think about it.

But then he met Kizzy.

⚜

On Saturday morning, Dec. 6, 1941, Stefan went with Fritz to Biggers Hardware to get a new hinge for their garden gate. Fritz parked the truck and as soon they got out a high school boy wearing a sandwich board approached Stefan. The colorful boards—front and back—were advertising an event at Fat Daddy's Dancehall that night, and the boy handed Stefan a cheaply printed leaflet:

Tonight 7 p.m.
Bob Eddy and the Troubadours
All the way from Texas
Little Jimmy Daniels on the Fiddle
$3 Fat Daddy's Dancehall $3

Stefan showed the leaflet to Fritz. "I'd like to go hear the fiddler, but $3 is a lot of money."

Stefan's interest in the fiddler took Fritz by surprise. Annemarie had told him how Stefan quit playing his violin at age 8, the day his father died in an accident. She had given the violin to Fritz for safekeeping, and on her deathbed she pleaded with him to encourage Stefan to play once again.

Fritz dug into his pocket and pulled three one-dollar bills from a wad of money. He handed the bills to Stefan. "Your mother would want you to go, Stefan. She told me how you used to play for her."

⚜

When Stefan got to Fat Daddy's that night the bouncer would not let him enter, and told the ticket seller to refund his money.

"You're too young, kid, this dance is for grownups."

"I only want to hear the fiddler. I'll stay out of the way of the dancers if you'll just let me in."

At that moment, Fat Daddy himself waddled up. "Ain't you Fritz's kid?"

"Yes, sir." Stefan was surprised to see that the fat man had a very friendly face.

"Fritz told me you were comin'—said you used to play the fiddle."

"Yes, sir."

"Here's the deal, kid. I can't let you in if I charge you admission; the sheriff would get me for that. But if you'll help me pick up trash every time the band takes a break, I'll let you stand down front so you can get a good look at Little Jimmy Daniels."

"Thank you, sir."

⚜

When Bob Eddy's band struck the first note of their opening number that night, Stefan was right down front, as close as he could get to the stage. He watched Little Jimmy Daniels like a hawk and thought of the last time that he played his violin.

Stefan moved his fingers and bow hand in time with the fiddler, picturing the beautiful moment when he played for his mother and father on the little farm near the Neander Valley.

Mother always wanted me to play again. And Kizzy wants me to play. She sings, and I could play. We could make music. Together. Yes. Yes.

He smiled, but suddenly the pain of his father's death came slinking back, vying for its place in his mind. He was on the verge of letting it overwhelm him, as it had for so many years.

Then he noticed something odd about the fiddler.

The fiddler is very good, but he is not showing how he feels. When Father played, he moved, he swayed, he showed his love for the music, and that's what he taught me to do. But Little Jimmy doesn't do that. He doesn't smile or anything. He moves his bow hand and his fingers, but he doesn't move anything else. Hmm ... Maybe that's how they do it around here, but I like the way Father did it. When you're playing, you must show that you love the music.

The band finished the song and the crowd cheered. Little Jimmy cracked a big smile and took a bow. Stefan smiled too.

I'm going to play again. Father wants me to play, Mother wants me to play, and Kizzy wants me to play. And I want to play!

Then the band started playing a lively version of the popular ballad "John Henry," and the crowd let out a whoop.

XXVI

Rape

Kizzy cooked a pot of beans and some stovetop cornbread for dinner, and when it was ready, she dished up a plateful for Cormac and set it on the table. "After we eat and I clean up this mess I'm going to go up to Fat Daddy's to hear that band from Texas. I'm just going to listen from outside—it costs too much to get in."

Cormac did not respond right away, but when he finished his beans and had sopped up the juice with a last bite of cornbread, he said, "It's gonna be cold tonight so you ain't gonna be up there very long."

"I know, but I'm going to listen as long as I can." She got up, and took the dirty dishes to the sink. And as she washed them, she thought of Olivia Decker, wishing she could have seen her before she left for Norfolk. *I hope she comes back. I like the story of old Phileas and Passepartout, and I'd like to tell her.*

Cormac got up from the table, and stood so close behind Kizzy that he interrupted her thoughts. "That was a good dinner," he said as he slid his hands around her waist and pulled her against his body, so tightly that she could feel the beat of his heart. He purred, and whispered. "You remind me more and more of your ma."

Kizzy stiffened, but kept on with what she was doing. Cormac backed off and started sweet-talking. "I've been learning you a little bit every night now for two weeks. So tonight, when you get back, I'll show you how to do the real thing, and how to do it right—like a real woman—not like Boopie with all that talk. It'll feel good. It's a way we can show that we care about each other."

Kizzy finished the dishes and turned to face Cormac. "I gotta go, the band's already started playing." She grabbed her coat and headed out the door. And as she stepped off the boat she got that tingly feeling again, and thought of the promiscuous Elsie Sue Pardee. Then she had a passing thought about Olivia. *She's with her husband and they're probably doing it. I don't know. I ain't for sure about this. But it's what people do.*

❧

When Kizzy got close to Fat Daddy's the music and the crackle of life inside the dancehall washed away the thought of what Cormac had said to her. She peeped in, savoring the sounds of merriment and country music.

I'll be danged. There's Stefan, and he's right down front. She grinned big. *I betcha he's gonna start playing the fiddle again.*

She listened to several songs, and just when she thought they were going to take a break, the Troubadours began playing an extra-loud version of "John Henry."

The dancers let out a whoop. Kizzy whooped too.

"John Henry" was her favorite. It was a sad ballad, but she liked the snappy old version they were playing. Kizzy sang along, adding a touch of gloom in just the right places.

Just as she was singing the final lyric, "There lays that steel drivin' man," she began to shiver. She wanted to hear more, but the band was taking a break and the night air of Dec. 6, 1941, was getting colder by the minute. She slammed her hand on the fender and muttered. *Dang it.* Then she slid off the fender of the bus and walked slowly across the road to the woods. She paused, then entered the thicket and started down the footpath that twists its way to the river and the houseboat.

❧

Cormac's waiting for me. Kizzy pushed her hands between her legs and shivered. *He's gonna do the real thing tonight.*

She thought of the times she had listened as her mother and Boopie were doing it with Cormac, and what Elsie Sue had said about doing it.

MeeMaw and Grandpa did it too. And Shirley Barden's done it with lots of men ... It's the way of the river all right ... but Olivia ... she's a townie ... but she's doing it too.

⚜

When the houseboat came into view, Kizzy stopped. The music of the night had long since given way to the ominous quiet of the river.

That peculiar feeling—the awkward quivering—swirled around her midriff. *There it is again. What would MeeMaw say?* Then she thought of Stefan, and the rich kids from school, and Olivia. *What would they think?*

Kizzy pursed her lips and sighed, letting a last good breath of fun and music fly away. She slumped a bit and stood still for a moment longer; then she lifted her chin and stood tall, dabbing her eyes and brushing back the curlicues of red hair.

She inched her way down the path to the boat, crossed the wiggly gangplank and stepped on board. *I got nowhere else to go.*

Part Three—The War Years

"The only victories which leave no regret are those which are gained over ignorance."

Napoléon Bonaparte

XXVII

Pearl Harbor

Sunday, Dec. 7, 1941, began perfectly for John and Olivia Decker. They attended the 11 o'clock service at an old Methodist church situated on a promontory near the inlet to Lynnhaven Creek.

The sky was clear and the waters of Chesapeake Bay were calm when they left the church shortly after noon. They paused to enjoy a magnificent view of the bay, then walked to the nearby Angler's Inn, a rustic eatery that claimed to have the best oysters and crab cakes on the East Coast. The young lovers—an alluring sight—strolled along, smiling, chatting, and clinging to each other. Olivia wore a short red coat over a green dress, a red scarf and a green plaid tam o' shanter that gave her a Christmas look, especially beside the formal look of John, elegant in the dress blue uniform of a Navy ensign.

The Deckers talked about their future as they feasted on the unique cuisine of the Chesapeake. The Navy would be their life. They would live in Navy housing, but later on, they might buy a place off base. And they would start a family, making every effort to time her childbearing with his sea duty. A Navy career can involve months, sometimes years of separation, but the Deckers focused on the positives. They were certain that the Navy was right for them.

They left Angler's Inn and returned to the furnished room that they had rented from a retired admiral and his wife. It was on the top floor of a white-frame, three-story Federal-style home. Their room had a fine view of Lynnhaven Creek, so John and Olivia made themselves comfortable. They would listen to the Sunday afternoon radio shows and continue their dreaming.

⚜

Kizzy woke up at 9:30 a.m. that day; it was later than she usually slept. Cormac was sprawled next to her, naked and snoring. She raised up to sit on the side of the bed, taking care not to awaken the huge man. Then she found her dress, pulled it over her head, and stepped to the sink to wash her face. She gazed out at the river; it looked the same as always, but Kizzy felt different.

She put on her shoes and coat as quietly as she could and slipped out the door. Then she headed for her thinking place in the woods. It was a fine morning; the birds were in full voice and it was cool, but there was no breeze. The forest floor was damp and that allowed her to move quietly to Grandpa's stump, her favorite spot.

Kizzy hooted to the owls, but there was no answer. She tried thinking about school, the library, Olivia and Stefan; and she thought about MeeMaw and Ma, and all the times they had gone toe-digging and fishing. Then she thought of Elsie Sue Pardee and Boopie. And as she did she pressed her hands against her inner thighs and thought of the many times she had heard her mother and Boopie having sex with Cormac. Now she had done it with Cormac, and she needed to think about it.

It hurt a little bit at first, but then it didn't. Doing it is just part of what he's teaching me about growing up—about how to be a woman. I ain't got anyone else to learn from—he's my make-do stepfather.

⚜

Private First Class L. W. "Birdie" Barden had been with the Third Defense Battalion at the Marine Barracks at Pearl Harbor Navy Yard for almost a year, but on Dec. 7, he was in the second month of a temporary assignment to the Marine Aircraft Group 21 at the Marine Corps Air Station at Ewa, Oahu.

It was a day of rest for most Marines, but Birdie had been getting up early every Sunday morning to study reading and writing. On this day he intended to write a letter to his mother to tell her that the commanding officer had chosen him as the Third Defense Battalion's outstanding Marine for the month of November 1941. Winning the award virtually guaranteed that Birdie would soon be a corporal, with an increase in pay and responsibility.

Birdie had found a home in the Corps, and the Corps had found itself a natural-born Marine. Everything was looking up for the poor river-rat boy from Big Pearl, Ark.

⚜

Stefan and Fritz slept late on Sunday, Dec. 7, then went to Curly's Fish Market for a cup of coffee and some of Curly's homemade cinnamon rolls. One apiece would be enough since each roll was as big as a man's hand and twice as thick. They ate their rolls and listened to Curly and some fishermen tell a few stories, then they went back home.

Fritz intended to loaf around the house, but Stefan had other plans. He went to his room and closed the door. Then he opened the long mirrored door of a chifferobe and carefully removed the violin that had been in storage for years. He sat on the side of his bed and gently opened the case. Then, as he was about to take it from the case, he bowed his head and said a prayer for his father and mother in memory of the last time that he had played for them. He tuned the violin carefully and took a deep breath. *Now, let me see if I can remember the second movement of Mendelssohn's Concerto in E minor.*

⚜

Admiral Chūichi Nagumo, Commander, First Air Fleet, Imperial Japanese Navy, launched the first wave of a sneak attack on the United States Pacific Fleet at Pearl Harbor. The warplanes struck their targets minutes before

8 a.m. Hawaiian time. It was almost 1 o'clock in Washington, D. C., and Norfolk, Va., and it was almost noon in Arkansas.

The Marine Corps Air Station at Ewa, Oahu, was the first target of the striking Japanese bombers and fighter planes. Minutes later the attack reached its main objective, Pearl Harbor, where scores of Navy ships lay at anchor or alongside piers.

President Franklin Roosevelt was having lunch with his aide Harry Hopkins at 1:40 p.m. when a telephone call interrupted their meal. The Secretary of the Navy, Frank Knox, was on the line, relating dire news from the Pacific. The Navy had just received a radio message from Hawaii saying that Pearl Harbor was under attack by the Japanese.

The raid lasted two hours, and when it was over 21 vessels lay sunk or damaged, including the *USS Arizona* and seven other battleships. The attacks destroyed 202 aircraft and killed 2,388 men, women, and children.

⚜

At 3 o'clock Shirley Barden stood at the gangplank and hollered as loud as she could. "Kizzy, are you in there?"

Kizzy got up and opened the door to the aft deck. It was unlike Shirley to get excited about anything, particularly on a Sunday afternoon.

"Have you heard? The Japs bombed Pearl Harbor."

Kizzy gave her a dumbfounded look, so Shirley said, "It's in Hawaii—where Birdie is."

Kizzy was not sure what to say. "Is he OK?"

Shirley mussed her hair, and sobbed. "I don't know. The man on the radio said the first place that got bombed was a Marine Corps base."

XXVIII

War

Kizzy, Shirley Barden, the Deckers, Fritz and Stefan, and the townspeople of Big Pearl—like most Americans—were not thinking about war on the morning of Dec. 7, especially war in the Pacific. That was the farthest thing from their minds.

The American people *had* thought about Hitler's evil aggressions, but they were *not* thinking that the United States would actually enter the war in Europe.

But within hours of the sneak attack at Pearl Harbor, America moved quickly to get on a war footing.

⚜

When Kizzy got to school on Monday, Dec. 8, the hallways were noisier than usual; World War II had come to Big Pearl Junior High School. Boys struggling with puberty pretended to march and salute as they jostled one another, spewing an assortment of epithets they had learned overnight from their elders. "Dirty Japs" and "Sneaky Little Bastards" seemed to be the most popular.

The girls also talked about the war, but in other ways: "My dad says it won't last too long." "Mine says we'll be all right." "My mother says it's just something we've got to do." And they still found time to talk about makeup, clothes, boyfriends, and movie stars.

When the first bell rang Kizzy went to her homeroom, and she was surprised to see that Horace C. Ayers and his followers seemed eager to listen to their teacher. The mousey Bertha Mae Tyler stumbled at first—expecting distractions—but she got her message across: "At 1 o'clock this afternoon, we will tune to radio station KPRL to hear President Roosevelt make an historic speech to a Joint Session of Congress. You must be on time ..."

Just then, the door to Bertha Mae's classroom opened and Stefan came in and headed to his desk. Horace C. Ayers gave Stefan a horselaugh, and mocked Bertha Mae. "You must be on time." And his toadies did not miss their cue—they horselaughed in unison.

"I'm sorry," Stefan said. He took his seat and a semblance of order returned to the classroom.

Kizzy ignored the antics of her nemesis, using the successful technique she had mastered in the fifth grade. But the sight of Stefan gave her a start; she sensed that something had changed. *Hmmm ... He's the same, but I'm different now. I bet he ain't ever done it. Hadn't thought of that before. Hmmm ... I never even thought of him that way before. I wonder who teaches him about stuff like that? That guy Fritz? That's his stepfather.*

In the meantime, Bertha Mae had lost control of the class to Horace C. Ayers, but Kizzy was not distracted. She played with a curl of hair and kept her eyes on Stefan. *He's got a new look about him—a sort of fresh, nice look—I can see it now that I ain't a virgin.*

When homeroom class was over and it was time to change rooms Stefan came to where Kizzy was standing, and he had a big grin on his face. Kizzy thought, *I'm thinking about sex and stuff like that, but he ain't. He's excited about something else. Surely it ain't the war ...*

Stefan spoke first, babbling. "I've started playing the violin again." Then he babbled some more about how he had not forgotten how to play. "It all came back—pretty easy."

Kizzy complimented him, but the words were barely out of her mouth when he said, "Can you go to my house after school? I'll play for you, and you can sing." And when she nodded yes, Stefan said, "Do you know

'O Tannenbaum'?" Kizzy gave him a blank stare, so he translated. "Oh Christmas Tree."

She laughed and nodded. Stefan's enthusiasm had washed away Kizzy's thoughts about what she had been doing with Cormac. *There ain't no need to dwell on all that. It is what it is—and what I'm doing with Cormac is just the way of the river.*

✤

Shortly after noon that day—less than 24 hours after the start of the Japanese attack—President Franklin Roosevelt entered the chamber of the United States House of Representatives to address a joint session of Congress, and via radio, the nation.

The president's speech was direct and short, only seven minutes.

"Yesterday, Dec. 7, 1941, a date which will live in infamy, the United States of America was suddenly and deliberately attacked by naval and air forces of the Empire of Japan.

"The attack yesterday on the Hawaiian Islands has caused severe damage to American naval and military forces. I regret to tell you that very many American lives have been lost.

"The people of the United States have already formed their opinions and well understand the implications to the very life and safety of our nation.

"We will not only defend ourselves to the uttermost, but will make it very certain that this form of treachery shall never again endanger us."

The Senate responded with a unanimous declaration of war on Japan, and only one member of Congress, Montana pacifist Jeanette Rankin, dissented in the House of Representatives. At 4 p.m. that same afternoon, President Roosevelt signed the declaration of war.

Thus the United States entered World War II, determined to fight to the finish.

The Imperial Japanese Navy had scored a brilliant success at Pearl Harbor, but the tactical victory assured its ultimate defeat. And it assured the defeat of Hitler as well.

⚜

Three days later, on Dec. 11, Japan's allies, Germany and Italy, both declared war on the United States. The United States Congress responded immediately by declaring war on them.

And from coast to coast, volunteers jammed the recruiting stations of the Army, Navy, and Marine Corps.

⚜

On Dec. 16, just eight days after the declaration of war on Japan, John Decker and Olivia stood on the dock in Norfolk alongside the *USS Yorktown*. The aircraft carrier would sail that day for duty in the Pacific.

It was time to say goodbye, and they wanted to make the most of it. They spoke of love and loneliness, and exchanged promises to write and pray for peace, but their lives were going to be different, and they knew it. The demands of war—duty, honor, and country—had muscled their way into the sweet dreams of too many young lovers.

Ensign John Decker was going off to the Pacific to fight the Japanese, and Olivia was going home to Big Pearl to wait for him.

A high-pitched whistle sliced through the pulsing clamor of sailors and loved ones—hundreds of them—saying their last goodbyes.

"That's the bosun's final call," John said. "I have to go."

They hugged with a sense of urgency; Olivia knew she had to let him go. He gave her a last kiss and made a beeline for the gangway. Then he turned and waved just before he stepped aboard to salute the flag and the officer of the deck.

Olivia stayed on the dock, hoping for a last glimpse of John. *Dear God, please take care of John and bring him home safe. I could not bear to lose him ... but, I know he must go ... and I must go on here at home. And, please God, let me have his child ...*

The *Yorktown* eased away from the dock, and just as Olivia was about to give up, she spotted John. He was by the rail on the quarterdeck, waving madly. Olivia waved with both arms, and like so many others on the dock, she cheered and cried at the same time. John saw her, and as the ship pulled away, he blew her a kiss.

XXIX

Fear

In Washington, D. C., Franklin Roosevelt signed Presidential Proclamations 2525, 2526, and 2527 pertaining to the arrest and detention of certain Japanese, German, and Italian aliens.

"All alien enemies are ... to refrain from actual hostility or giving information, aid or comfort to the enemies of the United States or interfering by word or deed with the defense of the United States or political processes and public opinions thereof ...

"All alien enemies shall be liable to restraint, or to give security, or to remove and depart from the United States."

Director J. Edgar Hoover, Federal Bureau of Investigation (FBI), sent a teletype to all field offices authorizing Special Agents of the FBI to arrest such aliens if "information indicating the arrest of such individuals is necessary for the internal security of this country."

And within days FBI agents arrested 1,002 German aliens, 169 Italian aliens, and 1,370 Japanese aliens.

The roundup was underway.

⚜

In Willich, Pa., on Wednesday, Dec. 17, Horst Bachmann placed a long-distance telephone call to Fritz Halder in Big Pearl.

Fritz answered the call. "Hello?"

"Fritz, this is Horst—don't talk, just listen."

"OK."

"The FBI is everywhere, asking questions. And they have already arrested some Germans, saying they are a risk to national security. This reminds me the last war. It will get worse. Remember what I said. Just keep saying you are Pennsylvania Dutch, and never say or do anything to suggest you are sympathetic to Germany.

"That's it. That's all I wanted to say. I was worried about you and Stefan, but I feel better now that I've called."

"Thanks, Horst, but I think we will be fine," Fritz said. "There are no other Germans here, and so far as I know, everyone thinks we are Dutch, not German."

"Good. By the way, Fritz, I visited Annemarie's grave yesterday and promised her I would call you. Give Stefan my love. And take care, dear friend."

⚜

On that same Wednesday, Shirley Barden came to Kizzy's boat and hollered for her to come out.

As soon as Kizzy opened the door, Shirley said, "He's OK! I got a letter from Birdie. The postman read it for me. He's OK!"

Kizzy ran across the gangplank yelling "Whoopee!" And as soon as she got to ground, Shirley threw her arms around her and they did a little jig.

But all of a sudden, Shirley stopped dancing and slumped. She pulled Kizzy close, murmuring the way mothers do when they worry about their babies. "I been worried sick about Birdie. And I'm still scared about them other boys of mine. They ain't like Birdie—they never write. He says he thinks they might go to England or somewhere over that way 'cause that's where everybody is saying the Army will go first—but Birdie says he's just guessing."

Kizzy hugged Shirley as snugly as she could. "Being scared is a terrible thing, but MeeMaw always said being scared is just the other side of caring—and caring's a good thing."

"I know my boys is doin' their part, but this better not turn out to be another rich man's war—I don't want my boys to get killed for the likes of Bully Bigshot."

"Cormac says he ain't going. He says, 'it ain't his fight.'"

Shirley nodded. "He's smart."

Kizzy pondered, and then said, "Did Birdie say anything about what happened in Pearl Harbor?"

"Here, read it for yourself."

Kizzy unfolded the letter and began to read to herself. Then she giggled. "He says, 'I nearly got my ass shot off.'"

"That ain't funny, Kizzy."

Kizzy stopped laughing and read on, paraphrasing Birdie's account of what it was like when the attack started. "He says he was working on his reading and writing when the Japs attacked ... says he had just finished writing a two-page letter to you when a bomb hit his barracks and started a fire."

She kept a somber look on her face so as not to irritate Shirley. "He says he went back into the barracks after it was blown up to look for the letter, but the fire and water had messed it up."

"Go on. You are comin' to the part I like."

Kizzy read the next paragraph of Birdie's letter just as he wrote it: "I worked all morning on that letter. Now I'm really pissed off."

Shirley cackled. She had memorized the last words of Birdie's letter. "I like the way he ended it: 'Now I'm ready to go kill them Japs.'"

Kizzy and Shirley laughed, but then Shirley whimpered. "Ain't that just like Birdie?"

XXX

Volunteers

On Wednesday afternoon, the day after their husbands shipped out on the *Yorktown*, Olivia Decker and Susan Porter, a new friend from Lynchburg, Va., took a taxi from their hotel to Union Station, the elegant eight-story headquarters of the Norfolk and Western Railway. The young Navy wives, like so many others, were going home to wait and pray for the safety of their loved ones.

They gave their bags to a redcap, and as they followed him into the station Olivia said, "What a difference two weeks can make. When I came to Norfolk to meet the *Yorktown* this place was half-full, but look at it now—it's jam-packed and noisy as all get-out."

"It's the damn war, Olivia. It's going to change everything." Susan kept slapping her hand against her hip as they walked farther into the station. Her husband was a newly commissioned ensign, a recent graduate of Virginia Military Institute, and they had only been married for three months. Susan, like Olivia, had come to Norfolk hoping to make a home, not to see her husband off to war.

The porter led them through the huge main lobby of Union Station to the platform where they boarded the *Pocahontas*, Norfolk and Western's premier westbound passenger train. It would get them to Lynchburg just after dark, and Olivia planned to spend the night there with Susan and her parents. Then she would continue her train trip to Arkansas on Thursday.

At 2:40 p.m. the train pulled out of the station. Olivia and Susan left their coach seats and went to the observation car, but they did not stop or sit down. They went outside to the aft deck—a sort of canopied porch—to watch the Norfolk station fade into the distance. It was their last glimpse of the city that they had hoped to call home.

They braved the cold as long as they could, then went back into the observation car. Susan asked the steward to save them a place at the first seating for dinner, gave him a tip, and then led Olivia back to their seats in coach. Then she said, "My dad works for the railroad—there's not much he hasn't taught me."

When the train stopped in Petersburg at 4:30 p.m., Olivia looked out the window. The platform was full of men in civilian clothing shuffling about in ragged formations, each under the obvious control of a recruiting sergeant. A small group of black recruits was off to the side, segregated, as were the families who had come to see their loved ones go off to war.

Then, at 5 o'clock sharp, Susan gave Olivia a nudge, and they headed toward the front of the train, passing through two coach cars, to the dining car. The steward, a white man, welcomed them and showed them to their table. Three waiters—black men dressed in black trousers, white shirts, black bow ties, and white jackets—were just beginning the first serving of dinner. And the waiter assigned to their table, a distinguished-looking man with grey hair, wore a name tag: Samson.

Their table was perfectly set: White tablecloth and napkins, dinnerware initialed N&W, heavy silverware, and a white porcelain bud vase with fresh-cut flowers. Samson helped the women take their seats, and when they were comfortable he handed each of them a meal-order card and put two small pencils on the table. Susan looked at Olivia. "The food is very good, all fresh-made here on the train." They placed their orders and began to talk about their husbands.

When Samson returned to pour them a glass of water he said, "I'm not supposed to say anything that's not about your dinner, but I heard you all talking about your men going off to war."

Olivia could see that Samson wanted their permission to say more, so she said, "Yes, we're worried, but isn't everyone?"

"Yes, ma'am," Samson said. Then he straightened up as tall as he could. "My boy volunteered for the Navy right after Pearl Harbor, and my wife and I saw him off yesterday. It broke our hearts to see him go. I pray that he will be all right, but we've all got to do our part, don't we?"

Olivia and Susan gave a nod of approval, then Olivia smiled as graciously as she could. "You must be very proud of your son."

Samson gave her a beamy grin. "Thank you, ma'am. I am. But now I better get back to work or the steward will dock me for breaking the rules."

As soon as he was out of earshot Susan said, "He's a nice man. He has probably been working in this same dining car for 30 years, existing mostly on tips. I don't know how he manages to keep a smile on his face."

⚜

After dinner the two returned to their seats in coach and continued to talk. Soon the *Pocahontas* pulled into the station at Appomattox, and they saw the same scene they had seen in every town along the way: Young men bunched up, going off to war—whites in one formation; blacks in another. Olivia thought of Samson, and she pointed to the black men on the platform and asked Susan, "Will they be segregated when they are in the service?"

"I don't know." Susan thought about her answer for a second, and then added, "I don't know how the military handles that. But I know for sure that when this train is passing through a segregated state, it has to follow the laws of that state."

They sat still for a while, and then Susan said, "It's a mess, isn't it—this race problem?" She sighed and pointed toward the Appomattox Depot. "Thank God, it's only 30 minutes from here to Lynchburg. I'm ready to get home, aren't you?"

⚜

At noon the next day, Olivia stood on the platform of the Kemper Street Station in Lynchburg, waiting for the arrival of the *Tennessean*, Southern Railway's newest passenger service between Washington, D.C., and Memphis, Tenn. And, right on time, the huge engine pulled into the station, shaking the earth and making a deafening racket—the sound of escaping steam and squealing brakes.

Olivia tipped the redcap and climbed on board to find her seat. She had arranged a Pullman berth for the overnight trip to Memphis, but she did not plan to go to bed until 9 o'clock.

During the long trip home, Olivia worked crossword puzzles and read, but her thoughts kept coming back to John. She had gone to Norfolk dreaming of life as a Navy wife, but now she was returning home with a prayer on her lips: *God, please keep him safe, and let me have his child.*

At 8:11 p.m. the *Tennessean* pulled into the station at Jefferson City, Tenn., and when Olivia looked out she saw a sight she had not seen. The crowded platform had the usual clusters of young men going off to the military, but she saw no black men. Instead, a cluster of 20 Cherokees waited for direction from an Army sergeant wearing a campaign hat. Behind the young men were scores of sad-faced Cherokee women, children, and elderly men who had come to see their young men off. Some wore pieces of native clothing, and the oldest man slowly waggled a colorful medicine-stick adorned with leather, fur and feathers.

Olivia thought about Samson and the pride he showed. Then she wondered about his son and the Cherokees. *Why do they volunteer?*

⚜

At 7:30 a.m. the next morning, Friday, Dec. 19, the *Tennessean* pulled into Union Station in Memphis on schedule. Olivia found a porter who put her luggage on a Frisco train bound for points west, and soon she was on her way across the Mississippi River and into Arkansas. The train made a brief stop in Jonesboro, and Olivia got off when it stopped in Hoxie. Her mother, Matilda Joyce, was there to meet her. It was a short drive to Big Pearl.

XXXI

Christmas

It was mid-afternoon when Olivia and her mother got to the Joyce family home in Big Pearl. Olivia unpacked her bags and freshened up while her mother made a pot of tea and a plateful of finger sandwiches. Then they arranged a white porcelain tea service on a coffee table in the parlor, their favorite place to sit and talk.

They spent the rest of the afternoon talking about all that had happened in the three weeks since Olivia left for Norfolk. But every time their tête-à-tête broached the subject of war, and the madness of it, a wistful Olivia steered the conversation to the First World War, wondering how it had affected her mother's marriage. Olivia's father had enlisted as soon as the United States entered the war in April 1917, just two months before she was born. The Army sent him to a camp in Texas, but the conflict ended a year later and he did not have to go overseas.

Matilda Joyce soon realized that her daughter did not want to talk about the war in the Pacific and John's hazardous duty on the *Yorktown*.

Melancholia, albeit subtle, seldom escapes the loving eye of a mother. So as it began to get dark outside, Matilda said, "Why don't you go to bed early, Olivia? Things always look better after a good night's sleep."

Olivia nodded, but did not answer right away. She helped her mother clear the table, and then she stretched and faked a yawn. "I think I will, and I'm going to sleep as long and as late as I can tomorrow."

Her mother gave her a hug. "That's my girl." She kissed her on the cheek, and then said, as if it were an afterthought, "Let's go to church tomorrow night—it's the Christmas Cantata. It will be beautiful and it will lift our spirits."

Olivia nodded, went into her bedroom, and closed the door.

⚜

The ushers roamed up and down the aisles of the First Methodist Church of Big Pearl looking for places to seat latecomers, but by 6:45 the sanctuary was completely full. Olivia and her mother, expecting a good turnout, had arrived a half-hour early to visit with friends and get a good seat down front. The choir was going to perform a selection of sacred music by Felix Mendelssohn, but the church was filling up for another reason. Olivia's mother explained it best: "It's the war; people turn to God when the world goes mad."

The cantata was beautiful, and when the choir sang "Hear My Prayer" with its haunting verse—"O for the wings of a dove"—Olivia noticed a young blond-headed boy sitting in a nearby aisle seat. *The music has cast a spell on him, and he shows it.* She nudged her mother, and motioned for her to watch the boy. He seemed to have an endless repertoire of facial expressions and gentle movements. And that prompted Olivia—after they had sneaked several looks—to whisper, "Now there's a boy who loves music."

⚜

When the cantata was over, Olivia and her mother walked a few blocks in the chilly night air to view the Christmas display at the library. Several people had gathered in front of the building to enjoy it, and that pleased Olivia. But when they got close enough to stand amongst the onlookers, Olivia shook her head and whispered to her mother, "I've got to change it."

"Why? Everyone seems to like what you've done. It tells the Christmas story, and it encourages people to read. Isn't that what it is supposed to do?"

"Yes, but I did it before Pearl Harbor. Everything has changed. I hate this war, but it is on everyone's mind. The display should connect—somehow—to the war."

Her mother shook her head. "War and Christmas? That'll be some combination."

⚜

On Sunday morning, Reverend Hershel Garland stepped to the pulpit of the First Methodist Church and began his sermon with a proposition that shocked every member of the congregation.

"Is God on our side in this war?" He paused for effect, and then answered his own question with an emphatic "No!"

He let his words sink in, then proclaimed with certainty. "God does not take sides."

A murmur of impatience swept through the congregation.

"But he is always on the side of what is right. Because, after all, it is God who makes up the rules about what is right and what is wrong."

With that, the congregants settled down, waiting eagerly for the preacher to finish his rhetorical exercise.

"I am certain that God wants people to be free, so when people like Hitler and Mussolini and Hirohito use force to take away our freedom, then God will be for protecting freedom."

The congregation murmured its approval, so Reverend Garland moved on. "So, you see, God does not take sides." Then he pointed to himself and smiled. "But that does not keep us from taking sides."

Then he told a story. "Some time ago, a parade of well-trained soldiers passed through a town. The soldiers were on their way to war, and they marched by an old woman's house. She was so proud of the men that she grabbed her broomstick, placed it on her shoulder, and started marching right beside the men in uniform. Someone shouted from the crowd, 'Old woman, you can't go to war with them!' And the old woman said, 'I know I can't go, but I can let the boys know whose side I am on!'"

The congregation jumped to its feet, cheering and applauding. Olivia stood with them, but her mind was grinding, testing a fresh idea for the display that had come to her in a flash, like an epiphany.

❖

Olivia made a beeline to the Veterans' Center as soon as the preacher finished the benediction. She wanted to reveal her new idea for the Christmas display to "Uncle Mac" to get his blessing.

Mac Thornton and Olivia's father, Arthur Joyce, were boyhood friends; so friendly and close that they joined the Army on the same day in 1917. The Army sent Arthur to Texas, and he was fortunate enough to stay there for the duration of the war. Mac was not so lucky; the Army sent him to France to serve with General Pershing's First Army. And it was there, on Oct. 4, 1918, that Corporal Mac Thornton lost both legs, a hand, and an eye in the desperate Meuse-Argonne offensive, a major action that broke the German lines and led to the end of World War I. Mac came home, broken and scarred, to spend the rest of his life in a wheelchair. He was only 52 years old, but the ravages of war made him look 70. Even so, his voice was deep and strong, and when Olivia's father died, Mac delivered a powerful eulogy, a testament to the power of love and friendship so moving that people quoted it for years.

Olivia called the beloved veteran Uncle Mac, but everyone else called him Old Mac. And when his name was mentioned someone was sure to add, reverently, "He's the smartest man in Jasper County."

❖

Olivia pulled a straight chair alongside Mac's wheelchair and gave him a kiss on the cheek. They exchanged the usual formalities, but he could see that she had something else on her mind, so he let her run on without interruption.

Finally, she got to her point. "Uncle Mac, I've got a new idea for the Christmas display."

He winked, but said nothing, and Olivia carried on. "I'm going to keep three windows for Christmas, but the other three windows will invite passersby to bring us mementos and photographs of the men and women from Big Pearl who are going off to war." She stopped to catch her breath, and then said, "I'll arrange all of it to honor them. What do you think, Uncle Mac?"

Mac grinned, but as he did, he used his right hand to trace the lines of a deep jagged scar that started at the corner of his left eye and disappeared beneath the collar of his shirt. Olivia shut up and settled back in her chair. She recognized the gesture: Uncle Mac was about to deliver a diplomatic rebuke.

"Everyone is in the fight, Olivia. It's not just the men and women in uniform. I like your idea, and I think it is OK to connect the war effort to Christmas, but be sure to include those who will stay behind—they will not do the actual fighting, but they will sacrifice a lot, and that's why they also deserve to be honored."

She thought he was through, but just as she was about to speak, he continued. "And be careful, Olivia. We are engaged in a cause greater than self, but don't glorify war—this one or the last one. Most of us Veterans'—especially me—don't like all the folderol. We just did our duty. We don't expect accolades, or special benefits, we just want to get on with life.

"And, finally, think of the little kids. Get them involved somehow; it will give them a way to deal with their fears. God knows what'll go through their little heads when the news reports start coming in."

⚜

Olivia spent half of the afternoon clearing out three of the six Christmas display windows to make room for her new idea. Then she made a paper-mâché replica of the old woman in the preacher's story—a craggy matron marching with a broomstick on her shoulder. She positioned the figurine in front of a large picture of soldiers marching off to war and painted a sign that showed the old woman saying, "I know I can't go, but I can let the boys know whose side I am on."

Then, taking Mac Thornton's advice, she painted attractive signs for each window inviting the men, women, and children of Big Pearl to bring photographs, letters, exhibits, and other items to show their support for the war effort.

She worked into the evening hours and as she worked, she thought of the scenes she saw on her trip home from Norfolk. At every train station there were men going off to war, but in the background there were the loved ones—blacks, whites, Cherokees, all Americans—who would, like the old woman with the broomstick, stay behind. *Uncle Mac is right—we are all in this together and this is no time for hand-wringing. John is going to be out there somewhere in the Pacific, but so are many others. I've got to stop feeling sorry for myself.*

⚜

At 9 o'clock Olivia finished her work, and to demonstrate what people should bring for the display, she created a montage of photographs of her family. There was a photograph of John in uniform with his arm around her, and one of John's mother and father and Olivia's mother and father. She positioned them around a poster showing the *USS Yorktown* leaving port and put John's high school ring beneath his photo.

Olivia went outside to admire her work, and just as she was nodding her approval, she realized she needed to lock the door to the library and go home as quickly as possible.

She would not have John's baby, not this time.

⚜

Kizzy met Stefan at Curly's Fish Market on Monday morning, Dec. 22, and they walked up the hill to the Veterans' Center and Library.

When they got close Kizzy broke into a run, and as soon as she could see into the display windows, she told Stefan, "She's back. Look, Stefan, she's changed it. She's inviting everyone to put stuff in the window. She must have worked on this over the weekend."

They went into the library, and Kizzy spotted Olivia right away. She was shelving books with her back turned to them. Kizzy put a finger to her lips, and signaled to slip up behind Olivia. When they were directly behind her, Kizzy said, "Hi," and it startled Olivia. She turned around, and when her eyes met Kizzy's, they laughed and gave each other a hug. Then Kizzy pointed to Stefan. "This is Stefan. He's my friend from school."

Olivia smiled and put out her hand to Stefan. "Hi, Stefan." Then she gave him a second look. "Didn't I see you at the cantata Saturday night?"

Stefan shuffled around, and then he grinned. "Yes, ma'am. I like music. My father taught me to play the violin. He liked Mendelssohn, and so do I."

Olivia noticed his accent, but did not let on about it. "I could tell."

Kizzy interrupted. "I like the new window decorations. My friend Birdie is in the Marines. He was at Pearl Harbor, but he's OK. His mother got a letter from him and it has a Pearl Harbor postmark on it. Can I put that envelope and a picture of Birdie and his two brothers who are in the Army in the window?"

"Yes, of course." She was about to say more, but Kizzy was too excited to stop talking.

"And can I put in one of Birdie's stuffed birds? He loves birds, and knows more about them than anyone. The one I want to put in the window is a white dove. It'd look real good, and it'd make Birdie proud. It was his favorite—an old man who was about to die gave it to him to take care of."

Stefan started humming, and Kizzy gave him a funny look. Then he said, "It's from Mendelssohn: 'O for the wings, for the wings of a dove!'"

Olivia smiled. "Yes. Yes, I think Birdie's dove would be perfect."

⚜

On Christmas Eve, after dark, Kizzy brought Shirley Barden and her two little girls up the hill to see the display.

The windows that Olivia had reserved for the display of local memorabilia were almost full. A light snow was falling, but it did not deter the people of Big Pearl. Scores went from window to window, pressing their faces against the glass and calling out the names of friends and relatives. The people of Big Pearl loved Olivia's idea; it was the talk of the town.

Kizzy pulled Shirley Barden and the girls to the window where she had put the pictures of Birdie and his half-brothers, and the envelope from Pearl Harbor. The little girls wiggled around and shouted their names, but Shirley could not speak. She was sobbing and clinging to Kizzy.

The oldest little girl said, "There's Birdie's stuffed dove—he'd like that."

Then she asked Kizzy, "What's that writing on that little boat paddle say?"

Kizzy laughed and read it for them: "THE RIVER BOYS ARE DOING THEIR PART TOO."

XXXII

Invasion

Vice Admiral Shimizu Mitsumi of the Imperial Japanese Navy ordered nine I-boats to attack the west coast of the United States on Christmas Eve. Shimizu directed each submarine commander to fire 30 shells on designated targets. The objective was to create fear and panic, but Shimizu had to postpone the surprise attack when he learned that the submarines had depleted their fuel reserves.

One month later, the Japanese tried again.

At sunset on Feb. 23, 1942, Commander Nishino Kozo steered his Japanese submarine I-17 into a channel near Santa Barbara, Calif., and at 7:10 p.m. he commenced firing at Ellwood Beach. When the last of 16 shells struck American soil, the I-17 submerged and fled to the open ocean. The shelling caused minor damage to an oil field, but the attack had the desired effect: The American people panicked.

A day later, false reports of enemy aircraft led to the so-called "Battle of Los Angeles." American troops, in the mistaken belief that the Japanese were invading, launched an anti-aircraft artillery barrage that lasted for several hours. When the barrage ended, Secretary of the Navy Frank Knox called the entire incident a "false alarm."

The panic was understandable. Just four days before the submarine attack on Ellwood Beach, President Roosevelt had signed Executive Order 9066 expressing concerns about Japanese attacks or sabotage. The president's order directed the removal of resident enemy aliens from places vaguely identified as military areas. The order most directly affected people of Japanese heritage, but it also applied to Germans and Italians.

⚜

On April 1, 1942, the *New York Times* reported that the FBI and local authorities throughout the United States were collaborating to "check up" on 1,100,000 aliens from Germany, Italy, and Japan to "choke off possible fifth-column activity."

The authorities planned to make complete dossiers of all such aliens, and the "checkup and dossier system" was only the beginning of a "more intensive watch on aliens." The system would enable "government operatives" to "put their fingers on any alien in any community at almost any time."

The roundup of aliens was in full swing.

⚜

It was recess time at Big Pearl Junior High School, and Horace C. Ayers was holding court on the playground. A dozen 13-year-old boys huddled around their leader, swapping hits to the shoulder and vying with one another to see who could display the goofiest facial expression. This ritualistic cluster—a sort of impromptu fraternity for pubescent boys—occurred each day below the overhanging branches of a huge oak tree in a far corner of the schoolyard.

Horace was bigger and stronger than the other boys were, but he did not rely on physical prowess to draw a crowd. He was a natural-born organizer, and the boys followed him because he always had the latest news about everything. Moreover, they knew that he would have the very best "Eight-page bibles," little cartoon booklets featuring lewd depictions of Moon Mullins, Popeye and Olive Oil, Tarzan and Jane, and other popular characters. Horace would let the boys pass the booklets around and they would flip through the pages, oohing and aahing and cackling with satisfaction, especially when they got to the predictable finales.

Horace would retrieve his booklets and steer the boys to other popular subjects, such as: Is the war going to mess up the baseball season? A topic like that guaranteed hot argument and occasional fisticuffs as the boys compared the Red Sox without Ted Williams to the Yankees without Joe DiMaggio.

Now, with the war in full swing, Horace made it his business to have the latest information, and if he did not have breaking news, he would make something up.

On this occasion, Thursday, April 2, Horace asked a scary question. What if the Japanese invade America and win the war? To fortify his theme, he told of an uncle who had supposedly seen an 8mm movie that showed Japanese soldiers beheading Chinese men, women, and children for sport. Horace said it was in a place called Nanking, and said his uncle had also seen movies showing Japanese soldiers tossing infants into the air and catching them on their bayonets.

The boys were horrified, so Horace played it to the hilt. "My uncle says we should have stopped them over there, but we didn't. And now they've gotten strong and they're going to come over here and chop off our heads."

Just then the bell rang, but the pubescents at Big Pearl Junior High—in the space of a 15-minute recess—had sampled a wartime mix of baseball trivia, squalid lust, and undiluted fear.

⚜

Olivia was having lunch with Mac Thornton in the Veterans' Center at noon on Friday. Mabel walked up and slammed a stack of posters onto the table.

"I'm not going to put these up in the library." She pointed to the poster on top, a grotesque cartoon of a scowling, buck-toothed Prime Minister Hideki Tôjô wearing oversized horn-rimmed glasses. "I'll put up the patriotic posters that are designed to keep our people unified, but I can't stand the posters that have no purpose other than to arouse fury." She put her finger on Tôjô's mustache, and then moved it downward and pointed to his unsheathed sword. "Look at this guy! He looks like he's ready to cut your head off—it'll scare the beejeebers out of the children. Hell, it scares me."

"I agree, Mabel," Mac said. "I'm mad as hell at the Japs, but we're better than that. And you're right; the kids are going to have enough nightmares without us making it worse."

"It's not just the kids," Olivia said. "There's a lot coming out about what the Japanese soldiers did to women and children when they invaded China. It's atrocious, and I think that's why everyone got so scared when that Japanese submarine bombarded California a few weeks ago."

Mac nodded. "Yes, but let's not forget the Germans. Their U-boats are sinking our ships in the Atlantic. And I won't be surprised if they try something like that on the East Coast."

"So," Mabel said. "Will you all back me up about the posters?"

Olivia looked at Mac. He lifted his right hand and touched the scar that ran from his left eye to base of his neck. "We're going to win this war. It may take a while, but ..." He pointed to the poster of Tôjô, and spoke in a solemn way. "We can win it without resorting to stuff like that."

⚜

In Berlin, Adolf Hitler ordered the training of saboteurs. Twelve carefully chosen men—all naturalized American citizens living in Germany—were selected to study chemistry, incendiaries, explosives, timing devices, secret writing, and techniques for blending into the American background.

The saboteurs memorized instructions and maps of American targets, critical railroad junctions, aluminum and magnesium plants, important canals, waterways, locks, dams and tunnels.

German U-boats would take the saboteurs to the East Coast of America and put them ashore in June to begin their operations.

Hitler was pleased. He bragged, in meetings at the Reich Chancellery, that his saboteurs would degrade American industrial capacity, gloating that the acts of terrorism would demoralize the American people.

XXXIII

Reading

Kizzy woke from a deep sleep just as the morning sun found its way through the big cottonwoods lining the Black River. A gentle ripple of current lapped against the houseboat, but the main attraction was the same as always—morning birds in full throat, singing their happy notes.

She listened for a moment, thinking of Birdie, and then she turned slightly to reach backwards, feeling to see if Cormac was in bed with her—but he was not.

Just then, he snored and sputtered, and rustled the covers of his own bed.

All right. He slept over there.

Kizzy pushed her covers away and sat up to slip on her dress and shoes. When dressed, she tiptoed across the cabin to put a good-sized piece of kindling in the cookstove and gently stoked the leftover embers. *That'll take care of the chill.*

Then she stepped to the sink to brush her teeth and wash her face. And as she did, she peeped through the window just in time to see the last bit of morning fog rising from the river, wafting away in the breeze.

Cormac rolled over and farted.

He's dead to the world. She shook her head slowly. *It's been almost four months. Dang. He's done it so many times I've lost count. ...I must be pretty good at it ... last night he said, "Any man would give his whole paycheck to get some of that."*

Kizzy smiled, brushed her hair and quickly made a sandwich for her school lunch. Then she grabbed her books and headed out the door.

Don't want to wake him up ... ain't got no time for any more of that. I need to get to school.

⚜

That afternoon when school let out, Kizzy went to the library to return her latest read, Jules Verne's *20,000 Leagues Under the Sea.*

Olivia was working behind the return desk, and she waved when she saw Kizzy entering the building. Kizzy smiled and held the book up for her to see, but when she got close, she did not give Olivia a chance to say a word.

"This makes three of his books that I've read. The first one you gave me—the one about old Phileas Fogg and Passepartout going around the world—I liked it so much that I read *Journey to the Center of the Earth,* and now I have just finished this one and I liked it the best of all—I guess because it's about the sea. I've always lived on the water."

Olivia did her best to listen, but Kizzy's liveliness trumped her words. *She's so fresh ... so enthusiastic ...*

"Captain Nemo and his struggle with Professor Aronnax on the submarine *Nautilus* is what made this book so interesting. Is there really an Atlantis? I'd like to go there, but it didn't end well for Nemo."

Olivia nodded in agreement, but let her go on. *What fun to be a teenager.*

"Is it true, Olivia?"

"Is what true?"

"Atlantis. Is that true?"

Olivia blinked. "I'm sorry, Kizzy, I ... No, Atlantis is fictional, but it's fun to pretend it's real, isn't it?"

Kizzy nodded, and then gave Olivia a serious look. "Yep, I like to pretend. I dream all the time and I like these stories because they are about people who are trying to do something hard and they don't give up. My MeeMaw always said, 'We got to look at the bright side of things, and keep on trucking.'"

"Would you like to read something entirely different?"

"Sure. Is it an adventure story?"

"Yes, in its own way." And she took Kizzy's hand.

⚜

Kizzy went with her to the stacks, and when they got to the end of a row Olivia stopped and pulled a book off the shelf. She placed it against her breasts as if it were sacred. "I read all the Jules Verne books, and lots of others when I was young, and I learned something from every one of them. But this book by Jane Austen really touched me."

She handed the book to Kizzy. "It's beautifully written ... you'll see."

"Thanks." Kizzy took the book and read the title. *"Pride and Prejudice."* She was about to ask what the book was about, but Olivia interrupted. "It's a classic, Kizzy. Look inside and read the opening sentence."

Kizzy turned to the first page and read aloud:

"It is a truth universally acknowledged, that a single man in possession of a good fortune, must be in want of a wife."

Olivia swooned, but she collected herself. "Let me know how you like it."

⚜

As she walked from the library to the boat, Kizzy kept looking at the book's title and thinking about the sentence that she had read.

I know Olivia loves it. That's easy to see. But I ain't sure I'm going to like it.

First of all, there ain't no single man on the river that's in possession of anything—much less a fortune.

And, I don't know any married folks. MeeMaw and Grandpa and Ma weren't married ... and Shirley's got five kids by five different guys.

But Olivia wants me to read it. So I'll give it a shot.

XXXIV

Worry

Kizzy hurried home after school, determined to start reading *Pride and Prejudice*. She had started it a time or two, but could not get past the first chapter. Today would be different. It was a mild mid-April afternoon; there was plenty of light left, and she planned to read outside, on the aft deck.

But when she pushed the door open and stepped inside the houseboat she stamped her foot, and shouted to herself. *Dang it, Cormac. This place is a mess!*

Kizzy stewed for a minute, then put her books down and got to work. She picked up several cans and jars—Pet Milk, peanut butter, beans, lard—and put them back on the shelf, then took a pile of Cormac's dirty clothes and put it outside, on the fore deck. She sorted out a mixed-up pile of fishing gear and put each piece back where it belonged—some went on the shelf, but she hung most of it on wall hooks.

He does it every time. He gets to looking for something and then he just plunders around—and he never puts anything back in its place.

Then she turned her attention to the dinner table. Cormac had eaten two leftover crappies that Kizzy had fried the night before. He had picked the bones clean, but there was still enough left to feed three big cockroaches, and they were busy eating, paying no mind to Kizzy who unceremoniously killed two of them and chased the third into hiding. Then she took

Cormac's plate outside and raked it clean, dumping the fish bones and cockroach carcasses into the river.

⚜

Kizzy finished cleaning the cabin and grumbled. *It's hard enough to keep this place straight, and I've told him before—you can't leave a mess on the table.*

Then she picked up her book and went out onto the aft deck to sit down and read. She wanted to forget about the cockroaches and Cormac, but a wave of nostalgia interfered.

She leaned against the stern railing and stared at the river, thinking about her family and reliving the good times they had had when she was a little girl. Toe-digging for mussels with MeeMaw, going to town with Ma, fishing, going to school, and just living free and independent like Grandpa said. But those pleasant thoughts gave way to reality: Her loved ones were gone, she would soon be 14 years old, and it had been eight months since they buried her mother.

Kizzy groaned. She was growing up, and realizing that led her back to thinking about her make-do stepfather, and soon she started thinking about sex. *It does feel good—I didn't like Elsie Sue's ways but she was right about that. And everybody does it—Ma and Boopie did it, and they seemed to like it too. Now I'm doing it. When he first started, it was just a pat on the butt and a little touching here and there, and it was about me learning some stuff for my own good. But now it's gotten more like what he was doing with Ma. It's just whenever he wants to do it.*

Suddenly Kizzy had a sneezing fit, and when she got control of it, she mused. The river—sporting a fine greenish veil—was carrying away the powdery springtime pollen of the oaks, the sycamores, and the cottonwoods. And the sight of it made her think of something else.

MeeMaw said the green stuff is how the oak trees get knocked up, but Cormac says that ain't exactly right ... anyway he says not to worry—he ain't ever knocked anyone up, and that includes the three years he spent in Ma's bed.

He says I can trust him and I reckon I ought to ... All the same, there's something that don't seem right about it, but I'm a little bit like Birdie's dove was when it was living in a cage—I got nowhere else to go.

⚜

Kizzy snuggled into a comfortable position on the aft deck, intending to read until sundown, but just as she got to Chapter 5, Cormac came chugging up the river in the workboat and coasted to a stop alongside the houseboat.

"I been down to Curly's."

Kizzy slammed her book closed and jumped up. "Well, while you've been down to Curly's I been cleaning up your mess. The cockroaches were all over the fish bones you left laying out."

"Yeah, I couldn't find that new box of trotline hooks. And then I didn't have time to put all that stuff back."

Cormac pulled himself aboard and went into the cabin, ignoring Kizzy's comment about the cockroaches. Then he guffawed and hollered back, "I got catfish for dinner—and there won't be no bones for the cockroaches on account of I fileted it."

Kizzy shook her head and mouthed her words. *There ain't no hope for him.*

⚜

After dinner, Cormac pushed back from the table and said, "What's that you're reading?"

"It's a book the lady at the library picked out for me. It's about people in England who are rich. The young girls in the story want to get married, so they go to dances and wear fine clothes so they can meet the right man. One of the men is very nice, but the other one is not ... that's about as far as I've gotten so far."

"That fancy stuff ain't for the likes of us—that's for rich folks—we're river folks and we've got our own ways."

"Well, I'd rather read adventure stories—but Olivia's been nice to me and I owe it to her to read this book."

Cormac shrugged. Then he took out his pocket knife and started cleaning his nails.

Kizzy cleared the table and washed the dishes. As soon as she was finished, she got into bed and turned her back to Cormac.

A half-hour later, he slipped in beside her.

XXXV

Need

Stefan stopped pacing the length and breadth of his front porch to check the time on his pocket watch, the Ingersoll Junior that Horst Bachmann gave him for Christmas. The little watch was a fine $2 timepiece, but Stefan gently shook it and put it to his ear to be sure it was still ticking.

Kizzy had promised to meet him at his house at 10 o'clock to make music and talk, but it was already 10:16, and there was no sign of her.

Stefan shook his head and whistled a sigh, but continued his patrol of the porch, stopping every time he got to the spot that gave him a good view of the street. Once there he would double-check the time and crane his neck to see if he could see her.

At 10:22 he shrugged and put the watch away. Then he took his violin from the case, tucked it beneath his chin, and played a mournful tune.

As time passed, the music revealed his mood: Mournful quickly became downright pitiful.

Then at 10:27 he saw Kizzy, and the sight of her gave him the jitters. He did a fancy dance step and fiddled the first part of an Irish jig. Then he waved to her and hollered, "Hey, Kizzy!"

She waved back, and with that Stefan put the violin down, vaulted the railing on the porch, and skip-hopped across the yard to greet her.

When they were close enough to touch, she gave him a big smile and brushed back a tangle of red hair. "Sorry, I got held up."

He pursed his lips to answer, but just then, Kizzy winked cutely and blew him a kiss.

Stefan—dumbstruck—endured a moment of goofiness. But he collected himself, and with dramatic flair he opened the gate and faked an aristocratic bow. Then he swept an imaginary musketeer hat from his head and swung it in a wide arc to greet his fair lady.

"*Willkommen!*"

Kizzy raised an eyebrow at his German, but she took his hand and they giggled and sauntered to the porch, jabbering about the music they planned to sing and play.

Stefan's house was their favorite place to meet. The small weather-beaten rent house was plain but unique. It was the only house in town with vertical bargeboard planking, slats of natural wood taken from an abandoned Black River flatboat. For most townspeople it was a relic at best, and an eyesore at worst.

But for Stefan and Kizzy the old house was idyllic. It was here that he first played for her and she first sang for him. To them the scruffy-white picket fence and the red-painted tin roof gave the place a smidgen of old-world charm, especially on a day like this when it was warm enough to enjoy the latticed porch swing. It was hanging empty, waiting for them to make music and memories.

⚜

Kizzy sat on the swing and rocked to get it going. Then she sang "Pretty Molly," one of MeeMaw's old songs about a girl who suddenly realizes that her boyfriend is going to kill her.

> *Oh, Molly, pretty Molly, you're guessing just right;*
> *I dug in your grave a part of last night.*
> *She threw her arms around him saying suffer no fear*
> *How can you kill a girl that loves you so dear?*

He stabbed his knife in her; the blood it did flow;
And into her grave her body did go.

Stefan stood by, grimacing and playing background as best he could. And when she sang the last lyric he said, "Good grief, Kizzy. Are all your songs so grim?"

Kizzy scoffed. "You sound just like my mother. She hated MeeMaw's old songs, but I think they're fun, and I know a bunch of them."

Stefan put a finger to his lips to shush her, and then he played a soothing melody from Mendelssohn. "I think there's a place for MeeMaw's folk music, but we need to take out the grisly stuff."

⚜

A late-morning rain put a stop to their music-making. It started as a sprinkle, but as the drops got bigger the tinkle became the most enchanting sound of spring: April rain falling on a tin roof.

Stefan put his violin away and sat beside Kizzy on the swing. They talked about the rain falling on the tin roof, about the war, and school and other things, but none of that mattered to him; it was just talk for the sake of talking. What mattered to Stefan was the flood of warmth that had overtaken him, and his sense that the hair on the scruff of his neck had come alive.

At that moment Kizzy touched his hand, and when she looked into his eyes Stefan saw them as never before—green, wild and enticing. He inched closer to her, and when their noses touched, his heart fluttered. Then they kissed for the first time, and whispered the sweet nothings of young love.

Stefan was sore tempted to touch her breasts, but he faced a greater challenge, one that required his immediate attention.

He wiggled and tugged at his britches, repositioning himself to hide the lump in his pants. When that failed, he made a Herculean attempt to hide the bulge with his hands, but the lump got harder and his face got redder.

I'm pretty sure she sees it, but she's acting like she doesn't.

God, what should I do now? I know what I would do if I was alone, but I'm not ...

⚜

When Stefan sat beside her on the swing, Kizzy felt stirrings deep inside that were new to her, and the good feelings got better when they kissed and whispered sweet words to each other.

I like Stefan, and he likes me, and ...

Mercy!

He's all worked up—anybody can see that. The sweet-talking and kissing has given him a hard-on ...

She chuckled to herself when Stefan started squirming and fooling around with his britches, trying to cover it up.

He's embarrassed by it. I bet he ain't ever done it, and that's got him bumfuzzled ...

What I'm doing with Cormac feels good, just like Elsie Sue said it would. But I ain't had this gushy feeling before—this is different—and it's better because Stefan's my boyfriend ... besides he's my age and all that.

Anyway, he's cute. There wouldn't be any harm in doing it, but he was raised different—more like the people in Jane Austen's book—more like Olivia.

⚜

Stefan decided that he needed to do something about the lump, so he got out of the swing and turned his back to Kizzy. "Look, it's about to quit raining. We can get back to our music."

"What's the hurry?" She patted the space next to her on the swing. "We can do music anytime."

"I know, but Fritz may come home for lunch any minute now—he does that sometimes."

Stefan's bland talk was not affecting her, but it did cure Stefan's immediate problem. The lump in his trousers was gone.

He took a deep breath, and then he turned to face her, letting the air whistle out all at once. Then he said, in a serious tone. "I just remember my mother saying that boys need to respect girls." He looked askance, searching for the right words. "So we ought to slow down. We're just kids."

She seemed puzzled by his outburst, so Stefan sat by her to explain. "I'm talking more to myself than to you. You're a nice girl; and I need to respect you for that, just like my mother said."

She started to say something, but instead she kissed Stefan on the cheek, and grinned. "You're different all right, but I like you the way you are."

⚜

Kizzy got up and walked to the other end of the porch, and looked out. "When you opened the gate for me you said '*willkommen.*' What does that mean?"

"It means welcome, that's all."

"Is that Pennsylvania Dutch?"

"Sort of, but I'm not supposed to say much about that. I should have just said welcome in English."

"It's good for people to share secrets," said Kizzy. "My MeeMaw used to get people to tell her the durndest things when she was doing fortune telling. She said everybody has secrets and that it's good to share them with people you trust."

Stefan did not respond, so Kizzy went on, "I ain't talking about all secrets—I'm just talking about the ones you want to share."

"What do you mean? What's the difference?"

"Well, MeeMaw said there's three kinds of secrets: There's those you'll share, those you won't share, and those you won't even admit to yourself. She said it's in that last batch where you'll find the truth about a person. That's why MeeMaw was such a good fortune teller; she knew how to get into that last batch."

"She sounds like a smart woman."

"She was. And she was making good money telling fortunes, but the sheriff put her out of business. After that she just told 'em for free. She said people need to talk about such stuff because misery loves company."

"I agree with that," Stefan said.

"OK, so tell me what's so secret about saying *willkommen* and then I'll tell you a secret."

Stefan hesitated, fidgeting with the buttons on his shirt. "You promise not to tell?"

She crossed her heart. "Yes, and you?"

He crossed his heart, and then he blurted out, "It's German. *Willkommen* is German for welcome."

"So what? Why's that a secret?"

"Because I'm German. After my father died, my mother married Fritz in Germany and we moved to Willich. I was 8."

Kizzy shrugged. "So what? I'm half Gypsy, and MeeMaw says my other half came from Scotland."

"That's different. People are mad at Germans because of the war, this one and the last one. And ever since Pearl Harbor the government has been arresting people from Germany and Japan and sending them to camps. That's why it's better for us to just say we are Pennsylvania Dutch. That's what they call Germans who live in that part of Pennsylvania."

"But you and Fritz are Americans now."

"Yes, but we have to be careful because the FBI has arrested some German people we know back in Pennsylvania, and they've questioned Fritz's friend in Jonesboro."

Kizzy pondered the situation. "Well, now you know how it feels. Us river people have had to be careful for years. Bully Bigshot hates us; he calls us 'river rats.' And he'd wipe us out if he could, and I know for sure he would like to send me to the poorhouse on account of I ain't got any real parents anymore. Cormac is just a make-do stepfather, but he's all I got."

She suddenly stopped talking, and tented her fingers. "So there, that's my secret."

"Your MeeMaw was right," Stefan said. "It feels good to figure out how much we are alike." He held up two fingers and folded one down as he said, "We're outcasts: I'm a German, and you're a river rat." Then he folded his other finger down. "And we both live with stepfathers and have nowhere else to go."

Kizzy laughed. "Don't forget Horsey Hairs and the rich kids. They don't like us because we're different."

"That's true," Stefan said. "But wait … my secret was bigger than yours. You need to tell me another one."

"Well, OK." Kizzy scrunched around and pointed upward. "I believe in monsters, and haints. MeeMaw taught me that too. But I have nightmares about 'em. There's the White River Monster and then there's the ghosts who haunt the river; they'll gobble you up if you try to get mussels from Mexican Bend. The river is full of spirits; mostly people who got murdered."

"I don't believe in such stuff," Stefan said. "But I confess that I have had nightmares about some old bones that were found in the Neander Valley— it's a place that's close to where I used to live in Germany."

"I want to hear all about those old bones."

"OK, I'll tell you some day if you will take me on the river and show me how to gather mussels and dig for pearls."

"All right, it's a deal." Kizzy said, "That'll be fun, but I'll have to borrow Shirley Barden's boat. Cormac would never let me take our workboat."

Kizzy's agreement to take Stefan on the river ended the talk of secrets and scary things. The teenagers—friends in need—were now bound together by music, natural affection, common enemies, and the secrets that they had decided to share. It was enough for the time being, perhaps forever.

⚜

"Let's get back to music," Kizzy said. "Let's do 'Barbara Allen.' It's a sad folk song, but it's pretty, and it ain't as grisly as the others."

Kizzy then sang the ballad about two lovers dying. Stefan accompanied her, and when they finished the song, he clapped his hands.

"Glückwünsche und bravo, liebe Kizzy."

"There you go again with that foreign talk."

"It was a compliment. What I said was, 'Congratulations and bravo, dear Kizzy.'"

She smiled and thanked him, but he was looking down. She said, "What's wrong?"

"Nothing, it's just that what I said to you in German is what my father said to me the last time I played for him."

She put her arm around him and pulled him close, and they sat still for a while.

Then Kizzy pushed to get the swing moving, faster than before, and when he began to help her swing, she said, "I agree. We need to make music that ain't depressing."

XXXVI

Homefront

"Look Mabel, here she comes." Olivia pushed a stack of returns to an out-of-the-way spot on the counter and waved to Kizzy as she entered the library.

"Yes, and judging from the way she's walking and the determined look on her face, I'm betting she's got something on her mind."

Kizzy walked right up to the counter and wasted no time. "Shirley got a letter from Birdie and it says he is somewhere in the South Pacific. Ain't that where your husband is?"

Mabel winced. "Isn't that where ..."

Kizzy frowned at Mabel. "Yep, right." Then she said to Olivia. "Isn't that where your husband is?"

Mabel nodded her approval, and Olivia smiled at Kizzy. "Well, yes, he's in the South Pacific, but that's a pretty big place, Kizzy."

"I'm worried about Birdie, but this war is driving his ma nuts. Shirley has three boys who have gone off to fight and ..."

Mabel interrupted. She pointed to the Veterans' Center and said, "Olivia, why don't you take her over there to talk to Mac Thornton. He's forgotten more than most people have ever known about war."

"Good idea."

"Let's go talk to Uncle Mac," said Olivia to Kizzy. "He'll have some words of wisdom for us."

⚜

Mac Thornton positioned his wheelchair so that he could watch the domino game, an all-day, every-day event at the Veterans' Center. Mac never played; he preferred to kibitz, especially when Charles "Dynamite" McFadden was in the game.

The players, all veterans of World War I, were shuffling the dominoes and mumbling to themselves when Mac launched his first bit of meddlesome advice. "You should have played the double six when you had a chance, Dynamite."

"Stay out of it you old fart, if you ain't got the balls to get in the game you got no right to tell me what I should have done."

Mac laughed. "It's my duty to help the mentally challenged."

Mac had known Dynamite since the sixth grade when he attempted to set off a homemade smoke bomb in Mrs. Rushing's art class. Alas, instead of making smoke, the earthenware jar—filled with a mysterious mixture of readily available chemicals—exploded. A large chunk of the jar lodged in the left buttock of Charles McFadden as he attempted to flee the scene. There were no other injuries, but after that his classmates nicknamed him "Dynamite," and it stuck.

When Olivia and Kizzy got close to the domino table the veterans cleaned up their language, but continued to play. Mac Thornton turned his wheelchair to face Olivia.

"Hi, Uncle Mac. This is Kizzy."

Kizzy smiled, but rubbed her smile away as she studied the deep scar that ran from the corner of Mac's left eye to his neck and disappeared beneath his shirt collar. "Hello, sir."

"He ain't no 'sir,' young lady. He never got past corporal." Dynamite chortled and slammed a domino onto the table.

"Never mind him, Kizzy," said Uncle Mac. "He's been addled ever since the sixth grade." He rolled his wheelchair to a quiet place and motioned for Olivia and Kizzy to follow him.

⚜

"Uncle Mac, Kizzy and I would like to talk to you about the war. Her friend is worried sick. She has two boys in the Army who may be going to

England, and another boy who is in the Marines. He's somewhere in the South Pacific, like John."

"God bless 'em." Mac saluted with his good right arm. "Army, Navy, and Marines—God bless 'em all."

"The boy in the Marines is like a big brother to me. We call him 'Birdie' because he knows every bird on the Black River. Will he be all right, Uncle Mac?" She caught her breath. "Is it OK if I call you Uncle Mac?"

Mac smiled and nodded, and then he raised his right hand and began to rub the scar of the left side of his face. Olivia patted Kizzy on the shoulder and signaled for her to listen. Uncle Mac was about to deliver a carefully worded sermonette about duty, honor and country.

"Let me answer your question this way, Kizzy. We didn't start this war. Our enemies did, and they mean to destroy us, and our way of life.

"Our boys—John and Birdie and all the others—know why they are fighting. The Japs bombed and strafed our troops in a sneak attack at Pearl Harbor, and Hitler and his Nazis are despicable; they have conquered all the countries we fought to save in the last war." Mac touched his scar again, and shook his head. "Evil is on the loose. We don't have a choice, and our boys know that. We've got to win this war.

"And if John and Birdie were here I bet they would answer you this way: 'Yes, we're in harm's way, but this fight is bigger than any one of us.'

"That's why—in place of worrying—those of us back here on the home front need to pray, stay positive, and do the best we can to keep our troops well fed and supplied. The outcome is in God's hands."

Kizzy moaned. "But I don't want them to get killed, or hurt like you."

Mac hesitated, and then he straightened up in his wheelchair. "Well, I'm not going to sugar-coat it, Kizzy. War is hell. Many will die and many will get hurt." He swept his good arm in the direction of the domino table. "All of us got shot up in the last war, but it was our duty to go, and if we could still fight we'd go again."

Kizzy stood up and stepped close to him. "I'm sorry that you got hurt, Uncle Mac." She leaned over the wheelchair to give him a hug, and then she sat down by Olivia.

Mac cleared his throat, and spoke softly. "Thanks, Kizzy. But those of us who got hurt aren't entitled to feel sorry for ourselves." He paused to let his words sink in. "That would be disrespectful to the thousands of good men we left behind; they're buried in the graveyards of France."

Kizzy frowned and snuggled closer to Olivia.

Mac realized that he had said enough, perhaps too much about dying and getting hurt, so he turned to Olivia. "Have you heard from John?"

"Yes, but the mail is slow. I know from newspaper reports that the *Yorktown* was in the fight at New Guinea, and there were reports yesterday that the *Yorktown* took part in a battle on the Coral Sea. That was in the first week of May." She lowered her eyes and bit her lip. "I haven't gotten a letter from him since then, but no news is good news."

⚜

When Kizzy got to the houseboat just before 5:30 in the afternoon, Cormac was sprawled on the aft deck with one bare foot dangling in the river, smoking a Bull Durham rollup. A half-empty squat bottle of Griesedieck Brothers beer sat amongst two empties.

When he saw Kizzy, he raised his beer in salute. "Good news! I got a job at the button factory."

"How'd that happen?" In all the time she had known him, Cormac had never applied for a steady job, arguing that it would interfere with his work on the river.

"The line boss saw me down at Curly's. He said all the men working there had signed up or been drafted." He took a swig of beer and shook his head. "Stupid bastards ain't smart enough to figure a way to stay out of it." He laughed and held his beer up high. "Their loss is my gain."

"I was just talking to an old soldier at the Veterans' Center and he said the boys are going because it's their duty. He says we ain't got a choice— we've got to win this war."

"Well, I don't give a shit about the Germans or the Japs, and I don't give a shit who wins the war. Win or lose, it won't make no difference in my life one way or the other. The hot-shot politicians who got us into this war don't give a care about us river rats, so why should we care about them."

"The old soldier said ..."

Cormac cut her off. "I don't give a damn what some old soldier said, Kizzy. This is going to put some extra money in our pocket and in times like this it's every man for hisself."

⚜

The *Big Pearl Free Current,* the oldest newspaper in northeast Arkansas, printed its first edition on July 4, 1854, and when the very first front page came off the press the editor tacked it on the door for the public to read, free of charge. It was a popular thing to do, especially during the Great Depression when people could not spare a nickel for a newspaper. In time, the promotion became a ritual, and on any given day a goodly number of Big Pearl citizens would gather outside, waiting to read the latest headlines.

On Tuesday at 10 a.m., May 26, 1942, a dozen matronly women—members of the United Daughters of the Confederacy—assembled near the front door of the newspaper, dressed as if they were going to church. They had volunteered to help administer the new rationing programs, and the editor wanted to interview them and get a photograph of them reading his latest story about sugar rationing.

His first question was to the president of the local chapter. "Mrs. Schoonover, how do you think it will go? The government has already rationed tires and sugar and they are getting ready to limit us to four gallons of gasoline a week. Will the people cooperate?"

Imogene Schoonover, a husky woman with blueish hair, puffed up and gave her members the signal to nod agreement with what she was about to say. "Of course we will! Our forefathers had to do with less during the War Between the States, and we can too. It's our duty to support the boys in uniform, and we believe the people of Big Pearl are ready to do their part."

The editor looked around the cluster of women, and then posed a tougher question. "But this is going to go on for a long time, and the government is saying it is going to ration nylons, cheese and butter, shoes, coffee, jams and jellies. And they're getting ready to issue rationing coupons so that people won't cheat and horde stuff. How do you feel about that?"

Imogene, who looked as if she had never missed a meal, said, "We'll do just fine. My granddaddy was at Port Hudson, La., when the Yankees took control of the Mississippi River. They were under siege for 48 days and got down to eating rats and horses and mules." The women behind her gave a cheer, and she continued. "The fighting spirit is in our blood. We'll do what we have to do."

A skinny woman chimed in: "Amen sister, Amen."

❖

In 1890 Carlton Biggers, at the insistence of his wife, built the Big Pearl Opera House, an elegant two-story Georgian-style theater that seated 350. The building was pleasing to the eye, and people came from miles around to attend a wide variety of performances: operettas, music recitals, lectures, and decent burlesque shows.

Carlton Biggers and his son, Carlton Biggers Jr., subsidized the performances to keep ticket prices low, but when Sully Biggers inherited the family fortune in 1920 he stopped the subsidies, forcing the opera house to offer minstrel shows and risqué burlesque to stay in business. The local preachers had a fit, and expressed their disapproval in sermons that had a common theme: "No good education ever occurred in theaters." From 1920 to 1927, the opera house survived, barely, by offering live wrestling, boxing matches, and an endless string of silent movies.

Then in 1927, Darryl F. Zanuck produced *The Jazz Singer*, a full-length motion picture with synchronized sound featuring Al Jolson singing catchy tunes: "My Gal Sal," "Toot Toot Tootsie (Goo' Bye)," "My Mammy," and several others.

It was the death knell for silent movies, but the "talkies" gave new life to the Big Pearl Opera House, and it survived the hard times of the Great Depression.

On Thursday evening, May 28, 1942, the patriotic citizens of Big Pearl queued up at the opera house. It was War Bond Night, and they were eager to see the popular movie *Sergeant York,* starring Gary Cooper.

The house filled quickly because the ticket price had been reduced to five cents for those purchasing at least 10 War Bond stamps. The 10-cent stamps could be pasted into a Defense Stamp Album and when it was full (187 stamps) the owner could take it and five cents to the Post Office and exchange the $18.75 investment for a $25 War Bond that could be redeemed in 10 years.

At 7 o'clock sharp, Imogene Schoonover waddled onto the stage to lead the pledge of allegiance, and then she told the audience about the rationing program. She wound up her remarks by saying, "We'll all have to do with less—it's our duty." Then, as she turned to leave the stage, she patted herself on the butt, and shouted out, "And that includes me."

The audience roared its approval, but the jubilant mood vanished when a trim Army colonel marched to the center of the stage.

⚜

Stefan and Fritz were sitting near the back of the theater, but it was easy for them to hear the colonel because he spoke as if he were delivering orders to a battalion of troops. He began with a plodding, over-long recitation of recruitment statistics. Then he set out to explain, in excruciating detail, the economic principles underlying the War Bond effort.

The audience tried to be respectful, but the citizens of Big Pearl had come to the opera house to see a good movie and show their patriotic support for the war.

The colonel's thunderous voice lost out to the tranquilizing effect of his message. The audience, at first eager and expectant, had sunk into a state of somnolence.

Fifteen minutes passed before the colonel realized that he had lost his audience, but to his credit he switched gears, and the first thing he said about the war caused Stefan to perk up.

"Ladies and gentlemen, German U-boats are sinking too many of our ships in the Atlantic, but the tide is turning. We are learning more about their tactics, and they are learning less about ours. As you know, the FBI broke up a German spy ring in New York City just before the war started, otherwise our losses might have been greater.

"Now, to prevent further spying and sabotage here on the home front, we are arresting thousands of German aliens and Japs, and we are sending them to internment camps for the duration of the war. Two of the camps are in south Arkansas—one at Jerome, and the other at Rohwer."

Stefan nudged Fritz, but Fritz put the back of his hand on Stefan's chest and shushed him.

The colonel continued. "The battle in the Atlantic is intense, but our Navy is doing its best, and the Army is getting ready to send troops. Soon we will take the fight to the Huns in Europe and North Africa.

"And now we will look at the most recent newsreels that tell about the War Bond drives and the great victories that we are winning in the Pacific."

⚜

Stefan scrunched down in his seat as the lights went down and the screen lit up with the sterile logo and familiar music of *National News*.

The first report showed several parades with the brightest stars of Hollywood riding in Jeeps, urging people to buy war bonds. Greer Garson, Hedy Lamarr, Judy Garland, Lucille Ball, James Cagney, Fred Astaire, and many other stars waved and gave the thumbs-up sign to the huge crowds that lined the parade routes. The announcer said Hedy Lamarr was offering to kiss anyone who purchased $25,000 worth of war bonds, and he told of a bond auction where the horseshoes from Triple Crown winner Man o' War fetched top dollar.

Then the scene abruptly shifted to the war in the Pacific, and the announcer gave a staccato summary of the Battle of the Coral Sea, a fight that ended on May 8. He portrayed it as a narrow strategic victory by first telling how American aircraft sank the Japanese light carrier *Shoho* and badly damaged the carrier *Shokaku*. But as his report wound down, the announcer said a Japanese bomb had struck the *USS Yorktown*, causing serious damage. Then, in a more somber tone, he revealed that the carrier *USS Lexington* had been sunk, lost to a barrage of bombs and torpedoes fired by Japanese aircraft.

The newsreel ended with the customary plea for every American to support the war effort, and as it faded from the screen, the crowd applauded and cheered.

Then the houselights came on and Bully Bigshot walked onto the stage. The cheering and applause stopped as suddenly as if someone had pulled the plug on an electrical device.

Bully's voice seemed high and squeaky compared to the stentorian tones of the colonel, and Stefan strained to listen.

"Ladies and gentlemen, I am Sully Biggers, and I am privileged to be the chairman of our local bond drive. And as such I am announcing tonight that I have bought a $5,000 war bond." There was a scattering of tepid applause, but Bully strutted and bowed as if the audience had given him an ear-splitting ovation.

Stefan whispered to Fritz, "I don't like him."

Fritz nodded his agreement as inconspicuously as he could and then, to the surprise of no one, Bully transitioned from war bonds to eugenics, his favorite subject.

"Ladies and gentlemen, another important way to win this war and make our country great is for the ne'er-do-wells to do their part. For too long we have stood by and let the deadbeats become a burden to society. I believe we can and should do something about that, so I hope you will support the work we do at the Big Pearl Eugenics Society. We are having a meeting this week where Herman Spence, a noted eugenicist, is making a return trip to Big Pearl to review the excellent work of Margaret Sanger and the organization she inspired. You are all invited to attend this important meeting."

There was a sprinkling of applause and as soon as Bully was off the stage, the houselights dimmed and the movie began.

XXXVII

Midway

In the spring of 1942, Fleet Admiral Isoroku Yamamoto planned a massive land, sea, and air attack on U. S. forces at Midway Island, a sandy atoll in the Pacific Ocean some 1,300 miles west of Pearl Harbor. He reasoned Japanese control of Midway would protect the homeland, enable a later invasion and occupation of Hawaii, and, most importantly, the attack would draw the U. S. fleet out of Pearl Harbor, making it vulnerable.

Yamamoto expected victory. Why would he not? Japan had seized vital oil fields and rubber plantations throughout the South Pacific, and the Imperial Japanese Navy had not lost a battle in 300 years.

Unbeknownst to the Japanese, U. S. Navy cryptographers had broken their operational code, and the analysis of several intercepted radio messages revealed Yamamoto's plan to attack Midway on June 4 from the northwest.

Admiral Chester W. Nimitz, commander-in-chief of the Pacific Fleet, knowing when and where the enemy would strike, formulated a simple plan: Get there first and ambush them.

Nimitz had two task forces available. The carriers *Hornet* and *Enterprise* were ready to sail, but the Battle of the Coral Sea had crippled the *Yorktown*. A Japanese bomb had plunged through her flight deck, causing damage that would take three months to repair.

Nimitz needed the *Yorktown*. He ordered emergency repairs, and the carrier steamed out of Pearl Harbor on May 30, three days after she had limped in. She headed west, ready to join the action at Midway.

Lieutenant John Decker was aboard the *Yorktown*.

⚜

On Thursday, June 4, 1942, Olivia Decker was at home having lunch with her mother, Matilda Joyce, when the postman stepped onto the porch and put their mail in a small box next to the front door. It was noon. "You can set your watch by him," Matilda said.

Olivia rushed to see if there was a letter from John, and there was. It was the first she had received in weeks, and she was anxious to know that he was alive and well. News reports about the Battle of the Coral Sea, a fight that ended May 8, were purposely vague due to wartime censorship, but there had been credible reports that a Japanese bomb had damaged the *Yorktown*.

She carefully opened the letter and when she saw the date, May 27, 1942, she put the letter against her heart and plopped down on the sofa in the parlor. She read just a few lines and then shouted to her mother. "Thank God, he made it through the Coral Sea battle. John's OK, Mother."

The letter was only a page and a half long, but Olivia savored every word, and when she finished reading she bowed her head to say a prayer. Then she folded the letter and put it in her purse.

"Where is he, Olivia?"

"It doesn't say—they can't write about such things—but I bet the *Yorktown* is back in Pearl Harbor for repairs."

Olivia told her mother some of what was in the letter as she walked into the kitchen, but suddenly she turned and took a step toward the door. "I need to get back to the library, Mother. We have a busy afternoon planned."

Her mother glanced at Olivia's unfinished lunch, but said nothing. Then she got up and gave her daughter a hug. "It's in God's hands, Olivia."

"I know."

⚜

Olivia loved to walk the short distance from the Joyce family home to the library. The sights never failed to stir memories from her childhood: The old homes, familiar cracks in the sidewalk, one-of-a-kind fences, flower gardens and trees, especially the stinky eucalyptus in front of Doctor Satterfield's place. Each sight had painted a stroke on the canvas of her life, but on this day's walk a haunting thought kept crowding its way into the picture.

When she was three blocks from the library, Olivia turned onto Pratt Street. It would take her a block out of her way, but she wanted to read John's letter again in the sanctuary of the First Methodist Church. And she wanted to say a prayer for him at the altar.

She sat alone in the Joyce family pew and took the letter from her purse.

"May 27, 1942

Dearest Olivia:

I am fine, but I lost my best friend, Joe Harrison, in the Coral Sea. You met Joe when we were in Norfolk. He told me, just hours before the attack that killed him, that he had been meaning to write a letter to his wife telling her how much she meant to him. He didn't get around to it, and now he's gone. I will miss him, but his death makes me realize that the time may come when I will not be able to write to you.

I want you to know that I have no qualms about being here. It is the right thing to do. It is my duty and I am proud to serve. Please tell that to Mac Thornton and the men at the Veterans' Center when you see them. We owe so much to all those who have gone before. I now have a new appreciation and better understanding of what they went through.

It's hard to say how I feel on this beautiful summer night when we are safe and have time to think about home and the people we love. But the memories of you fill my heart each day. I think of the time we had in California and especially those last days we spent in Norfolk. I thank God that we have had that much.

Your prayers ring in my ear, Olivia. Over and over, I hear your plea for me to come home unharmed, and God willing I will. But if I do not return I want you to know forever how much I love you, and if we are parted do not mourn for me, for we shall meet again in a better place.

I love you,
John"

⚜

On June 4, Vice Admiral Chuichi Nagumo, commander of the First Carrier Strike Force, Imperial Japanese Navy, ordered the carriers *Kaga, Akagi, Soryu* and *Hiryu* to approach Midway from the northwest. At 4:30 a.m., Nagumo—in keeping with Fleet Admiral Yamamoto's plan—launched 108 aircraft. Their mission was to soften the atoll's defenses and eliminate its air strength, but Japanese intelligence had not discovered the presence of two American task forces.

The U. S. Navy attacked, surprising the Japanese. Dive-bombers from the *Enterprise* destroyed two Japanese carriers, *Kaga* and *Akagi*. And aircraft from the *Yorktown* inflicted such extreme damage on *Soryu* that she too sank that evening. A single Japanese carrier, *Hiryu*, escaped damage on the morning of June 4.

In the fighting, a Japanese bomb hit *Yorktown* and detonated deep inside the vessel. *Hiryu* launched a second strike and two torpedoes slammed into *Yorktown*'s port side, well below her waterline. The *Yorktown* listed heavily to port, and the captain ordered the crew to abandon ship.

The Navy attempted to save the *Yorktown*, but shortly after noon on June 6, Japanese submarine I-168 slipped to within 500 yards of her and fired four torpedoes. Two of the torpedoes ripped open *Yorktown*'s battered port side, and just before dawn on June 7 the *Yorktown* rolled over and sank beneath the waves.

Fleet Admiral Yamamoto—desperate to salvage victory—gave the order to destroy the Americans with a night attack, but he quickly came to his senses and ordered a general withdrawal.

❧

It did not take long for the news of an American victory at Midway to seep out, but wartime censorship made it hard to get particulars. Even so, the story was too hot to hold, and within days the news reached Big Pearl that several Japanese bombs had crippled the *Yorktown*, forcing the crew to abandon ship on June 4.

Olivia had been getting up early every morning to meet the paperboy, hungry for news about the war, but she had found precious little about the *Yorktown*. She wanted to know more, but she cringed when she saw the latest headline: "JAPS SINK THE *YORKTOWN*."

She took the morning paper into the parlor and closed the door behind her. For a while, she stood still, staring into the corner at the tiny antique rocking horse she rode as a child, reliving one of her earliest memories. Then she braced herself, sat down, and started reading the story. Suddenly, she gasped. *June 4? The attack on the Yorktown was on June 4! They abandoned ship on the 4th. That's the day I got John's letter. Please God, let him be safe.*

Olivia secluded herself at home—for days—pondering, praying, and thinking: *Irony? Fate? Woman's intuition? Premonition? A portent of things to come? Lord, let him be safe.*

Then, on Monday, June 15, Olivia received a Western Union telegram:

"SA2 89 GOVT=PXX NR WASHINGTON DC JN 15 111A
   MRS. OLIVIA JOYCE DECKER, BIG PEARL, ARKANSAS
   THE NAVY DEPARTMENT DEEPLY REGRETS TO
INFORM YOU THAT YOUR HUSBAND JOHN DECKER
LIEUTENANT USN WAS KILLED IN ACTION IN THE

PERFORMANCE OF HIS DUTY AND IN THE SERVICE OF
HIS COUNTRY. THE DEPARTMENT EXTENDS TO YOU
ITS SINCEREST SYMPATHY IN YOUR GREAT LOSS. ON
ACCOUNT OF EXISTING CONDITIONS THE BODY WAS
BURIED AT SEA. TO PREVENT POSSIBLE AID TO OUR
ENEMIES PLEASE DO NOT DIVULGE THE NAME OF HIS
SHIP OR STATION.
REAR ADMIRAL JACOBS CHIEF OF NAVAL PERSONNEL."

⚜

Kizzy heard about John's death from Shirley Barden who walked up the hill
every day to see if her boys were on the latest casualty lists posted on the
big front window of the *Big Pearl Free Current*. She would ask, "Any Barden
boys on them lists?"

On June 22, an elderly man checked the lists for Shirley and then said,
"No, but we lost John Decker—he got it at Midway."

Shirley hurried back to the river to tell Kizzy.

"Kizzy, they say there's a John Decker on the killed-in-action list. Ain't
he married to the lady you like so much—the one who works at the library?"

Kizzy nodded, and then slumped and shook her head. "She talks about
him all the time."

They stood still, looking at each other, speechless. Then Shirley said,
"They say there's gonna be a memorial service for him at one of the churches
on Thursday. Reckon we could go? I mean, I got three of my own over there."

"I'm sure it's OK. I'll go ask Mabel right now, she'll know."

⚜

The First Methodist Church was filling up when Kizzy and Shirley got
to the front door. Everyone was dressed for church, especially the women,
most of whom were wearing somber black hats of every size and shape.
Kizzy pulled Shirley through the door and when they were in the narthex

she whispered, "The man at the door said we ought to go upstairs. I ain't sure, but he doesn't seem too happy with how we look."

The balcony was about to fill up, but Kizzy saw a space at the end of the front row that looked big enough for the two of them. She took Shirley's hand and when they reached the open spot, they scooched their way into it, then did their best to ignore the stares they were getting.

Kizzy looked around, taking in as much as she could. It was her first time to be in a church. The choir and organ music excited her, but so did the cascade of flowers mixed amongst an arrangement of Navy blue and gold bunting. She was not surprised to see an altar and pulpit; she had read about those, but the picture-stories in the stained glass windows puzzled her. Stefan had told her a little about Christianity, but only that which he had learned in the Catholic church his mother attended back in Pennsylvania.

At that moment, a murmur and rustle swept through the sanctuary. Everyone stood up to respect the appearance of John's mother and father, a distinguished couple who looked young but seemed old. Then Olivia entered, wearing a black summer dress with a small black hat and veil covering her face. She clung to her mother as the pastor gave an opening prayer. Then the organist played "The Navy Hymn" and the choir sang:

> *Eternal Father, strong to save,*
> *Whose arm hath bound the restless wave,*
> *Who bidd'st the mighty ocean deep*
> *Its own appointed limits keep;*
> *Oh, hear us when we cry to Thee,*
> *For those in peril on the sea!*

The grown man next to Kizzy cried aloud, and Shirley cried too. All of it—the crying and the strange surroundings—caused Kizzy to think of MeeMaw. *She didn't go for all this religious stuff. And she never cried when someone died ... she'd just shrug it off. If she were here she wouldn't do all the singing and praying. She'd just say, "He's gone on down the river." But everyone here seems to think there's more to it than that.*

Just then, a young man in an Army uniform rolled Uncle Mac to a place in front of the altar and Kizzy whispered to Shirley. "That's Olivia's Uncle Mac ... well, he ain't her real uncle, but he's a war hero ... got all shot up in the first war."

Mac Thornton sat up as tall as he could, and when he spoke his voice was clear and strong.

"Yesterday, Olivia received a letter from John's commanding officer, and she has asked me to read you part of what he wrote. 'Dear Olivia, John died a hero. When the Japanese attacked the *Yorktown,* he went immediately to the flight deck to care for the wounded and help clean up debris so that we could stay in the fight. He was still there, doing his duty, when a second attack caused the explosion that took his life. We miss him greatly and know that your heart is aching even more. He spoke of you so often that I feel that I know you. John's mates on the *Yorktown* and I send you and John's family our condolences. Warmest regards, Alex Johnson, Commander, USN.'

"Folks, God works in mysterious ways. John Decker wrote a letter to his beloved Olivia before he left for Midway. The postman delivered it to Olivia on the day John died, June 4. She has asked me to read a part of what he wrote:

'I have no qualms about being here. It is the right thing
to do. It is my duty and I am proud to serve.'

"That simple but powerful statement tells you all you need to know about John Decker. He was out there for us, for his country. The battle at Midway was a brilliant victory for the United States. The Japanese carriers that we destroyed— *Kaga, Akagi, Soryu* and *Hiryu*—were the carriers that attacked us at Pearl Harbor. Thanks to good men like John Decker, the Imperial Japanese Navy has suffered its first decisive defeat in three centuries, and in a single stroke, the U. S. Navy has changed the course of the war.

"Godspeed, John Decker. Olivia was here in this church, reading your letter the day you died, perhaps the very moment you died. All of us will think of you and your sacrifice every time we come to this place of worship.

It is God's house, but your spirit is here, linked forever to your Olivia and to a grateful nation."

⚜

Kizzy and Shirley left the church intending to go directly back to the river, but it was a nice afternoon so they walked a few blocks out of their way to go by Olivia's house. The Joyce family home was a beautiful Victorian, white with green trim, and when they got close Kizzy pointed to the service flag hanging in the parlor window. "Look, Shirley, that white flag with the red border is for John Decker. But, wait, it's different than it was when I came by here a couple of weeks ago. The star was blue then, but now it is gold with a blue edge to it."

"I don't want no gold stars for my boys, Kizzy."

⚜

Two days later, 1,000 miles to the east, trouble was brewing for Fritz and Stefan.

J. Edgar Hoover, the director of the Federal Bureau of Investigation announced that German U-boats had secretly put saboteurs ashore at Amagansett, N.Y., and Ponte Vedra Beach, Fla. Hitler's well-trained teams carried substantial amounts of American cash and enough explosives to wage a long campaign of sabotage.

The FBI arrested the saboteurs before they could do any harm, but news stories about the surreptitious landing on the east coast spread like wildfire. Fear took hold, and people began to say, "The mainland is vulnerable. A Japanese submarine shelled the west coast in February; now, just four months later, a German U-boat has landed saboteurs on the east coast."

XXXVIII

Friends

Patriotism filled the air on Independence Day in 1942. Most people in Big Pearl spent the day parading, celebrating, and praying, but all was quiet at the Joyce family home.

Kizzy stood at the front gate of the huge green and white Victorian home, listening for the slightest sound. She had come to see Olivia, but she was having second thoughts. The elaborate arches, gables, and curlicues were easy on the eye and the pièce de résistance—an ornate balustrade—beckoned her to take a closer look, but an eerie stillness and the presence of a single gold star in the window marred the invitation to come in, to enjoy.

Maybe this is a bad idea; it's only been a few weeks since she found out that her husband got killed at Midway. I ain't seen her at the library, or anywhere else lately.

Kizzy sucked in a deep breath; she carefully lifted the latch on the gate and entered, walking quietly to the front steps. She stopped, listened again, and then tiptoed up the steps to the porch. There were two seating areas, one with wrought iron furniture and the other with elegant wicker. She half-chuckled to herself. *Whoa! That's some gangplank, and this is some aft deck.*

She looked around again, and then she stepped close to the front door and gave it three good knocks.

Olivia's mother, Matilda Joyce, answered; she was dressed in a dark outfit with a high collar and looked older than she did at the church. She gave Kizzy the once-over, but said nothing.

"Hi … I'm Kizzy."

"Yes?"

Uh-oh. She doesn't know me from Adam. Kizzy shuffled around, and then blurted out, "I just came by to wish Olivia a happy birthday. I know her from the library. She's been extra-nice to me." She shuffled some more. "July the Fourth is my birthday too. Is she all right?"

"Come in. Olivia's mentioned you."

Matilda led her to the parlor, a mid-sized room elegantly decorated in the Victorian style. It looked jumbled to Kizzy, but it was interesting. The room was full of paintings and odd-looking furniture, especially the weird chair for two people that had an armrest in the middle to keep them separated. She was not sure she liked the decorations until she spied the colorful little rocking horse in the corner and pointed to it. "Oh, that's pretty."

Just then, Olivia came into the parlor. "That's been in the family for years. I used to rock on it."

Kizzy wheeled around and said hello, then she abruptly handed Olivia the bundle she had been cradling in her left arm. "Happy Birthday!"

Olivia nodded, but she looked peaked. And before she could say anything Kizzy reeled off a string of explanations: "It's fresh catfish. I took 'em out of the live box just an hour ago. There's three of 'em, and they're fryin' size." Then she puffed up and spoke with finality. "I skinned 'em and gutted 'em myself."

Olivia's mother twitched and took a step back, wrinkling her nose as if she had smelled a batch of rotten eggs.

But Olivia said, "Thank you, Kizzy. How thoughtful. Come, let's sit down and talk."

Matilda Joyce took the bundle of fish from Olivia. "Here, I'll put those in the refrigerator." Then she left the room, holding the fish in front of her with an outstretched arm.

Kizzy frowned. "They're real fresh, ma'am. I cleaned 'em myself, just an hour ago." Then she turned to Olivia who was smiling for the first time. "Are you doin' all right?"

"Yes, it's hard, but we have to go on. John told me not to mourn him— that we'd meet again in a better place."

"That's what the preacher said at the memorial," Kizzy said.

"Well, yes. But enough of that—happy birthday to you, Kizzy. I wish I had a present for you, but I'm just now getting back on my feet."

Kizzy started to answer, but Olivia suddenly looked as if she had had a brainstorm. She pointed to a Sears, Roebuck catalog laying on the coffee table. "Wait … I've got an idea. I was looking through the catalog the other day and thought of you." She paused, and then said, "I'd like to get you a pair of school shoes for your birthday. Will you let me do that?"

"Well, yes. But I go barefooted most of the time." She pointed at her well-worn brogans. "These clodhoppers are two years old, but they're holding out pretty good—even if they ain't so pretty."

Olivia opened the catalog. "Well, let's look."

They poured over the catalog for the next half-hour and finally settled on a pair of smoke-colored leather oxfords with rubber soles that cost $2.95. Olivia tried to interest her in a pair of black patent leather slippers with a T-strap, but Kizzy talked her out of it. "I love those, but they wouldn't hold up 'cause I have to walk from the boat to school, sometimes in the rain."

Olivia winced and quickly changed the subject. "Have you been reading?"

"Yes, I'm halfway through *Pride and Prejudice.*"

"Do you like it?"

"I do, and I want to talk to you about it, but I gotta go. I promised Shirley—she lives on the boat next to me on the river—that I'd watch the fireworks with her and her girls, and then Cormac—he's my stepfather— told me to get home early tonight."

She thought for a second after mentioning Cormac, and then added, "Tomorrow's Sunday, and I think we are going to get up early and go musseling."

❖

On July 21, 1942, Kizzy went to the library to see Olivia. She did not see her at the desk, so she looked amongst the library stacks, and when she did not see her there, she headed for the stairs to see if she was working on the second floor. Mabel saw her looking and called out. "Olivia and her mother have gone to Hoxie to visit a sick friend, Kizzy."

"Oh. OK. Well, I'll see her tomorrow." Kizzy started to leave, but when she saw Uncle Mac in his wheelchair near the entrance to the Veterans' Center she waved to him, and he motioned for her to draw close.

"Good news today, Kizzy." He pointed to two separate stories on the front page of the *Big Pearl Free Current*. "The Germans have lost their edge in the Atlantic—our boats are getting through, and the Army is deploying the II Corps to the European Theater." He slapped a crippled leg with his one good hand. "We're on offense in the Pacific, and now we're going after the Huns."

"My friend Birdie's in the Pacific, but he thinks that's where his two brothers are going—to fight the Germans."

"God bless 'em, God bless 'em all."

"I was at the church and heard your speech about John Decker getting killed at Midway. It was awful sad—everybody was crying, especially Shirley. That's Birdie's ma—she's got him and two other boys who've gone to war."

"Wartime eulogies are always sad, Kizzy. We talk about the honor of dying for a cause greater than self, but that doesn't bring them back."

"Olivia's low sick about losing her man."

"Yes, but you can help her, Kizzy."

"How's that?"

"Well, being alone is different from being lonely. People can learn to live alone, but loneliness will destroy the strongest heart because it eats from the inside, where it can't be seen." Uncle Mac rubbed the jagged scar on his face, a sure sign that he was about to get to his main point. "That's where you come in, Kizzy."

"Me?"

"Yes, Olivia likes you. She lights up when she talks about you."

Uncle Mac rubbed the scar again, but before he could continue Kizzy said, "She gave me a pair of nice school shoes for my birthday."

"I know, she told me." Then he looked her in the eye and took her hand in his. "Let her help you, Kizzy. Be a friend to her. She needs you."

✤

Two days later Olivia and her mother walked from the Joyce residence to Sweetcheeks' Café to meet Kizzy for lunch. When the restaurant was in sight, Matilda said, "I don't know why you like this place—it's full of roughnecks and bumpkins. Look, there's Ivo Parker going in—he just got out of the penitentiary."

"Mother … Please … John and I used to come here all the time. I like it, and Kizzy will like it. That's why I invited her to join us here."

Sweetcheeks' Café, a working-man's eatery located a block from Curly's Fish Market, overlooked the river. John Decker had taken Olivia there when they were high school seniors and it quickly became their favorite place to have lunch. They would get the blue-plate special, study the colorful characters, and listen to coarse words of wisdom from the cadaverous Sweetcheeks. She was 82 years old and all bent over. The naturally rosy cheeks of her youth had given way to a heavy application of rouge, but Sweetcheeks was a trooper. She had a cheery smile and a friendly word for everyone, and the patrons loved her as much as they loved her "Southern fixin's."

Sweetcheeks met them at the door and gave Olivia a hug. "God bless you dear, I'm so sorry about John." Then she turned to Matilda. "Hi, Matildy."

"Matilda."

"Yes. Well. Here, sit here." Sweetcheeks steered them to a table near the front. "We've got liver and onions today." Then she slithered her way back to the front door to shout a gravelly welcome to the crew of the local garbage truck. "Hi, boys, sit yourself down—I've got liver and onions today."

Matilda scrunched her nose and lifted her chin.

"Mother … Please … Relax … Kizzy will be here in a minute and I want her to feel comfortable."

"I think it's good for you to help her, and I'll do my best to be nice, but don't get your hopes up. You can do certain things to change people on the outside. But can you change them on the inside? That's the hard part."

"It's not her fault that she was born and raised on the river. She's a beautiful girl, Mother. And she's smart, you'll see."

Just then, Kizzy came through the front door and waved to Olivia and Matilda.

Sweetcheeks led her to the table. "What's it going to be, girls?" She looked at Kizzy. "I've got liver and onions today, young-un."

"I'll have that, ma'am," Kizzy said.

Olivia looked at her mother and said, "Me too."

Matilda sniffed. "I'll have a grilled cheese sandwich."

⚜

By the time their food arrived, Olivia had managed to get Kizzy to tell a few stories about her family and life on the river, but it was not easy given the indifferent look that Kizzy was getting from Matilda.

Eventually, Olivia asked Kizzy to tell what she liked about the books she was reading, and that got her excited. "I liked the Jules Verne books a lot because I like adventure stories, but now I'm halfway through *Pride and Prejudice* and it's my favorite so far."

The mention of Jane Austen's famous book energized Matilda. "Yes. It's a lovely book." Then she waxed endlessly about the wonderful formality of life in early England—the elaborate dinners, parties, and dances. She described all of that in detail, and then she concluded: "In those days, people had such elegant ways of doing things, and because of that they lived rich and full lives."

"That's true enough, Mother," Olivia said. "But for me it's not the setting, or the formal way of life in England. It's the way Jane Austen tells the love story and how she shows the relationships of the characters. That's what matter the most to me."

Kizzy listened, somewhat intimidated by the fact that she was having lunch with two pillars of the community. It occurred to her that she needed to say something about the book, just to participate and show that she was actually reading it. But she was itching to say what was really on her mind: *Well, yes, there's the formal stuff and the love story, but the thing that comes through to me is how strange life was back then, in England, compared to the simple ways of the river. And I gotta tell you, those people wouldn't make it on the river.*

But Kizzy did not want Olivia and her mother to think she was actually talking about them. So instead she said, "I like the love story, but I also like the fancy talk and fancy ways."

They smiled at that, so Kizzy carried on. "I like Elizabeth Bennet a lot, but I don't like the way Mr. Darcy treats her—I'm hoping that things will work out all right in the end, but I haven't finished the book yet."

"Well, let's not spoil it for you," said Olivia.

"Oh, it won't spoil it for me. My grandmother, MeeMaw, taught me how to dream, and I've already thought up several ways for it to end."

"How do you want it to end, Kizzy?" Matilda said.

Kizzy thought for a while. "I want it to end good, that's all."

"I like good endings too," said Matilda. "What dreams do you dream for yourself, Kizzy?"

"Well, ma'am, like most folks on the river, I dream that one day I will find a big pearl and get off the river. I ain't found it yet, but I'm only 14."

Matilda gave her an admiring look, and Kizzy did not miss it. *She may be OK after all.*

Then the waitress brought their desserts—big slices of Sweetcheeks' special coconut cream pie—and the conversation came to an abrupt halt. When they finished the pie, Kizzy thanked Olivia again for the school shoes. "I try them on every night and walk around to break 'em in, but I'm saving them for school."

Olivia grinned. "Good. And, Kizzy, I want you to come by the house one day soon, before school starts. I've been cleaning out my closet and I have set aside a few things that I think you might like to have."

"Oh, thank you, I will for sure."

Matilda and Olivia did most of the talking after that, because Kizzy was thinking about the hand-me-downs that she was going to get from Olivia.

Soon the lunch was over, and when they left the café, Sweetcheeks winked at Kizzy, discreetly indicating that she wanted to talk to her.

⚜

Kizzy said her goodbyes to Olivia and Matilda, and as they walked away, she slipped back into the café.

Sweetcheeks had taken a seat on a barstool near the front door. She was smoking a cigarette, and hustling those who were leaving. "Y'all come back … chicken and dumplings tomorrow."

When she saw Kizzy she patted the empty stool next to her, and Kizzy headed to it, wondering what the old woman wanted. Just then, Sweetcheeks blew a huge puff of smoke toward the ceiling, and hollered to the head garbage man as he led his crew out the door. "Peewee, if you bring them boys back tomorrow—it's chicken and dumplings—I'll fix you a plate of fried gizzards."

Peewee gave Sweetcheeks a thumbs-up just as Kizzy, more curious than ever, climbed onto the barstool.

"Matildy is a good woman, Kizzy. She was raised rich, and she don't know no other way. She's prim and proper, but don't hold that against her 'cause she did a good job of raising Olivia … that girl's as good as they come."

Kizzy nodded. She was not sure what to say, so she waited for Sweetcheeks to say more.

The old woman sucked in the last puff of her cigarette, and then squashed the butt in a stinky half-full Griesedieck Bros. ashtray. "I heard y'all talking, and it sounds like they aim to help you."

"Yes, ma'am. Olivia's been real good to me, but I'm just now getting to know her mother."

"It's good that they want to help you. Friends like them are good to have. You take all the help you can get and put it to good use, but if you ever need some plain talk to keep you from gettin' too ritzy, you come see me. I knew your MeeMaw and grandpa, and I grew up on the river, just like you."

Kizzy gave Sweetcheeks a hug, and then left the café, her head bursting; full of random thoughts that were banging against each other, vying for attention: Ritzy dinners and dances, Peewee's garbage men, fancy women, British ways, the war, Stefan, Jane Austen's love story, war widows, Sweetcheeks' fried gizzards, music-making, hand-me-downs, new shoes, plain talk, and having steamy sex with Cormac.

XXXIX

Guilt

Two weeks before the first day of school, Stefan and Kizzy went to their favorite spot downriver from Curly's to have a picnic lunch. A lonely picnic table in the shade, 20 feet above the river, gave a clear view of the Garhole, a place on the river where a local man once caught a record-breaking alligator gar.

They sat down, spread their lunch on the table, and Stefan pointed to a solitary fisherman, an elderly man with a huge potbelly. "He's at it again. That's the guy who caught the big one last year—seven feet long it was— the biggest ever."

"Well, he ain't doing any good today," Kizzy said. "He's just cussing and carrying on. I don't get it. Gars ain't no good for nothing. He just fishes for 'em for the fun of it. If he worked half as hard at real work he'd be rich."

Stefan laughed, and that ended the discussion of gar fishing.

"Olivia and her mother took me to lunch at Sweetcheeks'," Kizzy blurted, and then bubbled on, letting loose a string of pent-up news. "We talked about a lot of interesting stuff. And I'm going over to her house. She's got some hand-me-downs for me. She wears pretty things ... things like I ain't ever had."

Stefan could see that Kizzy wanted his approval. "That's good."

Then she turned solemn. "Uncle Mac says she's taken up with me because she's hurtin' and needs somebody to do for ... It must be terrible to lose a loved one in the war—I'd die if anything happened to Birdie—but Olivia does seem to be doing better."

Stefan swooned. *Kizzy's beautiful. And it doesn't matter whether she is happy or sad—it's her eyes, the red hair.* He could resist no longer; he leaned over to kiss her on the cheek, but she pulled away and changed the subject.

"I've got an idea for a song."

Drat. "What is it?"

"It's about MeeMaw's fairy, the spirit-lady that I've always gone to for answers."

"Sounds like praying to me. My mother used to pray all the time."

"Well, MeeMaw was different. She had a connection with spirits and haints of all kinds. She didn't go in for church and that kind of stuff. She said dreaming about the fairy works better because you can turn your dreams on or off and you ain't owing to anybody."

"My mother would say that's a lot of hokum."

"MeeMaw's way ain't nonsense! For years I've been dreaming about finding a big pearl and making enough off of it to get off the river—maybe buy a place of business like Curly's or Sweetcheeks.' I like to dream. It gives me hope." She stopped and began to wring her hands. "My only problem is that the big pearl in my dreams is at Mexican Bend, and we ain't supposed to go there—it's hainted."

Stefan chuckled. "Well, I don't see anything wrong with your dream. It's just a Black River version of Cinderella."

Kizzy cut her eyes toward him, and huffed. "Well, I like it, and that's what my song is about."

Whoops. Now I've made her mad. She's clinging to what she learned from her MeeMaw—the way of the river ... but that's OK ... I like her no matter what she believes.

He smiled. "Well, if we are going to do a song about the river, fairies, and dreams of finding a big pearl I need to know more about it. Will you take me out on the river someday and teach me how to gather mussels and dig for pearls?"

Kizzy looked at him, and then she gave him a kiss on the cheek. "Yep. Someday. But we ain't going to Mexican Bend!"

⚜

Olivia was sitting at the far end of the porch reading when Kizzy got to the Joyce home. Kizzy did not see her, but when she knocked on the door, Olivia got up and started toward her. "So, you're ready to try on some clothes?"

Kizzy was startled to hear her voice, but she smiled and nodded. Olivia put her hand on Kizzy's shoulder. "Well come on. I've set them out in my bedroom. Let's go upstairs and see how they look on you."

Kizzy pointed to a sack that she was carrying. "I brought my new school shoes."

"Good," Olivia said. She led the way into the house, and Kizzy followed. But she slowed to look around as they passed by the parlor and dining room, and when they were in the hallway she stopped to take a close look at a colorful assortment of bric-a-brac—several fine china and ceramic swans, cherubs, and flowers.

Olivia waited for Kizzy to look her way; then she signaled for her to follow her up a magnificent circular staircase.

When they were halfway up the stairs, Kizzy stopped again, just to look around, and she could not contain herself. "It's awful pretty, Olivia … everything … especially the little glass pieces downstairs. We can't have stuff like that on our boat. All our extra space is full of fishing gear and staples—stuff we have to have."

Olivia smiled. "Yes. I was lucky to grow up here." Then she stepped onto the second floor, walked to the end of the hall, and opened a door. "This is my bedroom."

Kizzy gulped as soon as they entered the room. *Oh my gosh, look at this room. It's bigger than our boat.* The canopied bed, rich furniture, lamps, and dressing table caught her eye, but then she saw the clothes on the bed:

Sweaters, blouses, skirts, and a coat. *Oh my gosh.* Kizzy was scared to ask if all of it was for her, so she just grinned and made nice.

"Here, let's start with these," Olivia handed her a light blue skirt with a matching blouse and pointed toward her bathroom. "Go on, Kizzy. Go in there and try these on for size."

Kizzy shut the door behind her and took a moment to savor the elegant plumbing. *This is fancy stuff ... better than the stuff at the school or the library ... better than anything I've ever seen.* Then she pulled her faded Sears, Roebuck dress over her head, and sat down to change shoes. She took off the brogans, and put on her new school shoes, and then she got up and turned around.

Holy smokes! Is that me?

Kizzy was standing naked, except for her panties and shoes, looking into a full-length mirror. *First time I've ever seen myself from top to bottom.*

She took a moment to cup her hands beneath her breasts and then she slid them slowly to her waist and then down to measure the new fullness of her hips. *Hmmm.*

Then she put on the light blue skirt and blouse and when she looked into the mirror, she laughed aloud. "Well, look at you!"

⚜

Olivia heard Kizzy's laugh, and wondered what was taking so long, but her curiosity vanished as soon as Kizzy opened the door. Olivia whistled to herself. *Goodness gracious—we need to fix the hair ... but what a difference.*

Then she gave Kizzy a big smile, and said, "You look like a New York model."

Olivia thought Kizzy would laugh again, but she did not. She just stood there, looking to be on the verge of tears, or laughter; it was hard for Olivia to tell which because Kizzy was holding back her true feelings, sheepishly biting her lip and twirling a lock of hair.

Olivia felt a tiny pang of conscience. *Maybe I'm being too pushy? No. No, I'm not.* She put her arms around Kizzy and whispered, "It's OK to be pretty, Kizzy." Then she held her at arm's length, and took on a cheery air. "So let's have fun. Let's try on some more clothes."

Kizzy nodded. Olivia thought she was getting ready to say something but instead Kizzy began giggling, a contagious giggle that quickly infected Olivia and turned into a full-blown fit of uncontrollable laughter. The two of them doubled over, laughing without knowing why they were laughing. Finally, Kizzy caught her breath long enough to say, "I'm sorry, Olivia. My tickle-box got turned over."

Olivia snickered some more, but managed to say, "Mine too."

Soon the giggling settled down, and the lull that followed yielded an oddly somber moment.

"No one's ever been this good to me."

Olivia paused and teared up. "You're good for me too, Kizzy." She fended off a touch of nostalgia about John and pointed to the clothes on the bed. "There, try on the black outfit. Let's see how that looks."

Kizzy took the skirt and blouse into the bathroom and when she came out Olivia said, "Wow. It's a perfect fit; your red hair and green eyes really set it off."

Kizzy guffawed, and did a perfect pirouette.

Olivia then asked her to sit at the dressing table and she stood behind her to brush and arrange her hair. They tried several styles, but soon agreed that the classic chignon at the nape of the neck was the best. Olivia secured it with a large black bow barrette and then asked Kizzy to walk around the room so they could admire their work.

"What do you think?" Kizzy said.

Olivia watched her spin around the room, relishing the transformation. "Perfect, Kizzy. The black bow makes it perfect." But Olivia's self-satisfaction quickly turned to doubt about what she was doing. *Am I trying to change her on the outside or inside? She loves her MeeMaw and the river, and it's not my business to fool around with that. Does Kizzy want this? Is it for her, or for me?*

Then she rationalized. *But I don't have to knock down her love for the ways of the river, do I? There's no harm in getting her to think about changing—a little at least.*

And it was then that Olivia decided to delve into Kizzy's thoughts about *Pride and Prejudice.*

"Have you finished the book?"

"Yep, I've finished it. I liked the way it ended, but the book started out with everyone wanting to marry someone rich, and the whole story builds on that. On the river nobody gets married—leastwise none of mine did—and nobody's rich." Kizzy pondered what she was going to say next. "So, it sure ain't the way I was raised, but I kinda like it."

Olivia thought. *There's a lot going on in that red head. This is all new to her. She has a fondness for the ways of the river. I need to respect that. Mother is right. It's hard to change someone on the inside. I need to be patient, let her decide what she wants to leave behind, and what she wants to bring with her.*

I'm sure she wants something better. She is reaching for the stars, and that is good. I should just listen, and let her ramble on. Let her talk it out, and think her way through it.

They tried on the rest of the clothes, and when they had talked about all of the outfits Kizzy expressed her gratitude and left, her arms full of sweaters, blouses, skirts, and a coat.

⚜

Stefan got to school early on the first day of the 1942 fall term, and went immediately to his locker, No. 102.

The main hallway of Big Pearl High School—a perfect echo chamber—rumbled with a mishmash of teenage racket. Ear-splitting shouts, foot shuffling, chatter, and laughter ricocheted off the concrete floors and cinderblock walls as hundreds of students jerked and slammed the doors of metal lockers.

Stefan was about to open his locker when the lull came. It was as if the power had gone out, or Principal Agee—also known as "The Paddler"—had unexpectedly shown his face. Stefan turned around to see what had happened and that is when he saw her.

Kizzy, dressed in a black blouse and skirt, had just entered the building. She was at the far end of the hall, walking toward him; ignoring the throng of dumbfounded students as they parted to give her a clear path. They gave her a close look, but as soon as she passed by, the mishmash of chatter would begin again, first as a murmur, then as loud as ever. There were a few whistles along the way, but overall the chatter had an incredulous tone to it as the students pondered the new Kizzy and prepared themselves to render judgment.

Stefan smiled and laughed to himself as Kizzy neared him. *Ha! Now they are seeing what I've seen all along, and they're stupefied. Horsey Hairs is just standing there with his mouth open. He looks like someone just gave him a high-colonic enema, and so do all of his stupid friends.*

When Kizzy got to Stefan's locker, she said, "Hi," and gave him a kiss on the cheek. Then she turned to look at the gawkers, and that is when Stefan saw the black bow barrette nestled into her new hairdo.

"You look terrific, Kizzy." He nodded toward the students. "They don't know what to make of you."

Kizzy smiled, and they huddled by Stefan's locker to laugh and talk until the first bell rang. Stefan stayed by her side for the rest of the school day, and a goodly number of kids—more girls than boys—went out of their way to speak to Kizzy. She was polite to all of them, but Stefan could tell that the newfound interest bothered her.

"Why are they being nice now?" Kizzy said it only once, but Stefan saw it in her eyes all day long; the question was on her mind and in her heart.

By the end of the school day, the early balloting on the "new Kizzy" yielded a predictable verdict, divided by gender. The boys, stunned and panting, liked the new Kizzy. But the rich girls did not. They doubled down, resorting to the line of gossip that they had used for years: "She's just a river rat."

⚜

When the bell rang ending the school day Stefan walked with Kizzy to the clearing by the bollards, and they stopped there to talk about their first day at high school.

The grass was damp, so Stefan put his satchel down to make a sitting spot for Kizzy. Then he dramatically swept the back of his hand over it, and said, "My Lady."

Kizzy feigned surprise. "That's the first time anyone's ever done that for me."

He winked. "It won't be the last."

They sat still for a long while, thinking about school, and watching as a logging boat came around the bend and drifted slowly downstream.

When the vessel was abeam of the bollards, Kizzy said, "You know, MeeMaw always said, 'People see things the way they want to.' Today, I got some of them to take a second look at me, but I'm still a river rat. Most of 'em ain't ever going to let go of that."

Stefan laughed. "You got a second look all right. The rich girls were jealous, but most of the boys just shuffled around, not knowing what to think."

"I've been waitin' a long time for this, but it ain't right to glory in it. MeeMaw and Grandpa said if we let ourselves get all puffed up we're sure to fall flat on our face."

Stefan said, "My mother taught me the same thing. She said it a million times: 'Pride and a haughty spirit goeth before a fall.'"

"That's the main point of *Pride and Prejudice*, the book I just finished." Kizzy started giggling as soon as she said it.

Stefan said, "What's so funny?"

"I loved the book, but I kept wondering what MeeMaw would have said about it."

"Would she have liked it?"

"Well, yes and no." Kizzy wiggled to adjust Stefan's satchel. "The book is about the manners and ways of fancy people in long-ago Britain. MeeMaw would have thought all of that—the formal stuff, ideas about marriage and courting—was silly, but she would agree with what the author, Jane Austen, was saying about pride and prejudice."

"I still don't see what's funny about that."

"Well, the people in the book choose their words carefully when they are talking to each other. I like that because it shows how words can hurt feelings, but it takes a long time for Jane Austen's characters to make their point. MeeMaw couldn't read, but if she could've read the book she would have pulled her hair out. She would have screamed at all the characters, especially Elizabeth and Mr. Darcy." Kizzy started giggling again. "MeeMaw would have said, 'Stop pussyfooting around. Get off your high horses and say what you mean. Get on with it.'"

Stefan laughed. "I think I would've liked MeeMaw."

"I miss her and Grandpa a lot. I'd like to talk to them about everything that's happened since they went on down the river."

"Yeah. I know. I'd give anything to talk to my real father."

⚜

Cormac got home from work at the button factory around 6 o'clock that day. Kizzy had just said goodbye to Stefan, and she was standing on the aft deck of the houseboat, enjoying a few more thoughts about her first day of high school.

She heard him before she saw him. "Whooeee! Look at you."

Kizzy watched as Cormac stomped across the gangplank and plopped down on the aft deck. *Uh-oh, he's drinking again.*

Cormac took a bottle of beer out of a paper sack, pried the top off, and took a long swallow. "I bet you turned some heads today."

Kizzy cracked a small smile, but looked away when she said, "Yep, I did." Then she went inside to change clothes and start fixing dinner, thinking to herself: *But I'm still a river rat.*

A few minutes later, just as Kizzy was about to pull an old cotton dress over her head, Cormac came in and sat beside her on the bed, his breath heavy and raspy.

Kizzy knew. *He's wantin' to do it.*

Cormac put his arm around her and pulled her back on the bed. "You're looking mighty fine these days, Kizzy. I could take you to Memphis and we'd be rich before you know it."

He keeps saying that. Oh, what the heck ... he's just horny. Just like the boys at school.

⚜

It was over in a hurry, and shortly thereafter Cormac was dead asleep, snoring and breathing deeply. Kizzy picked up her everyday dress from the floor and pulled it over her head. Then she slipped quietly out the door, barefooted, walking slowly toward her thinking spot in the woods, the old stump in the clearing where she last saw Grandpa.

Fall's coming soon. There are the cottonwoods, the oaks, and the sycamores. They're full now and the river's rolling along, lazy and tame, not wild and mean. And here I am, all alone, seeing life the way I learned to see it, through the eyes of MeeMaw and Grandpa, and Ma, and Shirley, and Birdie. But things are different now.

Kizzy knew what it was. Magic had made her young breasts soft, like the breast of Birdie's white dove. Her rich red hair, no longer girlish, was now brushing against her beautiful face. And her seductive legs peeked from beneath the old dress that seemed to know its fate, even as she did not know hers.

She stopped along the way to wade in a shallow pool of backwater, and stirred it with a bare foot, wagging it this way and that. Then, trembling, she thought of Cormac, and what they were doing, but there was no sense of shame. *It's just the way of the river.*

Kizzy went deeper into the woods, and when she got to Grandpa's stump she sat down and thought about Olivia. *She did it with John after they got married.* Then she thought of the book and Elizabeth Bennet's younger sister, Lydia, who did it with a soldier, then ran off with him. It disgraced her family, and everyone scorned her for breaking taboos and showing no regard for the moral code of society. But in Kizzy's mind poor Lydia was just like Kizzy's mother, Sarah, who did it with a Gypsy.

The clothes changed me on the outside, but I'm still a river rat, and we have our own ways. Grandpa said so. Us river people are free to live like we want to.

Just then, two hoot owls began to bark and cackle, and it disturbed Kizzy's reverie. She hooted back to them, but they did not answer, and it was then, in that quiet moment, that she felt a tinge of guilt about what she was doing with Cormac.

Kizzy ran out of the woods and along the bank of the river and made a beeline for the boat. Her cheeks were aglow, her body afire, and her legs were trembling. On she ran, crying out to the strange new ways that were crying out to her.

MeeMaw, you said there are things we don't want to know about ourselves. Should I peek behind the curtain?

She ran on.

Mercy, MeeMaw!

Kizzy's soul cried out.

What's happening to me?

XL

Jealousy

Just after dark on Halloween in 1942, Kizzy and Shirley Barden took Shirley's two little girls into the residential part of Big Pearl to trick-or-treat. It was a cool night; the girls, wearing disguises, could pass for town kids and gather a mother lode of free candy and other treats.

Kizzy and Shirley planned to stay in the background, out of sight while the girls knocked on doors and screamed, "Trick or treat." If asked to tell where they lived the girls would say nothing more than: "Over by the high school." And if they did not get a treat they were not—under no circumstances—to do any sort of trick or anything that would give the night law an excuse to arrest them; just leave and go to the next house.

On their walk up the hill to town, Shirley told Kizzy how nice she looked wearing the hand-me-downs that she got from Olivia. It was not the first time she had mentioned it, but Kizzy had not had a chance to tell her about the effect it was having on the girls and boys at school.

"The rich girls are shunnin' me, but the boys like the way I look."

"That ain't no surprise," Shirley said. "But they'll be trying to get in your pants. Boys is boys."

Kizzy laughed. "Yeah, I know. One of the rich boys, Horace C. Ayers—I call him Horsey Hairs—has been going out of his way to talk to me. And he ain't ever given me the time of day before now."

"Ha. I had a fling with a rich boy once," Shirley said. "But as soon as he got what he wanted I never saw him again."

Kizzy made a humming noise. "Well, I'm sticking with my boyfriend, Stefan. We've got a lot in common, and he liked me before I got the hand-me-downs, back when I was just another river rat."

"Well, if he's got a pecker you better watch out for him too."

Kizzy raised her voice. "No, he ain't that way, Shirley. We kiss and fool around a little, but his ma brought him up to wait before doing it."

"Wait for what?" Shirley guffawed as she said it.

"Marriage, I think," Kizzy said.

Shirley took on a serious tone. "Well, that's real special. You ought to hang onto him, and he's cute to boot—I've seen him hanging around with you."

"Did you ever get married, Shirley?"

"Naw, never even got close. And I gave up on it a long time ago. In the eyes of most men us river women is only good for two things: Fishin' and fuckin'." Shirley broke into a fit of laughter, and then as an afterthought said, "And I never was any good at fishin'."

"Well, I'm still dreaming about finding the big pearl and getting off the river one day," Kizzy said. "And lately I've been reading books that Olivia told me about and I'm seeing how the other side lives. That way of life wouldn't have worked for MeeMaw, and it might not work for me, but I'm thinking about it."

"Every one of us river rats dreams about stuff like that, but it never seems to work out. But it sounds to me like your best chance of moving up is to stick with that boy you're going with."

Kizzy gave Shirley a hug. And when they broke apart, Shirley stopped and took Kizzy's face in her hands. "And, Kizzy, keep your guard up with Cormac. They say he's screwing some of the girls at the button factory, and if you ain't careful he'll be trying to screw you. He's the horniest stud in these parts, and I heard he used to pimp out young girls in St. Louis."

Kizzy nodded as if she understood, but to change the subject she quickly pointed to the girls. "Look, they're getting too far ahead of us. Let's catch up."

⚜

A few days before Thanksgiving Kizzy went to school with an exciting piece of news that she was itching to tell Stefan, so she cornered him before the first bell.

"Cormac got us a radio, and we tuned it to the *Lum and Abner* show last night." Kizzy giggled, and pretended to turn imaginary dials. "It's a battery job that Cormac got from a girl who works at the button factory. Her husband got drafted and bought her a new electric one before he went overseas." Kizzy rambled on, telling about the radio; all the ways it was going to make her life better. "It's a Silvertone. Cormac says we can listen to the *Grand Ole Opry* with Roy Acuff and The Smoky Mountain Boys, and Minnie Pearl, and Bill Monroe, and other shows too—but we have to turn it off quick after we get through listening so that we won't run the batteries down."

Stefan interrupted. "Our radio is electric, and we keep it on pretty much all the time until we go to bed."

"Well, we ain't got electric on the boat."

Stefan shook his head. "I don't know how you get along without electricity."

"We get along—it's all in what you get used to. That's what Grandpa always said."

Stefan shrugged, and then said, "My favorite show is *Jack Armstrong, the All-American Boy*."

"But you're born German, you said."

"Yep, but I like Jack Armstrong because he goes all around the world, to strange places, and Wheaties gives away good stuff that you can send off for. Pretty soon they're going to start giving away cardboard models of fighter planes."

"I'd rather listen to Lum and Abner talking about the Jot 'em Down store. They're from Arkansas, you know."

"They're OK, but Jack Armstrong makes me dream about going around the world someday."

"Reading is what makes me dream. I'm glad we got the Silvertone, but it's mainly just for listening to shows and music."

"Did you start that new book?" Stefan said.

"Yep, it's called *Sense and Sensibility*." Kizzy waited a moment to see if Stefan would show further interest, but he did not and that bothered her. "So were you just asking to be nice? Or would you actually like to hear what it's about?"

Stefan grimaced. "Sorry."

"It's another Jane Austen book."

"OK, but what's it about?"

"It's about this: Should a girl marry a rich boy who will set her up for life even though she doesn't love him? Or should she marry a boy she loves who ain't got a pot to piss in?"

Stefan laughed. "What if the poor boy promised to work hard enough to get a pot to piss in?"

Kizzy giggled, and gave him a kiss on the cheek just as the first bell rang.

❧

On Thanksgiving Day, Cormac and Kizzy lazed around the boat for most of the morning. She read two more chapters of *Sense and Sensibility*, and Cormac piddled around, working on the outboard motor.

At 11o'clock Cormac came into the cabin, washed his hands, and pulled a box from the cabinet beneath the sink. He handed it to Kizzy and said, "Surprise!"

"For me?" And when Cormac nodded yes she tore the box open. It was a brand-new pair of athletic shoes with white duck uppers and rubber soles.

"You can wear them instead of the old brogans. Now that I'm working I'll be getting you some more nice things."

Kizzy put the shoes on and laced them up. Then she gave Cormac a hug, strutted around the cabin, and said, "Now I've got three pairs of shoes counting the brogans."

"See, that Olivia woman ain't the only one that likes to see you looking nice."

"She's been real good to me, all right."

"But we're family, Kizzy. And that's the difference. It's one thing to give you some hand-me-downs, but I been taking care of you for a long time now—just me and you—and when you get right down to it nobody else cares whether we live or die."

"Olivia does, and so does Stefan."

"Bullshit. You can't trust strangers like that. We got a good thing going on here and the way we live ain't none of their business." Cormac voice got husky. "You ain't told them about us doing it, have you?"

"I wouldn't tell that to anybody. MeeMaw said you never tell stuff like that about yourself."

"You ain't lettin' that boy screw you, are you?"

Kizzy snickered. "No, we just horse around and make music. Anyway, he's made up different than we are. He says it ain't right to do it without being married."

"Sheee-it." Cormac wheezed. "You sure he ain't queer or something?"

"Ain't nothing wrong with him. It's just his way of thinking. Anyway, I like him and Olivia and I'm learning a lot from them. So don't be running them down."

Cormac winked and tweaked Kizzy's breast. "Well, you're learning from me too, ain't you?"

"Stop it, Cormac. I'm having my period."

⚜

At noon that day Cormac told Kizzy that he was going to be gone for the rest of the day. He said the woman who gave him the radio wanted him to come over and help her hang some wallpaper.

Cormac spruced up and put on a clean shirt, and as he was leaving he gave her $1 and said, "Here, you can go over to Sweetcheeks' and get a good Thanksgiving blue plate. I'll probably be late getting back, so don't forget: If you play the radio be sure to turn it off so the battery don't run down."

⚜

Kizzy spent the rest of the afternoon reading and rearranging her new wardrobe on the shelves between her bunk and Cormac's. And when she was done she went to the aft deck and thought about what Cormac had said to her, and what he was doing that afternoon.

Shirley said he's screwing some girls at the button factory. If he's doing it with someone else he won't be doing it with me as much, but that's OK. We been doing it enough to suit me, and we ought to cut back on it anyhow. Cormac says he can't knock anyone up, but who knows.

Kizzy's thoughts then turned to the story line of Jane Austen's book, and she thought about Horsey Hairs and how he had been playing up to her. *It's because of the hand-me-downs; he's a spoiled rich boy who ain't ever given me a look, but now he wants to get in my pants, just like Shirley said. Yep.*

MeeMaw always said girls ought not to get too dolled up; said they're just asking for it. Hmmm. Jane Austen called it vanity, but it's the same thing. It's me caring too much about what others think, especially boys. I could never marry someone like Horsey. Ughh.

A cool breeze made the aft deck uncomfortable, so Kizzy went back inside and lay down on her bed. She began to read, and as she did, she let her fairy take her away, to her lifelong dream of finding a big pearl and getting off the river. *Who needs a rich man? I just need to find a pearl.*

Then she turned to Chapter 6, and that is when she discovered Barton Cottage. She let her fairy take her there, to a place that would change her life.

XLI

Operation Torch

In June 1940, the German Luftwaffe began bombing airfields and other targets in England in an attempt to gain air superiority. But the Royal Air Force stood fast, forcing Hitler to abandon his idea of invading the British Isles.

A frustrated Hitler ordered his Luftwaffe to bomb British cities and towns, and the indiscriminate German *blitzkrieg* killed more than 12,000 civilians in London alone.

When America entered the war in December 1941, the American generals wanted to gear up for an early invasion of the European continent, but the British—remembering the enormous casualties of World War I—urged caution. Churchill preferred to strike the Germans and Italians in North Africa with the hope of bringing the Vichy French forces located there back into the war on the side of the Allies.

Months of debate followed, but President Franklin Roosevelt sided with Churchill. He ordered General George Marshall to plan and carry out amphibious landings on the coast of North Africa before the end of 1942.

Early on the morning of Nov. 8, 1942, a massive allied invasion force assembled off the coast of North Africa. The *USS Leonard Wood*, a troop carrier, slipped in close to the beaches of French Morocco, and at 5 a.m. 1,900 fighting men from the Third Infantry Division deployed to land at Fédala.

Not all of them made it ashore. An unruly surf swept 21 of the landing craft out of control, throwing them against a rocky shore. The boats capsized or sank, and the troops, heavily laden with arms and ammunition, drowned.

Two half-brothers from Big Pearl, 20-year-old Layton Barden and 21-year-old Milton Barden, were among those who drowned without ever firing a shot at the enemy.

⚜

Early on Saturday morning after Thanksgiving, Kizzy walked over to Shirley Barden's to help her with the girls and to talk some more about boys and sex.

Shirley fixed a pot of coffee, but before they could pour themselves a cup, a man wearing a Western Union cap knocked on the side of the boat.

As soon as Shirley saw the emblem on the man's cap, she shivered. "Uh-oh, Kizzy. This ain't no good." She took two telegrams from the man and handed them to Kizzy. "I can't bear to look."

Kizzy tore open the envelopes, and said. "It's the boys—it ain't Birdie." Shirley slumped and went inside, and Kizzy followed. "You want me to read them to you?"

Shirley nodded, and Kizzy said, "They're the same, but one's for Layton and the other one is for Milton."

"Go ahead, let's hear it and get it over with."

Kizzy read the first telegram:

"GA2 89 GOVT=PXX USA WASHINGTON DC NOV 15 111A
MRS. SHIRLEY BARDEN, BIG PEARL, ARKANSAS
THE DEPARTMENT OF THE ARMY DEEPLY REGRETS TO INFORM YOU THAT YOUR SON, PRIVATE LAYTON BARDEN, WAS KILLED IN ACTION IN THE PERFORMANCE OF HIS DUTY AND IN THE SERVICE OF HIS COUNTRY. THE DEPARTMENT EXTENDS ITS SINCEREST SYMPATHY IN YOUR GREAT LOSS. BECAUSE OF EXISTING CONDITIONS THE BODY WAS NOT RECOVERED. TO PREVENT POSSIBLE

AID TO OUR ENEMIES PLEASE DO NOT DIVULGE THE CONTENTS OF THIS MESSAGE.

GENERAL JOHN GARDINER, DEPARTMENT OF THE ARMY"

Kizzy started to read the second message about Milton, but Shirley broke down. "Stop, Kizzy. I can't take no more." She sat down on the bed and Kizzy sat beside her, consoling Shirley as best she could; she let her remember, and she let her cry.

"Them boys was never very lovey-dovey, but they was mine and I did the best I could for 'em." Then she told a string of stories about the boys when they were little, stopping to cry between episodes.

By mid-afternoon Shirley had collected herself, and she showed a bit of pique. "I didn't know where they were or nothing. They never wrote 'cause they never learned to write, but they probably wouldn't have wrote even if they could've. They weren't like Birdie—they never was."

"Is there anything else I can do, Shirley? You want me to go or stay a while?"

"Stay, Kizzy. I ain't got nothin' to hold onto except the girls and you. And I got an awful feeling about Birdie. All I know is that he's out there somewhere fighting the Japs."

⚜

Later that day Kizzy went to the library to tell Olivia about Shirley's boys; she wanted to know how to get a service flag for Shirley so she could show that she had lost two sons in the war.

"Let's go see Uncle Mac. He got mine, the one for my John."

They found Uncle Mac in his usual spot, and when they told him about the boys he shook his head in sorrow. "Leave it to me; I'll have it in a couple of days. And I'll arrange a memorial service for them. It's what we are doing for all the boys we lose."

A week later a few Big Pearl citizens, mostly veterans from World War I, attended a brief memorial service at City Hall for Private Layton Barden and Private Milton Barden. There was no preaching, but Uncle Mac made a fine speech and presented Shirley with a service flag like the one Olivia got for John, except Shirley's flag had three stars on it—two gold ones for the boys, and one blue one for Birdie.

⚜

After the memorial service Kizzy walked with Shirley and the girls back to Shirley's boat. They fixed lunch and then talked until mid-afternoon when someone knocked on the side of the boat and called Shirley's name.

Kizzy gave Shirley a quizzical look.

"That'll be Doodle Lee," Shirley said. "He was at the memorial service." She arranged her dress, and fluffed her hair. "He said he might come down to the river to see me, but I didn't think he would." She shrugged her shoulders and hollered. "Come on in, Doodley. It's just me and Kizzy and the girls."

The boat tipped slightly as the big man stepped aboard. He was at least six foot six and well put together. He had long dark hair and steel-blue eyes that seemed friendly, but the layout of his face gave him a goofy look. He was about Shirley's age—mid to late 30s—and he had a beat-up sea bag over his shoulder.

Kizzy could see that Shirley wanted to explain further. "Me and Doodley used to mess around some, but it's been a while."

Kizzy gave Shirley an understanding look, but said nothing.

Doodle gave Kizzy a toothy smile and tossed his sea bag in the corner. Then he stuck his hand out. "Shirley tells me you live over there." He thumbed in the direction of Kizzy's boat.

"Yep, I've been on that boat all my life."

Shirley laughed. "Me and Kizzy look after one another." Then she turned her back to Doodle, lifted her head slightly and winked, motioning to the door.

Kizzy got the message. She said, "Nice to meet you, Doodley," and went outside.

Shirley followed her, and when they were out of earshot to Doodle and the girls Shirley said, "Doodley has hit on some hard times, so he's going to stay with me and the girls for a while."

Kizzy nodded, but gave Shirley a worried look.

"I could use some help around here, Kizzy." Her voice trembled. "But the truth is I need someone to love on me. I lost one baby at childbirth, my two boys is dead, and I'm worried sick about Birdie."

Kizzy put her arms around Shirley. "I just want you to be happy."

"I will, Kizzy. But, hey—I ain't no numbskull. I know Doodley's probably heard that I'm supposed to get some sort of death money from the Army on account of my boys getting killed, and he may be after some of that, but I don't care. I like him, and I need a man right now. If it don't work out I'll run him off. Of course, he'll most likely run off on his own—like all the other men in my life—if I get knocked up."

XLII

Semite Secrets

At 8 o'clock sharp on Tuesday morning, Stefan stood outside Eli's Dry Goods Store, peering in to see if Eli Schulman was alone or busy serving customers.

Stefan hoped to get a part-time job for the Christmas season, but he knew better than to interrupt the old man if he was helping a customer.

He put his face close to the window to shade his eyes. It was hard to see what was going on inside the store because Eli saw no reason to use electric lights during daylight hours. He had been in business since 1905, cutting costs and keeping prices low for his customers.

There ... There he is, and he's alone.

Stefan took a deep breath as he opened the door and headed to the back of the store. Eli, hunched over the register, was sorting out the cash drawer.

"Good morning, Mr. Schulman, I'm Stefan Halder." He waited; the old man gave him a friendly look, but said nothing.

"Do you need any help for the Christmas season?"

Eli smiled, but he panned Stefan's approach. "Of course I need help, but if you are asking for a job don't beat around the bush—just ask for a job."

Stefan blinked. "Yes sir. Can I have a job, working for you?"

"You're hired; 25 cents an hour. Come in after school today, and we'll see what kind of worker you are."

⚜

"Are you German?" It was the first thing Eli asked when Stefan reported for work that afternoon.

Stefan knew that Eli was a Jew, and that he had come to Arkansas from Europe when he was a teenager. Everyone in town knew that, because Eli still had an accent, and Bully Bigshot and his sycophants constantly referred to him as "a foreigner and a Jew."

But their slurs had very little effect: The people of Big Pearl loved Eli's Dry Goods Store. He had the best line of merchandise in northeast Arkansas—shoes, millinery, hats, lingerie, student apparel, linens, and real Levi Strauss jeans from San Francisco. A shoe repair stand in the back of the store gave the place the pleasant aroma of glue and fresh-cut leather, but Eli was the main attraction. The grownups loved his affable manner, and the children relished the way he laughed when they rode the large mechanical ride—a bucking Arkansas mule—that stood near the front door.

Something told Stefan to answer truthfully. "Yes sir, everybody around here thinks we are Dutch, but I was born in Germany." He shuffled and looked down. "But I'm an American now."

"Good answer." Eli pointed to an old photograph of his family on the wall behind the cash register. It was in an antique frame ornamented with gold Hebrew letters that spelled Chai. "My homeland is Belgium, east of the city of Liége, very close to the Rhineland. I recognized your accent, and have known for some time that you and your stepfather Fritz are German."

"Yes, sir. But we were told when we first got to America that it would be best to just say we are Pennsylvania Dutch ... because of the war and all."

"I agree, and your secret is safe with me. I know about prejudice." Eli pointed to a broom and said, "Now sweep out, and then we'll talk."

Stefan swept the entire store, and then he stepped behind a counter—out of Eli's sight—to reach beneath the collar of his shirt and touch his Chai pendant.

I promise, Mother ... I promise.

❖

By Friday, Stefan had proven himself a hard worker. Eli liked the boy; he enjoyed their talks about Eli's early days in Big Pearl, their recollections about the Rhineland, and the years Stefan spent in Pennsylvania Dutch country. And when Stefan compared the *Kristkindlmarkts* in Germany to those in Pennsylvania, Eli listened carefully, and then he said, "Are you a Christian?"

"My mother was. I went to the Catholic Church in Pennsylvania with her almost every Sunday, but I haven't been since coming here."

"I am a Jew," Eli said. "But I love the Christmas season. It is a good story and it perks people up, even in a time of war." He pointed to a Jewish calendar on the wall behind the cash register. "You know, Stefan, this is the eighth and last day of Hanukkah. I will be closing the store a little early, at 4:30. Would you like to come to my house and have an early dinner with me and my wife, Rachel? You'll be home by 7 o'clock, I guarantee."

"Yes sir, I'd like that."

⚜

Rachel Schulman, a wiry woman bent slightly by age, reminded Stefan of his schoolteacher in the Neander Valley. Her voice was soft, and she had a kindly manner, but the thing that struck Stefan was the warmth of her home. It was a red-brick Federal on the outside, but the interior decorations were eclectic, an indefinable mix that matched her personality.

"Welcome to our home, Stefan." Rachel led him to the living room, and the three of them sat on a sofa that faced a fireplace, close enough to feel the warmth and hear the crackle of a log that had just begun to burn. In the background, Rachel's Victrola was playing an assortment of chamber music by Felix Mendelssohn.

"I like Mendelssohn," Stefan said. "Especially his chamber music."

"Yes, me too," Rachel said.

Stefan then pointed to a little toy—a four-sided spinning top—that was laying on the mantle. "That's a *dreidel*, isn't it?"

Eli and Rachel looked at each other, and then Eli said, "Yes, it is. We actually played with it on the first night of Hanukkah—it's traditional to do that." He paused, and then said, "You know the *dreidel* game?"

Stefan looked like someone who had spilled the beans, but he quickly recovered. "I had a Jewish friend in Pennsylvania; he showed me how to play."

Eli rubbed his chin, and changed the subject. "Yes, there is much to learn when you are young. My family brought me to America when I was 16, and Rachel and I moved here when I was 28. That's when we opened our store, 37 years ago.

"Enough, already," Rachel said. "Let's move to the dining table. This is the last night of the Feast of Lights and it is time to light all the candles and have dinner."

⚜

Dinner was an assortment of potato cakes, fried breads, and pastries with different fillings, and as they began to eat, Eli told the story of Hanukkah. "Our people rebelled against the Greeks and needed to cleanse and rededicate the temple, but they only had enough consecrated oil to keep the lamp burning for one day." He paused for effect. "But the small bottle of oil miraculously lasted for eight days, and that is why we light eight candles." He pointed to a ninth candle that was shorter than the others. "That's the *shamus* candle. If we need to do something useful with a candle we must do it with the *shamus*; in that way we will not accidentally use one of the Hanukkah candles."

"That's enough of that, Eli. It's a good story, but let's let Stefan get a word in edgewise." Rachel smiled. "Do you have a girlfriend?"

"Yes, ma'am, Kizzy is her name. She's beautiful, and very smart." He blushed, then said, "We make music together. I play the violin and she sings, and we are working up an act for next year's talent contest—the one at the high school."

"Where does she live?" Rachel asked.

"She lives down on the river, ma'am. The bigshots in town call her a river rat, but she doesn't deserve that. She can't help it that she's poor."

"I've been locking horns with bigshots for years," Eli said. "And Sully Biggers is the worst of them. His father and grandfather were good men. They welcomed me to town and helped me get started. I don't know what happened to Sully, but he is no good."

"Kizzy and the river people call him Bully Bigshot."

Rachel squealed and clapped. "That's perfect!"

And Eli guffawed so hard that he nearly choked on a piece of pastry, but he recovered and took on a serious air. "If Bully had his way the government would be sterilizing poor people. I have heard him say, 'They breed like rabbits, and they don't contribute a damn thing.'"

"Eli, enough." Rachel gave her husband the small eye.

"It's OK," Stefan said, "My stepfather heard him say the same thing, and the night he said it he also took out after the Germans, the Negros, and ..." Stefan hesitated, but Eli signaled for him to go ahead, "... and the Jews."

"Well, he can't hurt us, Stefan—we've made too many good friends in Big Pearl and people love my store. But you and your stepfather need to keep your guard up because the government is sending lots of Germans to internment camps, just like the Japanese."

"That's why we say we are Pennsylvania Dutch. So far it's working. But our good friend back in Pennsylvania, Mr. Horst Bachmann, says the FBI is rounding up more Germans than they did during World War I."

Eli grimaced. "If that becomes a problem for you and Fritz you let me know. Will you do that?"

"Yes, sir."

"Eli, you promised Stefan we would be through by 7 o'clock, and it is now 7:30."

❧

When Stefan left, Eli put his arm around Rachel and they went back to the living room. He put another log on the fire and they sat down to talk.

"He's a fine young man, Eli."

"Yes, he is, but there's something about him. He looks like one of Hitler's 'Aryans,' but he seems so comfortable with our ways, our traditions." Eli got up, poked the fire, and took the *dreidel* from its place on the mantle. "He knew about this, and he likes Mendelssohn. Hmmm."

Eli rolled the little square top onto the table next to the sofa, and it came to rest with the Gimel side showing. "Look, Rachel, the *dreidel* has landed on Gimel—we would win the whole pot if we were playing—it's a good sign."

XLIII

Reproduction

A fierce February storm whipped its way north along the Black River, pushing the houseboats closer to shore, rocking them to and fro as the strong winds crashed against the current.

Inside Shirley Barden's boat, a fire was burning in the cookstove. It was bedtime and her girls were in their bunk playing with rag dolls, oblivious to the sound of passionate sex coming from their mother's bunk.

Doodle Lee, a foot taller than Shirley, could have passed for a prize-fighter. He was all muscle and no fat, but his sculptured physique had not come from hard work. Doodle was sorry to the core—always broke and often drunk—but he was just what Shirley wanted at this low point in her life. His appetite for raw sex had no boundary, and to that extent, he was a perfect match for Shirley.

On this cold winter day, Doodle was fully naked and mounted up, giving Shirley his best.

I need this. Doodley hits the spot.

⚜

A short letter from Birdie was on the table. It had come a few days before, on Feb. 2, just before the storm set in.

Shirley asked Kizzy to read it for her, and she did.

"Dear Ma,

I herd about Milton and Layton in North Africa, its sad but Im proud they were doin their part.

"I cant rite no detales or they wont let this go thru. But I can tell you for sure that it is plum scary when you first get out of the boat to toe dig—trying to get as many mussels as you can get. Particlar when you are the first to start diggin—but we is Marines—so there.

"A lot of my buddys has gone on down the river as MeeMaw sez, but thats how it is out here.

Say hello to Kizzy for me. Im OK.

I luv you, Birdie."

The letter puzzled Kizzy, so she took it to Mac Thornton for interpretation. "Uncle Mac, what does this mean? Where is Birdie, and what's he doing?" She pointed to the red ink-stamped markings on the envelope: "Somewhere in the South Pacific."

"They censor mail, Kizzy. The military cuts out anything that might help the enemy if the letter were to fall into the wrong hands. The boys can't write where they are or tell what they are doing. But we know that Birdie is with the First Marine Division, and they have been fighting on Guadalcanal for several months. It's been a bloody battle, but our boys won it, and now they are mopping up—and that's just about over."

Kizzy pointed to the text of the letter and guffawed. "Ha! Birdie's smart—he told us about the fighting in his letter, using river talk."

⚜

The storm passed, and on Saturday morning, Feb. 6, Kizzy walked over to Shirley's boat to tell her what Uncle Mac had said about Birdie. Doodle had gone to town to get some bread, and the girls had gone with him.

They had a good laugh about Birdie using river talk to fool the censors, and then Kizzy asked Shirley to sit down by the light of the window. Shirley gave her a questioning look, so Kizzy said. "I want to give your hair a good brushing and put it up in a bun like Olivia did mine. OK?"

Shirley made a face, but she did not protest when Kizzy started brushing. And for a while they did not speak.

She's a pretty woman—nice face and figure—and this rich black hair is going to look real good when I get done … She ain't got the right clothes, and she doesn't use lipstick and stuff like that, but if she did …

"You're too good to me, Kizzy. I ain't worth the trouble."

"Hush." Kizzy tried several different chignon styles, and as she worked, she thought how hard it must have been for Shirley to have all her sons go off to war, and then lose two of them on the same day. *She was down low after that happened, but she looks better now. At least her body looks alive. I think Doodley is doing her some good on that account. But she ain't got no shine to her … she still has that hangdog look that she got the day the telegrams came. Somethin's eatin' on Shirley.*

Kizzy put a barrette in the bun to hold it, and then she held a mirror so that Shirley could see her new hairdo. "You look beautiful, Shirley."

Shirley studied herself, but the look of satisfaction turned quickly into a whimper.

"Hey, stop that," Kizzy said. "Let's fix a pot of coffee and tell some of MeeMaw's funny stories about fairies and haints; that'll get you out of the dumps."

Shirley looked Kizzy in the eye. "I love MeeMaw's old tales, but I'd rather hear you tell about that place you been talking about—that Barton Cottage place—the one that's in your book."

Kizzy did her best to match MeeMaw's storytelling skill by adding a fairy to Jane Austen's story about Barton Cottage, and Shirley loved it.

Kizzy started her story in the classic fashion, "Once upon a time …." And when she got to the end she turned it into a great victory for the poor: "And the river girl used the pearl that the fairy helped her find to buy Barton Cottage."

Shirley squealed and took a sip of coffee, but it went down the wrong way. She sputtered, and that sent the two of them into a fit of giggling. But they collected themselves, and their conversation took a solemn turn.

"I love to hear you talk about your dreams, Kizzy, but those places ain't for the likes of me."

"Pshaw." Kizzy wrinkled her nose and shook her head.

"You deserve better, Kizzy, but I don't. I'm just an ole river rat. Always have been—always will be."

Kizzy started to speak, but Shirley cut her off.

"I'm knocked up again, Kizzy."

Kizzy was not sure what to say, so she waited.

"I missed my period right before Christmas … I ain't purified since Doodley moved on board. I keep hoping I'll start 'cause I've been late before. Remember that time I gave you my whole box of Cellu-ettes 'cause I thought I was pregnant? Well, that was a false alarm."

Shirley winced. "But I don't think this one is."

⚜

On Thursday, March 11, a cluster of 10 men hovered around a table near the meat counter in the back of Biggers Grocery & Market. They gathered there every weekday morning at 8 o'clock to drink coffee, talk, and tell lies. The men were old or otherwise exempt from the draft, and most of them wore business suits, although a few wore work clothes. Their common trait was volume; shoppers at the front of the store could hear everything they said, particularly words spoken in the heat of an argument.

Bully Bigshot was the ringleader of the coffee klatch, mainly because he owned the store and provided the coffee free of charge. That entitled him to set the agenda, and on this day he wanted to talk about what General George Patton was doing in North Africa.

"Patton is the best general we've got. He's going to drive the Krauts out of Tunisia. He knows as much about fighting with tanks as Rommel does, and I'm betting he's going to kick their ass. That'll be a good day for the U.S.A."

"It ain't all Patton, Bully. The Brits are there too, and they've got Montgomery."

"He's a pussy." Bully never allowed favorable comparisons to Patton.

Thus the argument began, but Bully got distracted when he saw Shirley Barden walk into the store. It was an unseasonably warm day, and she was dressed in a lightweight cotton outfit that did little to hide her pregnancy.

Bully moved away from the table to get a better look, watching her like a hawk as she shopped. After a few minutes, he stepped to a wall-mounted telephone behind the meat counter, placed a call, and spoke in a hushed voice.

⚜

On Saturday, March 13, a black 1936 Dodge pickup eased its way north on the state road that ran alongside the Black River. When the driver was abreast the narrow path leading downhill to the river, he pulled onto the shoulder and parked, and a small old woman got out of the truck on the passenger side. She motioned to the driver to stay put, and then she started down the path to Shirley Barden's boat.

It was not cold, but the woman wore an ankle-length dress that had the look of an old-fashioned nurse's uniform made of heavy gray woolen broadcloth with buttons in the front that ran from neck to hem. The cuffs and the oversized lapel—once white—had yellowed and were blotched with stains.

She inched her way down the path and when she got to Shirley's boat, she hammered on the railing with her walking stick and hollered.

"Shirley. Open up!"

⚜

"I'm knocked up, Doodley, and you done it." It had been two days since the old woman in the strange outfit had come to the boat, and Shirley could wait no longer; it was time to talk to Doodle Lee.

"They're saying I shouldn't have no more babies, and I don't know what to do."

"Who's saying?"

"I ain't for sure, but I think it's coming from them people at the Eugenics Center." She rubbed her swollen belly, fretted a bit, and then said, "They say me and you is living in sin and if I go on and have this baby by you they's gonna take my girls away."

Doodle got up and walked around the cabin. "Well, get rid of it. We don't need no trouble from the law."

"It ain't right to get rid of it, Doodley, and they ain't got no right to make me do it."

Doodle sat down by Shirley. "I don't want no trouble, Shirley."

Shirley backed off, and they did not talk about it for the rest of the night.

❖

When Shirley awoke the following morning, Doodle Lee was gone.

Shirley raised up in bed and looked to the corner where he kept his sea bag, but it was not there.

The son of a bitch. He ain't worth the powder it'd take to blow him up.

❖

On Wednesday, March 17, Shirley walked up the hill to town and stopped in front of a door to the left of the entrance to Booger's Pool Hall. A sign on the door showed an upward-pointing arrow and the words "Rooms for Rent."

Shirley pushed the door open and climbed the stairs to a hallway that had two rooms on the left and two on the right. She found the one marked No. 3 and knocked on the door. A runt of a man she did not know cracked open the door, and Shirley said, "Nurse Dagny told me to come here."

He nodded and opened the door wider. Shirley handed him $50 in cash and said, "She said I should give this to you to get things started."

The man took the money. "I'm Slim. I'll pick you up Friday morning at 8 o'clock. You be up on the hard road, standing right there by the path that goes down to the river. I'll be in a black Dodge pickup."

"OK," Shirley said. Then she left and went back to the boat.

❧

Late Thursday afternoon Shirley asked Kizzy if she would take care of her girls for the weekend, but she did not level with her about what she was going to do. Instead, she made up a cover story.

"Kizzy, Doodley's run off on me. He ain't no better'n the others. But I got a chance to go to Jonesboro for the weekend with an old boyfriend and I really need to go. I just need to get away so's I can think and get back to normal."

Kizzy did not hesitate. "OK. I'll watch them for you, and we'll have a good time too; the weather's supposed to be real nice."

❧

At 8 o'clock Friday morning, Shirley headed up the trail to the state road, and when she got to the top of the hill, she saw the black pickup. She climbed in on the passenger's side, and Slim pulled onto the road and headed north.

It was a half-hour drive to Leadwood, a small town on the north edge of Jasper County. Shirley tried to be nice, but Slim, who looked to be at least 65, was not a talker. He stared straight ahead the whole way, and when they entered the little town he made several turns that made no sense to Shirley. Then suddenly he pulled into the dirt driveway of a small run-down clapboard house. He parked alongside a tan Ford four-door sedan and motioned for Shirley to get out and go to the front door.

Nurse Dagny came to the door. She was in the same gray World War I nurse's uniform that she had on the day she came to Shirley's boat.

"This is the laying-in house. We'll be here all day, and we'll go see the doctor tonight." She took Shirley past a room where a young girl was lying in bed, writhing and softly moaning. "She'll be all right in a little while; it's always a little sore at first."

She led Shirley into a small bedroom and told her to sit on the side of the bed. "I'm going to put in a luminaria stick. It won't hurt, it's just dried seaweed, but it will swell up and that will open things up."

Shirley spent a boring day at the laying-in house, sleeping and worrying about what she was doing. Then, an hour after dark, Nurse Dagny came back into the bedroom. "Let's go, Shirley."

They got into the Ford sedan and drove a few blocks to a small cinder-block building that was set back off the street. A medium-size sign near the front steps said Dr. Marvin Quigly, M.D. General Practice, but a "closed" sign was hanging on the front door.

Nurse Dagny unlocked the front door to the clinic, looked over her shoulder to check the street in both directions, and then motioned for Shirley to come inside. It was a few minutes before 9 p.m. The lights were off in the reception area, but the lights in the rear of the building shone brightly enough to light a hallway that extended along the right side of the building.

Shirley followed Nurse Dagny down the hallway, but the old woman stopped abruptly when they were halfway to cuss and stomp at a half-dozen cockroaches that were scurrying for cover. Some escaped, but four did not. Nurse Dagny kicked the squashed bugs to the side, muttered a string of invectives, and signaled for Shirley to follow her to the end of the hall.

⚜

They entered what appeared to be an examination room, and Nurse Dagny pointed to a straight chair. "Sit there," Then she left the room.

Shirley looked around. A jumble of medical tools lay on a linoleum-covered counter to the left of a rust-stained porcelain sink, and a stack of hand towels and a large box of cotton filled the space to the right of the sink. The centerpiece of the room was a metal and porcelain examination table—with stirrups—that sat directly beneath a very bright light.

I ain't so sure about this.

She bowed her head to think, and that is when she noticed the mouse-trap in the corner to the right of her chair. There was a splotch of dried blood on the wooden base, but the trap was baited and set, ready to catch its next victim. Shirley looked away. *Yuk.*

Just then, Nurse Dagny reentered the room, followed by Doctor Marvin Quigly, a five-foot-two, 39-year-old man who had just made the news for crash-landing a single-engine Cessna airplane on the street in front of his ex-wife's house. The doctor told the authorities that he did it in a fit of jealousy, but there was more to it than that. Doctor Quigly, a manic depressive, frequently suffered week-long episodes of grandiosity, non-stop talking, and stupid risk-taking. He had managed to keep most of it away from the Medical Board, but those who worked around him knew the truth. Nurse Dagny once told Slim, "Doc's crazy as a road lizard."

Shirley knew none of that, so when Nurse Dagny introduced the doctor to her, all she saw was a middle-aged little man with disheveled hair. He seemed friendly enough, and he looked smarter than most of the men she had known. *He's OK, I guess.*

"Let's get started," Doctor Quigly said. And Nurse Dagny helped Shirley onto the examination table.

The doctor then started a rapid-fire conversation with the nurse, using medical terminology. Shirley could not keep up. *The man is a motor mouth.*

Finally, after saying the same thing in several different ways, the doctor concluded: "So, let's be sure we have this straight, Nurse Dagny. This pregnancy is about 13 weeks, but the patient has had a lot of trouble lately, and it appears from examination that the fetus is dead. We need to do a D&E to save the life of the mother—don't you agree?"

Nurse Dagny said, "Yes sir," and as she spoke, she put a wire-mesh mask over Shirley's face.

Shirley forced her words through the mask. "It ain't dead … and I ain't been havin' no trouble," but they ignored her.

"Breathe in and out, Shirley—I been givin' ether since I nursed in the First World War and it works real good." She dripped ether on the mask and began singing the nonsensical words of a new popular song, "Mairzy doats and dozy doats and liddle lamzy divey."

Shirley breathed the ether and a weird white line appeared in her mind's eye. It was making a circle, slowly, and short white cross pieces—laid across the line, one after another—gave it the look of a railroad track.

Doctor Quigly giggled for some reason. Then he started the abortion.

⚜

Shirley woke up at the laying-in house early Saturday morning. She remembered leaving the clinic and something she saw on her way out, but the rest of the night was a blur.

She spent all day Saturday and most of Sunday in bed, balled up in the fetal position, fighting cramps and suffering. Every so often, an episode of intense pain would pulse through her belly, and she would scream as loud as she could. Nurse Dagny would come to her side to console her, but she could not stop the painful attacks.

By mid-afternoon on Sunday, Shirley began to feel better. She went two hours without severe pain, and told Nurse Dagny she wanted to go home.

As soon as it got dark, Nurse Dagny helped Shirley into the Ford sedan, and a half-hour later they drove into Big Pearl. Slim met them at the path to the river and helped Shirley get down the hill and across the gangplank.

When Shirley stepped onto the boat, Kizzy opened the door. Shirley, hunched over and limping, cracked a tiny smile.

"What's wrong, Shirley?" Kizzy put her arm around Shirley's waist and together they got inside.

"What's wrong?" she asked again. But Shirley just shook her head, eased her way onto the bed, and then laid back. She whispered, "Don't wake the girls up … let 'em sleep."

Kizzy wet a towel and put it on her forehead, but Shirley said, "That feels good, but that ain't it, Kizzy. I ain't got no headache. It's something else." And she began to sob, softly at first, and then the tears came.

Shirley reached up and put her hand on Kizzy's cheek. "I didn't go to Jonesboro, Kizzy. I flat-out lied to you about that, and I feel awful about it."

"What's wrong with you, Shirley?"

"I got rid of the baby, and it's made me sore as all get-out."

Kizzy gave her a puzzled look.

"I had to do it. They get mad at me every time I get knocked up, but this time they was more serious. They was going to take my girls away from me for living in sin with Doodley."

"But he's gone."

"It wasn't me living with Doodley that pissed 'em off. It's us river rats having kids. That's it in a nutshell. Anyway, maybe they're right, maybe it was the best thing to do. All's I know for sure is that I don't want to lose the girls—not after losing my two boys."

Shirley sighed and turned her eyes away from Kizzy.

"You want me to tell you some stories like before—that'll perk you up."

Shirley did not answer, so Kizzy made up a funny story, complete with fairies and haints and wove it around Jane Austen's character, Lydia, and her elopement. She ended it with a punch line, "And the fairy made the soldier marry Lydia, and she did it without a shotgun."

Kizzy laughed at her own story, but Shirley did not. "It was a little boy, Kizzy. They tried to hide it from me, but they put it in a pan and I seen his little pecker." She broke down, sniveling and shaking her head. "I ain't no good."

Kizzy leaned over and kissed her on the cheek. "Don't say that, Shirley. It ain't so."

Shirley scooted over in bed to make room for Kizzy, and when she did, she grunted and winced in pain. Then she put her hand on Kizzy's heart and made her promise that she would not tell anyone about the baby. "Promise me, Kizzy. Doodley's gone and I ain't knocked up no more, so everything is going to be all right now. Promise me you won't ever tell anyone about what I done. It would just make trouble for the girls. Promise, Kizzy."

Kizzy nodded yes, and then she put a blanket over Shirley and lay down beside her. "I promise, Shirley."

❧

A ray of sunshine peeped through the riverside window of Shirley's house-boat and flashed across Kizzy's eyes, waking her from a deep sleep. It was eerily quiet. The girls were still asleep, but they would wake up soon. Kizzy leaned close to Shirley and put her hand on her forehead. She heard a faint rasping and smelled the foul odor of her breath, but Shirley seemed to be fast asleep. She was not groaning as she had the night before, but her lips were blue and she was sweating even though her face was cold and clammy.

Kizzy eased out of bed and made two peanut butter and jelly sand-wiches for the girls, taking care to be quiet. Then she rustled the girls to wake them up, and when they opened their eyes she put her forefinger to her mouth and said, "You all be quiet. Don't wake your ma up—she ain't feeling good. I've made you some breakfast, so you all take these sandwiches and go on up to the bollards and have a picnic."

As soon as they were dressed, she handed them the sack of sandwiches and shooed them out the door.

Then Kizzy went back to caring for Shirley. It was nearing 9 o'clock, and Shirley was groaning again. Kizzy sat by her and called her name, but Shirley did not respond. *It's like she's knocked out or something ...*

Kizzy pulled the covers back and that is when she saw a pool of blood beneath Shirley's hips that reached to her knees. It scared her so she tried to awaken Shirley, shaking her gently and calling out, "Shirley, Shirley."

Kizzy pulled the covers back up and said, "I'll be back, Shirley. I'm gonna go get the doctor."

⚜

Kizzy found Albert Monk sitting on the front stoop of his house, sipping coffee and reading the morning paper. The hand painted sign on his front door—Albert Monk, M.D.—spoke volumes. Everyone in town knew it was the very sign that had graced the front door of his medical office. But a dwindling practice forced him to vacate the space to save on expenses.

He was a bit of a legend in Big Pearl. Carlton Biggers—the philan-thropist who built the town—recruited Albert fresh out of medical school in 1899. And his practice flourished until 1920 when 35-year-old Sully Biggers inherited the Biggers fortune and seized control of the town. Sully did not like Albert; he steered patients to other doctors and did what he could to make life miserable for "Doctor Al," but he could not run him off.

Now, at age 68, Doctor Al worked out of his home, taking care of poor people. If a patient offered to pay, he would take a small amount of money, homegrown vegetables, or whatever, so that they would not feel like free-loaders. Doctor Al accepted the token payments graciously; he understood that the patients meant them as a tribute of respect.

"Hi, Kizzy." Doctor Al recognized her as soon as she rounded the corner, running full speed. "What's the hurry?"

"Shirley's bad sick, Doctor Al. Can you come down to the boat and see about her? Please, Doctor Al. She's out like a light."

"I'll get my bag."

⚜

"Hold on, Kizzy, I'm not as young as I used to be."

Kizzy slowed down several times to let him catch up, and when they started down the path to Shirley's boat, she stopped again to holler at the girls who were still playing around the bollards. "You all stay put until I come get you."

Doctor Al smiled and waved to the girls. *Those must be Shirley's girls— they look just like her.*

He knew Kizzy, but he had never treated her. MeeMaw would not let him doctor her or her mother, Sarah, because he once told MeeMaw: "There is no such thing as a haint." She never went back to him, nor would she allow her girls to see him. Even so, the attractive Kizzy had caught the doctor's eye, and he had said hello to her several times.

It's a miracle that they can live on fish and cornmeal and turn out so well. She must be close to 15 now ... I don't know how they live down here, particularly in the winter, but they're tough as a boot, that's for sure.

He followed Kizzy onto the boat and sat on the side of the bed next to Shirley. He took a stethoscope from his bag and put it against Shirley's chest, and Kizzy hovered behind him, wringing her hands. Then she blurted out, "She's bleeding real bad from down there, Doctor Al. Pull the cover back … you'll see what I mean."

He pulled the cover down. *Uh-oh. She's hemorrhaging—no telling how long it's been going on, but it's not good.*

"Shirley?" He called her name several times, but she did not respond.

"Did she say anything to you about this, Kizzy?"

Kizzy hesitated, and then said, "No, sir."

He looked Kizzy in the eye. "You're sure?"

She nodded.

Well … Kizzy's young. She probably doesn't know what's wrong, but I do. I've seen this before—too many times. There was the young girl who tried to do it herself using a coat hanger and then couldn't get the coat hanger out of her cervix. And the woman who tried to kill the fetus with a broken Coke bottle. I saved both of them, but they got to me sooner than poor Shirley.

Then there was that 25-year-old woman who got butchered by that quack who passes himself off as a doctor. He botched a D&E, but I saved her, barely.

I tried to get Bully's hand-picked prosecutor to charge that idiot, but he didn't give a damn because the girl was poor. He told me there was no way he could make a case against the quack. But he didn't give a shit—that was the real problem—and it still is. Bully's Eugenics Center is at the heart of all this. I've heard his speeches about breeding and the need for sterilization. What a fool.

Doctor Al leaned over and put his ear close to Shirley's face. Her breathing was very shallow and irregular, and her pulse was weak; she had gone beyond pain. *She's a goner. She's tough like all the river people, but she's not going to last much longer—she's lost too much blood and she's been in shock too long. I could send her to Jonesboro to cover my ass, but she'd never make it.*

I could turn this case in, but Shirley's going to die, and Kizzy doesn't know anything. It'll wind up just like the case against the quack—more trouble than it's worth.

I'll just put this down as a miscarriage, complications, shock and hemorrhaging.

"Kizzy, there's nothing I can do. She's too far gone. It's just a case of female trouble—that's what it is."

Kizzy collapsed on the girls' bunk and cried.

Doctor Al stayed, but Shirley Barden died just before noon on March 21. "I'm sorry, Kizzy. Shirley's gone."

⚜

"March 23, 1943

Dear Birdie,

Shirley's gone on down the river. I will miss her forever, and I know you will too.

They tell me that the Red Cross and the USO and the Marines will tell you about her passing, but I was with her at the end so I figured I should write to you about it even though I hate to.

The girls are going to be OK. My new friend Olivia has made sure that they are with good foster parents, and the money Shirley got from the Army for Milton and Layton getting killed in action will go for their upkeep.

Doctor Al was with Shirley and me when she died. He said she died of female trouble, but it all began with her getting pregnant again. I don't know much more that I can say about it that would make it easier to take, but I trust Doctor Al and he says things like this happen a lot.

We got her put away in a metal coffin, and they buried her real close to where they put Ma.

I put a memorial for Shirley in the library window for the Easter display. It's a picture of her and the service flag that she was so proud of. I'll make sure it stays up for the Fourth of July too.

Take care of yourself.

Love,

Kizzy"

XLIV

Talent Contest

"Oct. 4, 1943

Dear Birdie,

Guess what? I'm going to be in a talent contest at the high school next month. I'm going to sing and my boyfriend—his name is Stefan—is going to play the fiddle (he calls it a violin). We're going to do "The Magic of Your Eyes" It was one of MeeMaw's favorites.

I wish you could be here for it, but Uncle Mac says you and the Marines are beating the tar out of the Japs—so I know that is where you have to be.

I'm 15 now and in the 10th grade. Can you believe it? I like school—always have. And the town kids have been nicer to me since Olivia gave me some hand-me-downs to wear.

I went to the graveyard yesterday to see everyone. I put some late wildflowers—Black-eyed Susans—by Shirley's marker and said some words for you.

It's been almost seven months since she went on down the river and I still can't get over how fast it happened. I wish you were here so we could talk about her and old times, like we used to do.

Oh—I almost forgot—your boat's OK. Cormac and I have been taking care of it for you.

Be careful, wherever you are.

Love,

Kizzy"

❧

On Sunday, Oct. 10, the sound of music filled Stefan's house. Kizzy was singing a line from the second verse of "The Magic of Your Eyes."

She was pleased with her rendition, but Stefan suddenly quit playing. He took the violin from beneath his chin and frowned, shaking his head and mumbling.

Kizzy kept on singing. "Eyes that speak to me alone, of a secret of their own." But when she saw the look on Stefan's face she stopped and wrinkled her nose. "What's wrong?"

"It's just not right, Kizzy." He grimaced, and shook his head back and forth. I think we ought to do 'That Old Black Magic.' It's real popular right now."

"No. This is the song that MeeMaw used to sing to Grandpa when I was little. I love it, and I'm not changing."

"Then we need to pick up the tempo—do it in three-quarter time—make it peppy and interesting."

"I've been singing it this way all my life."

"That doesn't make it right."

She glared at him. "I'm doing the best I can, Stefan."

He gave her a sheepish look and laid his violin on the table by the bed. He reached out to hug her, but she wheeled away.

"I'm sorry, Kizzy. It's not you ... your voice is beautiful. I just think we can do better."

Kizzy plopped down on the bed to show her frustration. *Dang it. I like the way I've been doing it.* She looked Stefan in the eye and started to argue with him, but decided against it. *He ain't mad or anything. I ought to hear him out ... but first ...* She took Stefan by the hand and pulled him down beside her, and they did what they had done before. They kissed and explored each other, but they stopped short of serious sex. Kizzy thought to herself: *He wants to do it, I know that for sure—but he ain't going to—and I ain't going to push him.*

Stefan was aroused, as usual, and Kizzy teased him about having a hard on, but she had come to respect the limits that he had learned from his mother. *He ain't Horsey Hairs. That's for sure. That jerk's been trying to get in my pants ever since the start of school. Stefan's better than that. He says there's more to the boy-girl thing than just doing it.*

They lay on the bed for a while longer, but soon the fever cooled. And when it did, Stefan picked up his violin and began to play. Kizzy smoothed her skirt, and stood beside him. "OK, what is it you want to change?"

"We've been playing and singing the song just as it's written with no interludes, no creativity. I think the audience will like it better if we jazz it up, string it out, and toss in a little showmanship."

"Show me what you mean."

Stefan picked up his violin and sawed off a peppy version. "Now, you sing the first verse and then, while I'm repeating that melody, you do some play-acting to show how the magic is working on you."

She laughed. "I get it. I'll sing a verse about how the magic of your eyes has thrown me for a loop, then, while you are playing, I'll do my best imitation of MeeMaw rubbing on her crystal ball and talking to the haints."

"That's not exactly what I had in mind," Stefan said. "But it'll get us started."

⚜

The Big Pearl High School Talent Show began as a typical high school event, attended mostly by the relatives of contestants and a smattering of students. But in its 15th year the show filled the school's auditorium, thanks to a performance by Bubba Catlett, a rawboned cowboy type with a voice like Gene Autry. Bubba won first place and went on to a singing career at the Grand Ole Opry.

After that, the school moved the show to the Big Pearl Opera House, a facility that had better acoustics and 350 theater seats. The amateurish show caught on with the public, and tickets to the 1943 performance of "The Show" sold out weeks in advance.

Stefan and Kizzy arrived early even though they would perform last, a stroke of good fortune that Stefan attributed to the mysterious incantations that Kizzy muttered just before drawing for position. Bully Bigshot's granddaughter, Belinda Biggers, would be next-to-last. Her accordion number would follow a boy who was going to play the spoons in his fourth and final attempt to win first place.

Earlier acts, listed on the program, included a tap dancer, a ventriloquist using homemade FDR and Hitler dummies, a barbershop quartet, a boy playing the Jew's harp, and four singers including Horsey Hairs who planned to sing "Ol' Man River."

The Opera House filled 10 minutes before start time. Eli, Rachel, Fritz, Olivia and her mother, and Sweetcheeks were seated together on the front row. And just before curtain time Dynamite McFadden—hollering for people to clear the way—pushed Uncle Mac to a wide spot in the aisle by Olivia.

Bully Bigshot, his wife, and T. K. "Gunner" Brown, the sheriff of Jasper County, had the seats directly behind Fritz, but Bully was not sitting down. He was standing up, promoting his granddaughter to all within earshot, "She's the best accordion player in town. She ought to win this thing hands-down. You'll see." The people seated nearby granted Bully the tolerance customarily afforded to grandparents, but he kept it up, became obnoxious, and lost his audience. Then he sat down, and whispered to his wife, "I can't believe that our granddaughter has to perform on the same stage with a foreigner and a river rat; trash like that."

The crowd noise—a mix of laughter, loud talking, and shuffling—was an odd buzz by the time it reached the holding room where Kizzy and Stefan and the other contestants waited for their turn to perform.

Kizzy could not sit still. She had a case of stage fright that worried Stefan. "Relax, Kizzy."

She took a deep breath, but continued to hyperventilate and wring her hands. "I ain't got no business going out there in front of that crowd." She wiped her brow, and whispered to Stefan. "I'm just a river rat and that's all they're going to see."

Stefan put his arm around her to calm her down. "Everybody gets scared before they go on, but the only ones who need to worry about it are the ones who have no talent, and that's not you, Kizzy. They're going to love you."

The show started and the chairs in the holding room began to empty. Finally, it was time for Bully's granddaughter, and as she left the room she wished Kizzy and Stefan good luck, and they returned the courtesy.

Belinda Biggers had a pretty face that favored her mother, but she had Bully's pudginess, and that gave her a homely look. But the girl could play. Her accordion solo was the best act so far, and the corny polka she played had the audience rocking, stomping, and clapping.

Stefan and Kizzy were in the wings, just offstage, when the audience called Belinda Biggers back to take another bow. Kizzy's heart sank. But suddenly it was their turn, and when they walked onstage they got a polite welcome, tepid in contrast to what they had just heard.

Kizzy was wearing her black outfit with a small witch's hat perched on her head, and Stefan had a shawl around his neck to which Kizzy had attached a score of MeeMaw's most colorful tarot cards. Stefan carried his violin in one hand and a pedestal stand in the other. When they reached stage center he sat the pedestal down and Kizzy sat a crystal ball on it. The audience stirred as the theme of mysterious magic began to sweep away the memory of Belinda's polka.

No one in Big Pearl had ever heard Stefan play, so the audience was shocked when the boy who had mastered Mendelssohn at the age of 7 played the song that Kizzy would sing. They noticed how he showed his love for the music as he played, but they could not keep their eyes off Kizzy when she took a few tarot cards from the pedestal and fanned them in her hands as if she were telling a fortune.

Stefan neared the end of the melody, and when he winked at Kizzy, she smiled. Her stage fright was gone, and when she sang the first verse of "The Magic in Your Eyes," another kind of magic swept through the crowd.

Kizzy's voice was clear and full of feeling. The cute couple—a blond-haired boy and a redheaded girl—had captured the audience.

Then they did what they had practiced. Stefan played an interlude, and as he did, Kizzy rubbed the crystal ball, pretending to be a fortune-teller. Then at the perfect moment she sang the next verses, and when she got to the final lyrics she belted them out, strong and full of meaning. "All my soul is yearning for the love-light burning in the magic of your eyes."

The audience shouted "Bravo," and gave them a standing ovation. And when they tried to leave the stage the audience called them back, twice.

The judges quickly announced the five finalists, and the performers came on stage, waiting expectantly.

Bully's granddaughter got second place, and the crowd gave her a nice round of applause. She bowed and shrugged politely as she looked at her grandfather.

Stefan and Kizzy won first place, and when the master of ceremonies asked them to do a short encore the audience cheered. Stefan played and Kizzy sang the last verse, but the audience noticed a difference. Kizzy was smiling from ear to ear, and so was Stefan.

⚜

Bully Bigshot was livid. He tried to hide it when the master of ceremonies announced the winners, but his heart was too full of hate, perplexed that a foreigner and a river rat could outdo his blood kin.

As the crowd started to leave, Bully spoke to the sheriff in a stage whisper, "Can you believe it? They gave first place to a river rat and that tow-headed boy. What's this world coming to?"

Fritz heard Bully's diatribe and gave him a dirty look, but it had no effect. Bully continued to gripe to the sheriff, and by the time he reached the exit, he was looking and sounding like Rumpelstiltskin. He nudged the sheriff and pointed at Fritz Halder. "Who does that guy think he is?"

The sheriff nodded to show his sympathy, and then Bully said, "Who is he anyway? And where in the hell did he come from?"

XLV

Spies

Sheriff T. K. "Gunner" Brown was the ringleader of Bully Bigshot's political hierarchy. He was the lickspittle-in-chief—second to none—and every elected official from governor on down knew it. Gunner was Bully's eyes and ears; he marked the sparrow's fall. Every political tidbit—important or innocuous—flowed first to the sheriff. It was he—and only he—who decided what to tell Bully. And if Bully wanted something done, he would tell Gunner, who would pass the order to the appropriate lackey.

The sheriff was born to be a toady. His was not a case of wanting praise; Gunner Brown needed praise. He fed on it, and when it came from the exalted one—Bully Bigshot—it slaked his thirst, but always left him wanting more.

Thus, the only thing that was better than getting praise from Bully was the expectation of it. On those occasions, Sheriff Gunner Brown could not hide his excitement—his unbounded pride.

On Monday, Nov. 29, a week after the talent contest, Gunner burst out of his office and began a two-block strut that would take him to Bully Bigshot's office. Everyone in his office, and everyone he met on the street, recognized the giddy look. The sheriff was on to something. He was puffed up and reared back, and his step had a dancelike cadence. He was tipping his hat and grinning big, and the show continued until he was standing before Bully's secretary.

"Is Sully in, Sweetie?" Gunner asked only as a formality; he could see that the door to Bully's office was half-open.

"Come on in, Gunner."

Gunner pushed the door open, took the last few steps of his satisfying strut, removed his hat, and stood at attention—a wide grin on his face.

Bully knew the look. "OK, let's have it."

"He's a German. The smart-ass at the talent contest—he ain't no Dutchman. He's a goddamn German!"

Bully said. "Well, I'll be damned." He paused, squinting his eyes. "How'd you find out?"

"I asked Hoot—the guy, Fritz Halder, works for him—and Hoot says he came here from Willich, Pa. So I called the police there and they knew right away who I was talking about. They said he and his wife came from Germany about six years ago with a little boy, but she died and he and the boy moved away."

"I bet the son-of-a-bitch is a spy," Bully said. "Why else would he tell us he's Dutch, and all that. Damned Krauts …"

He picked up the phone and dialed a number, and when the call went through he said, "Put Joe on the line … this is Sully Biggers calling, and it's important."

It had taken Bully 20 years to build his finely tuned political machine. Unlike his father and grandfather, who left a legacy of philanthropy and good works, Bully's claim to fame was a disciplined machine that took no prisoners and tolerated no disloyalty or procrastination.

Congressman Joe Pratt understood the rules; he won his seat in Congress only because Bully's machine got behind him.

"Yes sir, Sully, what can I do for you?"

"We've got a German in Big Pearl that has been passing himself off as a Dutchman. He must be hiding something. We need to get this Nazi-lover and his boy out of town."

The congressman listened as Bully told him what the sheriff had learned from the police in Willich.

"This is something the FBI needs to know. I'll call Clyde Tolson and tell him; he's J. Edgar Hoover's right-hand man."

⚜

A few days later Fritz and Stefan were home listening to *The Adventures of Ellery Queen*, their favorite nighttime radio show. The announcer had just read a Bromo-Seltzer promotion, and it was time for the show's celebrity panel to solve the mystery. Stefan loved this part of the show; he and Fritz would listen to the panelists, and then they would disclose their own solutions before Ellery Queen solved the case.

Stefan did not wait for the show's last panelist to finish talking. "No, that's not right. The clues are plain as day ... Ellery Queen will ..."

Just then, someone banged on the front door three times so hard that it shook on its hinges. "Fritz Halder, open up!"

Neither Stefan nor Fritz heard Ellery Queen's solution to the mystery that night because the door banging continued, louder than before.

Fritz headed toward the door, "*Verdammt!* It's almost 7:30, who could that be?"

Fritz opened the door, but before he could speak, the smallest of three big men flashed a badge. "FBI! Are you Fritz Halder?"

As soon as Fritz said yes, the men pushed their way into the house. The smallest man turned the radio off and told Stefan to sit down and stay put. Then he turned to Fritz. "I am Special Agent Lenny Langford. Let me see your alien registration card."

Fritz walked across the room and started to open a roll-top desk, but the agent told him to back away. Agent Langford opened the desktop, looked for weapons, and then motioned for Fritz to get the card.

Fritz opened a small drawer, removed the card, and handed it to the agent. "You are not properly registered."

"But I am. As you can see, I registered in February of 1941 before the deadline. My wife, Annemarie, was sick, but I went to the Post Office in Willich, Pa., and registered as soon as I could."

"Yes, we know," Langford said. "But you have not filed a change of address notice since you moved to Arkansas on Aug. 15, 1941, more than two years ago."

"Can't I do that now?"

"It's too late for that. Besides, you have violated another registration law. After Pearl Harbor, President Roosevelt signed a proclamation requiring people from Germany, Japan, and Italy to register again, as "enemy aliens."

Fritz looked at Stefan, and shrugged his shoulders in a nonchalant manner.

One of the larger agents took offense, braced Fritz up against the wall, and got in his face. "You shrug your shoulders, but this is serious. You did not register, and you have been telling everyone around here that you are Dutch."

"I have never said that," Fritz said. "I told everyone I was Pennsylvania Dutch and people began saying that I was Dutch. My boss even started calling me 'Dutch.'"

Agent Langford scowled. "Why did you come to Arkansas?"

"I have a friend in Jonesboro who encouraged me—he said it is a good place to live, and it is." Fritz pointed at Stefan. "His mother, my wife, died of cancer and we couldn't get her off our mind. We needed a change of scenery."

"We know about your friend in Jonesboro. We arrested him last week, and he is on his way to a relocation camp in Texas."

"For what?"

The third agent, who had said nothing, spoke. "We'll ask the questions, Herr Halder." He looked around. "If you want to help yourself I'm sure you will not mind if we search your house."

"Go ahead," Fritz said. "I don't have anything to hide."

It took the agents less than an hour to search the small house; they seemed to know what they were looking for. They collected a stack of books, magazines, and letters, and took several photographs. Fritz and Stefan sat on the couch, waiting, and when the search was over Special Agent Langford pulled a folded paper from inside his suit coat.

"Fritz Halder, you are under arrest for violating the Alien Registration Act of 1940, and failing to register as an enemy alien as required by Presidential Proclamation 2537 and orders issued thereunder. We will hold you in the county jail; there will be a hearing in a few days to determine your status. The boy can stay here at home tonight, but he must report to the sheriff's office tomorrow at 4 p.m."

"What will happen to us?"

"That's not for us to say."

⚜

Stefan spent the night with Eli and Rachel, but at first light he slipped out of the house and went down to the river to tell Kizzy that he might be in trouble for not registering as an enemy alien.

He stood at the gangplank and called her name, but there was no answer.

Inside the boat, Kizzy lifted Cormac's arm from around her waist and got out of bed. She hurried to the door and peeped out just as Stefan hollered for a second time.

"Hey, Stefan. What's wrong?"

"The FBI came to our house last night and arrested Fritz for not registering as an enemy alien." He kicked at the gangplank, but missed. "They may send him away, and I may be in trouble for the same thing."

Cormac suddenly appeared in the doorway, bare-chested, towering over Kizzy. "Don't bring your troubles down here, boy."

"I don't mean to, sir. I just wanted Kizzy to know in case they take me away."

Kizzy pushed Cormac back, and fussed at him. Then she said, "Wait for me up by the bollards, Stefan. It's almost time to go to school; you can tell me all about it on the way."

Kizzy got dressed, and as they walked to school Stefan told her what the FBI said, and what they did, but he could not answer when she asked what might happen to him. "I don't know, but Eli has called a lawyer in Memphis who is going to help us."

"MeeMaw said lawyers can't be trusted."

"Eli says this one's OK. He's a young Jewish guy who's done something for the Japanese people who've been sent to those camps in south Arkansas."

"I heard about the Japs being sent to camps, but why are they taking Fritz? And why would they take you?"

"We're German, Kizzy. The government is sending Germans to camps too." Stefan wrinkled his brow. "That's what Eli says, but I don't know much more about it than that."

Kizzy and Stefan talked again at morning recess, and they planned to eat lunch together. But when they walked into the lunch room the students shunned them. Then the razzing began. Word of Fritz's arrest had reached Big Pearl High School shortly before noon and it was spreading like a bad rash, gathering malice as it traveled through the student body. Hateful epithets—Nazi, Kraut, and Heinie—were part of every accusation. Stefan could do nothing to stop the onslaught, and when Kizzy tried to help him the students turned on her; she became a "Nazi-lover."

⚜

On Friday, Dec. 10, 1943, a five-member civilian hearing board, hastily convened by the Department of Justice, held a hearing. A lawyer from the United States Attorney's office in Little Rock called and questioned the witnesses against Fritz Halder.

Special Agent Lenny Langford testified first. He said Fritz had failed to register as an enemy alien, that he was hiding out in Big Pearl, posing as Dutch instead of German, and that he had attended a meeting of a German front organization—The Brandenburg Social Club—when he lived in Willich.

Then he told what the agents had found in their search of the house: A shortwave radio, a postcard from an uncle in Hamburg dated June 23, 1938 that had a picture of Hitler on it, and a letter from a cousin in Berlin dated January 12, 1938 praising Hitler for bringing Germany out of depression.

After Langford's testimony the board members, two of whom were part of Bully Bigshot's political machine, seemed to lose interest.

Eli's young lawyer friend, Ruben Levy, managed to make a brief opening statement. He claimed the process was a denial of due process. He said he was appealing several similar cases for Japanese internees, but he spoke overlong and the board members began to squirm. The government attorney interrupted him, saying his time had expired, but Ruben kept on talking until the chairman ordered him to "Sit down and shut up."

Ruben was not allowed to question Agent Langford or a damaging witness—a full-time employee of Bully Bigshot—who testified that he heard Fritz express sympathy for what the Nazis were doing in Germany.

Fritz did testify, briefly. He apologized for not registering as an enemy alien, saying he was unaware of the requirement to register a second time. He denied the other accusations, said he got the shortwave radio from Sears, and pledged his loyalty to the United States. When he finished the chairman asked why Stefan did not register, and Fritz took the blame for that.

Lawyer Ruben Levy called Eli to the stand. He vouched for Stefan and told the board he would serve as his foster parent and be responsible for his actions.

The board was ready to make its decision, but Dynamite McFadden stood up in the back of the room and hollered as loud as he could. "Hold on!" He pushed Uncle Mac down the aisle in his wheelchair.

When he was close to where the board members were sitting, Uncle Mac said, "I want to testify in this kangaroo court."

The government lawyer did not know Uncle Mac. He objected, but the chairman knew Uncle Mac and realized it would be a mistake to prevent a war hero from testifying.

Uncle Mac wasted no time. He pointed to his scars and said, "The Germans shot me up in World War I and I've been in this wheelchair for 25 years, but I don't hate them for it. People on both sides get caught up in war, but that doesn't make them bad people. I know Fritz Halder and Stefan, and they are good people. Fritz is a good bricklayer and an asset to the community. Some of the best people I know are the Germans who live up in Pocahontas and over at Subiaco. Let this man register, but don't send him away. He is not a danger to the United States. That is poppycock, and you all know it."

The chairman thanked Uncle Mac, then the board retired to deliberate, and 10 minutes later they returned. The lawyer for the Department of Justice read the finding of the board:

"Fritz Halder, the board finds that you did not register as an enemy alien as required by law. Furthermore, we find that you purposely claimed to be Dutch instead of German, and that you have done and said things that are potentially dangerous to the peace and security of the United States. The government will transport you to Fort Lincoln, Bismarck, N.D., and you will be interned there for the duration of the war, unless these findings are changed by the Alien Enemy Control Unit in Washington, D. C."

And, in a split decision, the board decided to let Stefan stay in Big Pearl with Eli and Rachel; however, as a 15-year-old born in Germany, he was required to register as an enemy alien.

⚜

On Christmas Eve 1943, Stefan was sitting at the dinner table with Eli and Rachel Schulman. They had just celebrated the third day of Hanukkah with the customary serving of potato cakes, fried breads, and pastries.

Stefan read from a letter he received that day from Fritz. "He says it is very cold and snowing in North Dakota, but he has made a place for himself in the barracks with other Germans. He says he is doing fine and wishes me a Merry Christmas."

Rachel frowned. "I feel sorry for him and all the others who have been locked up as if they are criminals, and now Ruben Levy says there is talk of sending some of the internees back to Germany in exchange for Americans."

Stefan was listening, but he was also thinking. *Thank God I'm not locked up, but I'm catching hell at school, and that's not going to get any better.*

Kizzy and I made many new friends after the talent contest, but this has turned everything around.

Eli bowed his head. "Let's pray for Fritz."

"And for all those who are victims of the war," Rachel said as she bowed her head.

Stefan thought to himself, but he did not pray with Eli and Rachel. *Merry Christmas, Fritz.*

XLVI

Shame

On New Year's Day, 1944, Cormac left the boat just before sunup to go squirrel hunting. As soon he stepped off the gangplank, Kizzy got out of bed and tuned the radio to a Memphis station that played rhythm and blues music. And it was not long before Louis Jordan was singing "Ration Blues," the No. 1 song on the charts.

Kizzy smiled; she loved the song. The government was rationing tires, gasoline, shoes, sugar, coffee, meats, cheese, even bicycles and typewriters. It was hard on the townspeople, but it had not been that much of a burden for river people. They knew how to get by on the basics: cornmeal, flour, lard, dried beans, wild meats, and fish.

This was a big day for her. Olivia had persuaded Mabel to hire Kizzy for 25 cents an hour to stack books, do odd jobs and run errands. Mabel agreed upon the condition that she would stop saying "ain't," and Kizzy readily agreed to her terms.

She was dressed and ready to go by 7:30, eager to start her first day's work. But the library was not going to open until 9 o'clock, so Kizzy did busy work on the boat to dampen her enthusiasm and kill time. By 8 o'clock, she had run out of things to do, so she sat down to read. Olivia had given her a book of short stories by Rudyard Kipling, and she had bookmarked "The Janeites."

It took the best part of an hour for Kizzy to finish the story, but she now had two reasons to get to work on time: The excitement of her first job, and an eagerness to ask Olivia about the Janeites.

⚜

Olivia and Mabel got to the library well before opening time; they had a number of New Year's Day events planned for the people of Big Pearl.

Olivia saw Kizzy at the front door five minutes before opening time, peering in and waving. *She's eager to get started.* She turned to Mabel. "There's Kizzy. Now be nice to her, Mabel. It's going to take a while for her to stop saying 'ain't.'"

Mabel laughed. "I will, but Kizzy's already figured out that my bark is worse than my bite."

As soon as Olivia opened the door, Kizzy said, "Are we Janeites, Olivia? I hope so."

Aha! She's read the Kipling story. "Well, you could say that, but it's best to simply enjoy Jane Austen's writing. We don't have to join the Janeites to do that.

Kizzy was crestfallen. "But I like the idea of a secret society of Janeites with a password, and all that. And I know MeeMaw would like it."

She's still hooked on MeeMaw's mysticism; it's ingrained.

Kizzy pressed on. "The password for the Janeites, 'Tilneys and trapdoors', was taken from *Northanger Abbey*. I'm getting ready to read it, and when I'm finished I will have read all of her books."

Olivia persisted. "I agree that clubs and societies like the Janeites can be fun. They allow casual friends to talk about politics, movies, and sports. But Kizzy, the human heart longs for intimate fellowship and the sharing of feelings without fear of judgment, and that requires loyalty, mutual trust, and love. That's what real friendships are all about—sharing the things that bother us, the things we'd rather keep secret."

Kizzy teared up and looked away.

Olivia paused. *Uh-oh. I've touched a nerve. I need to be more patient.*

✦

Kizzy wiped her tears away. *I want that kind of friendship, but she doesn't know about Cormac—nobody does—and I can't tell her about that, ever. They'd run me out of here on a rail, and I'm just getting started. Besides, there's more than one way of looking at such things.*

MeeMaw, Ma, and Shirley had their own ways, and so did Boopie and Elsie Sue.

I'd like to be more like Olivia, but she ain't ... isn't always right when it comes to us river rats and the way we live.

I see her point about the Janeites, but I like the idea of being friends with other Jane Austen fans. I've never been part of anything. Olivia has plenty of good friends and connections so she doesn't need the Janeites like I do. Besides, Jane Austen is for everyone, river rats as well as silk-stocking folks.

"Are you OK, Kizzy?"

Kizzy nodded, but looked down. "I was just thinking. All that talk about sharing our burdens and heartbreak made me think of poor Shirley Barden. I'll be OK in a minute."

"We can have a password if you want to. I think it would be fun."

"How about Barton Cottage?" Kizzy said.

"Good. We'll use that whenever we want to talk privately and share secrets."

✦

On a cold Saturday morning a month later, Kizzy was at the library shelving books with Olivia. Stefan came by just before lunch and asked, "Would you like to go to the picture show this afternoon?"

Kizzy looked at Olivia. "You can go, Kizzy; your work is all caught up."

Later, as they neared the Opera House Kizzy said, "I've loved this place ever since we won the talent contest."

Stefan smirked and pretended to play a violin. "That was before the FBI took Fritz away. If the judges had known that I am from Germany we would have come in dead last."

Stefan put 20 cents through a small semicircle cutout in the ticket window and held up two fingers. They handed the tickets to an usher, bought a bag of popcorn, and found two seats in the back, the notorious smooching rows where most of the high schoolers kissed and petted, undisturbed by the horde of screaming youngsters that filled the front rows.

The newsreel for Feb. 12, 1944, came on first. It told the sad story of the Bataan Death March in the Philippines. The atrocity had occurred a year earlier after thousands of American soldiers and Marines surrendered, but the U. S. Office of War Information delayed release of information about the event to protect those who were still in custody. Kizzy gasped when the announcer told how the Japanese forced the captured troops to walk 60 miles in blazing heat, and if they faltered they were tortured, shot or beheaded. *Birdie. Be careful, Birdie.*

She could not take any more; she closed her eyes and covered her ears and did not look up until she heard the introductory music for the weekly serial *The Masked Marvel.* It was a welcome relief; everyone knew that the hero—patterned after the Lone Ranger—was going to fight and defeat Japanese spies.

When the serial ended, they watched the entire *Bugs Bunny* cartoon. The feature films that followed—two cheaply made westerns—gave them plenty of opportunities to take full advantage of the smooching rows.

And when the matinee was over they hurried to a little ice cream parlor next door to the theater. The soda jerk was busy, and every so often he would shout, "One scoop per person—don't blame me, blame rationing." Kizzy ordered a root beer float, and Stefan got a small chocolate sundae.

They sat in a booth at the back of the store, away from the distinctive racket of kids screaming for ice cream. Stefan said, "I thought the Gene Autry picture was better than the ..."

"Better than what?" Kissy said.

"Don't look now ... here comes Horsey Hairs."

Horace C. Ayers stopped halfway to their booth. "I didn't know they served sauerkraut here."

Stefan did not respond. Horace sneered and roostered around, but the smattering of laughter that followed his insulting remark quickly gave way to the clamor of hungry kids.

"I'd like to punch him in the nose, or tell him to shove it," Stefan said. "But Eli says that's what bullies want you to do. Being a Jew, he has a lot of experience with that sort of thing. He says, 'Ignore the insults, do your best, and wait for people to come around.' I think he's right, but it's hard to do."

"Do you like living with Eli and Rachel?"

Stefan nodded. "I miss Fritz, but they're good to me, and I like them a lot."

"I feel the same way about Olivia. I ain't … I'm not living with her, but I talk to her about lots of stuff, especially Jane Austen's books. I think she feels sorry for me because I'm a river rat, but she never says that."

"Don't call yourself a river rat."

Kizzy laughed, "It's OK for me to call myself a river rat. It only makes us river rats mad when town folks call us that."

"I bet Olivia helps you because she likes you, not because she feels sorry for you."

"Maybe, but she gave me some hand-me-downs so I wouldn't look like a river rat, and now she's busy trying to change the way I think about things. She never runs down MeeMaw or the ways of the river, but Olivia's fancy, like the people in Jane Austen's books. I can tell that she wants me to be more like that."

Stefan laughed. "I can't see you wearing wigs and acting like they did 150 years ago."

Kizzy shook her head. "Jane Austen's books are about old times, but she mainly writes about the good and bad in people. Her books are really about how we ought to treat one another with respect."

"Well, that's a good way to be."

"Yep." Kizzy pondered for a second. "Olivia means well, but the ways of the river ain't … aren't all bad."

⚜

Olivia wanted Kizzy to go with her to church. She tried several approaches, but none of them worked.

In the days before Easter Sunday, she decided to try again. *I think it would be good for her, but I better not use the Jesus-saves approach; I've tried that before and she takes it as an attack on MeeMaw and the river way of life.*

On Good Friday morning they were shelving books in the music section; Kizzy was in an upbeat mood, talking about her songwriting. Olivia saw it as an opportunity. "We are going to have a beautiful service at my church this Sunday. It's Easter, and there'll be lots of fresh flowers, and the choir will be singing plenty of good music. Would you like to go with me?"

Kizzy did not answer right away. She squeezed a book into place on the shelf, and as she did she said, "OK."

Olivia did a double take, and then chuckled. "Good, meet me in front of the church a few minutes before 11 o'clock."

⚜

Easter Sunday was a beautiful spring day. Kizzy put on the light blue skirt and matching blouse, spent extra time fixing her hair, and then walked from the boat to the First Methodist Church of Big Pearl. She got there 15 minutes early but did not see Olivia.

Kizzy waited on the street near the entrance. The gathering churchgoers gave her curious looks, and a few told her they liked her rendition of "The Magic of Your Eyes" and congratulated her for winning the talent contest.

Olivia, uncommonly tardy, spotted Kizzy standing alone, looking out of place. *It's a wonder she didn't leave.* Olivia caught her eye and waved, and then hurried to where she was standing. "Sorry I'm running late. Let's go in."

They found two seats in the balcony next to a stained glass window depicting Jesus at Gethsemane, cloaked in a red robe. The seats were close to where Kizzy and Shirley sat for John Decker's memorial two years earlier. As they settled into their seats, a ray of bright mid-day sun shone through the red robe as if on cue. It swept across Kizzy's red hair, lighting it and her blue outfit, and as it passed Olivia mused. The congregants were transfixed, studying Kizzy; a girl transformed. *Aha, the ragamuffin in catalog clothes is no more, and they are stunned. The drab moth has become a butterfly of many colors.*

Olivia fought back a smile, and then she peeked at Kizzy out of the corner of her eye. *Look at that. She doesn't see or feel their astonishment or care about it. She's soaking up the sights and sounds of Easter Sunday: The stained glass art, the altar peeking from behind the wall of orchids and lilies. The choir cloaked in purple vestments ... their voices filling the sanctuary ... singing the Hallelujah Chorus in concert with organ music. And, yes ... would you look? Her nose is wrinkling, ever so gently ... it's the orchids... the candles ... the lilies ... the perfumed people ... Ha!*

The preacher told the resurrection story beautifully, but when he got to the subject of redemption, he surprised the worshipers by linking it to "forgiveness for the sins of sexual transgression." He railed against the evils of fornication, adultery, and other sins of the flesh. Then he compared grownup evildoers to the purity of children. The odd tangent worked; the worshipers squirmed, but they listened to every word the preacher said.

Kizzy listened too, but as the preacher wound down she began to tear up and sniffle, and Olivia noticed.

That was a strange sermon for Easter, but something the preacher said was bothering Kizzy. *It must be hard to have grown up on the river with a bunch of heathens. That's what got to her—she's trying to sort it all out. Maybe she'll come to Jesus, but it'll be harder for her than others.*

When church was over and they were outside, Olivia said, "It was a moving service, wasn't it?"

"Yeah, it was ... I cried a little bit because I got to thinking about how beautiful everything looked, and how my people never took up with such stuff. They saw beauty in the river, and that was enough for them."

She does want to change, I can sense it, and I want to help her.

"Barton Cottage," Olivia said.

"You're giving me the password?"

"Yes, because we are real friends, and we can trust each other with our secret thoughts."

Kizzy gave her a serious look. "Well, I just did. That's my only secret. I think a lot about what I learned by living on the river, and what I will have to give up if I change."

⚜

The sound and gentle wake of a small fishing boat going upriver woke Kizzy shortly after dawn on June 6, 1944. She climbed over Cormac, and as she did, he patted her on the bottom. She slapped his hand away, got out of bed, and went to the stove to put on a pot of coffee.

Cormac sat up in bed and lit a cigarette. He took a big puff, had a coughing fit, and then got up and turned on the radio. It took a moment for it to warm up and for the static to clear, but soon they heard the voice of an announcer reporting the latest war news. Cormac growled. "I don't want to hear that bullshit." He twisted the tuning knob, searching for country music, but every station was reporting the details of D-Day, breathless reports about the allied invasion on the beaches of Normandy in France. One announcer said that 155,000 allied troops have landed. "It is the largest amphibious military operation in history."

Cormac huffed. "The dumb bastards are getting killed for nothing." He turned the radio off.

"Uncle Mac has been saying the invasion would come, and this is it. It's important, Cormac."

"Bullshit. What does that old fart know? I'm going to work." He finished dressing, gulped down a cup of coffee, and left.

As soon as he was gone Kizzy turned the radio on and listened to the reports. She had intended to use the morning to finish *Northanger Abbey*, but decided that would have to wait. She dressed and headed up the trail to town at 11 o'clock, and when she got to the top of the hill, she saw a good-sized crowd gathered in front of the *Big Pearl Free Current*. The people were waiting to get a copy of an Extra edition that would tell the very latest about the invasion.

Kizzy stood with them for a while, but when she heard a morose one-legged man say, "The war is over," she decided to go see what Uncle Mac had to say about it. *He'll know the strait of it. And he'll know what this means for Birdie.*

Uncle Mac was in his usual place, watching the domino game. But he was not kibitzing with Dynamite. The players were just going through the motions; their main conversation was about the war. And Kizzy listened long enough to learn that Uncle Mac's principal point was a concern that our troops might get bogged down like they did in World War I. The other veterans, having served in the trenches, agreed with him.

Kizzy asked Uncle Mac how the invasion would affect Birdie, and he said, "It'll help, Kizzy. We have to take out Hitler, and once we get that done, we'll turn all our guns on the Japs, and that'll bring Birdie home."

Kizzy felt better about the news, but later in the day when she was shelving books, Uncle Mac's words—"bogged down"—haunted her.

I'm bogged down too. Been bogged down ever since that preacher said I was a sinner. I was doing fine until he said I'm going to hell for screwing Cormac. And then last night I went ahead and did it again. Ma did it with a Gypsy, and Shirley did it with lots of men … It feels good, but now I'm hearing that it ain't … isn't right. And the more I hear that, the worse I feel about doing it. Whew! I need to back away from all this talk about rules and stuff like that. There's something to be said for being free … for living by the ways of the river.

⚜

Independence Day, 1944, was going to be the best ever, according to Uncle Mac. The celebration would begin with a parade, the biggest ever. Then there would be worship services at every church, political debates, bazaars, and games for the kids. And the day's events would culminate in a picnic at City Park. The format was always the same, but this year's celebration would have a special ingredient: Newfound optimism, the sense that America and the Allies were going to win the war; it was just a question of time.

For Kizzy the day would be extra-special. It was her 16ᵗʰ birthday, and in two months she would start her junior year at Big Pearl High School.

At 10:30 she gathered with Mabel, Olivia, Stefan, and some of the men from the Veterans' Center to watch the parade. They brought chairs from the library. It made Kizzy feel good to be part of a group; new friends that were like family to her.

A Marine honor guard led the parade, and when Uncle Mac saw them coming he tried to stand, but he could not get up. Dynamite pushed him alongside the Marines, but after a few steps, they turned around and came back. Uncle Mac was crying, but he was still saluting, and he held his salute in place until Dynamite got him back to where they started. Then came the bands—an Army band from Little Rock and another from Memphis. And Kizzy cheered when the Big Pearl High School band marched by. There were 20 floats in the "best float" competition; the Girl Scouts and the Rodeo Club had the best ones. Bully Bigshot's Eugenics Center had the worst float; the same one he had been using for years. Finally the horses came, a sure sign that the parade was about to end.

When it was over Kizzy turned to Mabel, Stefan, and Olivia and said, "Everyone is in such an upbeat mood. Uncle Mac says it's because the invasion is going well. He says the hardest part was the landing at Normandy."

"It's still a long way to Germany," Stefan said.

"Yes," Kizzy said. "But Uncle Mac says an invasion is like starting out in life—the hardest part is to get a toehold and not get bogged down. He says Patton has done that—he's broken out and he's sweeping across France toward Germany. Uncle Mac says he can see the light at the end of the tunnel. It won't be long until we win and the boys come home."

Mabel and Stefan cheered and clapped. Olivia nodded, but she had a glum look about her, and that bothered Kizzy. *She's smiling, but she misses her John. He's not coming home. He got killed at Midway and they buried him at sea.*

⚜

Later Kizzy and Stefan went to the picnic, but around 7 o'clock Kizzy said she was tired and wanted to go home. Stefan walked her to the bollards and gave her a goodnight kiss. She went aboard, changed clothes, and made a beeline for her thinking spot in the woods.

She sat on Grandpa's stump and listened to the sounds of life on the river. The critters stirred when she first arrived, but soon they quieted down, and that is when she conjured an image of the barefooted old man in his worn-out overalls. He was rising up as tall and straight as he could, getting ready to give his favorite Fourth of July speech. She knew it by heart, and mouthed it word for word. *Me and MeeMaw been on this river for 20 years. Some say it's a hard life, and I reckon it is, but nobody tells us what to do and we ain't owing to anybody. We live by the law of the river. We're free, and we aim to stay that way. Happy Fourth of July.*

Kizzy made a hard fist and socked it into the sky. Then she talked to Grandpa.

It's been a great day, Grandpa! The best Fourth of July birthday I ever had. I'm 16 now, can you believe it? Everyone says the war is going better. Uncle Mac says he can see the light at the end of the tunnel now that General Patton is on his way to Germany.

I hope you and MeeMaw and Ma are doing OK? I sure miss you all.

There's a nice lady that's helping me and she got me a job at the library, so that's good. I'm still living on the boat with Cormac, but sometimes I feel like that little white dove that Birdie used to have ... all cooped up. I've been think-ing that I need to break out too, maybe do things a little different. Olivia—she's the one that's being nice to me—thinks I ought to change. She ain't ... isn't pushy about it ... but there's a heap of difference in the way she lives and the way we've always lived.

You said nobody tells us what to do, that we're free, but that's the main thing that's got me buffaloed. Town folks have rules for everything. I went to church with Olivia the other day and the preacher called me a sinner because I've been doing it with Cormac. So who's right? Who decides what's right and wrong? If I knew the answer to that, I might could get out of the cage I'm in.

I think Jane Austen would take the preacher's side of things, but hers is not the way of the river, and it's sure not the way Ma and Shirley lived.

So that's what I'm sitting here thinking about. How to break out of the cage I'm in. I get out of it every so often when I'm reading, or singing, or dreaming about finding that big pearl, but there's got to be a better way.

One thing's for sure. I can't tell any of them about Cormac, so that's why I'm here at my thinking spot, wondering what you would say.

⚜

On Aug. 27, 1944, Kizzy took a break from working at the library's check-out desk to sit at a library table by the front window and read the Sunday paper. It was full of news about the war, and the lead story told about the liberation of Paris:

"The French Second Armored Division under General Philippe Leclerc was the first Allied force to enter the city, greeted by loud cheers from Parisians after many days of fighting between the Resistance and the German occupiers. The American and British forces followed the French, and at 8 p.m. General Charles de Gaulle, the leader of the Free French who has been living in exile in London since the Fall of France in 1940, entered the city."

The paper had two pages full of pictures from Paris, and there was a separate story with quotes from several American soldiers telling how grateful French women gave them wine and hugged and kissed them. And one of the photographs showed a lithe young French girl smooching with an American soldier, and it was not a Sunday peck on the cheek. Kizzy saw it as a serious "let's do it" kind of kiss.

She smiled and looked at all the other pictures. Then she pushed the paper aside, leaned back in her chair, and stared out the window, meditating, but her reverie did not last long.

Less than a minute later, she straightened up in the chair and pulled the paper back to take a closer look at the picture of the young couple. And her mind wandered. *I bet some of them were doing more than hugging and kissing.*

I bet some of them did it. But being happy about the war wouldn't make it right according to the preacher. He'd still call it fornicatin.' I bet Olivia wouldn't do it—even if she was a French girl. I might, but she wouldn't. And Jane Austen's Lydia might do it, but maybe not ... Anyway, that's not why I've been doing it with Cormac. I've forgotten how we got started. I was just a kid when he used to screw Ma. Then after she died he started taking care of me, and he started teaching me stuff—little stuff at first—and then we wound up doing it after Boopie left. But that was a long time ago. Here lately I've been doing it because he wants to do it and that's different from doing it because you are in love and married like Olivia was to John. Or doing it just because you're happy about something—like winning the war.

Olivia interrupted Kizzy's woolgathering. "You look worn out, Kizzy."

"Naw, I was just taking a break, reading about our boys going into Paris." She pointed at the photos. "Looks like those French girls are really happy to see our boys."

"They've been living under Nazi control," Olivia said. "I'd be happy too."

Kizzy looked at Olivia closer than before. She was wearing a light green high-collar blouse with a black ribbon around it. Her hair was done up in a tight bun, and she had an angelic look about her. *Nope, she definitely wouldn't do it.*

Kizzy put the paper back together and got up from the table. "I've got plenty to do, so I guess I better get back to work."

Later that day when the library closed she walked home. As she went down the hill to the river, leaving the town behind her, she began to think about the ways of the river and Olivia's ways, and that led to more thinking about the photograph from Paris. *Whew! I'm not making any headway on this fornication business, and I can't quit thinking about it. It's driving me nuts.*

⚜

At sundown that same day, after dinner Kizzy changed to her nightgown, got in bed, and turned her back to Cormac. He stayed at the table, drinking beer and listening to the Grand Ole Opry.

She was just about to doze off when she heard him turn off the radio. She perked up, but did not move a muscle. Then she heard the familiar sound of Cormac undressing—the unbuckling of the belt and the pants dropping to the floor.

She girded herself and waited. Then she heard him lighting a cigarette and in a moment she smelled Bull Durham tobacco burning.

Kizzy breathed deeply, as if asleep, but when he snuffed out the light she froze. And when Cormac lay down beside her she quickly climbed over him and got in the other bed, pulled a sheet over her head, and said, "That's it, Cormac. I'm done with that. I'm not going to do it any more with you. It's not right."

Cormac got out of the bed, and stood naked in the cabin. He pulled the sheet down and leered at Kizzy. "Why not? You been fucking that Kraut boy?"

"No. He's a nice boy."

Cormac tried to get in bed with her again, but she pushed him away. "I mean it, Cormac."

"I don't get it." Cormac took a step away from the bed, and made a full circle. Then he leaned over Kizzy, and with raspy words and the stench of beer, said, "Oh, now I get it. You been talking to the library woman and she's been putting crazy ideas in your head. Right?"

"No, I haven't told anyone about us doing it. It's just that I've decided that it's not right. And I'm not going to do it with you anymore."

Cormac climbed in beside her and whispered. "Come on, Kizzy. You used to do it to show how much you cared for me. I been takin' care of you ever since your mother died. I didn't have to do that but I did, and I got big plans for us."

"No, Cormac. It's over. Get out of this bed and leave me alone."

"I'll be damned if I will." He reached for her and they wrestled, but Cormac managed to grab her hands. He held them over her head with one hand, pinning her down. Then he began to rub her belly and talk ugly—the kind of dirty talk that he did with Boopie.

"Stop it, Cormac. It's not right."

"Well listen to Miss Van Astorbilt! Huh! You ain't no fancy town girl and you never will be. You're just a hot-blooded little river rat, just like your Ma, and Shirley, and Boopie."

It was rough sex, hard and fast with no pretense of caring. Kizzy let it happen, and when it was over, she pushed away from him and got in the other bed.

She whimpered and bit her fist, but then she cried and buried her face in the pillow so that Cormac could not hear. After a while she lay still, dozing off.

He's right, I ain't no good.

XLVII

Knuckles

Cormac was the first to get up on Monday morning. Kizzy heard him rustling around the cabin, and she knew without looking that he was naked and barefooted because that was his way.

The sight of Cormac in the raw had never bothered Kizzy. Her first experience with it came when she was only 8 years old, the day he moved aboard to live with her mother. But the night of mean sex and vulgar nightmares had changed everything. Cormac's nudity begat fear, and Kizzy worried that he might force her to do it again.

It was a sultry August morning. Kizzy longed to go outside for a breath of fresh air, but her comfort was at war with the need to hide. The cover sheet was clinging to her, damp with night sweat, but she carefully pulled it up and over her head. Then she quietly turned her back to Cormac and lay still to listen. She heard him strike a match and move something near the sink, but then the rustling noises stopped.

Kizzy held her breath, straining to hear the slightest clue, but none came. It seemed an eternity, but she did not move. Then, finally, she heard the welcome sound of Cormac getting dressed. Then he moved farther away, toward the door to the aft deck.

"You ain't fooling me, Kizzy. I know you're awake. I'm leaving and I'll be gone for a week." He paused, but she did not respond.

"Two of the girls at the button factory is quittin' and going to Memphis to make some real money. One of them has a pickup and I'm going with them to help them get started. And you need to get over the spell you're in before I get back."

Cormac pushed the door open and stepped out onto the aft deck. When he crossed the gangplank the boat rocked slightly, then it settled and the only sound was that of a lazy current lapping against the hull.

Kizzy jerked away the cover sheet and got out of bed. She waited to be sure he was gone, and then she went out onto the aft deck to cool off. She sat down, overcome with a spell of melancholy, and the feeling that she was tired and worn out. At times she would nod off, but she mostly stared at the river, and she did not move for the rest of the morning.

Noon came but she did not eat; she had no appetite. In mid-afternoon, she went back inside, got the book *Northanger Abbey* and returned to the aft deck. She calculated the time it would take to finish and read a few pages, but she lost focus and put the book down.

She kept telling herself to snap out of it, but the empty feeling would not go away.

She tried wandering off to fairyland, but that did not work either.

Finally, she tried singing a verse from "Lord Thomas," MeeMaw's favorite tragedy about a girl the lord planned to marry. In a fit of jealousy, the girl killed her rival, the Fair Elendor. Lord Thomas then beheaded his betrothed and killed himself.

> *She pierced Fair Elendor's heart.*
> *He took her by the hand,*
> *And led her through the hall,*
> *And with a sword cut off her head.*
> *And pitched it against the wall, wall, wall.*

Kizzy did not finish the ballad. Her shame craved empathy, but the sad song was not helping because the dead cannot empathize. *Those girls had it worse than me. If they were here they'd tell me to get over what Cormac did and go on with life, but they aren't here and I can't fool myself into thinking that they are.*

Besides, it's not the sex I'm trying to forget. Hell's bells, it was mean and different, and it was a hard screwing that did not feel good. But that's not what's bothering me.

It's me that's bothering me. I'm the problem here.

⚜

Stefan was whistling and stepping lively when he entered the library Tuesday at noon. He waved to Olivia, but turned left into the Veterans' Center and headed for the domino table.

Uncle Mac was harassing Dynamite for misplaying the Double Six, but as soon as he saw Stefan he rolled his wheelchair away from the table and said, "You look mighty happy this morning."

"Yes," Stefan said. "The paper says the Germans have surrendered at Toulon and Marseilles in southern France and Patton's tanks have reached the Marne. And I wanted to see what you think about that."

"We've got them on the run—that's what I think." Uncle Mac then recapped the action since D-Day, and wound up on a high note. "It'll be over by this time next year." Then he looked past Stefan and bellowed, "I better get back to my post. Dynamite needs me."

"Bullshit." Dynamite cackled and slammed a domino down for emphasis.

Uncle Mac rolled his eyes and wheeled himself into position behind Dynamite.

Stefan laughed, waved goodbye to the veterans, and went back into the library to talk to Kizzy. Olivia saw him coming and pointed to the stacks in the back of the library.

Kizzy was so busy rearranging a shelf that she did not see or hear Stefan when he slipped up behind her.

He put his arms around her, and leaned to kiss her, but when his lips touched the nape of her neck, she wheeled around and pulled him close. Kizzy held fast, but said nothing, and when Stefan started to speak, she whimpered and kissed his lips as if she might never see him again.

"Well, hello." Stefan said as she loosened her hold.

He kissed her again, and she returned the kiss with uncommon fervor, so much so that it made him wonder. *Is this the same Kizzy? She is as bright and beautiful as ever, but something is bothering her. There's a flicker of distress that I have never seen or felt before. It was just a flash, a wisp, but yes, it was real.*

He kissed her again and whispered, "I love you," and it was just what Kizzy needed to hear.

"You're the best, Stefan. I'm just down in the dumps today."

"I can tell, but I've got the perfect solution for that." Stefan rubbed his hands together and winked.

"What?"

"I want you to take me on the river. You promised, but we've never gotten around to it. The weather's perfect right now and we start school next week, so let's do it—let's pack a lunch and go tomorrow; you can teach me how to gather mussels and fish."

Kizzy hesitated, but then she said, "OK, Cormac's gone until Sunday, so we can take the workboat."

⚜

It was pitch dark when they loaded the workboat, but when they released the mooring lines and pushed off the indigo sky had faded to denim blue.

Kizzy used the sculling oar to reach the main current, and when it had them in its grasp she leaned back, lifted her face to the sky, and closed her eyes. Then, as they drifted slowly downstream, she took in a deep breath of river air and savored it as if it were Holy Communion.

Stefan watched as she studied the bouquet, sifting and scrutinizing its makeup, separating the fragrances. "You love it, don't you?"

Kizzy nodded, ever so slightly. "The river has been my life, Stefan. It's what I know."

"It is beautiful—a tonic for what ails us." Stefan sniffed the fresh air, and watched Kizzy as she worked the oar. "Tell me about the river, Kizzy."

She began with the fish. "Without them—the catfish, buffalo, crappie, bream, the good-eating fish—we couldn't make it. We catch them, eat what we want, and sell the rest to Curly. The fish are our mainstay."

"What about fish that aren't good to eat?"

Kizzy guffawed and slapped the steering oar against the water.

Stefan had hit a nerve. Kizzy launched into a full lesson about the fish she hated. She called them "no-good fish," and the more she talked about them, the madder she got.

Stefan grinned; Kizzy was back—acting like herself.

"Then there's the slimy green grinnel, an ancient fish that swam with dinosaurs. They're horrible, and I hate them! They have hundreds of tiny sharp teeth. When I was 7, I tried to take a one-footer off Grandpa's trotline. It bit me and brought blood, and I can feel it to this day." She caught her breath and calmed a little; Stefan thought she was through, but then she started in on the alligator gars. "They are the biggest, ugliest fish on the river; all they do is eat the good fish."

Stefan chuckled and let her rant; the tonic was working. Kizzy was out of the doldrums, at least for now.

Soon the sun rose high enough to cast shadows. The blue herons were working the river, looking for breakfast. Kizzy described their habits, and she was halfway through a detailed lesson about the other river birds, talking nonstop, when Stefan interrupted.

"Can I steer?"

Kizzy squinted as if she was going to object, but she checked their position on the river and changed places with Stefan. "Use the sculling oar to keep her in the middle—the current will do the rest."

When she finished telling about the birds, Kizzy started in on the critters. "We eat a lot of rabbits; the cottontails are better than the swampers. And the squirrels ..."

Kizzy suddenly changed the subject. "We're half a mile from Hog Head Bend. It's a good place to toe-dig for mussels, so that's where we'll stop. We'll dig up a few and I'll show you how to open them. We might not find a pearl, but the sand bar will be a good place to spend the day."

Stefan looked downriver. "We're coming to a bend, is this Hog Head? I see a sand bar." He pointed downriver. "There, on the right."

"Mercy no—this is Mexican Bend. We can't stop here, and we've got to hold our breath until we get around it."

"Why? Isn't that the place you dream about—the place where you'll find your big pearl?"

"Yeah, but MeeMaw swore it's hainted, and she knew about such things."

"But if we stop we might find the big pearl you've dreamed about."

"I don't care, there's a crazy man that lives here. I saw him when I was little—he was naked and wearing a funny hat, and I don't want any part of that."

Stefan sculled the workboat toward the sandbar. "You're 16 now, Kizzy. Let's go ashore and look around."

"Dang it, Stefan! Get back out in the current. I'm scared of this place."

"It's too late."

The workboat scrunched onto the sand bar.

Kizzy gave Stefan a dirty look, but he had already stepped into the shallow water and was pulling the workboat farther onto the sand bar.

"Come on, Kizzy. There's no such thing as haints. I'll look around, and if I see anything scary I promise we'll leave and go to Hog Head Bend."

Stefan did not wait for Kizzy's permission to reconnoiter. He took off running, splashing along the water line, heading downstream. When he reached the apex of the bend he looked back and waved, but Kizzy had not moved, nor did she wave back.

Stefan continued round the bend, but he stopped before losing sight of her. He returned on the high side of the sand bar until he was even with the workboat, then he rushed downslope to the boat and slid to a stop by her. She gave him another dirty look, but he gave her a breathless, upbeat report: "All clear!"

Kizzy looked away, stone-faced. But Stefan could tell that she was mellowing because she did not ask to leave.

"It's beautiful, Kizzy. The sand is warm and clean, and I didn't see a single track. We are all alone."

Kizzy looked downstream, past Stefan, to see for herself, but still she said nothing.

"If you will show me how to toe-dig we might find your big pearl. What do you say?"

Kizzy took off her shoes and stood up, but before she stepped onto the sand, she unfastened her belt and took off her jeans. Then she walked out into the river in her panties and when she was knee-deep, she turned toward Stefan. "What are you waiting for?"

Stefan was dumbstruck. It was the first time he had seen so much of Kizzy.

She laughed. "Take your shoes and pants off and come on in, Stefan. Time's a-wasting."

⚜

"My grandpa used to tong for 'em or rake 'em, but MeeMaw and I got 'em this way." She showed Stefan how to scratch the bottom with his toes until he felt a mussel. "Once you feel it you work it loose and then reach down and pick it up."

Kizzy demonstrated, and then she said, "MeeMaw and I used to make a game out of guessing the size and shape before we laid hands on it. Since you're new at this you can just say it's a big-un, a middle-sized one, or a little one." She handed the mussel to him. "That's a big-un."

Stefan felt something beneath his foot. He dug around it and said, "This is a big one." He reached down and brought it to the surface.

Kizzy laughed. "That's a little one, Stefan, but I'll give you credit for a middle-sized one."

The toe-digging went on for an hour, and that gave Kizzy a chance to explain the economics of musseling. "Finding a pearl is everyone's dream, but it's like finding a needle in a haystack." She hesitated, and then she said, "I've got another big-un." Then she reached down, pulled it up, and put it in the burlap bag that was now a quarter-full. "Selling shells to the button factory—as you can see—is a lot of hard work for very little money."

"How much is a big pearl worth?" Stefan asked.

"It depends on the size, shape and color. The biggest one was found right near here." Then she told Stefan the story of Tum-Tum, the black man who found a pearl that sold for $5,000. Kizzy shook her head, "He squandered the money on whiskey and whores and came back to the river, penniless." She chuckled, and shook her head again. "The only good that came out of that is that the newspapers called Tum Tum a 'fisherman' instead of a river rat."

"Maybe that's all he ever wanted." Stefan said.

"I wouldn't waste the money," Kizzy said. "I'd use it to buy me a place like Barton Cottage."

⚜

By 10 o'clock they had a good-sized batch of mussels. Kizzy opened one to show Stefan how to do it, and then she maneuvered her fingers around the plump, watery meat with the delicacy of a brain surgeon. "It's easier to feel a pearl than it is to see it, Stefan."

They worked for a half-hour, and when they got to the last mussel, Kizzy paused for a second. Then she deftly opened the mussel and probed, but there was no pearl. She tossed the shell onto the two-foot-deep pile of empty shells and sighed. Then she looked at Stefan, and shrugged her shoulders in resignation. "Let's wash up."

She took him by the hand and they walked into the river; when they were knee-deep Kizzy laughed and splashed water on him. He jumped, lost his footing, and fell backwards into the water. Kizzy screeched in delight, but as soon as Stefan surfaced he rushed toward her, splashing her and giggling. They embraced, oblivious to everything, and then they lay down on the sand to rest and sun themselves.

Kizzy broke the silence. "See, finding a pearl isn't easy and musseling is hard work. Here we are at Mexican Bend and we didn't even find a little burying pearl."

Stefan made a hoarse whistling sound. "Well, there are more mussels out there; let's don't give up."

"I'll never give up, Stefan; I ain't made that way."

Stefan propped himself up so that he could look into her eyes. "That's what I love most about you."

She pursed her lips and faked a kiss, but there was a tear in her eye.

He twirled a lock of her red hair and the magic of love took over. Words could not say what they were feeling, so they did not speak. But the spell soon gave way to Stefan's self-consciousness. He gave her a silly, coy smile, and said, "You know, I was embarrassed at first, but I like being undressed with you."

"Well, we're not naked, Stefan." She put her hand on the nape of his neck, pulled him close and kissed him, and then she sniggered. "You want to get naked?"

Stefan gasped. "No," and then he jumped up and pointed to the woods. "Let's go look around." He pulled Kizzy to her feet, and kissed her on the cheek. "If we stay here I'm pretty sure I'll disappoint my mother."

⚜

They dressed and walked along the tree line, looking for a path or a break in the brush that would give them a way into the thick grove of pines, syca-mores, and cottonwoods.

On the downstream side of the bend, Stefan spotted a small, well-beaten path nearly obscured by its quick turn to the left. "Here's a path. Let's see where it goes."

He went into the woods, but Kizzy did not follow.

Stefan turned around and came to where she was standing. "Come on, Kizzy."

"I'm not going. I saw an old man standing right here when I was little. Grandpa said he's been living here ever since he got out of the insane asy-lum, and MeeMaw said the place is hainted."

"I bet this just leads to a place where people can park their cars," Stefan said.

"I'm scared."

"Come on, Kizzy." Stefan tugged on her hand, and she followed, looking to the right and left.

As they got farther into the woods the trail got wider, and then it circled around a steeply banked knoll.

Stefan was about to declare victory over the haints, but when they got around the knoll they were just yards from where Knuckles was sitting.

"Hi-dee."

The grey-bearded old man was sitting in a rocking chair near the front door of a decrepit one-room scrap-wood shack. A dozen discarded tin signs—7 Up, Nehi, and Orange Crush—nailed to the walls and roof gave the place a bit of color.

"Welcome to Moralitas." His voice was shaky, but it had a touch of authority in it.

Kizzy turned away, but Stefan put his arm around her to keep her from bolting back into the woods.

"Hold on, Kizzy. Let's see who he is before we cut and run. He seems friendly enough."

XLVIII

Moralitas

Knuckles struggled to his feet as Stefan and Kizzy walked toward him. He was wearing a faded knee-length tunic made of coarse wool with a leather sash about the waist, and it gave him the look of an Essene hermit.

Kizzy inched closer to Stefan.

"We're just looking around," Stefan said. "Is this your place?"

Knuckles smiled and swept his arm across the horizon as if displaying a royal domain. "Yes sirree; all two acres of it. I've been here for 15 years."

Stefan shook hands with Knuckles and tried to make small talk. "I'm Stefan and this is Kizzy. She's been showing me how to toe-dig for mussels."

"That's fine—toe-digging is fine," Knuckles said. "It's the pearlers who come in the big boats that I don't like. They don't care nothing about the river." His eyes narrowed, and turned hostile when he spoke of the commercial pearlers.

Kizzy could hold back no longer. "People say you're crazy."

Knuckles horselaughed, but his eyes turned friendly as quickly as they had turned hostile. "I ain't gonna deny that."

"I saw you once before. You were as naked as a jaybird, and you were wearing a funny hat, waving your finger in the air. MeeMaw—she's dead now—told me the boogers had got to you."

"I get spells now and then so your meemaw had a point, but a lot of us caught the Cuban fever and it comes back every once in a while. And it makes us do crazy things. Heck, they found Teddy one night just walking around in the snow in his bare feet, holding his dog Skip to his chest."

"Who's Teddy?" Stefan said.

"Teddy Roosevelt. You know … he wound up as president, but it was because of him that I went to Cuba. I was young and working as a cowhand in Texas and joined the Rough Riders—signed up at the Menger Hotel in San Antonio in 1898."

"But they put you in the insane asylum, didn't they?" Kizzy said.

"That was for what happened in Little Rock. But just because folks think you're crazy don't make it so."

"People shouldn't hold a sickness against you," Stefan said.

"What did you do in Little Rock that got you locked up?" Kizzy said.

"That takes some explaining." Knuckles pointed to a big hunk of drift-wood lying next to his rocking chair. "Let's all sit down and I'll tell you about it."

He cleared his throat and spat. "I was born in Pocahontas in the dead of winter 1877, but as soon as I was old enough to get a job on a riverboat I left, and wound up in Texas punchin' cattle and doing a little bare-knuckle boxing on the side. I cowboyed for 30 years, except for the time I went off to Cuba with Teddy and the Rough Riders.

"I married a woman when I got back from Cuba, but it only lasted a month because she ran off to Mexico with a gambling man." He chuckled. "I swore off women after that.

"I was always searching for something. A Ford car, a ranch of my own, but I was never happy. Then along about Christmastime in 1925 a tent preacher came through town talking about the old-time desert hermits. He said John the Baptist started out with them—eatin' locusts and honey.

"Man, that preacher could lay it out. He said them hermits was deter-mined to get away from what he called 'worldliness.' He said man is eaten up with wanting stuff and thinking that he can figure out right from wrong on his own. That's what I was guilty of, and it had me all tore up inside. The preacher said it happens every time man starts thinking he knows more than God—he messes everything up and winds up sinning."

Kizzy interrupted. "My grandpa used to say, 'Nobody tells us what to do and we ain't owing to anybody. We live by the law of the river. We're free, and we aim to stay that way.'"

"Well, that's OK so far as it goes, but God's the only one that can set up what is right and wrong. The preacher called the business of knowing good from evil 'moralitas.' That's a Latin word, but it has stuck with me because that was the part of his preaching that got to me. And it's the strait of it from all I've seen."

"That's what my mother believed, but she was a Catholic."

"Well that's the strait of it no matter if you are Catholic, Jew, or whatever."

Kizzy measured what Knuckles was saying against the ways of the river, but she did not pursue the subject. "So what's all that got to do with getting put in the insane asylum?"

He gave Kizzy a knowing look. "Well, the preacher said John the Baptist got tired of just being a hermit so he went out and started telling everyone that they had to repent and get baptized. If the preacher had left it at that I probably would have gone back to punchin' cattle, but he pointed right at me and said I was supposed to 'go forth and spread the word.'

"So I took the little dab of money I'd saved up out of the bank and bought a brand new Ford Model A pickup for $395 cash. Then I went on a mission, driving all across Texas, Louisiana, Mississippi, and Arkansas to spread the gospel."

He seemed pleased with himself, and then he told how he did it.

"I came up with an idea for the shortest sermon ever, something that would get everyone's attention. I'd dress up like John the Baptist, find me a busy street corner, point at people, and shout 'Guilty!'"

Knuckles heehawed. "Boy, you should have seen the look on their faces. I could tell that I was doing some good. I was hittin' them right where they needed it."

Then he lowered his voice, and sounded a sad note. "My mission was working real good until one day I wound up on a street corner by the Capital Hotel in Little Rock. I was doing what I had done everywhere else, but all of a sudden I got a bad spell of Cuban fever. All I remember is that the police came and put me in the insane asylum. And it took me two months to prove that it was the fever—not religion—that had got to me."

"So it was after you got out of the State Hospital that you came here?" Stefan asked.

"Yep, when I got out I figured I better stick with just being a hermit. I gave up the preaching and came here, bought this two acres for $50, built my cabin, and I been here ever since." He pointed toward the river. "I can walk down to the river and fish, I've got a little garden, and this turned out to be a good place to hole up during the Depression. I drive my old A-Model to Newport once a month to get spuds and onions and other staples, but I don't go anywhere else." Then he added an afterthought. "And I don't go into Big Pearl on account of Sully Biggers. That scalawag owns everything in town and he don't like folks like me."

"Anybody that doesn't like him is OK with me." Kizzy said. "I call him Bully Bigshot."

Knuckles laughed and gave her a wink, but she had another question on her mind. "MeeMaw said this place is haunted because of the lynching that took place here."

"I don't believe in haints. There ain't no room for them if you believe in God, but it suits me if people don't want to come here to live on account of that man who got lynched. But there weren't no mystery to that killing. He got strung up because he was a messican, that's it—pure and simple."

Kizzy was beginning to identify with the old man. *The houseboat I was raised in isn't much better than his shack, and I've got more in common with him than most folks. He's dressed poor, Bully doesn't like him, and his being barefooted reminds me of Grandpa even though they'd argue about who gets to figure out what's right and wrong. But Knuckles has a good heart, and that's what is most important.*

"Are you ever going to leave here, maybe go out on another mission?" Stefan said.

Knuckles wrinkled his brow. "No, I'm here to stay. I live like the old-timey hermits, hand to mouth. I've found the Holy Spirit and I ain't going to let go of it. I might not be as pure about it as John the Baptist and the hermits he lived with, but I'm doing my durndest. Besides, that preacher down in Texas said, 'The worst hypocrite who pretends to be good does less harm than the open sinner.'"

"Would you leave here if you found a big pearl and came in to a lot of money?" Kizzy said.

Knuckles smiled. "I've done found the pearl I was looking for."

⚜

In mid-afternoon Stefan and Kizzy bade farewell to Knuckles.

When they got to the workboat they pushed it into deep water and Kizzy lowered the outboard motor. She fiddled with the controls then pulled the starting cord. It took three tries and a few cuss words that she had learned from Grandpa, but the old engine started and quickly settled into the steady putt-putt that would take them back upriver.

She turned the workboat into the current and took a long look at Mexican Bend as it slowly disappeared from sight.

"What a day!" Stefan said. "I learned to toe-dig, we met a crazy man who turned out to be a wise old hermit, and I got to see you in your panties."

"I'm glad we stopped there," she said.

⚜

They motored on, savoring the August afternoon sights but saying little. If Stefan had a question about the river, she would explain it, but the two of them seemed content to ponder all that had happened that day, especially their meeting with Knuckles.

When they were halfway home, perplexity got the best of Kizzy. She blurted out the question that was on her mind. "What did Knuckles mean when he said he had found the pearl he was looking for?"

Stefan did not answer right away, but after a while he said, "He said he was guilty of wanting stuff and thinking he was smarter than God. That seems to be what was bothering him. He said he was all torn up inside until he heard the preacher say that God is the sole judge of what is right and wrong. It was after that that he started living like John the Baptist, and that seemed to fix what was bothering him."

Kizzy thought for a second, and then she said, "So, if something is tearing us up inside and we want to stop it, do we have to become hermits?"

"Well, it worked for Knuckles. I think he is content with himself. And I think that's the pearl he was looking for."

"I don't want to be a hermit."

"The priest at my mother's church back in Pennsylvania, Father Joseph Meissner, made it seem easier. He said if you are guilty of doing something wrong, all you have to do is repent and ask God to forgive you. You don't have to go around in sackcloth or eat locusts."

"Olivia's preacher said the same thing when I went to church with her on Easter Sunday."

Kizzy used an empty coffee can to bail out water that had collected around her feet, and grimaced as she poured it into the river. *MeeMaw and Grandpa would roll over if they knew I was even thinking about such stuff.*

⚜

The rest of the trip was as quiet as it had been before Kizzy's question about Knuckles, and at 6 o'clock they pulled alongside the houseboat. They offloaded the stack of mussel shells and the gear they had taken downriver, then walked up the hill towards town to sit by the bollards. They did some billing and cooing, but when the shadows began to lengthen, Stefan went home and Kizzy went back to the houseboat to do something she had been thinking about all afternoon.

Kizzy took MeeMaw's fortune-telling books off the shelf and spread them out on the table. Then she made herself a peanut butter sandwich, poured a glass of water, and sat down to do some serious thinking about haints, spirits, and religion, the conflicting thoughts that were bothering her.

The first book, *Old Egyptian Madge's Fortune Teller and Dream Book,* was MeeMaw's bible, her guide for measuring the worth of all other spiritual works, including her other favorites: *Bonaparte's Oraculum* and *Are You Mediumistic.*

The books covered everything: Crystal gazing, slate writing, telling fortunes by reference to moles and lines on the hand, choosing lucky lottery numbers; and there were complete lists of the spells, charms, and incantations used by the Egyptian Magi and other oracles.

Kizzy had read the books to MeeMaw several times, and she relished the nostalgic moment. But after a while she tired of the project and began to talk aloud as if MeeMaw was present.

"It doesn't have to be the way of the river and nothing else, MeeMaw. Today I figured out two things: There ain't any haints, and the way of the river is not the only way. There's some good to it, but it's not the only way."

Kizzy made a fist, tapped on the stack of books, and pushed her chair back. She stood up, gathered MeeMaw's books and went out onto the aft deck. The moonlight, having found a crease in the tree line, brightened the river.

"I ain't throwing you and Grandpa over the side, MeeMaw, and I ain't forgetting what I learned from you all, but people have to change. Everyone around here is changing because of the war. Poor Olivia lost John and Stefan has changed too. He lost his mother and his real dad, and he came here, all the way from Germany. Now Fritz is locked up, and Stefan is living with Eli, who is a Jew. Everything is different.

"The truth is, there's a lot of racket going on in my head, but if everyone else can change then I ought to at least think about it."

Kizzy sighed, then tossed *Bonaparte's Oraculum* over the side. As it floated away, she tried to hit it with *Are You Mediumistic.* The books quickly caught the current and started their journey downstream. Then Kizzy took a big windup and threw *Old Egyptian Madge's Fortune Teller and Dream Book* as far as she could. It landed aside the others, and as they drifted away it reminded Kizzy of the scene on that cold February day in 1937 when MeeMaw fell overboard and waved goodbye as the floodwaters carried her on down the river.

Kizzy hustled forward to stand on the fore deck so that she could get a last glimpse of MeeMaw's books. She stood next to a big plant—a cardinal—that had lived for years in an 18-gallon wash tub. The tough old wildflower was to Kizzy's way of thinking a perfect tombstone for MeeMaw—blazing red, woolly, living defiantly against all odds.

She took a long look at the moonlit sky and rubbed her hands together as if to cleanse herself of lingering spirits. Then she spoke in earnest. "MeeMaw, I know you're out there, and I need to tell you something that I've been keeping secret."

Kizzy gently lifted one of the delicate red petals and studied it as if it was the story of her life. Then when the books were out of sight, she said, "I ain't as pure as your cardinal flower, MeeMaw. Not no more."

She toyed with the broad red petal, comparing it to the bevy of smaller upturned red petals, and then she whispered. "I've been doing it with Cormac … but I reckon you know that, don't you? When Ma died, he brought Boopie on board and they did it nearly every night. I could hear them going at it, and it got me all hot and squiggly inside. So when Boopie left and Cormac said he wanted to teach me about such things, I let him start playing with me. And pretty soon the playing turned into sure-enough screwing."

Kizzy took a deep breath, and then spoke louder. "Here lately, I've been reading and paying attention to Olivia—she's my friend at the library—and she and her preacher say it's a sin to screw when you ain't married, particularly when you are just a kid.

"Her preacher says sinners ought to repent, and I'd do that in a jiffy, but I'm having a hard time seeing how anybody is going to forgive me. What I've been doing with Cormac is just too terrible.

"I didn't think this way for the longest time, MeeMaw, because it feels good to do it. Shoot, I never even thought much about it being wrong. Besides—it's as I said—I know for a fact that Ma and Shirley liked it … and I reckon you did too before you got too old.

"I'd like to fix things, MeeMaw, but it's not like I just made a mistake. The truth is, I'm hot-blooded and I like doing it. But now that I know it's wrong, I can't tell anyone about it, and the shame of it is eating me up."

Kizzy bowed her head for a second, and then she huffed and jerked the red flower, pulling it off the large plant. She touched the petals to her lips, whimpered, and then sat down on the fore deck.

The familiar night sounds—crickets, frogs croaking, water lapping against the hull, fish flopping, and hoot owls fussing—were good accompaniment, but the late-summer mosquitoes showed no respect for the music of the river or Kizzy's deep thoughts. They pestered her unmercifully and drove her inside.

She turned the radio on and scanned through a half-dozen stations, hoping to find something that would give her peace of mind. She tried music, and the ever-present half-hour shows, but nothing worked. Finally, she turned the radio off and went to bed, and in that shadowy moment before sleep she made a wish. *Somebody—MeeMaw, Knuckles, Grandpa, God, anybody—please send me a sign.*

⚜

Just after midnight a huge log, half-submerged, floated downstream and banged into the side of the houseboat. It was not as violent as when MeeMaw got knocked overboard, but the collision shook the old wooden vessel from stem to stern, and it sounded like a cannon shot. Kizzy sat bolt upright in bed, and she rushed outside to see if the heavy log had done any damage. She walked all around the deck, looking over the side to inspect the hull. There was no serious damage to the boat, but the jolt and the cool night air had awakened her.

She sat down on the aft deck and dangled her feet in the current. The early sounds of nightfall had given way to the eerie stillness of midnight, and it was in that quiet moment that Kizzy's mind cleared and the truth came to her.

Wake up, girl! She batted her fist against her head and stared into the dark water. *I gave in to Cormac that last time only because he forced me to do it. I didn't do it because it feels good, or because I wanted to do it. He made me do it. He's been using me from the very beginning. It wasn't about teaching me.*

That was just an act to get me feeling as if I was just as much a part of it as he was.

It was a mistake to let him do it, but there is nothing wrong with me, and it is not wrong to like the way it feels.

I just need to live up to the way Olivia thinks about doing it. Stefan's mother felt the same way.

Besides all that, I get a better feeling just fooling around with Stefan than I do when Cormac actually does it to me.

It's not going to happen again.

I'm 16 now. Cormac will be back Sunday. I'll talk to him then.

I'll just tell him flat out: No more sex, Cormac. I'm not gonna do it with you ever again.

XLIX

Struggle

Kizzy got up early on Saturday. She cleaned the cabin, stowed all the gear that she and Stefan had taken with them on their trip down the river, then sat down to finish *Northanger Abbey*. In late afternoon she closed the book and smiled. Jane Austen had ended the coming-of-age story on a happy note, Catherine's marriage to Henry.

She put the book down and picked up *Juvenilia*, a collection of short stories written by Jane Austen when she was a teenager. Kizzy flipped through the pages out of curiosity. She did not intend to read any more that day, but then she saw the story of "Jack and Alice," and realized that it dealt with drinking to excess.

Cormac will be back tomorrow. He drinks too much, so I ought to read this.

The story was a tongue-in-cheek mockery of alcoholism in the fictional British town of Pammydiddle, but it was also about an envious and malevolent young woman, Sukey Simpson, who poisoned a 17-year-old girl because she was jealous of her superior charms. In classic Austen style, Sukey got her just deserts: "The perfidious Sukey was … exalted in a manner she truly deserved. Her barbarous murder was discovered, and in spite of every interceding friend she was speedily raised to the gallows."

The gallows! Kizzy shuddered. *Hankering after something that someone has is no reason to kill. That doesn't make any sense, even for someone as meanhearted as Sukey.*

She pondered Sukey's fate for a while, but fell asleep thinking of ways to deal with Cormac. She had fought his drunken advances the night before he went to Memphis, but the more she resisted, the madder he got. In the end, he had used brute strength to have his way with her, and Kizzy did not want to go through that again.

By mid-afternoon Sunday, Kizzy had decided that force would not work. Cormac was six foot four and strong as an ox. She would try a different approach.

He might have a change of heart if I can just slow him down and get him talking about other things. I'll start by telling him about the log that hit the boat, and the new school term that's about to start. Then I'll talk about how I'm going to graduate and get a job, maybe in Jonesboro or Newport— stuff like that. Then when he's listening, and we are talking like grownups, I'll look for a way to tell him ... I'll just explain why I don't want to do it anymore.

❖

It was turning dark Sunday afternoon when Cormac got back from Memphis, and the instant he stumbled through the door, Kizzy detected the god-awful stench of beer, rank body odor, and garlic.

She tensed up, doubting the wisdom of her plan.

Then, to her surprise, Cormac mumbled something about having a flat tire and being tired. He gave her a goofy grin, lurched across the cabin to sit on the side of his bunk, and wrestled with his shoes. When he got them off, he lay back on the bed, and passed out. And after a few deep breaths, he began to snore.

Kizzy relaxed and fixed herself a sandwich. She read for a while, and then got in the other bunk.

Her talk with Cormac would have to wait.

❖

On Monday morning, Sept. 4, 1944, Kizzy awoke as soon as she heard Cormac moving around.

She blinked and frowned. Then she raised her head to see what he was doing. *He never gets up before me.*

Cormac, still dressed in the clothes he slept in, was leaning over the sink, washing his face. Between splashes he said, "This is Labor Day. The button factory is closed today, but that don't matter—I ain't going back to work there no how."

He wiped his face dry and turned to face her. "You fix breakfast, and while you're doing that I'll tell you the good news." Then he tossed his towel on the counter and went outside.

When Kizzy heard him peeing off the side of the boat, she got up, sat on the side of the bed, and pulled an old cotton dress over her head. Then she got up, put a pot of coffee on the stove, and pulled a slab of bacon from the coolbox; she was about to start slicing it when Cormac came back inside.

"I drove back in Susie's truck to get you. We're leaving this dump." He was talking louder and faster than usual, barking orders like a drill sergeant. "I've got a job in Memphis starting next week; there's real money to be made there. Susie and Josie, another girl from the button factory, are all set up; they'll show you the ropes, and before you know it we'll have more money than we could ever make digging for pearls."

Kizzy did a double take. Her plan to get Cormac talking so that she could calmly explain why she did not want to have sex with him was not going to work. She put the knife down and turned to face him. "I don't want to move, Cormac. I've got friends here and this place is all I know. This is home." She caught her breath, and then added as forcefully as she could. "I ain't gonna be a river rat forever, but I love Big Pearl and I don't want to leave right now. This is where my memories are."

"None of that matters. Besides, you won't be in Big Pearl if I ain't here. You'll be in the poorhouse—just another orphan."

Kizzy shuddered. *The poorhouse! A fate worse than death ... that's what MeeMaw always said about it.*

Cormac continued in earnest. "Besides, there's lots of soldier boys in Memphis, and they've all got cash that's burning a hole in their pocket. The button factory girls is already in business, and they're making a buttload of money. But they is second rate compared to you, Kizzy. Them boys'll pay a fortune for a short time with something as fine as you."

Kizzy gasped and sputtered. *Oh, my God! He means it. And he ain't heard a word I've said.*

When she hesitated, Cormac switched to a softer, pleading tone. "The war will be over soon, Kizzy, and we'll miss our chance."

The words were barely out of his mouth when Kizzy slammed her hand against the counter and stamped her foot. "No, I ain't going."

Cormac screwed his face into a grotesque look that she had never seen, and raised his hand as if he was going to hit her. Instead, he bellowed. "Pack up, we're going! I'll get Curly to watch the boat, and later on I'll come back to get the rest of our stuff."

Kizzy noticed a small patch of froth in the corner of his mouth. She had not seen that before, and his lips were tightly closed and bluish. She had been living with this man since she was 8 years old and having sex with him since she was 13, but suddenly he had the look of a stranger, a crazy one at that.

She whimpered, and to hide her tears she turned her back to him and fiddled with the slab of bacon. "I've got school getting ready to start. I'm going into the 11th grade, and I don't want to go."

Cormac mocked her whimpering.

Kizzy took a deep breath. *I've got to be strong. I can't let him think I'm scared of him.*

She began slicing the bacon, and—in her most determined voice—said, "I'm not going. And I ain't ever going to sell myself to no one, not for no amount of money."

Cormac towered over Kizzy, and he moved so close behind her that she could smell his sour breath and hear the irregular, raspy sound of it. Suddenly he put his arms around her and began to rub her breasts. "Come on, Kizzy. I bet you missed ole Cormac, didn't you?"

She spun around and pushed him back. "Stop it, Cormac." Then she turned back to face the counter, and cut three pieces of bacon from the slab. She put them in a heavy iron skillet, and said, "Leave me alone. I'm having my period."

"Well, that don't matter to me."

"Well, it does to me, and besides, I ain't gonna do it with you anymore, Cormac. It ain't right."

"Here we go again. That's the same right-and-wrong bullshit we went through the last time."

He got behind her again and pressed his body against her rear, so close that she could feel his hardness. Then he slid his hands down to her inner thighs. "Huh! You're lying to ole Cormac—you ain't wearing no rag."

He pulled her dress up, cupped his right hand between her legs, and began to rub her.

"Stop it, Cormac."

But he did not stop; he held her tighter, pushed her against the counter, and forced his finger into her.

She pushed back, wheeled around, and hit his left knee with the iron skillet. The blow made a dull crunching sound, and Cormac screamed like a wounded razorback hog.

He grabbed his knee and swung wildly at her with his free hand.

She leaned backwards to avoid the blow, and then swung the skillet at Cormac's head. He saw it coming and raised his right hand to fend off the blow; the skillet turned in her hand, but the edge of it struck him squarely in the left temple.

He staggered back a step, addled but still conscious, and a heavy stream of blood seeped through his fingers as he rubbed the wound. It ran down his arm and dripped on the floor. When Cormac saw the blood, he howled and tried to speak, but his words were slurred. His eyes were open double-wide, and they appeared to be spinning in opposite directions.

Kizzy shivered and struggled to catch her breath. She started to run away, but the odd look on Cormac's face had morphed into a queer smirk that she mistook for a smile until Cormac opened his mouth and howled.

A thick layer of bloody mucus covered his teeth, and red drool spilled onto his chin.

Kizzy took a step back, but it was too late. Cormac doubled his fist and hit her so hard on the left cheek that she dropped the skillet and fell.

She looked up from the floor, expecting him to hit her again. But he was holding his head with his left hand, and the counter with the other, trying to keep his balance.

Kizzy struggled to her feet. She gave him a defiant look and raised the heavy skillet high above her head. "Leave me alone, Cormac. I mean it. Leave me alone."

Cormac picked up the butcher knife she had been using to cut the bacon and pointed it toward her, but he was convulsing wildly, waving the knife as if conducting an orchestra. Suddenly, he gave her a bizarre look, and jabbed the knife toward her.

Kizzy did not hesitate. She hit him with the skillet as hard as she could.

The death blow landed squarely on the upper left side of Cormac's forehead, and he collapsed in a heap. She stood over him, quivering and sobbing. She was ready to strike again, but there was no need.

Blood oozed from his head, making a puddle that slowly found its way around three misshapen pieces of bacon and several clusters of pulpy grey matter.

⚜

Outside, the air was still. All was quiet on the river. The morning sun was breaking through a dark grey sky, lighting the river and making shadows.

Now and again, a fish would jump or wallow, ending the life of a little bug or a smaller fish.

In the nearby woods, the little birds and critters searched for food while keeping a close lookout for their natural enemies.

The beautiful river flowed on, undisturbed, accepting the little cocoons of cruelty as part of the natural order.

⚜

The killing in the houseboat was of a different sort.

Cormac was dead, and Kizzy stood over him, frozen in place, staring trancelike at his body, crying and rubbing the left side of her face.

The ugly memories—Cormac jabbing at her with the knife, the crunching blow to his head, and the sight of him twitching, gasping, and struggling as he took his last breath—would not go away.

A bewildering spell took possession of Kizzy. It fogged her mind, and made her legs go wobbly. She jerked backwards, away from the corpse, and sat down on the bed.

Then she groaned, doubled over, and clasped her hands beneath her legs. At times, she would rock from side to side, moaning softly. After a while, the cycle of misery would start all over again.

⚜

A canoeist paddled by the houseboat, heading upriver. He rounded the bend and disappeared. A few minutes later, a huge barge piled high with timber came around the same bend, heading downstream. The captain of the unwieldy vessel mismanaged the turn and lost control; the heavy barge was heading directly toward Kizzy's houseboat. The captain panicked, blew an ear-splitting blast on the ship's horn, gunned the engine, and turned the wheel hard to port.

The startling noise shocked Kizzy, but it broke her spell; she came to her senses and jumped up to see what was going on. She looked through a small window just in time to see the big vessel pass within a yard of the houseboat, a near miss.

Kizzy shook her fist at the barge. *Damn! That was close.*

Just then, the wake of the barge rocked the houseboat, and Kizzy fell backwards onto the bed. When the rocking stopped, she sat up, and made a resolution.

I've got to get ahold of myself and figure out what to do.

She thought for a while longer. Then she stood up and bent over to take a closer look at the corpse and the mess on the cabin floor. The grisly sight of blood and brains turned her stomach.

She rushed outside to suck in a deep breath of fresh air, but she could not hold back the sickness. She leaned over the aft railing and threw up, heaving and gasping with each wave of nausea.

When the sickness passed, Kizzy splashed cold water on her face and returned to her seat on the bed, determined to reconstruct every detail of the ruckus that led to the killing: Cormac's plan to move to Memphis, the threat that she would go to the poorhouse, his plan to prostitute her, and his attempt to rape her.

The more she thought about what he had said and done, the madder she got.

Then she thought about what she had done to him, and when she visualized the death blow, her anger turned to fear.

A cold sweat broke out on Kizzy's forehead. She shivered, and a chill danced from the nape of her neck to the pit of her belly. When the chill completed its journey, a scary thought crossed her mind.

I'm gonna wind up like that stupid Sukey Simpson. She got herself hung for poisoning a girl. So what will they do to me for beating Cormac to death with a skillet?

Kizzy groaned and got up. She turned her back to the mess on the floor, picked up a hand mirror and used it to look at her face. The cheek that Cormac hit was a little puffy and pinkish, but the injury was hard to see and it looked as if it might not leave a bruise. Her eyes were red and teary, and when she wiped them dry she saw the image of Cormac's body in the mirror.

Kizzy jerked. *Did he move?*

She turned around, bent over the body, and held the mirror close to Cormac's mouth. Then, holding her breath, she looked and listened in vain for signs of life. *Nope. He's dead as a doornail.*

Kizzy stepped over the corpse, put the mirror away, and went out onto the aft deck to get away from the gruesome scene. The river was still once again, but the current had a batch of driftwood in its grasp. Kizzy watched it come her way, and she studied it carefully as it passed by the houseboat and headed downriver.

I could wait until dark and then put the body in the river. It would be pretty near to Mexican Bend before daylight, and by then I could have the mess in the cabin all cleaned up.

I could say I hadn't seen Cormac in days and don't know anything about how he got killed. But wait, there's that truck he drove home from Memphis; I'd have to explain that.

Just then a fishing boat, chugging its way upriver, changed course and headed in her direction. Kizzy squinted, but she could not identify the small man in the boat. *Uh-oh, he's coming over here.* She waved to him, and then quickly stepped backwards to close the cabin door.

The fisherman drifted alongside, took hold of the houseboat, and pushed his ball cap back on his head. Kizzy relaxed a little. It was Peewee, the head garbage man; she remembered meeting him at Sweetcheeks' Café.

"Hey, Kizzy, when're you and that German boy going to sing us another song?"

She tried her best to be nonchalant. "We're working on a new one, but it will be a while before it's ready." She gave him her best smile, but her stomach was churning. "Where're you going, Peewee?"

"It's Labor Day. I'm gonna catch me a mess of catfish. You got any tips?"

Kizzy forced another smile, and pointed north. "Try that spot upriver where Muddy Creek comes into the Black. It's always good for one or two nice ones."

Peewee nodded his thanks, pulled his cap down, and pushed off. As she watched him motor his way upriver, she realized that she could wait no longer.

What am I going to say if someone comes looking for Cormac? What if they find him before I tell someone what I've done? I can't wait all day and put him in the river tonight. There's too many people working the river. Somebody will find him, and then they'll start asking me a lot of questions.

She went back inside.

I've gotta do something. I can't run off because I got nowhere to go. Maybe I ought to just throw myself in the river and be done with it ...

She had a pang of guilt for thinking such a thing, but it did not last.

No! I ain't thinking straight. I ain't ready to go on down the river.

Besides, I got reasons. Cormac was fixing to move me to Memphis to screw for money. I'd never do that ... not in a month of Sundays.

And I'm not a mean person. I ain't ever hurt a fly. Oh, I've killed an ugly grinnel fish or two—that's true—but I ain't ever hurt anything else. Me and Birdie are alike when it comes to that. Now he's over there killing Japs, but that ain't much different than me killing a no-good grinnel—it's just something you have to do ...

She sighed. *This ain't getting me anywhere.* She ran her fingers through her hair, and then bent over and screamed aloud at the corpse, as if Cormac was still alive. "Dammit, Cormac, you might have been my make-do step-father, but you're the worst thing that ever happened to me."

She hissed, and turned her back to the body. "I may have done wrong by doing it with you, Cormac, and I oughtn't to have killed you, but I'm not a bad person. There ain't anything wrong with me."

Kizzy paused, took a deep breath, and whispered aloud, "Except for the mess I'm in right now."

She pushed the door open, stepped out, and hustled across the gangplank. *I've got to go find Stefan.*

⚜

When Kizzy rounded the corner that led to Eli's house she saw Stefan on the porch playing his violin, and she heard the sweet melody of "The Magic of Your Eyes," the tune they had performed to win the talent contest. Kizzy mouthed the lyrics, but she stopped; she did not feel like singing.

She bit her lip and trudged on. *God knows I need some help, but how am I going to tell Stefan what I've done? What'll he think of me?*

As soon as Stefan saw her, he stopped playing and waved. Instead of waving back, Kizzy ran toward him as fast as she could.

They met at the foot of the porch steps, and she threw herself into his arms. Stefan hugged her and smiled, but she was crying and trembling.

"What's wrong, Kizzy?"

⚜

She did not answer right away.

He'll never understand. I ought to just go back to the boat, wait for dark, and throw Cormac in the river.

Stefan took her hand and led her to a seat on the porch; they sat down and he put his arm around her.

Kizzy stopped crying and laid her head on his shoulder. She wanted to answer, but she needed more time to finish the debate she was having with herself. *I need to tell because this ain't gonna go away ... and I sure need help ... but how much of it should I tell?*

She wrung her hands, mulling the pros and cons. *I'll tell about the fight and how Cormac knocked me down, but I can't tell Stefan or anybody else about Cormac wanting to whore me out. I just can't do that. People would wonder why Cormac ever thought about such a thing, and pretty soon they would figure out that it's because we'd been doing it ... and that would ruin me forever with Stefan ... and Olivia ...*

Kizzy lifted her head off his shoulder, and when she did, Stefan put his hand beneath her chin, turned her face to his, and kissed her gently. "I love you, Kizzy."

"I love you too, but ..." She looked away, then finished what she was going to say. "I've done something awful, Stefan."

He pulled her closer. "Don't worry, Kizzy. It's OK to tell me."

"I ain't so sure about that, Stefan." She pushed back from him, swallowed, and looked down. "I got in a fight with Cormac."

Stefan wrinkled his brow, but before he could say anything, she continued, talking faster than usual. "He came back from Memphis last night, drunk as usual, and this morning he said he was gonna move over there. And he said if I didn't go with him I'd get sent to the poorhouse. I said I wasn't going anywhere, so he got rough with me, and I busted his knee bone with a skillet."

"No one will blame you for that. He's a big man."

"Well, there's more." Kizzy sucked in a breath. "He took a swing at me and I hit him in the head with the skillet. It was a glancing blow, but it staggered him. Then he hauled off and knocked the whey out of me. I got up off the floor and told him to stop. He poked a knife at me and I hit him again with the skillet."

She hesitated, sniffled a little, and then said with finality. "It was a hard lick to the head, and it killed him outright."

She got up, stepped to the edge of the porch, and looked toward the street. "I can't believe this is happening. Just when everything was looking up for me, I've gone and gotten myself in a bunch of trouble."

She turned to face Stefan. "Wait 'til Bully Bigshot hears about this. He'll be telling the lawmen to hang me, or put me in the electric chair."

"It sounds to me like Cormac had it coming."

She shrugged, and he went to her side. "I think you ought to tell Eli. He'll know what to do."

L

Reckoning

Eli hung up and turned away from the wall telephone.

"Ruben says we have to tell the authorities right away, but he says we shouldn't go into the details of how or why it happened. He says we should just say that there was a fight and that Kizzy fought back to defend herself."

"Is he coming over?" Said Stefan.

"Yes, but this is Labor Day; he'll drive over tomorrow."

"Will they put me in jail?"

"Ruben said he'll call the judge if they do, but he doesn't think they will because you're only 16."

"MeeMaw got thrown in jail once for telling fortunes. She said it was the dirtiest, stinkiest place she'd ever been."

"Ruben's a smart lawyer," Stefan said. "He brought up lots of good points when he represented Fritz."

"They sent him to prison."

"That was different, Kizzy," Eli said. "We are at war. Fritz got sent to North Dakota for being a German who didn't register."

"Well, Bully Bigshot hates us river rats worse than he hates Germans."

⚜

Rachel Schulman came out of the kitchen just as Eli dialed the sheriff's number.

She put her hand on his to stop the call. "Don't call Gunner Brown."

Eli raised an eyebrow. "Why not?"

"Because Sully Biggers owns him—lock, stock, and barrel. I've been listening to you all ... I think you ought to call that new city policeman, Butch Jansen."

Eli looked at Stefan and Kizzy, and shrugged. "I learned long ago not to question Rachel's intuition."

"It's not intuition, Eli. I was on the Welcome Wagon committee that visited him and his wife when they moved to town last week. He was with Patton's tank corps in North Africa, but he got hurt. The war is over for him."

Rachel took Kizzy's hand. "They seem like good people to me, Kizzy. Your 'Bully Bigshot' may get to him eventually, but right now I think he just wants to be fair and do a good job."

Kizzy said to Rachel. "I need to tell Olivia about this before she hears it from someone else."

Rachel looked at Eli, and when he nodded, she said, "I'll call her and ask her to come over."

Eli headed for the door. "And I'll go find Butch Jansen."

⚜

Olivia was in the middle of making a batch of cookies for a church social when Rachel called and told her that Kizzy was in trouble. Rachel did not go into details, but Olivia sensed urgency in her voice; she stripped off her apron and left immediately.

She walked, half-running most of the way, to the Schulman house; Rachel was there to meet her.

"What's going on Rachel?"

Rachel put her finger to her lips. "Kizzy wants to tell you herself ... she's in the parlor with Stefan."

Olivia gasped. *What on earth?*

The Schulman parlor, a darkish room stuffed with French provincial furniture, was on the shady side of the house. An ornate chandelier cast a small circle of yellowish light, just enough for Olivia to see Kizzy.

She was sitting next to Stefan on a deep purple French settee, tense and fidgety. Her face was ashen, uncommonly sullen.

Olivia winced; she could not speak. *Oh, Kizzy.*

You look like you did that night I saw you on the street and invited you to come into the library ... you're wearing that old dress ... but now your hair is all mussed up and you're barefooted. And you're scared ...

Olivia stopped that line of thought. *No. I'm judging her, and that's not right. She needs love.*

She took a step forward and opened her arms. Kizzy went to her and whimpered as they embraced. Olivia held her tight and let her sob, then Kizzy told her about the fight with Cormac. It was the same story she told Stefan, and when she finished she broke down again, crying and apologizing. "I'm sorry, Olivia." Then she looked at Stefan and Rachel and spoke in a raspy voice. "I've let all of you down."

Olivia consoled Kizzy, but on the inside she struggled to understand. *How could this happen? I don't know the ways of the river people ... but there's more to this than meets the eye.*

⚜

John "Butch" Jansen was all alone, sitting behind a desk and listening to the radio, when Eli Schulman entered the police station.

Eli introduced himself and was quick to add, "My wife was one of the Welcome Wagon ladies who came to your house last week."

Butch smiled. "Yes, they were real nice. What can I do for you, Mr. Schulman?"

Eli turned serious. "Officer, there's a fine young girl at my house who lives down on the river. This morning she got in an argument with the man who has been raising her, and it turned into a fight. He hit her and jabbed a knife at her, so she hit him in the head with a skillet, and it killed him."

Butch winced and turned off the radio. "Where did this happen?"

"In the houseboat where she's lived her whole life; it's the first boat upriver from Curly's Fish Market. I can take you there."

"I'll call the coroner. He needs to go with us." Butch made the call, then told Eli, "He'll be here in five minutes."

While they waited, Butch gathered the things he might need, talking aloud to himself as he put various items in a canvas bag: Eastman Kodak camera, a fresh tablet of writing paper, tape measure, and evidence collection dishes.

Eli studied Butch as he worked. He was handsome in his way, 27 years old with wide-set eyes and a high forehead. The brand-new police uniform, blue with black trim, gave him a look that seemed out of sorts with his soft voice and friendly countenance. For a big, broad-shouldered man—six foot two at least—Butch moved easily about the room.

He was a picture of health except for the grotesque burn scars that disfigured the right side of his face and neck. The scarring did not end there; it reappeared beneath the hem of his short-sleeve shirt and ran down his arm to the tip of his fingers. Eli could only imagine what lay beneath the young veteran's shirt and trousers; he assumed the worst, and was right to do so.

Butch was part of a tank crew that took a direct hit from German artillery fire during the Battle of El Guettar in North Africa. He pulled two members of his crew to safety, but when he tried to save a third man a hideous fire broke out. Butch managed to get out of the tank, but he spent six months at Walter Reed Hospital recuperating from burns that covered the right side of his body.

Eli recognized the Silver Star and Purple Heart ribbons pinned just above the breast pocket of Butch's police uniform. He was just about to praise Butch for his service when County Coroner Mutt Falwell barged into the room.

❖

"The killings around here have slacked off since the war started, but I can always count on the river rats—they're good for one or two a year." Mutt feigned sadness, then laughed so loud and hard that it triggered a coughing fit. Eli and Butch took a quick step backwards to let him catch his breath and let his remark about the river rats go by; it was ghoulish and proprietary, but not out of character for the jaded little mortician. His life depended on death, and he looked and acted the part.

The three men walked from the police station to the houseboat; it was less than 200 yards, and most of that was on the narrow foot trail that led from the state highway down to the river.

Eli and Butch talked about the war and their families, but Mutt walked ahead, constantly urging them to pick up the pace. When he got to the houseboat he held his nose and hollered, "Whooee, it's going to be a scorcher today. Let's get this over with. This place will be stinking to high heaven before you know it."

The scene inside the houseboat was just as Kizzy had left it. Butch told Mutt and Eli to stand back so that he could take photographs. He shot the scene from every angle, and when he finished he bent over the body; it was time to start the methodical process of collecting and marking items that might be evidence.

Mutt shuffled around, complaining about the heat, and then he leaned toward Eli and spoke in a stage whisper, "The rookie doesn't know what he is doing."

Butch ignored the slur and took his time; he was busy scooping up a tiny piece of bone from the pool of blood by Cormac's head.

Mutt spoke to Eli again, this time out of the corner of his mouth. "He's taking way too much time."

Butch marked the bone as evidence, and when he set it aside Mutt tapped him on the shoulder. "Move over, buddy. Let me examine the body so we can wrap this up and I can get out of here."

"I'll move over when I'm done."

Mutt huffed, and pointed his finger in Butch's face. "I've had enough of your bossiness. I'm the duly elected coroner in this county, and I've worked every killing for the last 40 years. I ain't ever been treated like this."

"Maybe so, but it's my responsibility to collect and preserve the evidence; when I'm done with that I'll let you examine the body."

Mutt sneered. "You're working this case like it was the killing of the president or something. This is just another river rat killing. That goo there on the floor is brains, any fool can see that. You can fiddle around playing policeman but believe you me, the prosecuting attorney and the town fathers know how to handle these people."

Eli butted in. "This involves a 16-year-old girl; her name is Kizzy. She is not 'these people.'"

Mutt stared at Eli and faked a salute. "Yes sir, Mr. Eli Schulman."

"Knock it off, Mutt," Butch said. He worked a while longer, and then stood up. "There, I'm done. Now you can examine the body."

Mutt glared, but said nothing. Then he squatted down by the body to start his examination.

Eli and Butch stepped out onto the aft deck, and Eli said, "What happens next?"

"That'll be up to the prosecuting attorney, but if the girl's story holds up it looks like a case of self-defense to me."

"I've got a lawyer, Ruben Levy, coming over from Memphis tomorrow. Will it be all right if Kizzy stays with me tonight?"

"That sounds OK to me, Eli. This is Labor Day and she's not going anywhere. I can't see anything wrong with that."

Just then, Mutt came outside. "Whooee! That little river rat girl sure packs a wallop. She busted his skull twice … either one of the licks was enough to kill him. I'm done here, so I'm going home to listen to the baseball game—it looks like the St. Louis Browns are going to the World Series."

He started across the gangplank but stopped when he was halfway to shore. "Oh, by the way, Butch, I heard you telling Mr. Eli Schulman that the girl can stay with him tonight. That ain't your call, bigshot. That'll be up to Sheriff Gunner Brown and the prosecuting attorney, and they'll listen first to me and Mr. Sully Biggers, who by the way ain't got no use for river rats."

It was shortly after lunch when they heard a car door slam. Rachel, who was sitting by the front window, parted the heavy drapes and peeped out.

"It's the sheriff, Eli."

Eli got up and went to the front door, signaling for everyone to stay calm. "I'll see what he wants."

Kizzy gave Olivia a worried look, and then nestled closer to Stefan.

Eli watched through a glass panel as the sheriff got out of the car and started toward the house, hitching his pants and straightening his hat. After a few steps, he seemed to puff up and his stride became a swagger—the unmistakable mark of an overly proud lawman.

As the sheriff neared the porch, Eli opened the heavy front door, but he left the screen door closed.

The sheriff said, "Is the girl here?"

Eli pushed the screen door open and stepped onto the porch. "Why?"

"Because I need to talk to her about the killing, that's why."

"Can't that wait, Gunner? I've asked a lawyer friend to come over from Memphis. He'll be here by noon tomorrow, and then we can get this cleared up."

"That's not the way it works around here." Gunner Brown sneered. Then he looked through the screen door, and said in a loud voice. "I've got orders to take her in."

Kizzy cringed when she heard that, but Olivia did not. She jumped up and headed for the porch, pushing the screen door open so violently that it almost came off the hinges.

Olivia got in the sheriff's face. "You can't be serious, Gunner Brown. Kizzy is only 16 years old. She has every right to talk to a lawyer before she talks to you."

"I ain't saying she can't talk to a lawyer, Olivia. She can do that tomorrow, but right now she is going to jail."

Olivia exploded. "Jail?" She glared at the sheriff. "Why?"

He backed up a step and gave Olivia a softer look, but that did not slow her down. "I'll vouch for her, and she can stay with me tonight."

"I already told Eli it don't work that way. The prosecuting attorney told me to put her in jail and hold her on suspicion of murder."

"Murder?" Olivia wagged her finger at him and shouted, "You're as dumb as you look, Gunner Brown."

"Well, there's things you don't know, Olivia. The coroner says the girl hit Cormac three times with a heavy iron skillet ... hit him so hard that it busted his head open and knocked his brains out."

"It was self-defense, you nincompoop."

The sheriff chortled. "It may be, and it may not be; that's why the prosecutor said to hold her 'on suspicion.'"

Olivia looked at Eli. "Can't we call somebody? Judge Barnhart?"

Gunner butted in. "Won't do you no good, Olivia. It's Labor Day. Besides, he wouldn't go against the prosecutor."

Olivia's knees wobbled, but she hid it from the sheriff. "I'm going to tell everyone in town about this, Gunner Brown. You'll pay in the next election."

Just then, Kizzy and Stefan came onto the porch, and Kizzy put her arm around Olivia. "I'll go with him, Olivia. It'll be all right."

"No it's not all right." Olivia stamped her foot. "It's all wrong."

Kizzy kissed her on the cheek. "Thanks for fighting for me, but I better go."

The sheriff stepped close and put his hand on Kizzy's arm, and tugged her in the direction of his patrol car.

Kizzy shook his hand loose and gave him a defiant look. Then she hugged Stefan and nodded thanks to Eli and Rachel.

"Don't worry, Kizzy," said Olivia. "We're going to get you out of there."

Kizzy winked, then she threw her head back and laughed aloud. "It ain't gonna be like Barton Cottage, but it's not anything that I can't take."

⚜

The Jasper County Jail, an ugly two-story building made of native stone, was built in 1894, just a few months after a gang of desperados robbed a passenger train and killed the conductor in nearby Oliphant. The robbers were caught and hanged, but the people of Big Pearl wanted to do more; they built a new jail and put it in the center of town on a prime piece of property overlooking the Black River.

The 50-year-old jail was an eyesore, but it served a purpose: No one wanted to be locked up in the Jasper County Jail.

It was designed to hold 20 prisoners, but a raucous weekend could swell the population to as many as 30. The war and the draft relieved the overcrowding somewhat because many of the "regulars," the young men who got locked up on Saturday nights for drinking, fighting, or just "acting funny," were now in the Army.

Sheriff Gunner Brown brought Kizzy to the jail and turned her over to Roscoe Jones, the jailer. "Put her up on the second floor, Jonesy."

The first floor was off limits to the likes of Kizzy. The entire space was devoted to the jailer's living quarters, storage, and a small private sleeping room that the sheriff reserved for special people, friends of Sully Biggers, and others who could and would make a financial contribution to the sheriff's campaign fund.

The jailer booked Kizzy and wrote her name and date of birth in a well-worn journal. Kizzy stood by, wrinkling her nose and sniffing. *Sauerkraut and weenies.*

"Come on, girl." The jailer pointed to a medieval stairwell. "I'm gonna put you in with Gertie."

The smell of sauerkraut and weenies followed them up the steep circular stairs. But when they stepped into the dimly lit corridor that gave access to the cells, the odor of food gave way to the stench of urine, feces, soiled bedding, and body odors.

Kizzy rubbed her eyes and strained to see.

The second floor was one big room with steel bars that divided it into three cells, all on the river side of the building. Each cell had three double bunks, a small sink, and a toilet bowl with no seat. A small-wattage light bulb dangled above the corridor; the only other light came through small barred windows, one in each cell. The windows were positioned near the ceiling so that prisoners could not see out or be seen by people on the outside.

Kizzy heard a jumble of talk and the rustling sound of prisoners moving about, all straining to see if the jailer was alone. Was he coming to release someone, or was he bringing a new cellmate? Kizzy was close enough to see the look on their faces—forlorn, desperate, hopeless—and she cringed when they reached through the bars, whistling and pleading for her to touch them. But once she had passed them by, their pleas for a simple touch turned into crass offers of sex.

The jailer rattled his nightstick on the bars and barked orders. "Get back to your bunks. This one's going in with Gertie, and I'm gonna move Duncan from Cell No. 2 to Cell No.1."

"That'll make five of us in No. 1, Jonesy."

The jailer said, "If she bonds out I'll move Duncan back, but for tonight there's gonna be an empty cell between you horny bastards and the girls."

Kizzy waited in the corridor as the jailer moved Prisoner Duncan to Cell No. 1 and slammed the door shut. The clanging noise, unique to jails, did not scare Kizzy. She twitched slightly, but she had steeled herself, determined to take whatever might come her way.

But when the jailer pushed her into Cell No. 3 and slammed the door Kizzy felt all goose-pimply. The ear-splitting clang of the steel door closing behind her sounded the same, but the meaning was different, and that is what scared her.

Dang, Grandpa. I get it now. This here is what you meant when you made your July Fourth speeches ... the ones about us living free on the river ...

The racket of that first door shuttin' was about someone else losin' their freedom. This last clang when the door closed behind me was the sound of me losing my freedom, and that's sure enough scary.

⚜

"Hey kid, I'm Gertie." The gravelly voice, loud in the stillness that settles over a jail as soon as the doors are locked shut, came from the shadows.

Gertie Gazaway, spread-eagled on the lower level of a double bunk, raised up just enough to let the light strike her face. It was round and jowly, a good match for the rest of her.

"Whatcha in for?"

Kizzy moved toward her to get a better look, but stopped when she saw that Gertie was playing with herself.

"I'm not sure," Kizzy said. "The sheriff said they're holding me on suspicion."

"Ha!" Gertie stopped playing with herself and pulled her dress down. "I been in here for three weeks 'on suspicion.' They say I know something about my boyfriend being in on a bank robbery, but they can't prove nothing on me so they are just holding me without no papers being filed." She sat up in bed. "They do whatever they want ... they don't give a shit about folks like us."

"My Grandpa and MeeMaw told me the whole thing is rigged, and it's run by Bully Bigshot—that's what we call Sully Biggers, the man who owns everything around here."

Gertie cackled and lay back. "Perfect. Well the joke's on them, I'm knocked up. So, in three months they're either gonna let me out or there'll be two of us for them to take care of."

Duncan shouted from Cell No. 1. "I heard you got busted for killing a man."

Gertie growled. "Don't answer that asshole. He's just wants to get you talking so's he can tell the sheriff what you said. Then if they can use it against you in court he'll get time off for rattin' you out."

Kizzy nodded thanks, and then she climbed to the top level of the double bunk farthest away from Gertie and turned her face to the wall. *I've just got to wait it out. Maybe I'll get out tomorrow. But right now I've just got to wait.*

Duncan was tireless; he kept baiting Kizzy, trying to get her to talk about the killing. The others goaded her with endless offers of sex and vivid descriptions of their anatomy.

At 5 p.m. the jailer brought trays of sauerkraut and weenies for the inmates, but Kizzy did not eat. She stayed where she was, thinking about the sudden turn in her life. Less than 12 hours ago she had been steeling herself to tell Cormac that she was through having sex with him; now he was dead and she was in jail and might be charged with murder. *Tomorrow. Tomorrow will be better.*

At 8 o'clock that night Kizzy awakened to what she thought was more goading, but it was not that. The prisoners in Cell No. 1 were carrying on conversations with people outside the jail. Shouts from the prisoners were being answered by shouts from friends and loved ones on the outside.

Kizzy sat up on the edge of her bunk. "What's going on Gertie?"

"It happens every night after dark when it ain't too cold or rainy. It's the easiest way for folks to talk to someone that's locked up in here—it's a helluva lot easier than trying to get a sure-enough visit. It's been going on for 50 years ... next best thing to having a telephone."

Kizzy lay back and dozed off. But just before 10 o'clock she awoke to a familiar sound, one that warmed her heart and gave her confidence.

Stefan was outside, playing "The Magic of Your Eyes." And when he finished, he shouted, "Tomorrow, Kizzy. They're gonna get you out tomorrow." Then he played the tune that meant so much to him, the second movement of Mendelssohn's Concerto in E minor.

The prisoners in Cell No. 1 stopped kibitzing. Thoughts of magical eyes quieted them, and the strains of Mendelssohn lulled them to sleep.

Kizzy smiled and slumbered, thinking of Stefan.

⚜

"You have to charge her or let her go," said Ruben Levy. He had been on the phone with Prosecuting Attorney Sam Lookadoo for 10 minutes, trying to get Kizzy out of jail, but he was not making any progress.

Lookadoo laughed. "I'll charge her when I get good and goddamn ready."

"You've got no case, Mr. Prosecutor. The city policeman himself said it looks like a case of self-defense."

"He's new around here. I pay more attention to the sheriff and Mutt Falwell; they have their hands on the pulse of the community."

"You mean they have their noses up Sully Biggers' ass."

"You big-city lawyers just don't get it, do you? You think you can come over here and tell us how to run our county."

Ruben Levy had had enough. "I'm going to file a petition for habeas corpus. I've already called the judge, and he's agreed to hear my petition at 1 p.m."

⚜

Judge Roger Barnhart, a longtime member of Sully Biggers' good-old-boy network, did not like big-city lawyers, particularly Jews from Memphis. The only thing he hated worse was for one of them to get him reversed on appeal. He was finishing up his last few months on the bench, having been defeated in the recent election by a last-minute surprise candidate. So, as soon as he saw Ruben Levy's petition for habeas corpus he called the prosecuting attorney. "Sam, you've got to file a charge or I'll have to grant the petition and let the girl go. I've only got a few weeks left as judge and I don't want to get reversed by a Jew boy."

At 1 p.m. Ruben Levy went to Judge Barnhart's office, and as soon as he walked through the door Sam Lookadoo handed him a copy of the information that he had just filed charging Kizzy with second degree murder.

Judge Barnhart did not give Ruben time to react. "Now that there is a charge filed, Mr. Levy, wouldn't you like to withdraw your petition for habeas corpus?" He looked over his glasses and grinned, daring Ruben to say no.

"If I do withdraw it, can we use this meeting to set bail? I want to get Kizzy out of jail."

The judge looked at the prosecuting attorney, who nodded. "Your Honor, the state asks that bail be set at $50,000."

"That's outrageous. The girl is a pauper and she's not going anywhere. Furthermore, Olivia Decker has agreed to take her in until this matter is resolved."

The judge rubbed his chin. "Olivia Decker is a fine woman, highly respected, Mr. Levy. I'm surprised that she would be involved in a case like this. You say she is willing to vouch for the girl and sign her bond?"

"She will sign for the girl, Your Honor. And if that is not good enough, Mr. Eli Schulman, Mac Thornton and two other Veterans' at the Veterans' Center have said they will sign."

The judge thought for a moment, then said, "That won't be necessary, Mr. Levy."

⚜

At 3 p.m. on Tuesday, Sept. 5, Kizzy stood in the doorway of the Jasper County Jail, blinking and shielding her eyes from the sun. She took a deep breath, and when she stepped clear of the jail Olivia and Stefan swarmed her.

"Thank God you are free," Olivia said.

Kizzy put her hand on Olivia's cheek. "I was right—it ain't Barton Cottage." Then she burst into laughter.

"Did you hear me playing last night?" Stefan asked.

"Did I? Are you kidding? It was the only good thing that happened to me yesterday … I was feeling pretty low until you started playing."

⚜

Kizzy heard Olivia calling her name, but she did not want to get out of the bathtub. She had been soaking for a half-hour, letting the warm sudsy water cleanse her. The grime and stench of the Jasper County Jail had washed away quickly, but Kizzy could not forget the sights, sounds, and smells; that would take a while, perhaps years.

Olivia called again, and Kizzy sat up in the tub. *Dang. I'm loving this— sure beats the spit baths we had to take on the boat when it was too cold to get in the river.*

She splashed a final rinse on her arms and stood up. Then, as she was drying off, she saw herself in the full-length mirror. *Hmmm. There I am again … looking pretty much like I did the last time I was here.*

She stepped out of the tub and sneaked another look at herself. She started to smile, but sulked instead. *I'm the same on the outside all right, but I ain't the same on the inside.*

She went into the bedroom. Olivia had taken away the old cotton dress that she had worn for two days; in its place was a light green smock, undies, and a pair of slippers.

She dressed and went downstairs. Olivia was in the kitchen. "Well, look at you—all cleaned up, and no worse for the wear."

Kizzy laughed, then sighed. "Maybe so, but I sure don't want to go through that again."

"We're going to fight this thing, Kizzy." Olivia pointed to the table, inviting her to sit down. "Eli and Ruben believe they're trying to make an example out of you, and that doesn't make any sense to any of us."

"You all ain't … you all aren't river rats. If you were it'd make sense to you."

"That's all the more reason to fight. They've suspended you from school, but we're going to get a tutor for you so you won't be put back a grade when this is all over."

Kizzy teared up and looked away. "I'd be up the creek without a paddle if it weren't for you all."

That night Kizzy enjoyed another luxury. She propped herself up in a real bed to read by the light of an electric lamp.

Just before midnight, she put the book aside and turned out the light. The dreaded image of Cormac—dead on the floor—darted across her mind.

Kizzy sighed. *I ain't ever gonna tell what me and Cormac were doing, and I sure ain't gonna tell that he was wanting to whore me out in Memphis.*

⚜

On Wednesday, Sept. 6, 1944, *The Big Pearl Free Current* had a five-column banner stretched across the front page, above the fold: LABOR DAY SKILLET KILLING.

A two-column story beneath the banner was headlined: RIVER GIRL CHARGED WITH MURDER.

The wire services did not move the story; they were too busy with war news. But it was big news in Big Pearl.

At 8 a.m. the coffee klatch gathered at Biggers Grocery. The "skillet killing" was the topic of conversation, and the klatchers were siding with Bully who had quickly turned the killing of a "no-good river rat" into a holy cause.

"We gotta do something about the river rats. They breed like rabbits; before you know it there'll be more of them than there are of us, particularly if you count the niggers and the white trash that live down south of town. We need to get rid of 'em, and we'd be doing better at it if those idiots in the legislature would make it legal for us to sterilize 'em."

"Amen, Sully," said the butcher from behind the counter.

The other klatchers picked up on Bully's theme, and that gave him a chance to say what was really sticking in his craw: "The girl that Gunner Brown arrested and threw in jail for the killing is a good example of what I'm talking about. She's been mighty uppity ever since she won the talent contest and started working over at the library with those women who think they know everything."

The local postman, a regular at the table, said, "Well, I like Olivia, but that girl does have her buffaloed. I don't know why she keeps trying to help her; it sure ain't working."

Pretty soon the klatchers were ready to hang Kizzy even though most of them agreed with a point the butcher made about Cormac, "He needed killing."

⚜

"September 6, 1944

Dear Birdie,

I think about you all the time, and I hope you are doing OK.

I'm doing all right, but I just got out of jail.

Day before yesterday—it seems longer ago—Cormac tried to make me move to Memphis, and I didn't want to go. We got in a fight about it and I hit him a pretty good lick with a skillet.

I didn't mean to kill him—I was just fighting back—but he's dead and now the law is going after me for it.

Olivia and Mr. Eli Schulman are standing by me and they got a lawyer for me. Uncle Mac and the vets at the Center are also helping. They all think I will get off, but I ain't so sure. If Bully Bigshot has anything to say about it, I'll wind up in prison.

Anyway, the judge is letting me stay with Olivia until the trial and that's a good thing. I've got my own sleeping room and there's a flush toilet right next door so I'm living pretty high on the hog—right now anyway.

Oh, I almost forgot. The judge has set my trial for February 5. They say he put it after the first of the year because he won't be judge then—there's a new judge coming in.

Anyway, it's just five months from now.

Take care of yourself.

Love,

Kizzy"

LI

Peleliu

The war in the Pacific was fought island by island.

The Japanese—faithful to the ancient code of *bushido*—began World War II with a false sense of superiority, dedicated to the principle of death before dishonor or defeat. They often launched suicidal attacks on American forces, waving samurai swords, screaming their blood-curdling cry: *"Banzai!"*

During the Battle of Guadalcanal on Aug. 21, 1942, Colonel Kiyonao Ichiki ordered 800 soldiers to launch a *banzai* charge. The Americans were ready for them. Most of the Japanese soldiers were killed, and the disgraced Ichiki committed *harikiri*.

The *banzai* attacks continued, but desperate fighting on Saipan in the early summer of 1944 convinced the Japanese that the ancient tactic was no match for modern infantry weapons in the hands of a determined, well-trained opponent. They ordered their commanders to stop the *banzai* attacks.

Lt. General Sadao Inoue, commander of the Palau Island Detachment, the site of the next major battle, issued a proclamation to his troops: Utilize the terrain to best advantage. Dig in and hunker down. Make carefully coordinated small-scale counterattacks at night. Fight a war of attrition. Use snipers and terroristic atrocities. Make no *banzai* attacks, but honor our revered code of *bushido* by fighting to the death. Our goal is to delay and bleed the enemy.

⚜

On Aug. 7, 1944, 2,100 miles to the southeast, at a rest camp on the island of Pavuvu, Corporal L. W. "Birdie" Barden was eating lunch when an excited private ran into the mess hall hollering, "Bob Hope is coming—Bob Hope is coming!"

Birdie cheered along with others in the mess hall, but he asked, "When?"

"They say he's on the way right now, and Frances Langford is coming with him."

The mess hall cleared out immediately; the First Division Marines, to a man, were in general agreement: "Eating can wait ..."

The USO show gave the men a chance to laugh, and they saw the first white women they had seen in months. But when the show was over and the entertainers were gone, a sense of nostalgia settled over the island.

Birdie's gunny sergeant said, "I'm glad they came. It gave the men a boost, but it hurts to see all those good-looking girls when you're stuck out here, thousands of miles from home."

⚜

Meanwhile, the American commanders were planning their assault on the Palau Islands chain. The main objective was to capture the airfield on the tiny island of Peleliu; that would protect General MacArthur's right flank in the liberation of the Philippine Islands.

The planners did not know that General Inoue had changed the way the Japanese would fight. The Marines expected them to continue the fool-hardy *banzai* tactics that they had used all across the South Pacific.

By the end of August the plans were ready; rumors spread quickly through the ranks of the First Marine Division: "We are going to Peleliu. They say it will be a quick victory; the fighting will be rough, but short. It will take only two or three days to defeat the Japanese."

⚜

Birdie and Private First Class Henry "Hank" Moses leaned against the star-board rail of *LST-117* as she eased away from Pavuvu and headed for deep water to join a massive convoy headed to the Palau Islands chain. Their outfit, the First Marine Division, would assault White Beaches 1 and 2 on Peleliu.

Hank Moses—an Alabama farm boy fresh out of boot camp—was a good mechanic, thus he had been chosen to carry a Browning Automatic Rifle, a complex weapon that was difficult to clean. He liked being the BAR man; to him it was a badge of honor.

Hank tossed his cigarette butt into the clear water, threw his head back, and breathed deeply through his nose. Then he nudged Birdie. "Fresh air— finally! Pavuvu's pretty, but the whole damn island smells like rotten coconuts and land crabs."

Birdie looked askance. "Maybe so, but as soon as we hit the beach in Peleliu you'll be wishing you were back here."

"Not me. Me and my BAR are itchin' to do some fighting."

Birdie gave Hank a knowing look. Then, to change the subject, he pointed to a flock of drab-colored long-winged seabirds that were gliding close to the surface behind the LST. "They're hunting, looking for fish stirred up by our wake."

"What are they?"

"They're called shearwaters. They can fly for thousands of miles; sometimes they'll follow whales to get the fish that they stir up."

Hank watched and pointed as the shearwaters caught one fish after another. "Wow! You can't see that back where I come from."

Birdie smiled, then brooded. "There won't be any birds to see on Peleliu. They'll leave as soon as the Navy starts shelling the island." He waved his hand across the horizon. "It's a cryin' shame, Hank. This whole place is as pretty as anything you'd ever see, and there's more birds here than I ever saw ... but we ain't here to look and enjoy. We're here to kill."

Just then a blast of foul air belched from a deck vent that was just upwind of them. Hank pinched his nose. "Whew! Let's go forward. That vent is pumping out the smells from down below. It stinks like a mix of farts, puke, and B.O."

Birdie laughed. He took a final look at the shearwaters, then the two men headed for the bow of *LST-117*, a vantage point from which they could see the best and worst of the South Pacific in 1944. Birdie took off his dungaree cap and ruffled his hair in the breeze. Pavuvu faded from sight, but as the LST headed toward the open ocean it passed close to other atolls and islands.

Soon they passed by the last bit of land that they would see for several days and sailed into the open sea. The deep blue water lay beneath a sky full of clouds, puffs of white lambswool scattered askance, casting shadows, but parting from time to time to allow blazes of hot shiny sun.

The endless ocean was littered with patches of white foam that danced and then vanished as the rolling waves made their break and then gathered to roll again.

Beauty gave way to reality. Scores of warships—troop carriers, aircraft carriers, battleships, cruisers, and landing craft—were gathering to pass through stretches of water patrolled by Japanese submarines. And beyond the far horizon, on the island of Peleliu, lurked a wily enemy dedicated to the code of *bushido*.

Just then the sun shone through the clouds. Birdie glanced up at it, thinking. *You're the same sun that shined on the Black River a few hours ago. I sure wish I was there instead of here, but I ain't. I can hear the June bugs humming, the frogs croaking, and the old hoot owls barking and fussing. It's making my heart ache.*

Maybe when this is all over I'll get back there. Wonder what Kizzy and all the other river rats are doing on a day like this?

It was Sept. 4, 1944. Back home the American people were celebrating Labor Day.

⚜

Early on Sept. 15, 1944, an AmTrac laden with Marines debouched from *LST-117.* Birdie and Hank were aboard, hunkered down near the stern. At 8:32 a.m. the landing craft reached the beach and the Marines went ashore amidst the sound of men shouting and screaming and the deafening roar of explosions and naval gunfire. The beach—a mixture of sand and coral rock cooked by the blistering sun—was exposed to heavy enemy fire and men were falling, some dead before they hit the ground.

Birdie and Hank moved forward with their unit; they would attack the Japanese on a front that was 1,000 yards wide. Their commanders had told them, "Get off the beach," so they did. Weaving to and fro they ran, but soon they were wilting, wet with sweat in the stifling heat. Even so they kept on running, side by side—firing as if they could see a target—gasping and looking for a safe place to kneel and catch their breath.

The enemy gave them hell on the beach, but it was going to get worse. When they turned north to begin their advance on the airfield the Japanese hammered them with heavy artillery fire, mortars, and a fusillade of small arms. The stubborn defenders, hiding in underground caves and fortifications, had not been hurt by the naval bombardment.

Ten thousand Japanese soldiers were dug in, ready to fight to the death.

⚜

Two hundred Marines died on the first day at Peleliu and 900 were wounded. Birdie and Hank, like many others, suffered from the heat. They were exhausted and thirsty, but there was very little drinking water; some idiot had stored the main supply in barrels that reeked of gasoline odors.

The purpose of the assault was to take the airfield, but the heavy fire pinned them down. Birdie and Hank dug a foxhole, sweating and wheezing as they hacked into the coral rock that lay just beneath the surface.

At twilight they hunkered down to spend the night, not too far from the shell-splintered shore where they had landed. They listened as the big naval guns boomed, percussion for the uglier and closer sounds of death and misery—the moans of those who would not make it through the night, the sporadic gunfire, and the irritating hum of gargantuan mosquitoes searching for the best place to bite and suck blood.

They did not talk until it was pitch dark; Hank broke the silence: "Birdie? I been dozing off, but it's been demon sleep. I'm thinking I've gone mad, and then I wake up to find it was just a nightmare."

"Everybody does that, Hank." Birdie said as he peeked out, straining to see if there was any movement near their foxhole.

"See any Japs?"

"No, it's too dark. We can look for 'em when the Navy sends up a star shell, but mostly we gotta listen for them. If they hear us yakking the next thing you know we'll have a short-fused hand grenade land right here in our hole."

"We got time for a prayer?"

"Make it short."

"Lord, please get me and Birdie back to Pavuvu without gettin' all shot up. It stinks there, but this right here is hell on earth. Amen."

Birdie did not say amen; he was thinking. *Hank was wantin' to get in on the fightin' … well, now he's here—just another heartbroke rookie with jellified legs. Wait'll he has to fight hand-to-hand with cold-bladed steel."*

❖

On the second day Birdie's outfit fought their way north, but once again they were bogged down by heavy artillery, mortars, and endless salvos of small arms fire from Japanese forces that were dug into caves on a 30-foot-high coral ridge called The Point.

All day long they fought in temperatures near 115 degrees; there was no water to drink, and men dropped like flies from heat prostration or gunfire.

And then it was twilight, time for another miserable night in the foxhole.

Birdie said, "It's going to be dark soon, but I been thinking about something ever since we landed here, and I need to say it."

"You fixin' to chew me out for something?"

"No, that ain't it." Birdie wiped the sweat from his brow. "This fightin' is different. The Japs have changed the way they fight. They're laying back and hitting us only when they can make it count. On Guadalcanal they'd run right at us hollering *Banzai* and waving their swords. But here they're doing sneak attacks at night, trying to scare the wits out of us."

Hank said, "They knifed a guy last night and cut off his balls."

"That's what I mean … the dirty sons-a-bitches are getting smart."

✤

On the third morning Birdie's outfit was still pinned down worse than ever; every time they tried to move, Japanese soldiers on The Point would hammer them with raking fire from heavy machine guns and artillery.

Birdie and Hank had just left the foxhole; they were crouched down, zig-zagging their way forward when an artillery shell shattered the ground next to them. Birdie shouted, "We got to get out of here."

The words were barely out of his mouth when a burst of machine gun fire tore into Hank.

Birdie pulled Hank to cover and kneeled down to say something to him. But his best friend—the farm boy from Alabama—had no face.

Birdie slumped to the ground. "Aww … no! He's just a kid." He lay still for a half-second, then he pounded the hot coral with the butt of his hand, screaming, "It ain't right. It just ain't right."

Birdie took Hank's ammo belt from his waist, and shook his fist at The Point. *So you bastards ain't gonna fight like you did on Guadalcanal. Huh? Well, ole Birdie's gonna turn the tables on you.*

He took a deep breath, and then he picked up Hank's BAR and rushed toward The Point, screaming as loud and mean-sounding as he could.

"*Banzai! Banzai!* You sons-a-bitches!"

A burst of machine gun fire ripped into the ground around him as he charged toward the cave that held the machine gun that killed Hank.

When he reached the entrance he fired point-blank into the opening to trap the Japanese. Then he hurled a grenade deep into the cave, and after it exploded he stood at the entrance, shooting the survivors as they tried to flee.

Birdie, the bird-loving river rat from Big Pearl, had had enough. He was determined to crush the Japanese singlehandedly, or die trying.

They fired at him from all directions, but he kept going—from one cave to another.

In all, Birdie stormed and destroyed six gun emplacements and killed 50 Japanese soldiers.

He would have done more but they finally managed to stop him with a volley of fire that knocked him to the ground. He tried to crawl to cover, but the enemy was peppering the area with machine gun fire. Then, just as it appeared hopeless, a corpsman pulled him to a safe place and applied a tourniquet to stop the bleeding.

The war was over for Corporal L. W. "Birdie" Barden.

⚜

Two weeks later Birdie was resting in the recovery ward at the U. S. Naval Hospital at Pearl Harbor. The surgeons there had just removed a slug that was lodged against his spine, but they were optimistic. They told Birdie that he was lucky; the shot had come within a hair of making him a paraplegic.

His left arm was another matter; the doctors at Peleliu could not save it. The elbow was shattered and the flesh and bone that dangled beneath the corpsman's tourniquet was hopelessly shredded. They amputated Birdie's arm just above the elbow, and it would be months before he could be fitted for a prosthesis.

"Mail call." The fleshy ward nurse had a cute smile on her face as she handed a well-worn letter to Birdie. She cranked his bed up a notch, and winked. "Well, Corporal, it looks like a girl's handwriting to me."

Birdie looked at the envelope. "It's from Kizzy. Me and her grew up on the Black River in Arkansas—the town folks called us river rats."

"Well, the town folks back in Georgia called me a hick, but look at us now."

Birdie smiled, and then he carefully tore open the envelope and removed the letter as if it were a delicate piece of fine-spun lace.

Jail? Killing? Prison? Birdie read as quickly as he could, and then he read the letter again. *She ain't kidding, but at least she's out of jail. It's that damn Bully Bigshot. The killing was on Sept. 4? That was Labor Day, the same day we pulled out of Pavuvu to go to Peleliu.*

"Nurse!" Birdie hollered so loud that everyone looked his way.

When the ward nurse got back to Birdie's bed he said, "I need some paper and something to write with."

⚜

United States Naval Hospital
Pearl Harbor, Hawaii
"October 1, 1944

Dear Kizzy,

I got your letter about being in jail. That aint no place for a good girl like you.

I dont blame you for hittin Cormac. He's bigger than you and who would want to live in Memphis anyway. Besides, he wernt no good to begin with.

Anyway, I'm glad you got some of the bigshots in town helpin you. Cause you never know about such stuff in Jasper County.

Im back here in Pearl just up the road from where I was when the Japs bombed us on December 7.

The doctors say I'm gonna live, so thats good.

The Marines say there gonna to send me to Washington as soon as I get back on my feet. They say the president is gonna give me a medal or somethin, but I don't know if that is so. I guess I will find out sooner or later.

I sure hope I can get home before your trial on February 5.

Take care.

Birdie.

P.S. Glad Im right-handed on account of I aint got a left one anymore. The Japs shot it off."

LII

Hills and Valleys

Matilda Joyce walked into the parlor; Olivia and Kizzy were listening to the radio. "Dinner's on the table, girls."

Kizzy's eyes opened wide as she entered the dining room; they always did. She was in her sixth week at the Joyce residence, but having dinner in an elegant room was still new to her. The chandelier, the French provincial furniture, and the room itself—a cozy oval with mahogany panels, Chesterfield rosettes, and luxurious moldings—awakened imaginings of Jane Austen's world.

Matilda's fancy cooking gave her the same feeling, a sense of aristocracy. Kizzy reminded herself: *Gotta mind my p's and q's in a place like this.*

When the meal was over Kizzy asked Matilda, "If it's all right, I'd like to go upstairs and read."

Matilda nodded; Kizzy thanked her and left the table without saying more. But when she got to the door, she turned and spoke to Olivia, "I've just started the new book you gave me—*Les Misérables*—and I think I'm gonna like it."

⚜

Olivia and Matilda cleaned the kitchen and went into the parlor to talk. Matilda looked around to be sure they were alone, then she nodded toward the stairs. "She loves to read herself to sleep, doesn't she? Well, I don't blame her; she's lived her entire life without electricity, something we take for granted."

"That's true, Mother, but I think she mainly wants to be alone. The last six weeks have been awfully hard for her."

Matilda nodded. "Yes, but she lives for Stefan's visits. He comes over every day after school to check on her. They talk and fool around, but I also hear him playing his violin for her. He's a good boy."

"Yes, he is," Olivia said. "But does she sing when he plays?"

"No, she doesn't."

"Stefan came to the library yesterday to tell me he is worried about her. He says when he plays for her she just sits there, staring off into space. He said, 'It's like she just wants me to finish and go home.'

"He said, 'She's upbeat one day—warm and loving like the old Kizzy—but the next day she's down-in-the-mouth—it's like she's off somewhere else.'"

"We have to trust God, Olivia. He knows what he is doing. Life's full of ups and downs, hills and valleys." She paused and then said, as an afterthought, "She'll get a fair trial, won't she?"

"She doesn't think so. Kizzy's greatest fear is that she'll be railroaded by Sully Biggers and his stooges. I asked her why she was so afraid of Sully—she calls him Bully Bigshot—and you know what she said to me?"

"What?"

"She said, 'MeeMaw told me Bully is evil and he's out to get us.' She said, 'MeeMaw figured out that he got possessed by haints because his numbers weren't right—that's how he got to be evil.'"

"You're kidding," said Matilda.

"No, I asked her how MeeMaw could know that, and she said, 'I don't know, but I believe it.'"

"No wonder she is scared and depressed. Isn't there some way we can gently tell her that MeeMaw's numerology and haints theories are all wrong?" Matilda asked.

"MeeMaw's theories may be screwball, but Ruben Levy came to see me yesterday, and he is worried about the trial. He says they are definitely after her, and there is a good chance that she will be found guilty. He wanted me to talk to her to see if there is something that she is not telling us about Cormac. Something that would justify killing him, something other than self-defense."

"Good gracious!" Matilda stiffened as she said it.

"Yes. I agree. Even so, I've broached the subject with Kizzy several times, but she just clams up and repeats the story that they got in a fight about moving to Memphis."

⚜

A week later, there was a knock on the door of the Joyce residence; Olivia's mother answered.

"Hi, Mrs. Joyce." The postman pulled a crumpled letter from his leather mailbag and handed it to Matilda. "This one's for Kizzy."

She looked at the return address. "Thanks, Charlie, it's from her friend Birdie. He's in the Marines."

Matilda closed the door and started toward Kizzy's room. *Please God. Let this be good news—she needs a boost.*

⚜

Kizzy's hands trembled as she slit the flap on the envelope and removed Birdie's letter. She carefully unfolded it, but before she started reading she looked upward, squinting her eyes shut.

Then she read to herself, mouthing the words, and when she finished she laughed aloud, danced a little jig, and shouted, "Hooray! He's coming home, Mrs. Joyce. Birdie's coming home!"

Matilda grabbed Kizzy and danced a few steps with her, then she said, "Praise God. Is he all right?"

"He says the Japs shot off his left hand. I hate to hear that, but he's doing all right and he's gonna live. And he's coming home!"

She giggled again, and gave a small cheer, but then she turned serious. "I've been worried sick ever since Uncle Mac found out that Birdie got wounded at Peleliu. He's like a big brother to me and I've been thinking the worst ... so many bad things have been happening to me ..."

She read the last part of the letter again. "He says they're gonna give him a medal, so as soon as Stefan gets here I'm gonna go see Olivia and ask Uncle Mac about that."

"Yes, you should." Then she mused as Kizzy read and reread the letter, shaking with excitement. *It's the first time that girl has laughed and smiled in seven weeks. Thank God.*

✤

Kizzy waited for Stefan by the door, and as soon she saw him coming she went outside to meet him.

She waved the letter, grabbed him by the hand, and headed in the direction of the library. "Birdie's OK, Stefan, the Japs shot off his hand, but he's coming home. Let's go. We gotta go tell Olivia and Uncle Mac."

Stefan gave her a bear hug and they kissed. Then the two of them hurried down the street, arm in arm.

Matilda Joyce, peeping out from the parlor, watched them go. She smiled, then let the drapery fall back in place.

✤

As soon as they entered the library, Kizzy shouted loud enough for all to hear. "Birdie's OK. He's coming home."

Olivia and Mabel stopped what they were doing and followed her into the Veterans' Center.

Dynamite got up from the domino table to push Uncle Mac in his wheelchair, and when everyone was all together in the reception area Kizzy spoke to Uncle Mac. "Birdie says he's gonna get a medal from the president."

"Good," Uncle Mac said. "All the boys who were at Peleliu deserve a medal. It's the toughest battle the Marines ever fought."

Kizzy handed him the letter and he read it. Then he read part of it to the others. "Here's what Birdie says about the medal:

'The Marines say they're gonna to send me to Washington as soon as I get back on my feet. They say the president is gonna give me a medal or something but I don't know if that is so. I guess I will find out sooner or later.'"

"Sounds like the big one, Mac," said Dynamite.

"What do you mean—the big one?" Kizzy asked.

"If the president is going to give a medal to a corporal it must be the Congressional Medal of Honor." Uncle Mac choked up, but collected himself and went on. "It's the highest honor our country can bestow, Kizzy." He patted his heart, and handed the letter back to her. "I'll run my traps to see if I can get a confirmation."

Olivia put her arm around Kizzy and pulled her close. "I'm so glad he's coming home; that's the main thing."

❦

On Saturday, Dec. 11, Kizzy and Stefan were in the parlor listening to the radio when a news reporter gave a breathless report: "American air forces have launched an intensive offensive against Japanese positions on the island of Iwo Jima."

"I'm so glad Birdie is no longer in the fighting," Kizzy said. "Why don't the Japs just surrender? Who ever heard of Iwo Jima anyway? It's all such a waste."

The news that Birdie was coming home was like a tonic for Kizzy. She still had spells of melancholy, but most of the time she was her old self. Stefan noticed it more than the others because Kizzy was laughing and joking again, and their spooning was as good as it had ever been.

And for the first time, Kizzy opened up to Stefan about her time in jail. She described the cells, the smells, the sounds, and the prisoners who groped and made lewd offers of sex to her. She also told Stefan about her pregnant cellmate, the savvy Gertie Gazaway, but she saved the worst for last.

"And when that jail door clanged shut behind me? That was the awfullest feeling I've ever had ... in my whole life."

Stefan pulled her close, and Kizzy laid her head on his shoulder.

She sighed and went limp, but then she perked up. "The only good thing about my being down in the dumps is that I thought of a good lead-in for a song. I won't be able to finish it until I know how my trial is gonna turn out, but here's how it starts:

I found my pearl on the river free
Where there ain't no secrets or shame.

She trailed off and looked up at Stefan. "So what do you think?"

"I like it," said Stefan, and he played a few bars of a melody on his violin. "I think we can make something out of it. Let me know when you are ready to finish it."

He started to play the melody again, but Kizzy put her hand on his bow hand to stop him and looked him in the eye. "I've been a bother, Stefan. I know that, but I'm ashamed of what I've done and shame's a wicked thing—it's eatin' on me."

"But your new song talks about a place 'where there ain't no secrets or shame.'"

"I know," Kizzy said, and then she chuckled. "I can dream, can't I? I want my song to say that there's a better way to live."

"That sounds good to me," said Stefan.

Kizzy snuggled closer; she started to say more, but hesitated. Then she whispered in his ear, weighing her words carefully. "Olivia wants me to tell her my deepest secrets. It might be a good thing to do, but there are some things way down inside us that we're better off to keep secret—that's what MeeMaw always said."

"MeeMaw's right," Stefan said. "There are some secrets that we just have to live with."

⚜

On Dec. 21, 1944, Uncle Mac received official confirmation from Headquarters Marine Corps that President Franklin Delano Roosevelt, in the name of Congress, would award the Medal of Honor to L. W. "Birdie" Barden, Corporal, United States Marine Corps, at a White House ceremony on Friday, Jan. 12, 1945.

He rolled his wheelchair up next to the domino table. "It's 100 percent official. Birdie's going to get the Congressional Medal of Honor."

"That's the big one. I told you so!" Dynamite slammed his hand down so hard that the dominos jumped an inch off the table.

The other veterans cheered, then Uncle Mac said, "We gotta get started with planning for a Welcome Home Birdie celebration—a parade, a speaking, and a reception here at the Veterans' Center."

⚜

At noon on Christmas Eve, Sweetcheeks rolled a cart laden with food from her café into the Veterans' Center: Fried catfish, hush puppies, potato salad, coleslaw, and coconut cream pie.

The members of the planning committee were already there: Uncle Mac, Dynamite, Mabel Swafford, Olivia, Matilda, the high school principal, and Officer John "Butch" Jansen. Conspicuously absent were the members of Bully Bigshot's political machine.

The group quickly designated Mabel—the best organizer in town—as their chairperson, and just as she was suggesting an agenda for the meeting, Sheriff T. K. "Gunner" Brown walked into the room, hat in hand, saying he would like to be heard when the committee took up the question of welcoming speeches. The members ignored him, but Mabel motioned for him to take a seat.

The first order of business was to set times for the parade, the reception, and the public speaking that was to be held outside or in the Big Pearl Opera House, depending on the weather.

The committee voted unanimously to make Uncle Mac the grand marshal of the parade, with the stipulation that his sidekick, Dynamite, be allowed to ride in the lead car with him.

Mabel then opened the floor for a discussion of who would be the appropriate person to give a welcoming speech. Several names were mentioned: The governor, congressmen, senators, and a half-dozen others.

It was then that the sheriff made his move. He stood up and said, "I'd like to suggest the name of Sully Biggers. He's the most important man in town, and he knows how to make a good speech. As a matter of fact, he made the dedication speech for this here Veterans' Center when it opened in 1923."

Uncle Mac had not said anything throughout the meeting, but the sheriff's bootlicking performance set him off. "Get lost, Gunner. Sully Biggers is a sorry SOB. He tried to undo his daddy's will to stop the building of this library and Veterans' Center, and he has made a fortune off of the war.

"So, Sheriff, the answer is not no. It's hell, no. You can go tell Sully Biggers that his days as King Kong are just about over, and you can tell him that I said so. The boys who are coming back home from the war are way too independent to let the likes of him boss them around."

Dynamite could not restrain himself. He pointed to the door, and said. "Hey, Gunner, there's the door—don't let it hit you in the ass on the way out."

The sheriff left in a huff, and the committee voted unanimously for Officer Jansen, a disabled Army veteran and winner of the Silver Star Medal, to give the main speech at the public event.

LIII

Hero

At 8 a.m. Jan. 13, hundreds of people gathered in front of the newspaper office, waiting for the editor of the *Big Pearl Free Current* to come outside and tack the first page of Saturday's paper on the front door. The ceremony at the White House on Friday had been broadcast live—everyone in town was listening—but the people wanted to see the story and the pictures in print. That would make it real.

Kizzy and Stefan got there just as the editor posted the front page. The crowd roared its approval. There it was, a banner headline and a photograph of President Roosevelt putting the Medal of Honor around the neck of a local boy. Corporal L. W. "Birdie" Barden was a national hero; he had put Big Pearl, Ark., on the map.

Horace C. Ayers and the sassy rich girls from school were there, right down in front, acting as if they had always known and cared about Birdie. The air was full of such comments—people claiming to have some recollection of him: "I remember him, he used to do this or that." Or, "He worked for so and so." Or, "He's smart, he went to the CCC as soon as he could." No one got close to calling Birdie a river rat. They would say, "He done us proud," or "This is the biggest thing that ever happened to Big Pearl," but no one mentioned Birdie's mother, Shirley Barden, his two half-sisters in foster care, or his two half-brothers—soldiers who died on the shores of North Africa.

❖

As soon as the White House ceremony was over the Marine Corps flew Birdie to New York City for a round of interviews with the media, then he made an intensive two-week railroad trip from Washington D. C. to St. Louis, touring with movie stars to promote the sale of war bonds. A reporter for the *New York Sun Herald*, Joe Thurmond, followed his every move, generating more stories, photographs, and publicity for Big Pearl.

On Monday, Jan. 29, an R4D Navy transport with Birdie aboard landed at the Marine Corps Air Facility in Walnut Ridge.

Butch Jansen, Uncle Mac, Dynamite, and Kizzy—dressed in the black outfit that Olivia gave her—were there to meet him. Kizzy wiggled around. "I can hardly stand it. I haven't seen him since he joined the Marines."

The plane taxied to a stop, and when the door opened she got a glimpse of Birdie and rushed forward screaming his name. But as he stepped onto the tarmac she stopped short to take in the sight. Birdie was in the classic forest green uniform of a Marine corporal, crisply pressed and bedecked with a perfect alignment of Marine Corps insignia and service ribbons.

The Medal of Honor, a five-point gold star with a light blue ribbon that had a field of 13 white stars, was suspended at the V of his blouse by a separate length of light blue ribbon that encircled his neck. His left hand, a prosthetic, was in a tan glove.

Kizzy cheered and jumped wildly into his arms, sobbing and calling his name over and over. Birdie caught her and took a step back to keep his balance, then they danced in a circle as if they were the only two people on earth.

Birdie's barracks cap came off and toppled to the ground, but he let it go. The hero of Peleliu was home, crying like a baby in the arms of his best friend.

⚜

Birdie and Kizzy held each other at arm's length and talked for a moment, then they turned and walked to where Uncle Mac, Butch, Dynamite, and a crowd of Marines were standing. The three veterans from Big Pearl snapped to and saluted Birdie as he approached, as did the others: the air crew, the ground crew, and every Marine—including the officers.

Birdie returned the salutes, then he hugged Uncle Mac and said, "I ain't ever gonna get used to being saluted, particularly by officers."

"Welcome home, Birdie. The boys at the Veterans' Center—hell, everyone in Big Pearl—we're all mighty proud of you."

Birdie shook Dynamite's hand, and then he looked at Butch and sized up the hideous burn scars. "You must be Butch Jansen. I heard what you did in North Africa."

Butch shrugged. "Just doing what had to be done."

"Amen, Brother, but we're the lucky ones. A lot of good men aren't coming home."

"We better get going," Uncle Mac said. "The parade is gonna start at 10 o'clock."

⚜

On the one-hour drive to Big Pearl thousands of people lined the road, waving and holding handmade signs welcoming their hero.

Birdie tried to pick out familiar landmarks as they approached Big Pearl, but it was hard to see. There were too many people—sometimes 10 deep—lined up, waiting for the parade to start.

They got a fair view of the river just before they reached the Veterans' Center, and Birdie looked out, straining to get a glimpse of his childhood home. The houseboat was still there, just upstream from the boat where Kizzy killed Cormac, and when he saw it he patted Kizzy's hand and said, "It's been a long time."

Kizzy studied him as he looked out the window. *I never paid attention to it before, but Birdie's right handsome. He's got the jut-jawed look of a Marine—that's for sure—but there's a friendliness about his face that reminds me of Shirley.*

⚜

Everything about the parade was perfect. Twenty thousand people turned out to welcome Birdie home. It was a nice day, cool but not cold. Scores of groups marched: The American Legion, Veterans of Foreign Wars, state and local police, service men on leave, a drum and bugle corps, Boy Scouts, Girl Scouts, Red Cross units, Air Raid Wardens, soldiers and sailors from nearby bases, and various marching bands led by the Marine Corps band and a company of Marines from Memphis.

Uncle Mac, grand marshal, rode in the lead car with Dynamite at his side. Birdie sat atop the back seat of a convertible halfway back, waving to the crowd and reaching out to touch the hands of the young boys who ran alongside. Butch Jansen sat to his left. The two men bonded the moment they shook hands at the airport, and the parade gave them a chance to share their deepest feelings about war, life and death, and the friends they left on the battlefield.

As they neared the end of the parade they passed by the main office of Biggers Enterprises. Sully Biggers was inside, sulking. He peeped through the venetian blinds and when Birdie and Butch passed by he grumbled, closed the blinds and turned away.

Everyone else in town walked to the open field on the north end of town to hear Butch and Birdie speak. They were not disappointed; Butch gave a moving tribute to Birdie and to all the men and women in uniform, especially those who would not come home. He also praised civilians on the home front for making Victory Gardens and "putting up with rationing so that the war could be won."

Butch then introduced Birdie, who did not say much, but what he did say brought tears to the eyes of young and old.

"Thank you for this welcome. I agree with Butch, the real heroes ain't here today. They ain't comin' home. I lost my two kid brothers in North Africa, and some of you lost loved ones too." He swallowed, and cleared his throat. "The honor you're showin' to me is really for them. And that's what this here medal means to me."

An old woman near the front was crying, and when Birdie saw her he straightened up as if a sergeant had called 'Attention.' He saluted the old woman, and then bowed his head. He was done, but he managed to whisper into the microphone: "God bless 'em all. And God bless America."

⚜

Sweetcheeks catered the reception at the Veterans' Center, serving fried fish donated by Curly. Five hundred invited guests came by to welcome Birdie home and shake his hand. Awestruck little boys wanted to touch the medal, and Birdie let them. And when they pulled their hands back as if they had touched a red-hot coal, he saluted them.

Several people offered for Birdie to spend the night in their home, but he politely declined. And when the reception was over Birdie and Kizzy spent an hour with his two half-sisters. Olivia took photographs of the girls with Birdie and Kizzy, and she listened as the four of them talked about Shirley and their "good old days on the river."

At 4:30 Olivia said, "It's time to go, girls. I promised your foster parents that I would have you home before dark." As they were leaving, Birdie hugged them and gave each of them a framed photograph of the White House ceremony. On each photograph President Roosevelt had written, "Your brother is my hero too," and he had signed it "FDR."

Then, for the first time all day, Birdie and Kizzy had a chance to talk privately. "I like your boyfriend, Kizzy. He sounds funny when he talks, but he's got a good heart and he's crazy about you. You stick with him, you hear?"

Kizzy smiled. "I plan to, if I don't go to prison."

"Pshaw, stop talking like that," said Birdie. Then he pulled another gift from his sea bag and handed it to her. It was a book, *Birds of the South Pacific*. "I love the birds here at home the best, but them birds over there—well—they're somethin' to see."

He showed her a picture of a shearwater, the long-winged seabird that followed the wake of his ship the day he left the rest camp at Pavuvu. That led to more talks about all he had seen in the South Pacific. Then, as it began to get dark, they left the Veterans' Center and headed to the river.

A number of curiosity-seekers followed them at a distance, but dropped off when Birdie and Kizzy went down the narrow path to Shirley's houseboat.

They stopped just shy of the gangplank to talk about old times, and Kizzy blurted out her favorite memory of Birdie: "I'll never forget that day you took me to the baseball game in Newport and then bought me a chocolate milkshake. It was something—a day I'll never forget. That's when I started thinking of you as my make-do big brother."

Birdie laughed and hugged her, but then he turned serious and nodded toward the boat. "It won't be the same for me, Kizzy, but I'm gonna spend a few nights on this old boat; Curly and Sweetcheeks cleaned it up for me." He tossed his sea bag aboard and pointed up the hill towards town. "I want the folks up there to know that us river rats is worth somethin' after all."

Kizzy blew him a kiss. "You're the best, Birdie. I'll come get you in the morning. I want you to see where I'm living, and then we'll go to the graveyard to see Shirley and everybody else."

⚜

Dozens of people, hoping to get a glimpse of Birdie, were gathered all along the state road, high above the river, when Kizzy arrived early the next morning. Several impatient young boys had gone down the path to stand near the houseboat where their hero had spent the night.

Kizzy laughed as she ran down the hill. "This is the first time anybody in Big Pearl ever wanted to see one of us river rats."

She shooed the boys away, went aboard, and knocked on the cabin door. "Birdie? You ready to go?"

"Yep," said Birdie as he came outside. He was in uniform, but the medal was not around his neck.

"Where's your medal?"

Birdie pointed to the rows of service ribbons on his chest; the top ribbon was light blue with five white stars. Then he pulled a garrison cap out of his pocket, carefully positioned it on his head, and winked. "We call this a piss-cutter."

As soon as they crossed the gangplank the boys converged on Birdie, asking: "How many Japs did you kill? Are you going back? What is war like?

He shook their hands, but instead of answering their questions he said, "You boys be sure to do good at school, that's more important than war."

The boys followed them to the Joyce residence, and all along the way people waved and shouted greetings to Birdie.

⚜

Olivia met them at the door and led them to the kitchen. "Mother's cooking breakfast for us and there is a fresh pot of coffee brewing."

Matilda Joyce was at the stove frying bacon when they entered the kitchen. She put the cooking fork down, wiped her hands, and gave Birdie a hug. "How about some bacon and eggs? And there's biscuits in the oven."

Birdie smiled and nodded.

A copy of the morning newspaper was on the table. The front page was covered with stories about Birdie's homecoming. There were several pictures of the parade, but the biggest photograph was the one of Birdie giving his speech. When Kizzy pointed to it he said, "I ain't much of a speaker, but I aim to get better at it."

Matilda smiled. "I thought your speech was just right—it's not how long you talk that makes a good speech."

Birdie thanked her, then he looked at Olivia. "President Roosevelt told me I ought to go to college on the GI Bill, and I'm planning to do that when I get out of the Marine Corps."

Kizzy broke in. "Birdie's real smart. He knows everything there is to know about birds."

Olivia smiled at Birdie and started to say something, but Matilda interrupted. "All right everyone, let's eat while the biscuits are hot."

After breakfast, when Kizzy and Matilda were clearing the table, Olivia asked Birdie if he would like to take a tour of the house.

"Show him my room, Olivia," said Kizzy. "And be sure to show him the tub."

✤

The tour of the house ended at the parlor, and when they entered the room Olivia showed Birdie the antique rocking horse that she rode as a child. Birdie smiled and pushed the little horse to make it rock. Olivia took that as a signal to talk about other interesting pieces of furniture, but Birdie raised an open hand to stop her.

He had two things on his mind that he was determined to say to Olivia, and he said them softly, with gratitude.

"It's real nice that you and your mother are helping Kizzy. She'd be in jail if it weren't for you all."

Olivia smiled and started to answer, but he raised his hand again. "And there's another thing I want to say that I've been thinking about ever since I got to your house this morning."

Olivia looked puzzled. "What?"

"It's about that gold star in your window. I know that's for your husband who was at Midway. Kizzy told me, and I wanted to say I'm sorry."

Her lips quivered.

"We were losing the war until your husband and the Navy whipped the Japs at Midway. That battle turned the war around. After Midway we started winning and now we've got them on the run. Pretty soon it will all be over and we can go back to living our lives."

"Thank you," she said, her voice raspy. "It helps to hear that from you."

✤

Kizzy and Birdie walked from the Joyce house to the graveyard; it was an unusually mild January day. Every car and truck that passed by slowed to a near stop. The drivers would honk and wave greetings, but it was not a distraction. The half-mile walk gave them a chance to talk privately about the trial.

Kizzy told Birdie the same story she had told the others. "The fight started because Cormac wanted to move us to Memphis, and he told me they'd send me to the poorhouse if I didn't go with him. He got rough so I hit him in the knee with a skillet. Then he took a swing at me. I whacked him in the head, but that didn't stop him. He knocked me down, and when I got up he poked a knife at me. That's when I hit him a real hard lick in the head. He went down and that was it. Cormac was dead as a doornail."

"I met your lawyer at the reception and he told me it's a case of self-defense. He thinks it will come down to whether the jury will believe you, and he asked me to be a witness for you."

"Will you?"

"You know I will. I'd do anything for you, Kizzy."

She looked away, fidgeting with the buttons on her jacket. "It's got me scared, Birdie. I'm doing better now that I know you are OK, but I get low sick when I think about going to prison. Some of the big talkers around town are saying they may not get me for murder, but Bully's got the thing rigged so's I'll be found guilty of something—enough to send me away."

"You gotta have hope, Kizzy."

"I had a bunch of hope until this happened. Olivia's been teaching me how to be a lady, but my dreams of making something out of myself are going up in smoke."

"When I was in the hospital at Pearl Harbor they told me I might not walk again and that knocked me for a loop. But I got through it by prayin'."

"I didn't know you were a praying man."

"I wasn't until Peleliu. That's when I learned how to do it from a buddy who was in the foxhole with me. He got his face blowed off, but I think the prayin' saved me ... something sure did 'cause what I did to win this medal didn't make no sense. Something just made me do it, and someone up there brought me through all of it ... and here I am."

"And here we are," said Kizzy as she pointed to a pea-gravel drive that passed beneath an entry arch bearing the name Big Pearl Cemetery.

⚜

Kizzy led Birdie to the back of the cemetery. "They buried Grandpa way back over here by the fence. Remember?"

"Yep. I was here. That was when I was in the CCC."

They stood over the grave for a while, telling Grandpa stories, and then Kizzy said, "Of course, MeeMaw isn't here at all. We lost her in the Flood of '37. She went on down the river—I mean sure 'nuff on down the river."

"Ma and Shirley are over there." She pointed to the right. "We had burying pearls for everyone, but the gravedigger called them 'charity cases.' He said we had to take whatever was available." She sighed, and as they walked away from Grandpa's grave she said, "I reckon it doesn't matter all that much since we never found MeeMaw anyway."

When they got to the gravesites for Shirley and Kizzy's mother, they sat down on a monument that looked like a bench.

Kizzy asked Birdie if he ever saw Tamás, her father.

"Yes, but I was only 8 when he took off … he wore a bright purple shirt all the time. That's what I remember about him. He was a Gypsy according to MeeMaw."

Then she laughed, "Men chased after Ma like flies to honey. Tamás was the only one she ever wanted to keep, but he up and ran off."

"Your ma and my ma were a lot alike," said Birdie, and he broke out laughing. "I reckon that's why I had a passel of half-sisters and half-brothers."

Kizzy giggled, but then she turned sullen. "Shirley was like a mother to me and I hate it that she died so young." She looked away. "Doctor Al said it was female trouble, and that's true. I told you that in my letter—that she was pregnant—but there was more to it than that."

"What do you mean?"

"Shirley made me promise not to tell anyone, but she's gone and it isn't right to keep it from you."

"Keep what from me?"

"She told me just before she died that they were going to take the girls away from her if she had another baby. So she went in for an abortion."

"They? Who's they?"

"I'm not for sure, but Doctor Al ought to know. I think it was somebody at the Eugenics Center. Shirley said they were mad at her because she was living in sin with a guy named Doodley."

⚜

When Kizzy and Birdie got back to the Joyce residence Olivia was waiting for them at the door.

"You had a phone call from a reporter in New York City, a John Thurmond."

"Oh that's the hotshot reporter from the *New York Sun Herald*. He was at the White House ceremony, and he went with us on the first week of the bond drive."

"You can use our phone if you want to; he said you could call him collect."

⚜

"John, it's Birdie Barden."

"What the hell is going on down there, Birdie? I saw a wire story this morning saying you are going to testify in some murder case they're calling the Skillet Killing."

"Yep. I'm going to be a witness for a good friend who's going on trial for murder. We grew up next door to each other on the river, and I'll tell you this for certain, John—Kizzy ain't guilty of nothing; she's a good girl."

When the call was over Birdie thanked Olivia and headed for the door.

"Where are you going, Birdie?" said Kizzy.

"I'm gonna borrow Sweetcheek's truck and do some runnin' around."

That night, when he was back at the boat, Birdie went out onto the aft deck. He had changed into civvies—grey work clothes, a stocking cap, and an old pea jacket saved from his days in the CCC.

The river was glossy in the moonshine. He looked upriver and down, and then went to the other end of the boat to look up toward town.

Good. There ain't no one around. I'll get up before it's light and get started. I got a lot to do.

⚜

Two days later, on Thursday, Feb. 1, 1945, the *New York Sun Herald* ran a story under the byline of John Thurmond. A five-column banner stretched across the front page, above the fold: HERO DEFENDS FRIEND CHARGED WITH MURDER.

There were separate two-column stories beneath the banner. The one on the left was headlined RIVER GIRL CHARGED IN 'SKILLET KILLING.' The story on the right was headlined FROM PELELIU TO BIG PEARL, ARKANSAS. Between those two headlines was a picture of Birdie with this cutline: Corporal L. W. "Birdie" Barden, winner of the Medal of Honor, rides in a parade in Big Pearl, Ark.

By noon the story was being told hourly on every national radio network. And newspapers all across the country were making plans to feature the story in their Friday editions.

The *Big Pearl Free Current* could not wait. The editor was working feverishly to publish an "Extra" edition that would be delivered that afternoon, just four days before the start of Kizzy's trial.

LIV

Trial

At first light on Monday, Feb. 5, 1945, a snub-nosed milk truck rattled and clattered as it entered the town square in Big Pearl, the site of the Jasper County Courthouse.

The driver slowed the old Divco to a stop and scratched his head.

It was a cold and windy morning, but scores of people—some dressed up, and some in overalls—stood in a queue that stretched from the front door of the old red-brick courthouse to the street.

There was no place to park; the quadrangle teemed with people. Some waited in their cars and trucks but others milled about, stamping their feet, hunkering over to keep warm. A half-dozen reporters stood in a tight circle near the statue of the revered town father, Confederate Colonel Carlton Biggers; they carried cameras and notebooks and seemed to be arguing about something, perhaps the Civil War.

The milkman shook his head and drove away.

Soon the principals would arrive and the courtroom drama, now dubbed the Skillet Killing, would begin.

⚜

A few blocks away, at a table near the meat counter in the back of Biggers Grocery, the morning coffee klatch was in full swing. The regulars—all lackeys for Sully Biggers—were flailing their arms and talking over one another; the decibel level was uncommonly high. The klatchers were arguing whether they should debate the likely outcome of the Skillet Killing, or the significance of yesterday's meeting of FDR, Churchill, and Stalin at Yalta in the Crimea.

The butcher suddenly stopped carving, came from behind the meat counter, and went to the front of the store. He looked out, and hollered back to the klatchers. "They're gathering up at the courthouse. That story about Birdie testifying was like putting a match to gasoline."

The war news—a Big Three meeting to discuss the final phase of World War II—quickly lost out to the Skillet Killing.

The local hardware man responded to the butcher. "Hero or not, there ain't nothing that Birdie can say that'll get her off scot-free. Ain't that right, Sully?"

The klatchers looked to their host for wisdom. "That's what Lookadoo says, and he hasn't lost a jury trial since he's been prosecutor."

The local plumber, a reliable jokester, spoke up. "Lookadoo? Shit, he ain't all that good. Hell, I could get a conviction if I was arguing a case to one of Sully's juries."

Several of the klatchers cringed, but Bully took the plumber's joke as a compliment. He laughed then said, "Lookadoo says they might not get her for murder, but he's sure they'll get her for manslaughter. She beat a man to death with a skillet and doesn't have a good excuse for doing it. That story about him poking a knife at her ain't gonna fly."

"What about the new judge?" said the hardware man. "He's from Cranford County."

"Yeah, he filed against old Judge Barnhart at the last minute," said Sully. "He caught us napping. We'll get rid of him in the next election; our circuit judge needs to be from right here in Jasper County"

⚜

The men at the Veterans' Center were also talking about the trial.

"The publicity is going to help Kizzy," said Uncle Mac.

"How's that?" Dynamite said.

"Because it's harder for Sully's machine to do its dirty work when things are out in the open."

Dynamite thought for a second. "Maybe so, but Sully Biggers still controls everything. There may be some on the jury who'll vote to let her go, but Sully will have two or three on the jury who'll hang tough. Trust me, I was on a jury last year, and I'm telling you: They won't vote for an acquittal come hell or high water."

One of the other veterans said, "Bullshit. Birdie's being here'll swing it for her. Where is he, by the way?"

"He's around," said Uncle Mac. "Olivia said he went to see his little sisters, and Kizzy thinks he just needs a little privacy. I'm guessing he doesn't like all the hullabaloo about being a hero ... and God bless him for it."

⚜

At 8:45 a.m., the custodian of the Jasper County Courthouse—a sway-backed old man with a beer belly as big as a bowling ball—opened the heavy double doors to the courthouse, and a swarm of people from every occupation and lifestyle scrambled upstairs to get seats.

The large courtroom filled quickly, but the four front rows did not. Cordoned off and marked "Reserved," the seats were for prospective jurors, local lawyers, and bigshots like Sully Biggers. The custodian allowed late-comers to stand in the back of the room, but when that space was full he herded the overflow back into the hall and closed the doors. The courtroom was jam-packed, a record crowd.

Lawyers, clerks, and other officials dribbled into the courtroom through a door to the right of the judge's bench, a regal structure designed to elevate the one sitting there. The first lawyers to come through the door were not involved in the case. They wandered around like popinjays, feigning importance. They would soon disappear, slipping out before their irrelevance became obvious.

The clerks and other court officials took their places, and when they were seated Prosecuting Attorney Sam Lookadoo and his deputy came in and put their books and papers on the counsel table nearest the jury box.

⚜

The room was abuzz, but when Ruben Levy and Kizzy came through the door the hubbub gave way to whispers and the sound of people stirring, straining to see.

Kizzy's blazing red hair, gathered at the nape of her neck, complimented the conservative outfit that Olivia had chosen for her to wear at the trial: A dark blue long-sleeve cotton dress with wide lapels and four well-placed white buttons that gave it a double-breasted effect. The belted dress had a pleated front panel skirt.

Ruben Levy previewed the outfit two days before the trial. He told Olivia, "It's perfect. This is going to drive Lookadoo crazy. He wants to present Kizzy as a low-life river girl, but she won't look the part."

Olivia had said, "Won't he try it anyway? I mean, he can just insinuate that she is a river rat."

"He could do that, but it's pretty hard to pick on river rats now that Corporal Birdie Barden has come home a hero."

⚜

Kizzy, eager to turn her back to the stares, sat beside Ruben at the counsel table farthest from the jury box.

Whew. They're giving me the once-over all right. Wondering what to do with me. I've been on a stage before—at the talent contest—but this is different. They're not going to be fooled by the way I look—everyone knows I'm a river rat, and ...

Just then, the bailiff disappeared though the door to the left of the judge's bench. Moments later, he reappeared. "All rise. Oh yez, oh yez, the Circuit Court of Jasper County, Arkansas, is now in session, the honorable Judge Forrest Wheatley presiding. God save this honorable court."

Judge Wheatley, black robe flowing, made a simple entrance. He stepped up onto the judge's bench, sat down unceremoniously, and told his audience, "Please be seated."

The reporters, seated on a bench near the defense table, scribbled notes as the judge spoke, and an artist put the last touches on a sketch of Kizzy. Then he turned the page, and started a charcoal of Judge Forrest Beauregard "Beau" Wheatley, who was a sight to see—handsome with prematurely grey hair and a black patch over his left eye.

⚜

The judge asked the clerk to draw 12 names, and the time-honored process of jury selection began.

Kizzy paid close attention to what each prospective juror said when the judge and lawyers asked their questions, but she learned more by watching.

It was half past noon when the lawyers ran out of peremptory challenges. The judge asked if there were further challenges for cause, and when the lawyers said no, the judge administered the oath to the 10 men and two women who would decide Kizzy's fate.

It was nearing 1 o'clock when the judge recessed for lunch; he told everyone to be back at 2 o'clock.

When the courtroom cleared out, Ruben and Kizzy huddled with Olivia, Uncle Mac, Sweetcheeks, and Dynamite. And Ruben said, "Well, what do you think of the jury?"

Dynamite grumped. "There's three Biggers men on the panel. They're hard cases, step-and-fetch-its for Sully. I wouldn't trust them any farther than I could throw them."

"I agree with Dynamite—100 percent," said Sweetcheeks. "Those three were lying through their teeth when they swore to be fair and impartial—they're Biggers boys, lock, stock, and barrel."

"I agree," Ruben said. "But I couldn't get rid of them for cause because Sully Biggers is not a party to this case in any way. And I used up all my challenges getting rid of eight others just like them."

"My MeeMaw, she couldn't read a lick but she always said, 'You can't tell a book by its cover.'" Everyone nodded agreement. "So I don't know for sure about any of them. The men on the back row—the ones that Dynamite and Sweetcheeks don't like—have given me some hard looks. They scare me, but the rest of them seem OK. The two women in particular have been looking at me nonstop from the start. I may be wrong, but I think they'll be fair."

"Well, there's nothing we can do about any of it now," said Ruben. "This is our jury, like it or not."

"They took an oath," Olivia said. "That ought to stand for something."

Dynamite laughed and then apologized to Olivia. "Sorry, Olivia, but I've been on one of these juries, and it ain't fair and impartial unless it comes out the way Bully wants it to come out."

Uncle Mac sighed. "You did the best you could, Ruben, considering how things work around here. Let's go to lunch."

⚜

At 2:30 p.m., Judge Wheatley gaveled the afternoon session to order, and said, "Mr. Prosecutor, you may make your opening statement."

Sam Lookadoo—a stubby man in his late 50s—sashayed to the lectern, smiling and making eye contact with each of the jurors. This would be his 55th jury trial since winning the office in 1935, and he had a knack for simplicity.

"Ladies and gentlemen. This is not a complicated case. Cormac Manatt risked his life to save this girl and her family during the Flood of '37. Then he took care of them, and when her mother died he stayed on so the girl wouldn't have to go to the poorhouse."

He said "poorhouse" oddly, rubbing his temples as if conjuring an image of the dreaded place. The two women jurors did not react, so he moved on.

"Cormac worked the river to make a living, and when the war broke out he took a job at the button factory so he could buy nice things for the girl. He bought her candy, dresses, and shoes, but he wanted a better life for her so he went to Memphis and got a good job in the munitions factory. He came home and told the girl that he wanted to move to Memphis so they could get off the river."

Lookadoo looked at Kizzy, and shook his head as if puzzled.

"And what did he get for it? He got beat to death with a skillet. That's what he got."

The prosecutor turned to look at Kizzy. "This ungrateful girl killed Cormac Manatt for no good reason." He pointed at her. "She is guilty of murder."

He glanced at the reporters, and then opened his arms to the jury. "So let's show the world how we deal with murder down here in Jasper County."

⚜

Ruben's opening statement lacked flair.

In a quiet manner, he told the jury that Kizzy loved Big Pearl, that she had overcome the hardships of river life to become a good student, and that she was a recent winner of the annual talent contest.

Then he got to the crux of her defense. "On Sept. 4, Cormac Manatt told her that he was moving to Memphis and she would have to go with him or go to the poorhouse. Kizzy told him she didn't want to leave Big Pearl and they got into an argument about it."

Ruben pointed at Kizzy. "Folks, Kizzy is 16 years old, and she is only five foot four inches tall. Cormac Manatt was a big man, six-foot-four, and strong."

Ruben pointed to himself, "I'm six foot two, but as you can see I'm scrawny, not big and strong like Cormac was. Just imagine the fight between him and Kizzy. She was trying to cook breakfast when the fight broke out. Cormac started roughing her up so she hit him in the knee with a skillet. That should have stopped the fight, but it made him madder. He took a swing at her, so she defended herself by hitting him in the head, but even that didn't stop him. He hit her so hard that it knocked her to the floor, and when she got up he tried to stab her with the knife that she had been using to slice bacon. Ladies and gentlemen, Kizzy did what any one of you would do to defend yourself. She hit him again and he went down, this time for good."

Ruben paused, then he stepped close to the jurors. "Please, in the name of mercy, let this girl go on with her life. I ask you to return a verdict of not guilty."

⚜

Judge Wheatley announced, "It is getting late. We will adjourn for the day, and begin tomorrow at 9 o'clock." He looked at Sam Lookadoo. "Will you be ready to start, Mr. Prosecutor?"

"Yes, Your Honor. The state will begin with the testimony of Big Pearl Police Officer John "Butch" Jansen, followed by the testimony of County Coroner Mutt Falwell."

The judge admonished the jury to not discuss the case, tapped his gavel, and stood up. "Court is adjourned."

Stefan was in the back of the courtroom with Olivia, waiting for Kizzy. He offered to walk her home, but Ruben said the three of them should go with him. "The town is full of curiosity-seekers. I'll give you a ride home."

Kizzy asked Ruben and Olivia, "Has anyone seen Birdie?"

Olivia shook her head.

"He'll be here for you Kizzy," Ruben said. "But he can't come into the courtroom until it is time for him to testify. Lookadoo has made sure of that by invoking what we lawyers call 'The Rule.'"

⚜

Kizzy and Stefan went to her room as soon as they got to the Joyce residence. They wanted to talk secretly, and as soon as Stefan closed the door Kizzy took his hand and pulled him onto the bed.

They kissed and snuggled, but not for long.

Kizzy lay back and stared at the ceiling. "The trial is getting to me. Ruben says it's going all right, but I'm not so sure. I was sky-high when

Birdie got all that publicity. Uncle Mac thought it would help me, but now I'm not so sure, and to make matters worse, no one has seen or heard from Birdie since the middle of last week."

"Everything will work out, Kizzy." Stefan kissed her and ran his fingers through her hair; he had been trying to cheer her up ever since they left the courtroom.

Kizzy slammed her hand on the bed. Then she sat upright, and lashed out. "I was doing all right until that Lookadoo man made his speech. He made Cormac out to be a saint, telling the jury that he raised me as his own when nobody wanted me … said everything he did was for my own good. He even told them how he'd get candy bars for me at Curly's, and how he bought me dresses and shoes.

"And I nearly puked when he said Cormac wanted to move to Memphis to better himself and give me a chance to get off the river. On and on he went, and then he said I had no reason to lash out at Cormac, much less kill him."

She took a deep breath, but then she slumped, and worry took the place of anger. "I was hanging in there pretty good until he turned and pointed right at me and said, 'She's guilty of murder.' That was hard to take, Stefan, and that's what's got me down.

"Lookadoo's words are banging around in my head like pinballs; I can't make them go away."

Stefan spoke softly. "My mother always told me, 'Do not worry about anything.' She said if we trust in God everything will work out."

Kizzy nodded, "Birdie says praying works. He said he learned how to pray in a foxhole, and he believes it helped him get well when he was in the hospital. And I know for sure that Olivia prays because I've been to church with her. But my folks, especially MeeMaw, didn't believe in such things."

Stefan did not react; he let her go on.

"I tried it," said Kizzy. "I've been praying to get out of the mess I'm in, but I've decided I'm not doing it right, or whoever's up there isn't listening to me because I've done wrong."

"My mother was Catholic. She said you can be forgiven if you confess your sins to God. Then He will hear your prayers."

Kizzy sighed. "Seems like everyone's got a different idea about it. There's Eli and his way, but how's that different from the Catholics, or the Methodists, or what old Knuckles told us? Remember the day we ran into him? He said he tried to figure all this stuff out for himself. He finally gave up and decided God's way was best."

She giggled. "Maybe I better pray to all of 'em—including MeeMaw's haints—just to cover all my bases." But then she turned sullen. "We only get one life to live, Stefan, and I've messed mine up something awful."

⚜

Stefan was halfway home when he got the idea.

One life to live. That's what she said, so maybe there's a way I can lift her spirits after all.

He turned around and ran back to the Joyce residence. Kizzy was in the kitchen with Matilda and Olivia when Stefan rang the doorbell.

"Did you forget something?"

"No, but I thought of something else I wanted to say."

They went into the parlor and closed the door. Stefan pulled her toward the antique loveseat that had the padded armrest in the middle to keep young lovers separated.

Kizzy sat down, a puzzled look on her face.

Stefan sat across from her, but for the moment he was in a distant place. *It's the right thing to do, Mother. She needs something to give her hope ... a reason to make the most of her life. Father's smiling, I know he is, so forgive me for what I'm about to do.*

Kizzy started to say something, but waited as Stefan reached to his neck and gently pulled a pendant from its hiding place.

He unfastened the clasp and spread the necklace out on the armrest.

"I want you to have this, Kizzy. It means a lot to me, because it belonged to my father."

"It's beautiful, Stefan. What does it mean?" Kizzy said as she pointed to the figure on the pendant:

חַי

Stefan smiled. "Life, Kizzy. It means life. The symbol is a Hebrew word—CHAI—and it means 'life.' Living a good life is very important to Jews, and they are encouraged to enjoy the time they have on earth. At celebrations they say a toast: *l'chaim!* which means, 'to life.'"

"Was your father a Jew?"

"I ... well ... yes. ... And that's my secret, Kizzy. I didn't tell you before because I promised my mother a long time ago that I would never tell anyone."

Kizzy wrinkled her brow, but there was love in her eyes.

"It all goes back to when we left Germany—before the war. Mother was afraid of what the Nazis would do to me. She was as afraid of them as you are of Bully Bigshot."

Stefan put the necklace and pendant around her neck and fastened the clasp.

"There! Now you're safe. Enjoy every day of your life."

Kizzy fondled the pendant, then kissed him. "But you have broken your promise to your mother."

"She'd understand; besides I feel better now that I don't have a secret. And the Nazis are done for anyway."

Kizzy nodded, then gave him an impish smile. "So this Jewish sign means life. Well, Knuckles believes in John the Baptist. Birdie and Olivia believe in Jesus, and so did your mother. And, of course, there's MeeMaw and whatever she believed." Kizzy chuckled. "Am I leaving anybody out?"

They laughed, and then they both got the giggles as they struggled to hug each other over the armrest. When they settled down Stefan said, "I just want you to be happy, Kizzy. It's not good for you to be down in the dumps."

⚜

Kizzy went to her room after Stefan left, pondering what they had talked about.

It's a lot to think about, but Birdie said it doesn't matter how you pray when you are in a foxhole.

So, OK. Here goes: God, I'm asking forgiveness for killing Cormac. I'm ashamed about that—even though everybody says he needed killing.

And I'm ready to take whatever the jury decides, so give me the strength to keep my head up and enjoy every day I have on this earth. Stefan's right about that.

And P.S. God: Please forgive me for doing it with Cormac.

But, God, I'm not ever gonna tell anyone about doing it with him, or that he wanted to whore me out in Memphis.

Stefan told me it made him feel better to tell his secret—but I can't tell mine.

Telling someone you're half-Jew isn't the same as me telling someone that Cormac started screwing me when I was only 13 years old.

⚜

That night at dinner, Stefan told Eli and Rachel the truth about his father.

"We knew it all along, Stefan," Rachel said. "You left a lot of clues."

"Your mother did the right thing," said Eli. "The stories coming out of Europe are ghastly, but you are safe now, so I'm sure your mother would understand."

"I hope so, but one thing is for sure. I feel better now that I am not hiding the truth."

"Jeremiah had a similar experience," Eli said. "He kept God hidden for a season to avoid persecution, but it became like a fire shut up in his bones."

LV

Truth

Birdie woke up just before daybreak on Wednesday, Jan. 31, five days before the start of Kizzy's trial.

It had turned cold during the night, but he was warm in the bunk that had been his as a boy. He had slept in his clothes—the old CCC khakis—covered with the only homemade quilt his mother ever made, a garish hodgepodge of scraps she bought at a rag sale. He was 8 years old when Shirley sewed the first squares together, and was at her side two years later when she put in the last stitch. That night, she had tucked him in and whispered in his ear. "It's yours, son. I made it just for you."

Now, 17 years later, Birdie was back on the boat—a war hero—but his mother was dead.

He kissed the hem of the old quilt and said a prayer for her. Then he remembered. *You were the best, Ma. No one ever had a better mother. We struggled to make it—that's for sure—but there was plenty of love, and lots of good times. I wish you'd been here for the big parade—I would've put you in the car, right there between me and Butch. That would've have been a sight for 'em to see: Two river rats and a burnt-up city policeman ridin' down Main Street in Big Pearl.*

He kissed the hem again and got out of bed. *I've got a lot to do.* He splashed a double-handful of water on his face, put on his pea jacket, and went outside to take in a deep breath of morning air.

He rubbed the stubble on his face and stared out at the river he loved. A lot had happened in the two days since the R4D dropped him off in Walnut Ridge.

Parades and gatherin's ain't my thing, but I'm done with all that, thank God. Kizzy seems OK, but she's in a heap of trouble.

She's got some good people on her side, especially Olivia, who's real nice. But yesterday at the graveyard I could tell Kizzy's worried sick. The trial ain't startin' 'til Monday, but she's already convinced herself that Bully Bigshot—that SOB—is out to get her.

But right now I gotta figure out who was out to get Ma.

Just then, he heard the first birdsong of the morning. *Ha ... a purple finch. I'd know that warble anywhere.* Birdie tipped his cap. *Good to hear you again, ole buddy.* He grinned and listened for others, but the racket of a big alligator gar, bursting through the surface in chase of breakfast, shattered his reverie.

It's time to go.

⚜

Birdie brought the truck to a quick stop when he saw Doctor Al's house. The old white-frame Federal that looked so elegant when he was a boy was falling apart. The paint was curling and half the shutters were drooping, hanging precariously from tired hinges; large patches of bare earth speckled the front yard.

Birdie gasped, then he saw a tiny stream of smoke rising from the chimney and the faded sign on the front door: Albert Monk, M. D.

Good, Doc's here. He eased the truck forward, rounded the corner, and parked in a vacant lot two blocks away. He pulled up the collar of his pea jacket and tugged down the bill of his cap as he got out of the truck. Then he walked back to the doctor's house and knocked on the door.

An emaciated old man, frail and hunched over, opened the door just wide enough to see out. His eyes, sunken and watery, had the empty look of those who know the end is near.

"Hi, Doc."

Doctor Al took a closer look. "Birdie? I'll be damned." He opened the door wide and motioned for Birdie to follow him, talking in a weak voice as he shuffled toward the living room. "I saw the pictures of you in the parade. We're all mighty proud of what you did over there." He smiled and pointed at Birdie's clothes and the stubble on his face. "But right now you look more like the boy who came home from CCC camp."

"That's because I ain't here on hero business, Doc. I'm here on river rat business, and I didn't want a bunch of people following me around like they been doing."

Doctor Al plopped down on a sofa and patted the cushion. Birdie sat by him, but the old man sighed, and looked away. "It's about Shirley, isn't it?"

Birdie nodded, but said nothing. He wanted answers, but he was not going to get pushy with Doctor Al; no one raised poor in Jasper County would think of doing such a thing. He was *their* doctor, and they respected him. Sully had tried to destroy him by steering Biggers Enterprise employees and political lackeys to other doctors. Doctor Al could have left town, but he did not; he moved his practice to his home, cut his overhead, and eked out a living taking care of poor people.

"It was a shame to lose her, Birdie. Kizzy came to get me, and I got to her as quick as I could—I got around better back then—but it was too late to save her."

"I know you tried, Doc. I ain't blamin' you, but Kizzy told me there's more to it than that."

"She had female trouble, Birdie. She was bleeding really bad, and that is what killed her."

"But what caused the bleeding? That's what I want to know, Doc."

"I asked Kizzy that morning if Shirley had said anything to her about what made her sick, and she said 'No.'"

Birdie waited; Doctor Al appeared to be thinking, searching for what to say next.

Finally, he spoke. "But I didn't need Kizzy to tell me what was wrong. I'd seen too many cases like hers. It was a botched abortion, Birdie. There was nothing I could do."

"Ma wasn't one to have abortions, Doc. She would've been happy to have a little baby to love on, especially since Milton and Layton had just got killed in North Africa."

Doctor Al looked down, and sighed. Then he struggled to his feet and went to the window; he stared out, pretending to have heard something.

Birdie got up, crossed the room, and stood close behind him. Then he spoke in a soft voice. "Kizzy told me the people at the Eugenics Center threatened to put the girls in the poorhouse if Ma didn't get an abortion."

Doctor Al moaned. "That's the truth of it, Birdie."

Birdie put his hand on the old man's shoulder. "What they did ain't right, Doc—it's bad wrong."

⚜

The simple but powerful assertion of right versus wrong touched the old man's heart. He turned to face Birdie, the sunken, sad eyes suddenly afire. He pointed to the sofa, and when they were seated he was the first to speak. "I tried to get something done years ago, but I ran into a brick wall. I should've raised hell right then, but I didn't. And I've regretted it ever since."

"The Marine Corps taught me that it ain't ever too late to raise hell."

The doctor studied Birdie's face. "Now I see how you won the Medal of Honor. But the truth is, Birdie, most of us don't have the balls to raise hell when we see wrong."

"Will you help me, Doc? I want to know why my mother died, and I've been thinking: If they forced her to get an abortion ... well, I figure they must have forced other women to do the same."

Doctor Al wept. "I'm on my last legs, Birdie, but it's a blessing that you've come. It gives me a chance to redeem myself. I turned a blind eye to what was going on, and the shame of it has been eating on me like a bad case of the dry rot."

"Tell me what you know, Doc."

"Some of what I know is firsthand, but I also know a world of hearsay that's 99.9 percent accurate."

"Fire away, Doc. I want to know the truth."

"I've been watching the Eugenics Center ever since Sully Biggers started it in 1932," said Doctor Al, speaking with the unbridled pep of a newly-forgiven man. "At first he called it the Big Pearl Fitter Families Clinic, but everyone around here calls it the Eugenics Center.

"Sully and Lookadoo are the main culprits. They're zealots, disciples of Madison Grant, the eugenics purist who once considered extermination as a possible solution. I've heard them praise Grant at public meetings, but they've never talked openly about what they've been doing here locally.

"When the eugenics movement began to lose steam in the late 1930s, a group down in Little Rock started a clinic that focused on contraception instead of sterilization. That pissed Sully off. He called it a 'watered-down version of eugenics that won't work.'

"Sully pushed hard to get a bill through the legislature that would've allowed the state to sterilize imbeciles and other undesirables—mostly poor people living on the margins of society."

"Like us river rats?" Said Birdie.

Doctor Al harrumphed. "Well … yes … but the legislature wouldn't go along; they said it was 'a form of socialized medicine.'

"Sully and Lookadoo were furious, so they started using the Eugenics Center to do exactly what the legislature had just rejected."

"It ain't right to go after folks just because they're poor, Doc."

"It's not just poor people, although they get the brunt of it. The likes of Sully and Lookadoo say they want to 'stamp out the impure.' Their goal is to 'stop the breeding of genetic defectives.' The 'feeble-minded and sexually wanton, criminals, epileptics, the insane, Jews, Indians, blacks'; their list goes on and on. These groups, they say, are 'passing on bad genes at the expense of good ones.'"

"Doc … who did the abortion on Ma?"

"I can't say for a fact, but I'm right sure it must have been a guy who has an office up in Leadwood. He's an oddball—some say he's a manic depressive—but the Eugenics Center sends women to him for abortions and tubal ligations. I don't know exactly how it works, but he's been hooked up with the Center for at least five years."

"What's his name, Doc?"

"Marvin Quigly."

✢

The two men spent the rest of the morning at a table in the living room, going through old files, looking for medical records to validate Doctor Al's recollections about women he treated for problems related to abortions. It was not an easy task; the records—covered with dust and mildew—were falling apart. Doctor Al had stored them in cardboard boxes—15 in all—in the basement of his house.

But their search bore fruit; the first record they found was Shirley Barden's. It contained Doctor Al's handwritten note about the cause of her death: "Miscarriage, complications, shock and hemorrhaging."

"I'm ashamed of myself, Birdie. I should've written, 'Botched abortion by a quack,' but I didn't." I took the easy way out."

"Ma's dyin' ain't your fault, Doc."

"What are you going to do?"

"I ain't sure yet, but I'm gonna do something."

"You've got to be careful, Birdie. They're all in on it—the prosecuting attorney, Sully, the judge, the sheriff, and Mutt the coroner. If you threaten them they'll find a way to take you down."

"I've faced worse, Doc."

"I know, but you need to be smart about it. Stay at my hideaway on Greystone Lake. I haven't been there in a good while, but there's canned goods there and I've got a slab of bacon you can take with you."

Birdie nodded. "I'll take you up on that, Doc. There's too many people watching for me at Ma's boat."

They found four more records in the boxes. One was for a 25-year-old woman, the victim of a "botched D&E." The other three were for women who complained of tubal ligations that resulted in serious infections.

All five women had one thing in common. Their doctor was Marvin Quigly of Leadwood, Ark.

⚜

Birdie spent Wednesday night at Doctor Al's place on Greystone Lake. The rustic two-bedroom log cabin—just steps from the water—was a quarter-mile from the nearest neighbor, surrounded by 40 acres of woodlands.

An hour before daybreak on Thursday, Birdie drove to Big Pearl and parked two blocks from Butch Jansen's house. He looked around, then walked back and knocked on the door.

Butch, in pajamas, cracked the door open to see who had knocked, and as soon as he did Birdie said, "It's me, Butch. I'm on to something and I need your help."

⚜

"Doctor Al is right," said Butch after listening to what Birdie had learned about his mother's death and the Eugenics Center. "You need to watch out. Everything in Jasper County is controlled by Sully Biggers, and Sam Lookadoo is his main sidekick."

"They killed my mother, Butch, and I aim to do something about it."

"What Doc told you is a good start, but you'll need hard evidence."

"Like what?"

"Testimony, documents, and official records. Doctor Al's old medical records are a good start, but an official record would be better. I'll look through the city police files to see what I can find."

"What if I get the truth out of Marvin Quigly … wouldn't that be enough?"

"Maybe, but who are you going to take it to? Lookadoo will bury it, and if that doesn't work he'll bury you."

"I've got some connections with newspaper guys who've been following me around. I could tell them."

"There may be a better way. Let me think on it. Meanwhile, you need to talk to the women Doctor Al told you about *before* you go see Doctor Quigly. If they'll back up what Doc said, it'll give you some leverage."

"All right. I'll find the women, and then I'll go see Quigly."

&

On Friday in the late afternoon, Birdie called Butch from a pay telephone in Tulip, a small town near the western border of Jasper County.

"Butch, I found 'em ... the two women who went to Doctor Al."

"Come to my house for dinner; we need to talk."

Later, when they were alone at Butch's house, Birdie lowered his voice. "Both women—Susie Hardeman and Peggy Trask—are poor, barely making ends meet. They're scared, but when I told them about Quigly killing Ma they opened up. They went to Quigly because someone at the Eugenics Center told them that if they didn't get fixed the state was going to take their kids away."

"I hit pay dirt too," said Butch. "Peggy Trask came to the police station in October of 1942, before she went to Quigly to get fixed. Someone made an entry in the log book by her name that says: 'State trying to take her babies / reported same to P.A.'"

"Birdie slammed his fist on the table. "Wait'll I get my hands on Quigly."

"I can't be a part of that, Birdie. I'd like to be, but I'm a cop."

&

Birdie tried to contact Dr. Marvin Quigly all day Saturday and Saturday night. He went to the doctor's home and to his office in Leadwood several times. It was a miserable day, freezing cold and windy. Birdie would bang on the doors, peep in the windows, and walk around the buildings, shouting the doctor's name.

He got no response at either place, nor did he get an answer when he dialed the doctor's telephone number.

On Sunday he tried again. He circled the block at both places, stopping first at the office. When he got no response there, he drove to the house, banged on the door, and hollered the doctor's name three times as loud as he could.

A next-door neighbor—a portly woman in her late 50s with stringy black hair—stuck her head out of her front door and hollered to Birdie. "For God's sake, buddy. Can't you tell? He ain't there."

Birdie looked her way, and shouted. "Do you know where he's gone, or when he'll be back?"

"Doc?" She horselaughed, "He's half-crazy. He gets in the car and drives around for hours. I've heard he'll drive as far as Chicago and then turn around and drive back, stopping only to pee and get gas. He's a nut job, buddy … tried to land an airplane on a city street a couple of years ago."

She started to close the door, but stuck her head out again. "It's Sunday, so he'll come dragging in around midnight tonight. That's what he always does. You can set your watch by him." Then, with the quickness of a snapping turtle, the stringy-haired woman pulled her head back into the house and closed the door.

❖

Butch came to the cabin at Greystone Lake after dark on Sunday. He brought the Sunday edition of the *Big Pearl Free Current*. The lead story had a banner headline: TRIAL OF RIVER GIRL STARTS MONDAY.

"It's the talk of the town," said Butch. "I saw Lookadoo at church this morning. He came late on purpose so he could preen himself. He was strutting around acting like he's got a conviction in the bag."

"He's the one that ought to go to prison, him and Sully Biggers, and all the others," said Birdie. "But first I gotta get ahold of Quigly, and he's off running around right now."

"You think he'll be back tonight?"

"That's what the neighbor lady said. And I'll be waiting for him."

❖

Birdie parked in front of Marvin Quigly's home at 11 p.m. and let the engine run to keep warm. Then, at midnight, he turned off the ignition and waited. *If the neighbor lady with the stringy hair is right, he ought to be coming home pretty soon.*

At 12:30 a.m., a 1939 Chevrolet coupe pulled into the driveway, and a diminutive man carrying a medical bag got out of the car and headed for the house.

"Doctor Quigly," shouted Birdie as he got out of the truck. "I need your help; it's an emergency."

When the doctor looked to see who had called, Birdie closed to an arm's length. "Can you come take care of my sick boy? It ain't far, and I'll bring you right back."

"Can't you bring him in this afternoon?" said the doctor as he studied Birdie's face. Then suddenly he said, "Who are you?"

"Everyone calls me Birdie."

"I thought so. You're the hero. I saw you in the parade."

"Yeah, but I ain't here to talk about what I did over there. I'm here to get you to do what you're supposed to do. Come take a look at my boy, Doc." He reached in his pocket and pulled out a wad of cash and handed it to the doctor. "Here's $50, and I'll give you another $50 when I bring you home."

"Where is he?"

"He's at my cabin on Greystone Lake. It ain't far."

"Oh, all right."

⚜

On the short trip to the cabin the doctor peppered Birdie with questions about the war and the boy's condition, but Birdie said as little as possible. Mostly he nodded, mumbling, "I don't know," or "You'll see."

As soon as they were inside the cabin, Birdie took off his cap and pea jacket, tossed them in the corner, and turned on the light.

"Where's the boy?" Said Doctor Quigly, as he looked nervously around the room.

"There ain't no boy, Doc. It's just you and me."

"What do you want with me?" said the doctor as he fidgeted and jiggled around to relieve a sudden burst of fear.

Birdie pulled a chair away from the kitchen table and motioned for him to sit down. And when he balked, Birdie barked at him, like a drill sergeant.

"Sit down!"

The little man gulped, and his face lost a shade. He started to say something, but sat down when he saw the determined look on Birdie's face.

Birdie got another chair from the table and sat down, facing the doctor.

"Let's talk, Doc."

"About what?"

"Well, let's start with what we do for a living." Birdie smiled big; the doctor half-smiled with quivering lips.

"I'm a Marine, Doc." Birdie smiled again, but then he leaned forward and snarled, "I kill bad people." The doctor tried to speak, but he could not make a sound.

"What do you do for a living, Doc?"

He stammered.

"Do you do abortions, Doc?"

"That's against the law," he said, his voice weak and hoarse.

"Stop the bullshit and answer my question, Doc. I know you fix women—tie their tubes—and do abortions for the Eugenics Center."

He shook his head, taking care to avoid Birdie's stare.

"You killed my mother, you worthless piece of shit."

"Your mother?" Quigly grabbed his crotch and wiggled as if trying to hold back pee.

"Yes, my mother." Birdie took a photograph from his breast pocket and held it in front of the doctor's eyes. "Remember her? Shirley Barden. You butchered her so bad that she bled to death, but before she died she told my best friend that you and those people at the Eugenics Center forced her to get an abortion."

Quigly sobbed. "I've never forced a patient to do anything."

"So you're saying you do remember my ma, but you didn't force her to have the abortion. Is that what you are saying, asshole?"

"Look, I just want to go home. You can't hold me here ..."

Birdie scooted his chair closer. "I know a story about a lot of Marines who also wanted to go home." He took on the style and sound of a storyteller. "But it's also a story about getting fixed when you don't want to be fixed."

He paused for effect, but none was needed; the doctor was on the brink of apoplexy.

"The Japs on Peleliu would hide in caves during the day, but at night they would sneak up on Marines who had fallen asleep in their foxholes. And they would do bad things to them just to scare the beejeebers out of the rest of us.

"You ever been scared, Doc?"

The doctor sniveled, and shook his head. "No? Well, I have. The Japs scared the shit out of me one night on Peleliu. You know what they did to one of our Marines, Doc?"

Birdie did not wait for an answer. He leaned close, and whispered in the doctor's ear. "They pulled his pants down and cut off his balls."

Doctor Quigly shivered, and peed in his pants.

"So, Doc. I need to know the truth, and I aim to get it from you—Japanese style if I have to."

The doctor could take no more. "Look, I just do the cases they send to me."

"Who sends to you, Doc? The Eugenics Center?"

"Yes."

"You're a miserable son-of-a-bitch, Doc. But you ain't the only one I'm after. If you want to save your balls you'll tell me everything you know about the Eugenics Center and how the whole thing works.

"Otherwise, I'll get on with fixin' you. I ain't no surgeon, but I'll be nicer than the Japs. I'll put your balls in a fruit jar so's you can take them with you."

⚜

It took a half hour for the doctor to resolve his dilemma. He worked his way through several stages of psychosis, chattering, whimpering, and acting out. There was hand wringing and eye-rolling as he compared one peril to another: The bad things that Sully Biggers and Sam Lookadoo would do to him versus Birdie's reminder that he had already said enough to incur their wrath versus the new threat of losing his balls. He bounced maniacally from one horn of the dilemma to the other.

Finally, like a man facing the hangman's noose, it all cleared up for Doctor Quigly. He stopped whimpering—apologized for what he had done to Shirley and her baby—and opened up.

Birdie did not forgive him. Instead, he said, "I need you alive, Doc, so stick with me; play ball and you'll live to see another day."

"It all started when Lookadoo caught me using drugs," the doctor began his confession with a babbling attempt to justify his conduct. "He had me dead to rights, but said he would let me go if I would agree to work with the Eugenics Center."

"Are you a drug addict or something?"

"They say I'm a manic depressive, and I guess that's true. I get excited and ramble and do stupid things. I just got back from St. Louis—drove round trip, nonstop. I don't know why I go on tears like that, but it's what I do, and I take drugs to keep me jacked up." He slumped, and then added an afterthought, "It makes me feel good."

"That ain't no excuse for killing," said Birdie.

"At first I was just tying tubes for women who told me that's what they wanted, but then I learned that Lookadoo and Sully were using the Eugenics Center to round up poor women that they considered 'undesirable.' They would find ways to scare them into getting tubal ligations and abortions. It was all part of their plan to improve the race through what they called 'better breeding.'"

The doctor, unleashed, rattled on. "It's not against the law to do a tubal ligation, but you can't make someone do it if they don't want to. Anyway, I went to Sully Biggers and told him to his face that I wanted out, but he picked up the phone and called the prosecuting attorney. Lookadoo came over and the two of them told me it was too late to get out. They said my hands were already dirty, and if I tried to back out they would send me to prison for using drugs."

"What about abortion, Doc. It's flat-out illegal to do abortions, ain't it?"

"Yes, but Lookadoo told me he would never prosecute a case of abortion—he said he believed in it, especially to control the 'undesirables.'"

"Meaning river rats and poor white trash?" Birdie said.

"Mostly, but Sully and Lookadoo are crazy-mad about eugenics, they're true believers. They want to go further: Jews, black people, social misfits. I heard them say it time and again: 'Sterilize them or abort them, we've got to get them off the dole.'"

"That's bad sick, Doc."

⚜

"Butch, this here is Doc Quigly," said Birdie. "We've been talking since early this morning and I've brought him to see you so's he can tell you what he's been telling me about the Eugenics Center."

Birdie looked at the doctor. "Ain't that right, Doc?"

Marvin Quigly, a small man to begin with, looked even smaller standing between two large decorated veterans. He looked up at Butch, who was still in his police uniform, and nodded.

"Then let's get busy," said Butch as he pointed to his kitchen table. "I'm testifying first thing tomorrow and I want to get a good night's sleep."

"How'd Kizzy hold up today?" Birdie asked.

"I was only in the courtroom once; they had just finished picking the jury, and the judge was swearing them in. She looked fine, even winked at me."

"Ain't she something?" Birdie said. "All right, Doc, tell him what you told me."

⚜

Three hours later, Doctor Quigly leaned back in his chair. "So that's it. That's all I know."

Butch continued to write, adding the doctor's final comment to a six-page statement. When he finished, he handed the statement to the doctor, and said, "Read it over, Doc, it needs to be correct from start to finish."

The doctor found five mistakes that Butch had made on purpose—one on each of the first five pages. He pointed them out to Butch, who feigned surprise and corrected the mistakes.

"So, Doctor Quigly, if you are ready to sign, I'll ask my wife, Ellen, to come in. She works at the bank and is a notary public. She'll be a witness to your signature. Is that OK?"

Doctor Quigly nodded. Ellen came into the room and smiled at the doctor. "Are you ready, Doctor? Have you read the statement, and is it true and correct?"

The doctor said, "Yes." He started to sign, but Butch stopped him.

"Wait, Doc. Before you sign you need to initial the changes we made. We don't want anyone saying I changed something without your OK. Right?"

"Right," said the doctor; then he scribbled his initials by each change and signed his full name on the last page.

Ellen instructed Butch and Birdie to witness his signature, then she signed it and sealed it with her notary stamp.

⚜

Butch signaled for Birdie to follow him to another room, and said to Ellen, "Pour the doctor a cup of coffee, Ellen. We'll be right back."

When they were out of earshot, Birdie said, "So are you going to give this to your State Police buddy?"

"No," said Butch. "I've decided that's a bad idea. There's no way he could keep it from the new governor, Ben Laney; he's a big fan of Sully's, and he might be a supporter of the eugenics movement for all we know. I learned today that he goes around praising Arkansans for being 'good and pure Anglo-Saxon stock.' If he hears what we're up to he'd find a way to stop it."

"So they control everything from the governor on down?"

"Not everything, and not everyone," said Butch. "I've had a brainstorm. Our new circuit judge—the man who's trying Kizzy's case—was a major in North Africa. I didn't serve directly under him but I knew about him, and everything I heard about him was good. I'm gonna call him right now and see if he will see us tomorrow."

"But it's almost 10 o'clock," said Birdie.

"He'll understand … I think," said Butch as he dialed the judge's number.

"Judge, this is Butch Jansen—I'm the city policeman in Big Pearl. Yessir, I know it's late. Yessir, but Major … I was in North Africa when you were. Yessir. Well, I'm calling to ask for a meeting with you. Sir, it's something I can't talk about on the phone, but it's something you need to know about, and you're the only person that I can tell. Yessir, Major."

Butch hung up the phone, and looked at Birdie.

"Four o'clock tomorrow afternoon. Judge Wheatley will see us at his home in Cranford County."

⚜

Ellen was in deep conversation with Doctor Quigly when Butch and Birdie came back into the room.

"You will be just fine, Doctor," Ellen said as she patted his hand. "Confession is good for the soul."

"Yeah," said Doctor Quigly. "So long as it doesn't get you killed."

"Don't worry, Doc." Birdie said. "You're gonna stay with me tonight at the cabin, and between me and Butch you are gonna be the safest man in Jasper County. It's like I said before—I need you alive."

LVI

Conundrum

On Tuesday morning, Feb. 6, 1945—a cold, clear day—hundreds of people gathered outside the Jasper County Courthouse. Most of them hoped to get a seat for the second day of Kizzy's trial, but some had come just to kibitz about the trial and the stories in the morning papers.

The out-of-town press and the Big Pearl Free Current carried a number of unbiased stories about the jury, the new judge, and the opening statements of counsel.

But the widely-read Jasper County Bulletin, a wholly-owned subsidiary of Biggers Enterprises, took a predictable approach. Prosecuting Attorney Sam Lookadoo's opening statement was printed word for word beneath a headline that stretched across the front page: PROSECUTOR TELLS JURY: THIS WAS MURDER!

A sidebar heralded Lookadoo's success as a crime fighter, with a pull-quote from his opening statement set in a mid-column box: "We can't turn a blind eye to evil; this was murder, pure and simple."

The Bulletin also carried a story about the work of the Eugenics Center. It was not on the front page, but it contained a quote from Sully Biggers, who linked the trial to his favorite cause. "This trial is a black eye for the good people of Big Pearl, but it proves the need for better breeding."

⚜

Birdie and Doctor Quigly were back at Greystone Lake, listening to the radio. An announcer—broadcasting live from the steps of the Jasper County

Courthouse—was giving a breathless report about the trial, relying mostly on the stories in the Bulletin.

When the announcer read the quote from Lookadoo: "We can't turn a blind eye to evil," Birdie kicked a trash can across the room. "That's pure-dee horseshit."

"What's that called, Doc?" Birdie snapped his fingers. "What's the fancy word for that? You know—when a no-good SOB like Lookadoo goes after someone as good as Kizzy."

"Hypocrite."

"Yeah, that's it," Birdie said as he turned the radio off.

⚜

At 9 a.m., the bailiff sang out, "Hear ye, hear ye. The Circuit Court of Jasper County is now in session, the Honorable Forrest Wheatley presiding."

Judge Wheatley entered the courtroom. He stepped up onto the bench in an unfussy way and invited the people to be seated.

"Ladies and gentlemen of the jury, today we will hear the testimony of witnesses. Ordinarily we would work until 5 o'clock, but I will adjourn court at 3 p.m. today because I have a previously scheduled meeting in Cranford County that I cannot miss.

"Mr. Prosecutor, you may call your first witness."

⚜

Lookadoo called Officer Butch Jansen as the state's first witness. He told about Eli coming to his office and then going to the boat with the coroner. He described the scene, authenticated the photographs he took, and identified the items he had collected and marked as evidence.

County Coroner Mutt Falwell regaled the jury with a down-home version of the cause of death, insinuating strongly that Kizzy used more force than necessary under the circumstances. He wound up his testimony with a personal opinion: "There weren't no need to call in the state medical examiner; that's a waste of money in a case like this." Judge Wheatley instructed the jury to ignore the unsolicited remark.

After lunch Sheriff Gunner Brown told the jury that Kizzy admitted the killing, and he twisted what she told him to favor the state's version of the case. He said Cormac had landed a good job in Memphis and suggested it was ungrateful for Kizzy to argue about it. He also said she did not look like she had been in a fight, which led him to opine that she had used more force than necessary to defend herself. And he admitted on cross-examination that he had not taken a written statement from Kizzy, saying, "I didn't take one because this case ain't complicated."

At 3 p.m. Judge Wheatley adjourned court, tapped his gavel on the sound block, and left the courtroom.

⚜

At 3:55 p.m., Butch steered his car into the driveway of the historic Wheatley home in rural Cranford County. Birdie was in the passenger seat; the hapless Doctor Quigly was in the back.

The home, an Italian Renaissance Revival, had been in the judge's family for a half-century. Elegant but understated, the old stone two-story was a perfect fit for Forrest Beauregard Wheatley, a temperate man of Scots-Irish heritage.

The judge met his guests at the door, and when he saw Birdie he snapped to attention and saluted. "It's a privilege to have you in my home, Corporal Barden." Then he said hello to Butch and Doctor Quigly and motioned for them to follow him.

"Sir, I think it might be best for Doctor Quigly to wait for us in another room, if that is all right with you," Butch said.

"Of course," said the judge, and he showed the doctor to the parlor.

Then he took Birdie and Butch into the library, and closed the door.

"Now, gentlemen, what's this all about?"

⚜

Butch laid it out for the judge, beginning with what Shirley told Kizzy on her deathbed and ending with what Doctor Quigly admitted in his confession. Then he said, "Judge, we've brought this to you because you're the only one we can trust.

"Lookadoo, the sheriff, Sully Biggers, the people at the Eugenics Center—they're all in it up to their ears. The coroner and the county judge are probably in it too, but that part needs more investigation.

"We thought about taking it to the State Police, but the governor would hear about it if we did, and he's all tied in with Sully Biggers."

"You say Doctor Quigly has signed a statement?" said the judge.

"Yessir." Butch handed the statement to him. "But we brought him with us in case you want to hear it straight from the horse's mouth."

The judge read the statement. Then he wrinkled his brow, looked at the ceiling, and mumbled, "This presents a conundrum."

"A what?" said Birdie.

"Sorry, I was talking to myself, working through some complicated legal issues."

"That conundrum thing, Judge—does it mean we've done something wrong?" said Butch.

"No, not at all. But this *is* a knotty problem. The prosecuting attorney is a constitutional officer. I have no authority to remove him from office, and we are in the middle of a trial that I can't stop; that wouldn't be fair to anyone.

"I've got to think about this, and do some research."

"What about Doctor Quigly, Judge? He's scared they'll come after him if this gets out."

"I may be on thin ice, but I'm going to write out an order right now directing you to hold him as a material witness. Then I'll start trying to figure out the best way to clean up this mess."

⚜

That night Birdie called John Thurmond, the reporter for the *New York Sun Herald.*

"There's something rotten going on in Big Pearl, John. And it's gonna be bigger news than the so-called Skillet Killing. I'm working on it, so stand by and I'll tell you about it soon as I can."

Thurmond fished for more, but soon gave up. "OK, we'll play it your way, but keep me posted, Birdie."

⚜

The next day Judge Wheatley tapped the gavel and said, "You may proceed, Mr. Lookadoo."

Lookadoo had no more witnesses to call, but he wanted the jury to think that he had something more up his sleeve. He went to the exhibit desk and shuffled through the documents and photographs, inspecting one with feigned care. Then he went to the counsel table, whispered to his deputy, and returned to the exhibits.

"Do you—or do you not—have another witness, Mr. Lookadoo?" asked the judge.

"Your honor, certainly there's more that the state can offer, but I'm just trying to make it easy on the jury." He smiled at the jurors as he spoke.

"We're here to do justice, Mr. Lookadoo," said the judge, scowling with his one good eye. "We are *not* here to admire your showmanship. Either call another witness or rest your case and sit down."

The women on the jury laughed, and so did three of the men.

The judge's sudden outburst and change of tone puzzled Lookadoo, but he quickly recovered. "I certainly agree that we are here to do justice, your honor."

He paused, glanced nervously at the judge, and then announced with dramatic flair: "Your honor, ladies and gentlemen of the jury—the state rests."

⚜

"Mr. Levy," said Judge Wheatley. "You may call your first witness."

Ruben stood up and called her name.

Kizzy rose and walked smoothly to the witness stand. Her red hair, hanging loose beneath a ribbon beret, stood out against the light blue skirt and matching blouse that Olivia had chosen for her to wear. She had the angelic look of a sweet 16-year-old, perfectly composed in the face of great danger. And when she took the oath and spoke her name she exuded class, sounding very much like a citified young woman.

But Kizzy wanted to scream. The tingly feeling racing through her bloodstream would not go away. Worse still was the hard knot in her belly and the tiny hairs on the nape of her neck that rippled back and forth, as if ruffled by a cold winter breeze.

Stefan, sitting between Uncle Mac and Olivia, saw what others did not. So when Kizzy looked his way, he winked and pretended to be playing his violin.

It was the perfect thing to do. Kizzy smiled, and a warm feeling gushed through her from head to toe. The shaky legs that were about to crumble stopped shaking. She heard Stefan's music in her head and giggled to herself. *It's my song*:

I found my pearl on the river free
Where there ain't no secrets or shame

"Kizzy?" Ruben called her name, but she was in a distant place with the boy of her dreams.

Ruben raised his voice. "Kizzy."

"Oh … yes sir, Mr. Levy."

"Tell the jury, in your own words, what happened on the morning of Sept. 4."

Kizzy looked each juror in the eye, and then she began. "Well, I won't argue with what the sheriff said yesterday, but I didn't like the way he said it. My MeeMaw told me it's *how* you tell something that matters most, so I'm going to tell it my way."

Ruben had coached her well. "Don't just talk to them, Kizzy—*visit* with them as you would visit with kinfolks."

Kizzy led off with a heartfelt account of her life on the river. She told about growing up with MeeMaw, Grandpa, and Sarah: "People called us river rats, and looked down on us because we were poor, but we didn't think of ourselves that way. We didn't have electricity, or plumbing, but we had love, and we had fun."

"Your honor, I object," said Lookadoo. "She needs to get to the point; all this stuff about toe-digging, fishing, and looking for pearls gets us nowhere."

The judge frowned. "Mr. Lookadoo, the sheriff testified that the deceased wanted to make her life better by moving to Memphis. This girl is on trial for murder, and she is entitled to tell why she wanted to stay in Big Pearl. Overruled!"

Kizzy studied the jurors as the judge spoke. *Some of them are out to get me, that's easy to see. But the women, I can feel it ... they're itching for me to tell 'em how Cormac treated me, especially when we were alone at night. It might get me off to tell 'em the truth, but I can't do that. Olivia and Stefan would drop me like a hot potato if I was to tell what Cormac was doing to me, and how he was planning to whore me out in Memphis. Maybe one day I can tell all that through my songs, but right now is not the time. I'm sticking to my story.*

She made some headway with the jurors when she told about the fight, but Lookadoo was merciless in his cross-examination. He made her admit that Cormac had bought her dresses, shoes, and candy, and that he had kept her from going to the poorhouse. Then he posed a string of questions: "Cormac took a job at the button factory so he could buy you nice things, didn't he?"

"Yessir."

"And the argument that led to the killing started because he got a better job in Memphis, and you didn't want to move. Isn't that right?"

"Yessir." But when it came to questions about the fight, Kizzy stuck to her story. "He's big and strong, and I hit him because he got mad and knocked me down. Then he jabbed a knife at me, so I hit him again because I was scared."

Lookadoo tried to get her to say she didn't need to hit him with the skillet, especially in the head. Kizzy admitted that she hit him three times in all, but fended off Lookadoo's contention that she had used more force than she needed to. Even so, Lookadoo was effective, and when Kizzy stepped down from the witness stand the women on the jury looked concerned, and the hard cases—Bully's boys on the jury—smirked.

When the judge recessed for lunch, Olivia, Stefan, Uncle Mac, Dynamite, and Sweetcheeks clustered around Kizzy, and they all told her that she had done a good job.

She smiled, and Uncle Mac said, "That's my girl. Keep hope alive. The Marines are coming!"

⚜

The courtroom filled quickly for the Wednesday afternoon session. Some who were there for the morning session never left; they had skipped lunch to save their seats. The standing room was soon packed with people who had fought their way into the room before the custodian closed the big double doors.

"Is he here?" The question circulated as people craned to see, but the answer was always the same: "No, not yet."

They had come to see the hero, but they would have to wait.

Olivia testified first, followed by Uncle Mac. They told of their love for Kizzy, describing her as "a peace-loving young girl determined to make the most of her life."

Lookadoo squirmed, but he did not cross-examine.

"Call your next witness, Mr. Levy."

"Your honor, the defense calls Corporal L. W. "Birdie" Barden as a character witness for Kizzy."

A hush, and then the custodian opened the double door. Birdie—dressed in the forest green uniform of an enlisted Marine—entered the room and walked smartly down the center aisle. His barracks cap was cradled beneath his left arm, and the Medal of Honor was around his neck, held in place by its light blue star-speckled ribbon. Several people stood as he passed by on his way to the witness stand, and some of them saluted.

Lookadoo rubbed his forehead and made the instant decision that he would not object or cross-examine Birdie, no matter what he said.

"Corporal Barden, do you know the defendant, Kizzy?"

"Yessir. I've known her all her life. We were raised right here on the Black River—our boats were sittin' side by each."

"Do you have an opinion, or know her reputation for being a peace-loving girl?"

"Yessir, I do. Kizzy's the sweetest girl in the world. She's like a little white dove that I used to have—she's full of love, and she wouldn't hurt a fly."

Birdie raised his hand. "But wait, that ain't altogether true. I did see her take out after a slimy green grinnel one day, but they ain't good for nothing anyway."

The audience cracked up laughing, and so did the jurors.

Lookadoo changed his mind, and jumped to his feet. "Your honor, I move to strike the last comment. It is an insinuation about the deceased."

Judge Wheatley said, "Well, Mr. Lookadoo, I don't think that is what he meant. In fact, I agree with Corporal Barden—I don't know a single thing that a grinnel fish is good for."

Everyone laughed again; Lookadoo slumped, and sat down.

When Judge Wheatley asked Lookadoo if he wanted to cross-examine the witness, he shook his head.

Birdie waved to Kizzy and blew her a kiss from the witness stand. Then he stepped down and marched out of the courtroom. More people stood than before, and once again the veterans saluted as he passed by.

The two women jurors and three of the men on the jury looked as if they wanted to stand, but they did not.

⚜

The judge declared a 15-minute recess and retired to chambers, but only a few people left the courtroom.

Lookadoo leaned over and whispered to Grant Phelps, his deputy, "The girl did better than I thought she would, but Birdie hurt us the most; he had the jury swooning. I expected those two women to wilt, but hell skatoot, our own hand-picked jurors—Sully's boys—were slobbering all over themselves."

He pushed his chair back and stood up. "I'm gonna go back to the judge's chambers and sniff around. Wheatley's been going against me all day for some reason, and I need to see if there's something I can do to smooth things over with him."

Lookadoo started to leave, but suddenly he sat back down and nudged his deputy. "Look at that," and he nodded toward Butch and the reporter John Thurmond. They were having an animated conversation near the judge's bench, speaking in hushed tones.

"They're up to something, Grant. What the hell is a New York reporter doing talking to a city cop? I've been feeling it all day long. Something's changed. Something's going on."

"They're probably just talking about the war. Thurmond is a veteran too."

"No, it's more than that," Lookadoo said.

"Everything's gonna be OK, Sam. You'll win the jury over with your closing argument; you always do."

"Maybe so, but I've never lost a jury trial, and I don't want to start now, not with the whole world watching." He got up and went to where Sheriff Gunner Brown was in a huddle with Sully Biggers and coroner Mutt Falwell.

"How's it going, Sam," said Sully. "I just got here. Gunner tells me the judge has been pissin' on us, but don't worry—our boys on the jury will hang tough."

Lookadoo fiddled with his tie. "Yeah, but I wish we had old Barnhart back on the bench."

"We'll take Wheatley out in the next election," said Sully. "I don't like him either."

Just then the bailiff entered the room and everyone returned to their places. He cried out, "All rise."

Judge Wheatley entered, took his seat on the bench, and told Ruben Levy to proceed. But Lookadoo stood up and asked permission for counsel to approach the bench.

The judge nodded his approval and the lawyers approached the judge. Ruben moved smartly to the bench, but Lookadoo oozed his way forward. And as he approached he cozied up to the bench, bowing deferentially.

"What is it, Mr. Lookadoo?"

"Nothing in particular, Your Honor, I just wanted to clear the air between counsel and court before we go on to the closing arguments."

The judge gave him a quizzical look, and so did Ruben. But Lookadoo pressed on, "Well, judge, it just seems to me that everyone is acting kinda funny. Is there something I'm missing?"

Judge Wheatley wrinkled his brow, and said in a voice loud enough to be heard throughout the courtroom. "Go on with your work, Mr. Prosecutor. When this court has something it wants to discuss with you I will let you know."

Lookadoo skulked back to the counsel table and sat down.

⚜

"Ladies and gentlemen of the jury, both sides have rested and it is now time for closing arguments of counsel. Mr. Lookadoo, you may proceed."

Lookadoo, ever resilient, rose and walked deliberately toward the jury box. He harrumphed, and thanked the jurors for their service in a booming voice, but the cockiness he had shown when the trial began was gone.

Even so, he made a convincing speech, using many of the tricks he had developed over the years to hide his loss of enthusiasm. He reviewed the evidence, wagged his finger in the air, and told stories that had never failed to get a conviction.

But there was no preening or smugness, and that was noticed, particularly by the two women on the jury.

Ruben also noticed, and he played it to the hilt in his closing argument. "The prosecuting attorney has no case, and he knows it. Kizzy is the only person in the whole world who can say what it was like to live with Cormac. And she is the only one who knows what happened on that fateful morning. The sheriff doesn't know. The coroner doesn't know, and it is for certain that Mr. Lookadoo doesn't know.

"So, ladies and gentlemen, if you believe her and the fine character witnesses who testified in her behalf, you must let her go."

Lookadoo gave a rebuttal, but it was a wandering repeat of his principle argument.

Judge Wheatley read the instructions of law to the jury, and when he finished he said, "You may retire to the jury room to consider your verdict."

✦

At 5:15 p.m., the jury returned, and the foreman reported that they were deadlocked.

Judge Wheatley said, "I am going to adjourn for the day, but you, ladies and gentlemen of the jury, must return at 9 o'clock tomorrow morning to resume your deliberations."

He gaveled the session to a close, but as he was leaving the courtroom he signaled for Officer Butch Jansen to meet him by the door. And when Butch got close, the judge whispered in his ear, "Bear with me, I'm working on a solution. Tell Corporal Barden."

✦

That night Butch stayed with Doctor Quigly at the cabin, and Birdie met with John Thurmond at Butch's house.

He pledged Thurmond to secrecy, and then told him everything he and Butch had learned about his mother's death, the Eugenics Center, Sully Biggers, Sam Lookadoo, and all the others.

"This is a bombshell, Birdie, but the *New York Sun Herald* will not go with it until you give us the OK."

They shook hands and Thurmond headed for the door, but he looked back.

"But I'm gonna write it up and have it ready."

LVII

Comeuppance

At 9:05 a.m. Thursday, Judge Wheatley sent the jurors out to continue their deliberations, and as soon as they were out of the room he declared a recess, tapped his gavel, and left the room.

The crowded courtroom came to life as soon as the judge was gone. First it was the sound of whispering, then murmurs, but within seconds the room pulsed with the familiar noise of people speculating aloud, wondering how long the jury would be out.

Kizzy wondered too, but for her it was different. The verdict would seal her fate.

She asked Ruben how long it would be, and when he said he did not know she pushed her chair back from the counsel table and stepped to the rail to visit with her friends.

Stefan reached forward to hug her, but suddenly there was a loud knock on the jury room door.

The jury had been out less than 10 minutes, but they had a message for Judge Wheatley.

⚜

"We are still deadlocked, Judge," said the foreman.

Judge Wheatley asked a few carefully worded questions to see if it made sense for them to continue their deliberations.

He could see frustration and touches of anger among the jurors as he asked his questions, but he could not tell which way they were leaning. He had learned long ago that no honest man would daresay which way a jury was leaning.

He decided to give them a nudge, so he read the Allen Charge, an instruction of law also known as the Dynamite Charge.

"Members of the jury, you have advised that you have been unable to agree upon a verdict in this case. I have decided to suggest a few thoughts to you.

"It is in the interest of the State of Arkansas and of the defendant for you to reach an agreement in this case, if at all possible. A hung jury means a continuation of the case and a delay in the administration of justice.

"You should consider that this case will have to be decided by some jury and, in all probability, upon the same testimony and evidence. It is unlikely that the case will ever be submitted to 12 people more intelligent, more impartial, or more competent to decide it.

"Under your oath as jurors, you have obligated yourselves to render verdicts in accordance with the law and the evidence. In your deliberations you should weigh and discuss the evidence and make every reasonable effort to harmonize your individual views on the merits of the case. Each of you should give due consideration to the views and opinions of other jurors who disagree with your views and opinions. No juror should surrender his sincere beliefs in order to reach a verdict; to the contrary, the verdict should be the result of each juror's free and voluntary opinion. By what I have said as to the importance of the jury reaching a verdict, I do not intend to suggest or require that you surrender your conscientious conviction, only that each of you make every sincere effort to reach a proper verdict.

"You may now retire and continue your deliberations."

⚜

Once again the courtroom came to life, an eerie replay of what had occurred just minutes ago. Wonderment ... again, but not a single person left the courtroom. There was a sense that the jury would not take long.

At 10:05 a.m. there was another knock on the door. The jury had been out for 30 minutes.

Kizzy, dressed in the belted blue dress she wore on the first day of the trial, took her seat by Ruben.

The courtroom noises faded to near silence as the jurors filed in to take their seats.

Judge Wheatley asked if they had reached a verdict, and in the moment it took for the foreman to stand, the courtroom went from near silence to total quiet.

"Your Honor, we have not. We are hopelessly deadlocked."

⚜

There were a few sounds from the spectators as everyone looked to the judge, waiting for him to rule.

Judge Wheatley declared a mistrial. He thanked the jurors for their service and discharged them. It seemed for a minute that he was going to comment further, but he did not; he simply stepped off the bench and stood to the side. An odd silence followed, but it was gone in a flash. The courtroom—pregnant with strong feelings that yearned to be free—became a hive of activity, with loud talking and noises to match.

The jurors filed out of the jury box. Three of the men went directly across the room to where Sully Biggers, Mutt Falwell, and the sheriff were standing. But the women on the jury went directly to Kizzy. They hugged her, and the older of the two said, "We did our best, Kizzy. It was 9 to 3," and she pointed to the jurors who were in the huddle with Sully Biggers. "But we couldn't get those hardheads to change their votes."

Meanwhile the crowd noise reached full force, a mix of anger and joy. Kizzy thanked Ruben, but soon she was surrounded by her excited friends: Olivia, Stefan, Birdie, Uncle Mac, Dynamite, Matilda, and Curly. Sweetcheeks, standing behind Curly, studied the crowd and quickly announced another verdict. "There's only a few in this room who ain't happy, and they're standing right over there." She pointed to Sully and his cronies.

The loudest and sharpest noise in the courtroom came from the gaggle of reporters who had worked their way to the prosecution table where Sam Lookadoo was gathering his papers and getting ready to leave.

"Will you retry Kizzy, Mr. Prosecutor?" asked the reporter from Sully Biggers' paper, the *Jasper County Bulletin*.

Lookadoo smiled, and with a confident look said, "It's my duty to get a clear resolution in all death cases, and I always do my duty."

He gave the *Bulletin* reporter a knowing wink, but the out-of-town reporters were not ready to let him go. They asked the usual questions about a hung jury: Shouldn't you have done this or that?

Lookadoo fended them off, putting the best face on his failure to get a conviction. He turned to leave, but another reporter shouted his name.

"Mr. Lookadoo. Mr. Lookadoo. I'm John Thurmond of the *New York Sun Herald*."

Lookadoo gave him a so-what sort of look and started to walk away.

"Sir ... I'm breaking a story on the Eugenics Center. It will say that poor women have been forced to get abortions and have their tubes tied. Some have died, and the story will say that you are involved. What about it, Mr. Lookadoo? Are you and Sully Biggers involved in this scandal?"

Lookadoo stuttered, and tried to dance around the question. "Well, I'll look into that if it's necessary, and if the sheriff and I, or the State Police for that matter, come up with anything we'll get back to you."

John Thurmond grinned and closed his notebook.

Lookadoo stuffed his papers into his briefcase, and rushed to tell Sully Biggers what the reporter had said.

⚜

"He's bluffing," said Sully Biggers. "Just stonewall him, and it'll all blow over. People around here like the way we're running things, at least that's what they keep telling me. It's just big-city bullshit."

Bully's diatribe made Lookadoo feel better. Servile as ever, he agreed. "Right, all these New York hotshots will go home and we'll get back to normal. Then I'll retry the girl. And I'll get her next time."

On the other side of the courtroom, Birdie had watched when John Thurmond confronted Lookadoo. And he knew why Lookadoo got a sick look on his face, and ran to tell Sully Biggers what the reporter had said.

But Birdie was not the only person in the room who knew about the Eugenics Center scandal.

⚜

Judge Wheatley was still in the room. He had not adjourned or recessed the court, so he stepped up on the bench and signaled to the bailiff.

"Quiet, please," cried the bailiff. "Quiet! This court is still in session."

Everyone in the courtroom stopped talking and people scrambled to get a seat, curious to see what the judge was about to say.

Lookadoo whispered to Sully Biggers, "What the hell is he up to now?"

"Ladies and gentlemen," Judge Wheatley spoke in the commanding voice of a soldier. "I am at this time issuing a call for a Special Grand Jury to look into allegations of wrongdoing at the Big Pearl Eugenics Center." The crowd buzzed, and people looked at one another in wonder. "And I intend to appoint a special prosecutor to lead the investigation and advise the grand jury."

The buzz got louder, and all eyes turned on Lookadoo.

Sully elbowed him. "Do something, Sam, don't just stand there."

"Your honor," Lookadoo said as he moved toward the judge's bench. "With all due respect, I am the duly elected prosecuting attorney for this judicial district and I have had no advance notice of your intention to issue such a call."

He feigned surprise and anger as he spoke, but the shakiness in his voice—the warble of a scared man—told a different story.

"I know that you did not know, Mr. Lookadoo."

Lookadoo blinked and cocked his head.

And the judge continued, "Plus I know something else that you do not know."

Lookadoo jerked back a step, and braced himself.

"Credible allegations have come to my attention that *you* and others may have violated the law. That is why you were not entitled to advance notice."

"Your honor ..." Lookadoo tried to speak, but the judge cut him off.

"This court has a duty to make certain that the laws of this state are faithfully and fairly administered."

"But, Judge, I am a constitutional officer. You have no authority to go around me or interfere with my role as prosecuting attorney."

"You are mistaken, Mr. Lookadoo. This court has the inherent power to do what I am doing because you, sir, along with several others, are under suspicion. No man is above the law."

⚜

Judge Wheatley called out, "Mr. Keith, will you come forward?"

"Yes, Your Honor," came a voice from the back of the courtroom. Everyone turned to look, but the lean, hollow-cheeked young man with neatly-coiffed blond hair was already halfway to the bench, striding down the center aisle with the gait and bearing of a soldier on parade.

"Ladies and gentlemen, I have asked Carson Keith of Dardanelle, who was in my unit in Sicily, to serve as special prosecutor."

"Your Honor, I object," Sam Lookadoo said. He approached the bench and stood close beside Carson Keith. The warble was now a loud squawk, the sound of panic. "I am a constitutional officer ..."

"Stand aside, Mr. Lookadoo," the judge said. "I have my duty to do." Then he asked Carson Keith to raise his right hand and swore him in as the Special Prosecuting Attorney.

Lookadoo turned a complete circle, and stepped closer to the bench.

The judge ignored him. "Mr. Keith, my order recites that I have called the Special Grand Jury to investigate—among other things—allegations that Mr. Lookadoo has misused the power of his office to ..."

Lookadoo squawked at the top of his voice. "Judge, you have no authority. I am going to seek a Writ of Prohibition from the Arkansas Supreme Court to stop this travesty."

Judge Wheatley struck his gavel so hard that it broke. He threw the handle aside, stood up, and leaned forward as far as he could.

"Sit down and shut up, Mr. Lookadoo."

Lookadoo went back to stand by Sully Biggers and the sheriff and the coroner.

The judge addressed Carson Keith. "Sir, I have chosen you to advise the Grand Jury because there are credible allegations that the Eugenics Center, with the help of Mr. Lookadoo, has been pressuring poor women to get abortions or be sterilized ..."

Lookadoo shouted from where he was standing. "Your honor, such things should be investigated in secret by the Grand Jury, not by you here in open court. This is all wrong."

"Maybe so, Mr. Lookadoo, but my God, man. If half of this is true, then it's not much different from what Hitler's been doing to the Jews, the Gypsies, and ..."

Judge Wheatley made a fist and hit the bench. "Court is adjourned." And he stepped down and left the courtroom amidst the drone of people murmuring about what had just taken place.

LVIII

Justice

On Friday morning, Feb. 9, the *New York Sun Herald* carried a front-page story under the byline of John Thurmond. A huge banner stretched across the front page, above the fold: ARKANSAS INVESTIGATES EUGENICS SCANDAL.

There were two separate columns beneath the banner. The one on the left was headlined CABAL FORCES STERILIZATION AND ABORTION. The story on the right was headlined PROSECUTOR AND PROMINENT CITIZENS SUSPECTED. Between these two headlines was a photograph of Shirley Barden with a cutline that said: Shirley Barden, the mother of Corporal L.W. "Birdie" Barden, Medal of Honor recipient, is said to have died at the hands of an abortionist.

The story was picked up by newspapers all across the country, and the radio stations led with it on the hour and half-hour. Only a few national outlets reported that Kizzy's trial had ended in a hung jury.

A pot of coffee was brewing in the back of Biggers Grocery near the meat counter. The butcher was cutting meat and talking to Sully Biggers, but they were alone. No one had come for the morning coffee klatch; the big table that had been full every morning for as long as anyone could remember was empty.

Nearby at the Veterans' Center, the domino room was packed. Kizzy, Stefan, Olivia, Matilda, Birdie, Sweetcheeks, and all the veterans huddled around Uncle Mac, who was waving a copy of the *Big Pearl Free Current*, with its full reprint of John Thurmond's latest story. The editor had changed the main banner to read GRAND JURY INVESTIGATES EUGENICS CENTER, and there was a separate story across the bottom of the page headlined HUNG JURY ENDS MURDER CASE.

Sweetcheeks yelled, "Three cheers for Kizzy." The room exploded with cheering and laughter, and when Stefan pulled Kizzy to his side and kissed her on the cheek, everyone cheered again.

"The jury should have let her go," Dynamite said when they quieted down. "The three stooges—Sully's boys—hung it up. But a hung jury is the best they're ever going to get because Lookadoo, Sully Biggers, and the rest of them are going down."

Again they cheered, but Uncle Mac cautioned, "Hope springs eternal, but let's not get ahead of ourselves. Sully still carries a lot of weight around here, and he's putting stories in the *Jasper County Bulletin*, denying everything and saying, 'Outsiders are trying to tell us how to run our county.'

"I think the Grand Jury will do the right thing, but we oughtn't dance on Sully's grave until we hear from them."

⚜

The Special Grand Jury for Jasper County met for two weeks. A parade of witnesses testified in secret proceedings: Nurse Dagny, Slim the driver, all the employees and volunteers at the Eugenics Center, the patients of Doctor Quigly, the coroner, the sheriff, and the county judge. Special Prosecuting Attorney Carson Keith spent hours with the jurors and more time with Officer Butch Jansen, investigating and compiling hundreds of records that were seized pursuant to search warrants.

The local paper speculated about the work of the Grand Jury, but very little leaked out; Carson Keith and Butch Jansen used the methodical approaches they had learned in the Army to secretly build an airtight case.

On Wednesday, Feb. 21, Carson told Butch, "We are ready to make our move. Lookadoo is the key. We don't have a lot of proof on Sully Biggers, but we have a strong case on Lookadoo. If he crumbles and implicates Bully, it will be over. We will nail Sully Biggers, and if he's got any sense he will work out a deal with us."

⚜

Early the next morning Sam Lookadoo barged into the Big Pearl Police Station. He paced around the front room, clearing his throat to announce his presence.

Carson came out of a back office. "We're back here, Mr. Lookadoo."

"OK boys, you got your headlines, and you've wasted two weeks with the Grand Jury, so what the hell does this have to do with me?" He plopped down and propped his feet on the conference table.

"That's what Sully Biggers has been saying, Mr. Lookadoo. The two of you have been going around the county badmouthing the press, the court, me and Butch, and outsiders in general. It has been a crass attempt to poison the jury pool and undermine what we are doing."

"I haven't been doing that, but I believe Sully is right. This is a put-up job that would have never seen the light of day if Judge Barnhart were still on the bench."

"I want to ask you some questions about the Eugenics Center, are you agreeable to that?"

"What the hell do you think I'm here for? You called this meeting, Mr. Special Prosecutor, so let's get on with it."

"You don't have to meet with us, and you can have a lawyer if you want one."

"You're telling me the law. That's a joke. I've forgotten more about prosecuting than you'll ever know, hotshot."

"We've located hundreds of records, and interviewed scores of witnesses. Are you sure you don't want counsel?"

"As I said, this is a put-up job, and you know it. You don't have anything on me or you would have already arrested me."

"Well then, let's talk lawyer to lawyer, and stop pussyfooting around."

"Fine."

"Doctor Marvin Quigly has told us everything, and he will be a witness against you. He says you coerced him to do abortions and tubal ligations, and he says you used the power of your office to force women to submit to such operations."

"He's crazy, everyone knows that." Lookadoo laughed dismissively.

"We know he has issues, so before the judge called the Grand Jury, even before I was involved, Officer Butch Jansen corroborated what the doctor said. He located and interviewed three women who said they consented for the doctor to tie their tubes only because you threatened to take their kids away if they didn't."

"They're lying. I never did that." Lookadoo tried to sound convincing, but Carson heard a slight warble in his voice.

"You're saying all three women lied?"

"Uh, yes … that's what I'm saying." Lookadoo's anemic denial signaled the end of his boisterous façade.

"Well, Mr. Lookadoo, at latest count we have 21 women who have testified against you." Carson paused, then added, "They've been coming forward in droves ever since this story hit the front page. And they all say they were coerced by you—some said it was to get an abortion, some said it was to be sterilized."

Lookadoo gulped, searching for something to say. "Women like that hate all of us who have the responsibility to make sure their kids are safe and well taken care of."

"Well, what about the testimony of Nurse Dagny, the coroner, the county judge, the sheriff, and all the workers at the Eugenics Center? Are you saying they are lying too?"

"Mutt and Gunner?" Lookadoo made a hard fist, then quickly hid it in his lap beneath the table.

"Yes, they have all confessed to the Grand Jury; they are throwing themselves on the mercy of the court."

Lookadoo, ashen, did not respond.

"Doctor Quigly says you bragged that you have never prosecuted an abortion case. So here's an irony for you: I'm toying with the idea of charging you as an accessory to abortion. That would serve you right, but I've got a laundry list of other charges that will be easier to make: Manslaughter, misuse of county money, abuse of office.

"The list goes on and on, Lookadoo, but the short story is this: I am going to send you to Cummins Prison to serve time with all the poor devils that you have sent down there since you've been prosecuting attorney. And I bet they will give you a very warm welcome."

Lookadoo stared down at the table and rubbed his temples.

Carson let him writhe, waiting for the perfect moment. It came when Lookadoo looked up; his empty eyes portrayed hopelessness.

"I want Sully Biggers, Lookadoo. He is the driving force behind this evil. Eugenics is a cultural disease that must be stopped, and I mean to tear it out by the roots.

"Here's my one-time proposition. You can take it or leave it. If you admit the charges, agree to testify against Sully Biggers, resign from office, and surrender your law license, I'll recommend to Judge Wheatley that you should serve one full year in the county jail instead of going to prison. After that, you will leave the state of Arkansas and not come back."

"I can't go to prison. There are too many there who would kill me on sight. It'd be like signing my death warrant."

He slumped down in the chair. "I got sucked into the eugenics thing, a lot of people did. I sent those women to Quigly, that's true, but I took no pleasure in it. I was just going along with the idea that there should be 'fewer births of unwanted children who can be cared for only at public expense.' Sully was different, he was evangelical about it; he despises the people he calls 'undesirables.' He actually enjoyed what we were doing. He kept detailed records for each woman—pedigree charts, personal traits, how they talked, what they looked like—and every time we sent one of them to Quigly to get an abortion or be sterilized, he would say, 'They're just trash. It's for their own good, and for the betterment of the race. We have to get rid of these undesirables through better breeding.'"

Butch Jansen wrote down what he said, inserting dates, names, and places. Then he read it to him to get his approval. Lookadoo corrected a few errors, initialed the changes, and signed the statement.

He left the police station a broken man, but Carson had what he needed to convict Sully Biggers, and Lookadoo promised to keep his mouth shut until it was time to testify.

✢

On Friday, Feb. 23, Sully Biggers and Dandy Dan Goodlatte, a cocky criminal defense lawyer from Little Rock, came to the police station.

Carson met them at the front door, and they went into the conference room.

"Mr. Biggers, I am Carson …"

"I know who you are, buddy. Let's get on with it, I've got a business to run."

Dandy Dan spoke up. "We are here at your request, but if you have targeted my client, then I am advising him to remain silent."

"Of course," Carson said. "He does not have to talk with us, but I wanted to give him a chance to clear this up before I ask the Grand Jury to indict him."

Sully horselaughed. "You lawyers. You're all the same. Ask your questions, Mister. None of us know what you've been doing behind closed doors, but I don't have anything to hide."

"I really don't have questions, Mr. Biggers. I just wanted to tell you about the evidence I have, and give you a chance to respond."

Dandy Dan intervened. "This is highly irregular. Let's go, Sully."

"Shut up, Dandy. I've read all the news stories, and this is all bullshit." He looked at Carson. "I don't care what you've got—it's just lies—and there ain't no way you'll ever get a Jasper County jury to do anything about it.

"Who in the hell do you people think you are? We Biggers' have been running this county since the end of the War Between the States. People around here like what we have done, and resent you people coming in here and telling us how to run our business."

Carson listened to his rant, then pretended surprise. "Oh, I see the problem now."

Sully raised an eyebrow, but said nothing.

"You have no idea that everyone has turned against you."

"Bullshit."

"OK, Mr. Biggers, I'm just going to lay out all my cards for you and Dandy. I have sworn statements from Sam Lookadoo, Mutt Falwell, Sheriff Gunner Brown, the county judge, Nurse Dagny, Slim the driver, and all the people at the Eugenics Center. They back up everything Doctor Marvin Quigly has told the Grand Jury, and they did it to save their own skins."

Carson read short, damning excerpts from the statements of Lookadoo, the sheriff, and he had just started to read from Doctor Quigly's statement when Sully Biggers exploded.

"All those people are weaklings. If it hadn't been for me this county would be overrun with trash."

He stood up, and motioned to Dandy Dan. "Let's get out of here."

The two men started to leave, but Sully stopped, pointed at Carson and said, "You can take those statements and shove them up your ass."

Carson and Butch stood up to face Sully and Dandy Dan, and that set Sully off again. He let loose with a speech that he had made many times, but this time the speech had an unintended consequence: It incriminated him.

"For years I tried to get those idiots in the Arkansas legislature to follow the lead of North Carolina and the other enlightened states that have passed compulsory sterilization laws.

"Hell, I wanted them to go a step further. We should sterilize *all* the undesirables. The problem goes beyond the Supreme Court case that dealt with imbeciles. Through scientific planning and intervention here in Jasper County we are weeding out the ne'er-do-wells, the lazy, the infirm, and the homosexuals. We are doing it because these undesirables—and that includes the Jews and the niggers—are corrupting our race.

"The river rats are a good example. They breed like a bunch of rabbits and we wind up taking care of them at the poorhouse.

"This is what we've been doing at the Eugenics Center since it opened in 1932, and by God, I aim to keep doing it. The women we have encouraged to get abortions don't know what's good for them, that's why we sent them to Quigly. And the same goes for the ones we sent to him to be sterilized.

"You people need to study the work of Margaret Sanger and all the others who have given this a lot of thought."

And with that he and Dandy Dan stormed out of the room.

❖

That afternoon, Carson went to the Special Grand Jury with Lookadoo's statement in hand. He read it to the jurors, then put Butch Jansen on the stand to tell what Sully Biggers had said that morning in the presence of his own attorney.

At 2 p.m. the jurors returned a True Bill charging Sully Biggers, Lookadoo, the sheriff, the county judge, the coroner, and Doctor Marvin Quigly with a variety of crimes based on the activities of the Eugenics Center.

At 3 p.m. they formally arrested Sully Biggers and the others, and by 5 p.m. all the defendants were released on bond.

❖

Sully Biggers dug in. He traveled from one end of the county to the other claiming that he had done nothing wrong. He made his favorite speech about eugenics to anyone who would listen, but most people treated him like a pariah.

He sensed hostility, so he changed tactics. He used his newspaper to circulate scurrilous rumors about Judge Wheatley, Special Prosecuting Attorney Keith, and Officer Jansen. He even turned against his longtime allies Lookadoo and Sheriff Gunner Brown. He wrote a column accusing them of lying to save their own skins.

All the while he asked numerous people to testify for him as character witnesses, but no one would do it.

❖

The national media would not let go of the issue. Newspapers, magazines, and radio stations carried stories and features casting light on the American eugenics movement, explaining how it got started and what it had become. Editorialists and commentators called for repeal of compulsory sterilization laws. And many politicians—including some who had supported the laws—railed against the practice and urged an end to it.

But locally, the newspaper stories and radio reports focused on the indictments of the Jasper County elected officials and the most prominent citizen of Big Pearl. The Eugenics Center had been closed and shuttered, but the townspeople were bracing for another notorious trial and days of bad publicity. They wanted the nightmare to end, but the stories kept coming.

Sully Biggers himself generated an endless string of negative news stories with daily invectives against "outsiders, do-gooders, and the need to weed out undesirables through better breeding."

Then, on Tuesday, Feb. 27, John Thurmond broke a national story saying that all the defendants, with the exception of Sully Biggers, were expected to plead guilty. His report was confirmed when Judge Wheatley set Monday, March 5, 1945, as the day when he would accept the pleas and impose sentences.

⚜

The square around the courthouse teemed with people eager to witness the fall of the mighty. The custodian did his best to keep order, but it was not easy. Carson Keith had reserved the front four rows in the courtroom, some 38 seats, for the victims and for Kizzy and her friends.

No one, including Judge Wheatley, expected to see Sully Biggers in the courtroom. Then, just before the time set to begin, Dandy Dan Goodlatte and Carson Keith asked to see the judge in chambers.

"What's this about, gentlemen?" Judge Wheatley said.

"Your honor, I am advised by Mr. Goodlatte that Sully Biggers may wish to change his plea."

"Is that correct, Mr. Goodlatte?"

"Your honor, the special prosecutor and I have been discussing a plea agreement that would basically give my client, who is 60 years old, a chance to get out of prison in eight years. You are new to the bench, Your Honor, so I do not know how you feel about such arrangements."

Judge Wheatley was noncommittal. "Go on, Mr. Goodlatte."

"Well, Your Honor, if you are amenable to accepting the prosecutor's recommendation, then my client would be willing to forgo his right to a jury trial and enter a plea of guilty today."

"Mr. Prosecutor?"

"Your Honor, the people are ready for this to be over. So if Sully Biggers will admit the charges set out in the indictment I will recommend five two-year sentences to run consecutively. It is my understanding that, with good behavior, he would be eligible for release in approximately eight years."

Judge Wheatley rubbed his chin. "Why the last-minute conversion, Mr. Goodlatte? Sully Biggers was spouting off as recently as yesterday afternoon, slandering this court, the special prosecutor, and making speeches about the virtue of eugenics."

"Your Honor." Dandy Dan fiddled with his tie. "This is off the record, but I know for a fact that the governor called Sully last night and told him—flat out—that he would not give him a pardon or take any other action to shorten his time in prison."

"Aha," said the judge. "That explains it."

"So if he pleads, Judge, will you go along with the deal?"

"Yes, Dandy, we need to wrap this mess up."

⚜

Everyone shushed when the judge came into the courtroom; the drama was about to unfold. Butch Jansen led the defendants into the room, and there was a gasp when the audience saw Sully Biggers.

Doctor Marvin Quigly surrendered his medical license and was sentenced to five years in prison.

Prosecuting Attorney Sam Lookadoo handed his law license to the judge, along with a letter of resignation. Sheriff Gunner Brown also resigned. Both men pleaded guilty to all the charges and the judge asked Carson Keith if he had a recommendation.

"Your Honor," Carson began. "Nothing is more pernicious than public officials who, in league with the most powerful man in a community, use the power of public office to coerce poor women—by threats, compulsion, or oppressive action—to be sterilized or get an abortion. But these two defendants have cooperated with the prosecution, and they would not last long if we sent them to Cummins Prison. For that reason, the state recommends that they be sentenced to a year in the county jail with no time off for good behavior. I also recommend that they be sentenced to 10 years in prison, but the prison sentence can be suspended as long as they behave."

The judge imposed the sentences, and then called Coroner Mutt Falwell and the county judge to the bench. They resigned from office and were sentenced to five years in prison, but the sentences were suspended.

The others, the women at the Eugenics Center, Nurse Dagny, and Slim the driver, received one-year suspended sentences.

Sully Biggers was the last to stand before the judge. When he approached the bench the crowd stirred, then quieted to hear every word. The sentiment was universal: *The most powerful man in the county is going down, surely he will say something in his own defense.* But the loquacious Bully stood mute, his head hanging.

Carson made a short statement, "The sentence I agreed to, 10 years in all, is fair, given his age. It gives him a ray of hope, but more important, it brings this sordid mess to a close."

Judge Wheatley sentenced Sully Biggers, then he praised the Grand Jury, Carson Keith, and Butch Jansen for their expeditious handling of a complicated matter. "You wrapped it up in less than a month. Good. We need to put this behind us."

Then he addressed the audience. "Ladies and gentlemen of Jasper County, there is no place in America for the kind of thinking that led to this tragedy. The fact that these people—those who believe in eugenics—can treat their fellow man with such heartlessness and savagery in what we call a civilized world is almost beyond comprehension. What the Eugenics

Center was doing here in Big Pearl could—if carried to extremes—lead to what Hitler has done in Europe. Somehow the eugenicists have come to see the poor people as 'undesirables.' They regard them as an enemy whose extermination is not only necessary, but just. They say these 'undesirables' must be removed in order to cure the ills of *their* nation, but today we are turning the tables on *them*."

He pointed to the prisoners. "Today we are removing the eugenicists to cure the ill that *they* have brought to *our* America.

"Court is adjourned."

Sully Biggers and the other prisoners were taken away, and the people filed out of the courtroom silently, contemplating the magnitude of what had just occurred.

Kizzy, Stefan, Olivia, and Birdie crowded around Uncle Mac for words of wisdom, and he did not disappoint them. "The people of Big Pearl have shown the world the best of our best with the parade that honored Corporal Birdie Barden. We've also shown them the worst of our worst with this scandal about the Eugenics Center.

"But God works in mysterious ways. Today we have dealt with our worst." He looked up. "Let it be a lesson to others."

⚜

On Sunday, March 11, the two most famous people in the history of Jasper County walked slowly down the center aisle of the First Methodist Church of Big Pearl with Matilda Joyce, Olivia Decker, and Stefan.

It was a sight to see: Corporal Birdie Barden, elegant in his forest green uniform, and Kizzy, beautiful in the dark blue dress she wore on the first day of her trial, were in the company of bluebloods and the nice boy who was living with Eli and Rachel Schulman.

The parishioners jostled for a better view, not to cast scorn but to offer geniality to a pair of river rats and a German boy.

Kizzy, who had been to the church for John Decker's memorial and on Easter Sunday, pulled closer to Birdie, and as they neared the front of the sanctuary she spotted a half-dozen rich girls from Big Pearl High School; they were dressed to the nines, as always, but they winked and smiled at her, seeking the slightest sign of recognition. Kizzy smiled to herself and resolved to be gracious. *Better late than never.*

The preacher addressed the subject that was on everyone's mind.

"Big Pearl is under a microscope; the American people have read the horrible stories about the Eugenics Center. I have heard many of you say, 'I am ashamed,' so I feel called to discuss the related issues of guilt and shame.

"Is there a difference? Learned scholars say there is a big difference. Guilt is when you say, 'I made a mistake.' Shame is when you say, 'I am the mistake.'

"Now that the Eugenics Center is closed, and the wrongdoers have been punished, each of us must ask ourselves: Did I turn a blind eye to this?

"If our answer is yes, then our indifference was a mistake, but that does not mean that we *are* the mistake.

"When we dwell on our mistakes it wears us down spiritually. Guilt then becomes shame, and we see ourselves as failures.

"But God has an answer for us. As believers, our mistakes have been forgiven. In Philippians 3:13, the Apostle Paul teaches us to forget the things which are behind, and reach forth unto those things which are before.

"So let's address our mistakes and seek forgiveness, but there is no call to be ashamed. Psalm 25:3 says, 'Let none that wait on thee be ashamed.'"

The congregation buzzed its approval. Kizzy liked the sermon for another reason. *I made two mistakes with Cormac—letting him screw me, and killing him—but I'm not the mistake. I'm not a failure. And best of all, the preacher says I'm supposed to forget all the stuff that's behind me.*

⚜

After church they all went to the Joyce residence for lunch, and Uncle Mac, a devout Baptist, met them there.

Olivia sat next to Birdie who was to the right of Matilda, and Uncle Mac took the end seat opposite the hostess. When Stefan held the chair for

Kizzy it puzzled her for a second, but she sat down, and quickly noticed that Birdie and Olivia were paying no attention to her or anyone else. *Good. They look good together, and they're getting along just fine. Birdie's rough as a cob, but she could fix that.*

Matilda told Uncle Mac he missed a good sermon, but he would have none of that. "I'm a Baptist, Matilda. I need my weekly dose of hellfire and damnation."

Matilda huffed up, ready to defend Methodism, but Olivia quickly changed the subject. She looked at Birdie, and spoke loud enough for everyone to hear, "It is a blessing that you came home when you did. Everything has changed … for the better."

Birdie blushed. "I'm glad you put it that way, because the man upstairs is in charge of blessings."

Everyone laughed, and Uncle Mac said, "Amen."

"By the way, I liked the way your preacher talks," said Birdie. "We had some chaplains in the Corps who used fine words like that, and when I get out I'm going to use the GI Bill to get some more education so I can make better speeches."

Kizzy liked the way Olivia nodded her approval when Birdie talked about his future. *She's definitely interested, but it's not a one-way deal. He likes her too.*

"Were the chaplains with you on Peleliu?" Matilda asked.

"Oh yes, ma'am, they were right there with us, but some of them ain't coming back."

"God bless 'em, God bless 'em all," said Uncle Mac.

"You know, Mrs. Matilda, we Marines ain't exactly known for being church goers, but most of the boys I served with were God-fearin' believers, especially when they were in a foxhole."

"God bless 'em, God bless 'em all."

LIX

Peace

On May 8, 1945, just two months after the sentencing of Bully Bigshot and the others, the war in Europe ended. Allied troops entered the heart of Berlin, and the madman, Adolf Hitler, cowering in a bunker deep below ground, committed suicide.

Celebrations erupted from Moscow to Los Angeles. In London—the target of Hitler's ruthless *blitzkrieg*—enormous crowds gathered from Trafalgar Square to Buckingham Palace. King George VI and Queen Elizabeth, accompanied by prime minister Winston Churchill, waved to the happy crowd from the balcony of the palace.

In the United States millions of people in cities and towns, big and small, stopped what they were doing and took to the streets to cheer and revel. In Big Pearl the men at the Veterans' Center, especially those who had been in the trenches during World War I, were overjoyed. "They'll stay beat this time," said Dynamite.

V-E Day was President Harry Truman's 61st birthday, but he dedicated the victory to the memory of President Franklin D. Roosevelt, who had died of a cerebral hemorrhage a few weeks earlier. "My only wish is that Franklin D. Roosevelt had lived to witness this day."

The allied forces liberated millions of grateful Europeans, but as they fought their way east and west to crush the German army they discovered the Nazi death camps. At Auschwitz, Dachau, Bergen-Belsen, Buchenwald, and other places they came face to face with inhumanity: Emaciated prisoners, hollow-eyed men, some no more than skin and bones, told stories of mass murder, gas chambers and ghastly atrocities. The allies found piles of decomposing bodies and scores of mass graves; all of it was a somber testament to the madness of eugenics taken to its extreme: genocide.

In Bismarck, N.D., the gates of Fort Lincoln opened wide; Fritz Halder walked out of the internment camp and boarded a train for Arkansas. The German-American internees were freed, but those who died in the camps will be there forever.

❖

On Aug. 6, 1945, a U. S. Army Air Force Boeing B-29 Superfortress rolled down the runway of North Field on Tinian in the Mariana Islands. Six hours later, the aircraft was over Japan, and at 8:15 a.m. the crew released an atomic bomb they called "Little Boy." Forty-three seconds later, the bomb struck the city of Hiroshima; the explosion and firestorm that followed killed more than 70,000 people and destroyed a five-square-mile expanse of the city. Of those killed, 20,000 were soldiers.

Three days later the United States dropped a second atomic bomb dubbed "Fat Man" on the city of Nagasaki, killing another 40,000 people.

The bastardized version of the ancient Japanese moral code of *bushido* that led to *banzai* attacks and the maniacal defense of Peleliu died in the mushroom clouds that rose from the ashes of Hiroshima and Nagasaki.

Thus, on Aug. 14, 1945, Japan surrendered, unconditionally, to the allies.

Victory over Japan marked the end of World War II, and V-J Day celebrations surpassed the revelry of V-E Day. People emptied out of theaters, stores, homes, government offices, and businesses to scream and shout, "The war is over! The war is over!" Photographers captured pictures of men and women—some total strangers—kissing as if they were long-lost friends. The end of the war was more than a moment to remember; it was a moment that could not be forgotten.

On Sept. 2, 1945, a formal surrender took place aboard the *U.S.S. Missouri* in Tokyo Bay.

The gates of the Japanese internment camps at Rohwer and Jerome, Ark., opened, as did the gates on other camps across America. Thousands of Japanese-Americans went back to their homes, but like the German-American internees, those who died in the camps will be there forever.

LX

Our First Weapon

As the sultry nights of August 1945 gave way to the clear, cool days of autumn, hundreds of ships converged on America. The troops were coming home.

Soldiers, sailors, Marines, nurses, and airmen from every theater of war hurried ashore, eager to see their loved ones. They scattered in all directions, to villages, farms, and cities. Some would seek fame and fortune, but most had a simpler goal; they just wanted to get a job and settle down.

A contagious can-do spirit—the progeny of a hard-fought victory—swept across the land, but it came face to face with an *old* worry.

At the train station in Jefferson City, Tenn., members of the Eastern Cherokee tribe stood apart from the whites to welcome one of their own, an Army corporal who had served with distinction in the Signal Corps. In Norfolk, Va., Samson Johnson, the N&W dining car waiter who served Olivia in the days after Pearl Harbor, hugged his son, a sailor dressed smartly in the bell-bottom crackerjack uniform of a petty officer, first class. And in San Jose, Calif., a young sergeant of Japanese descent was met at the bus station by his mother, father, and younger sister—American citizens who had spent three years at the War Relocation Center in Rohwer, Ark.

And there was a *new* worry: The Bomb. The mushroom clouds over Hiroshima and Nagasaki were gone, but the apocalyptic image of death and destruction had scorched itself into the memory of man. It would stay, perhaps forever.

Even so, the American people were determined to accentuate the positive. The war was over; there was much to do.

⚜

The colorful fall leaves soon fell to ground, and the air turned windy and cold.

Olivia and Kizzy spent the best part of two days decorating the Joyce residence. They arranged pumpkins and stalks of Indian corn on the porch and set the dining table with Matilda's finest china and silverware.

Kizzy made a huge centerpiece for the table—an assortment of apples, cranberries, pine cones, and gourds. Olivia made two paper-mâché figurines for the foyer and dressed them as a pilgrim couple. The man held a Bible; the woman had Birdie's white dove cradled in her hands.

⚜

On Thanksgiving Day, the elegant Victorian home was alive with warm talk, laughter, and music. Stefan wandered from room to room playing sweet refrains of chamber music, mostly Mendelssohn, but shortly after noon he put his violin away to announce, "Matilda says it's time to eat."

Uncle Mac rubbed his hands together. "Well, what are we waiting for? Let's do it. Rationing is over!" He sniffed theatrically and motioned for Birdie and Fritz to follow as he wheeled his chair toward the inviting aroma of roast turkey and fresh-made rolls.

When they were seated at the table, Matilda signaled for everyone to hold hands, then she nodded to Uncle Mac.

He bowed his head. "Lord, we thank you first for peace, and we pray for the souls of all the good men and women who gave their lives to defeat evil and keep us safe. We especially remember Olivia's beloved John, who died in the fighting at Midway, and Shirley Barden's boys, Milton and Layton, who died on the shores of North Africa …

Kizzy could not help herself. She peeped. *Olivia's OK. She's wiping a tear, but she's praying hard. And Birdie's OK too.*

She tried to refocus on what Uncle Mac was saying, but could not. *I'm lucky to be here ... I'd be in prison if it weren't for all of them ... 'specially Birdie and Olivia. ... Wait ... yep ... he's winding up now ...*

Uncle Mac thanked God for bringing Fritz home safe from North Dakota and for the food that they were about to eat. Then he intoned, "In his name we pray, amen."

Kizzy looked up just in time to see the old man wink and cackle loudly. "Now pass me some of that turkey and dressing!"

There was a flurry of small talk as the food was passed, but when everyone had filled their plate, Birdie blurted out, "I ain't supposed to talk about it yet, but I can't hold it any longer." Everyone stopped eating and looked at him. "Butch told me last night that he is going to run for sheriff."

Olivia clapped. "Yea! Things are looking up around here. I never paid much attention to politics until Lookadoo and that stupid sheriff Gunner Brown put Kizzy in jail. But now she's free for good, and they're locked up. Ha! Serves them right. They got what they deserve."

"Olivia!" Matilda shook a finger. "Mind your manners."

"Whoa, Matilda," Uncle Mac said. "A lot of us feel just like Olivia. We were all fast asleep, but we're wide awake now. We need to celebrate all the good things that have happened in Big Pearl."

"Amen," said Birdie and Fritz.

Uncle Mac leaned back in his chair. "I was going to let it be a surprise, but I wrote an article that will appear in tomorrow's paper. It's about how we need to stay on the alert. Look for it. I titled it 'Our First Weapon.'"

Matilda jerked backwards in her chair and frowned. "Sounds like it's about the bomb. I'm tired of hearing about that."

"No, it's not really about the bomb. It's about fixing the prejudice that led to all the trouble here in Big Pearl."

Uncle Mac waited until he had everyone's attention, especially Matilda, then he continued.

"We used the atomic bomb to *end* the war, that's true. But just the other day President Truman said 'unity' is the weapon that actually *won* the war for us. He said unity is 'our first weapon' both *here* and abroad, and that without it we are doomed."

Matilda looked puzzled. "So?"

"So, Matilda, my article is about how we need to stick together and speak out against the kind of prejudice that gave us the likes of Bully Bigshot. Unity will be our first weapon."

Matilda smiled and raised her glass. "Good for you, Uncle Mac."

Everyone nodded their approval, and the discussion turned to lighter subjects when Olivia served the pumpkin pie. And when they finished dessert, the adults retired to the parlor to talk. Kizzy and Stefan stayed behind to clear the table.

When they were alone Kizzy said, "I liked what Uncle Mac said about how to fix the sort of stuff that happened around here."

"I did too," Stefan said. "But it made me think of Eli and Rachel. I'm going over there tomorrow night for dinner. Will you go with me?"

"Yes, I'd like that."

⚜

At 4:30 Friday afternoon, Stefan and Kizzy walked to the Schulman residence. Rachel met them at the door and took them to the living room. Eli was reading, but he got up and gave Kizzy a hug. "We're so happy you came, Kizzy. In a little while we will celebrate Shabbat, but for now let's sit down and talk."

She sat between Eli and Rachel, but Stefan went directly to the fireplace and took the *dreidel* from the mantle. "Watch this, Kizzy." He spun the top on the table, over and over, until it landed with the Gimel side showing. "That's how you win the jackpot—when it lands on Gimel."

Eli snickered. "Stefan loves the *dreidel* game. And speaking of jackpots, Ruben called me today. He has filed a lawsuit against Sully Biggers, Lookadoo, and the others on behalf of all the women harmed by the Eugenics Center."

"They deserve to win," Rachel said. "And Sully Biggers certainly doesn't need the money, not where he is."

Stefan put the *dreidel* back on the mantle and sat down by Rachel. The four of them praised Ruben for what he was doing and Uncle Mac for his article in the *Big Pearl Free Current.* Then as it neared sundown, Eli turned to Kizzy. "We celebrate Shabbat on Friday at sunset—it's our belief that the day begins at sunset."

Kizzy smiled. "I don't know much about religion, but on the river we didn't have electricity, so shuttin' down at sunset is pretty much the way we did it."

Eli and Rachel laughed, then Eli became a teacher. "Shabbat is a holy day. There is to be no work, and no fires are to be kindled." He nodded to Rachel, and as she lit two candles, he said, "The two candles respect the commandments to remember and observe."

Eli recited a special blessing in Hebrew, then said, "Now it is time for the meal and quiet talk. We will have good food and enjoy the physical and spiritual love of family. Shabbat is our day of rest; it is a time for spiritual growth."

During the candlelight dinner Kizzy told some funny stories about toe-digging and MeeMaw's fortune-telling days. Then she and Stefan talked about their senior year at Big Pearl High School, their music, and their plans for college. Rachel interrupted. "I love your music. We already have our tickets to the Christmas Extravaganza at the Opera House."

"Everyone is coming—Olivia, Birdie, Uncle Mac, Fritz, everyone ..."

Rachel interrupted Kizzy. "Olivia is going to miss you when you go away to college."

"Maybe, but I think she's already found her next Pygmalion project."

"Birdie?"

"Yep."

Eli smiled and looked at Stefan. "The Shabbat meal is for the telling of heartwarming stories, Stefan. Kizzy told us about growing up on the river, but you have been awfully quiet."

Stefan hesitated, but Kizzy and Eli urged him to tell about his boyhood in Germany.

He started slowly, first telling about his grandfather's farm. Then, as he loosened up, he told about the day Annemarie and Victor took him to the Neander Valley near Düsseldorf for a picnic. He told of seeing fishermen and a *futbol* game and described the valley where laborers found the bones of the Neanderthal Man. "I was only 8 years old, but I remember asking my father if the bones were Aryan or Jew. He laughed, but I remember the exact words he said next: 'Nobody knows who they were or what they believed, but if someone says they were Jews the Nazis will not like the Neanderthal Man.'"

Stefan shrugged his shoulders and wrinkled his brow. "I asked why and my mother said, 'We don't know why.' That's when I learned that we were going to move to America ... so, here I am."

"That's such an important story, Stefan." Rachel put her hand on his, and so did Kizzy.

Stefan looked at Eli. "I would like to say the 'Our Father' for my mother, Annemarie. Is that OK?"

"Certainly."

"And then will you say Kaddish for my father, Victor? I know I should be the one to say it, but I don't know how."

"Yes, of course." Eli said. "We should have 10 people present, but we won't stand on formality."

Stefan's chin trembled, and his voice cracked as he prayed for Annemarie, but he made it through.

Then Eli said Kaddish for Victor. And when he spoke the last words— *aleinu v'al kol Yis'ra'eil v'im'ru. Amein*—Kizzy whimpered, "It's so pretty, all of it ... so musical."

"Yes, the prayers are beautiful," Eli said. "The Kaddish, a mourner's prayer, is interesting because it does not mention death or dying. We say it to affirm the holiness of God and the wonder of life."

"The wonder of life," Kizzy looked at Stefan and then Eli. "Like the Chai?" She reached beneath her blouse and showed Eli and Rachel the pendant that Stefan gave her.

Eli smiled and touched her hand. "Yes, Kizzy, *l'chaim*."

⚜

Later that night, as she lay in bed, Kizzy touched the pendant. *Olivia and Birdie are believers. So's Uncle Mac, and old Knuckles, and Matilda. Eli and Rachel have a different way, but they believe too. They're all saying there is a higher power who can fix things. It's all so different from the ways of the river. There's the Our Father and Kaddish, and so many other ways of doing it.*

I've got a lot more to learn about all this.

⚜

On Saturday night, Dec. 22, 1945, the Big Pearl Opera House was all lit up; people were converging from across Northeast Arkansas for the Christmas Extravaganza.

At 7 o'clock, a half-hour before show time, the house was packed. Everyone was there, even Horsey Hairs and the rich girls. The gang from the Veterans' Center was on the second row, but Dynamite had pushed Uncle Mac to a wide spot near the stage. Kizzy peeked through the curtain and saw Olivia, Birdie, Eli and Rachel. They were all sitting front row center. Sweetcheeks and Fritz were nearer to the aisle.

The first act was a baritone soloist who sang several popular tunes, ending with a beautiful rendition of the Lord's Prayer. He was followed by a 50-member gospel choir from Jonesboro that sang half their program before intermission and half after.

Finally, the master of ceremonies announced the featured performance: "Ladies and gentlemen, Kizzy and Stefan have been singing and playing music all over northeast Arkansas. They are seniors at Big Pearl High School but I'm betting it won't be long before they are signed by a Nashville recording studio. They are unique, and their music speaks to the heart. Please welcome Kizzy and Stefan."

They came on stage to rousing applause. Kizzy, dressed in the black outfit she wore for the Talent Contest, was holding hands with Stefan. He was wearing blue jeans and a gaudy purple shirt with baggy sleeves that Kizzy wanted him to wear in memory of her Gypsy father, Tamás.

They did three songs. The first was Mendelssohn's "Hear My Prayer." It gave Stefan a chance to show his mastery of the violin, and when Kizzy sang the words "O for the wings of a dove," she pointed to Birdie and the audience went wild. No one had ever heard Kizzy sing anything like that. Then they switched gears and she sang "Gypsy Girl," the song she learned from MeeMaw. And they finished with the newly popular "White Christmas."

When it was over the audience gave them a standing ovation with repeated shouts of "Bravo!" They left the stage and came back three times, finally realizing that they would have to do an encore.

The crowd quieted down, and Kizzy looked to Stefan to see what he wanted to play. Just then, a pretty red-haired girl who looked to be 12 or 13 years old shouted out, "Sing the song that means the most to you."

Kizzy looked to Stefan, who nodded his approval. "Here's one we just finished. It's about how we need to get along with each other and make the most of our differences." She looked at Olivia and winked. "I got the idea for it one day when I was talking to my friend Olivia about our special place: Barton Cottage."

Olivia smiled, then sniffled and pursed her lips.

"This'll be the first time we've played it in public, so I'd like to dedicate it to Olivia and my make-do brother, Birdie Barden, who's sitting right there next to her. Stefan wrote the music for this." She pointed to him and urged him to say something.

"I'd like to dedicate this to my mother and father, Annemarie and Victor, who taught me that love is 100 times more powerful than hate."

Kizzy looked at the red-headed girl, and then the audience. "We call this 'Kizzy's Song' but it can be your song too."

Stefan played the melody all the way through, and then turned to Kizzy, who sang with the passion of one who has suffered:

Some folks live in the great big city
and some folks live in town
Me and my kind keep to the river
and carry on somehow.

I love living on the river, free
Where you can be you
And I can be me
We can be different, that's alright
God made both weak and strong,
And rich and poor, and black and white
And bade us all to get along …

I can tell that it's Sunday morning
'cause the church bell's on the breeze
I'm in worship with lil green tree frogs
Amid the cypress knees

Some folks talk about their dear friend Jesus
like he ain't no friend of mine
But He says "Howdy" when I say "howdy"
We get along just fine

Some folks are going up Glory Mountain
to where there ain't no fields to plow,
Me and my kind will keep to the river
and carry on somehow

I'll keep living on the river free
Where there ain't no secrets or shame
I found my pearl on the river free
That's where I'll lay my claim

CPSIA information can be obtained
at www.ICGtesting.com
Printed in the USA
LVOW01s2251090317
526743LV00006B/118/P